DEADLY GAMES

'A dizzying but invigorating ride through the graft and
fleshpots of power'
Observer

'Full marks for plausibility . . . portrait of Russia's
black economy and underground world of graft,
viciousness and unacknowledged double dealing'
The Times

'Crammed with non-stop action and documentation'
Sunday Times

'Credibility and realism . . . the build-up of tension is
skilfully done and the sense of place and people very
persuasive and believable . . . recommended'
Glasgow Herald

Fridrikh Neznansky was born in 1932 in Zhuravichi, USSR. He obtained a degree in jurisprudence at the Moscow Law Institute in 1954 and subsequently worked as an investigator for the USSR Prosecutor's Office. After attending the USSR Institute for the Study of the Causes and Prevention of Crime in Moscow, he joined the Moscow City Collegium of lawyers and handled criminal cases among others. In February 1978, he emigrated to the USA where he lectures on crime in the USSR.

Edward Topol was born in 1938 in Baku, USSR. He attended the All Union State Institute of Cinematography in Moscow where he concentrated on creative writing. His play *Love at First Sight* was produced twice and was later made into a film. Seven of his scripts were made into feature films and *The Minors*, *Cabin Boy of the Northern Fleet* and *The Sea of our Hope* won national awards. He is a prolific writer in many genres including poetry. In 1979 he emigrated to the USA where he continues to write.

Also by Edward Topol and Fridrikh Neznansky

RED SQUARE

and published by Corgi Books

Deadly Games

Fridrikh Neznansky and Edward Topol

CORGI BOOKS

DEADLY GAMES

A CORGI BOOK 0 552 12584 9

Originally published in Great Britain by Quartet Books
Limited

PRINTING HISTORY
Quartet Books edition published 1983
Corgi edition published 1985

Translated from the Russian *Zhurnalist dlya Brezhneva*

This book is set in 10/11 Mallard

Corgi Books are published by Transworld Publishers Ltd.,
Century House, 61–63 Uxbridge Road, Ealing,
London W5 5SA, in Australia by Transworld Publishers
(Aust.) Pty. Ltd., 26 Harley Crescent, Condell Park,
NSW 2200, and in New Zealand by Transworld Publishers
(N.Z.) Ltd., Cnr. Moselle and Waipareira Avenues,
Henderson, Auckland.

Made and printed in Great Britain by
Hunt Barnard Printing Ltd., Aylesbury, Bucks

Deadly Games

Part 1

Moscow, Monday, 4 June 1979, 09.15 hours
'Shamrayev to the Chief Public Prosecutor's office!' boomed the intercom.

Kolya Baklanov fell silent. He had wandered into my office to tell me how he had spent his holidays. He raised his eyebrows in surprise, wondering what business this could be between myself and the Chief Public Prosecutor.

I didn't know either. I pressed a button on the intercom and said: 'I'll be there right away.'

'Igor Iosifovich,' came the reply. 'Come as quick as you can. He's got to go to the Central Committee afterwards, on Staraya Square.'

'All right, all right,' I said, stuffing into my briefcase the bottle of *Chornye Glaza*, a Soviet wine which Baklanov had brought back from the south. God knows what the prosecutor wanted me for!

I locked the door to my office, told Baklanov what he could do with his sarcastic 'Good luck!' and went towards the lift. On my right were the offices of other investigators, 'specials' like Baklanov and myself. The safes behind those doors contained the details of scores of sensational crimes, any one of which would have provided the plot for a detective novel or caused a huge stir in the much-vaunted Western press. The affairs of every department of state pass through this building, giving the Public Prosecutor's office enormous power. It's not surprising that when the MVD and the KGB joined forces a few years ago to take from

9

our hands responsibility for carrying out investigations, the Public Prosecutor made such a fuss that the whole affair reached the Politburo. After all, what would the Chief Public Prosecutor have become? A general without an army . . .

Now what could he want me for? I had only just completed work on a case involving the Ministries of Forestry, Inland Waterways and Railways. The noose had been drawn very tight, since there was evidence linking two ministers and four railway chiefs with illegal financial dealings involving hundreds of thousands of roubles. But being summoned to the Chief Prosecutor's office was a bad sign . . . I walked through the general office and into his reception room. Vera Petelina, his personal assistant, nodded urgently in the direction of the padded double doors which led to his office. I opened them and found myself in the Chief Prosecutor's modest room, which was quite small and not at all what you would have expected of someone in his position. All his deputies had enormous rooms, finished in walnut and fitted with soft furnishings, imported from abroad. But not the prosecutor himself. No, he was modest. And the secret behind his 'modesty' was quite simple. Immediately after the Revolution, in the 1920s, this very building had housed the Central Committee of the All-Union Communist Party (Bolsheviks), and this tiny room had been the office of the future CPSU Secretary-General, Joseph Stalin. So today's Chief Public Prosecutor finds himself 'modestly' sitting in Joseph Stalin's own office, and using the same desk.

The seventy-year-old prosecutor raised his ageing posterior from the sacred relic of Stalin's armchair, bumped up now with an extra cushion.

'Ah, Igor Iosifovich,' he said, offering me his flabby hand. 'Take a seat. You look the picture of health, and yet you're asking to go away on holiday. Do sit down.'

I am always amazed at how well informed he is. Sometimes he doesn't see his subordinates for months

10

on end, yet he knows every little thing about us.

'Well, it *is* my turn to have a holiday, Roman Andreyevich,' I replied. Realizing I was now on the defensive, I sat down in the chair next to his desk. 'And there happened to be a trip available to Gelendzhik . . .'

'I'm afraid it won't work out, old man,' replied the prosecutor sorrowfully. 'But how do you like your new flat?'

So he knew about that, too. After my divorce from Irina I had spent a couple of years moving about from friend to friend, renting a room here and there. Nobody paid any attention to it. The authorities and the party committee don't approve of people getting divorced. But a month ago, by some miracle, I'd managed to get a co-operative apartment – really out in the sticks, beyond the Izmailovsky Park. No sooner had I got it, it seemed, than the whole Public Prosecutor's Department was buzzing with the news: 'Shamrayev's bought himself a co-operative flat!'

'Thank you, Roman Andreyevich,' I replied cautiously. 'The apartment is fine. It's a little away from the centre, but that doesn't matter. It's habitable.'

'I should say so! With the park next door, fresh air, mushrooms! What do you need to go away on holiday for? Why waste your money?' His watery, bulbous eyes held me in their pale questioning gaze, as if he had summoned me with the precise aim in mind of persuading me not to travel to Gelendzhik and spend all my money, because the marvellous Izmailovsky Park was invitingly spread out there beneath my balcony. 'Or have you got more money than you know what to do with? You have just bought yourself an apartment, after all . . .'

I laughed. When you've got nothing to feel guilty about and you're as poor as a church mouse, you can afford to laugh, even in the face of a Chief Public Prosecutor.

'It's the local trade union committee's mutual benefit

11

scheme which has provided the money, Roman Andreyevich,' I replied. 'You can check, if you like.'

'My dear fellow, what do you mean?' he said, sitting back in his chair with a reproachful smile. But we understood each other and he finally adopted a more businesslike tone.

'No, Igor Iosifovich. Let us postpone your trip. There's no reason to blow the local trade union committee's money to the wind, either. You know the old expression: borrow other people's money, but give away your own. In any case, it's not right that a special investigator should be forced to buy a co-operative apartment miles from anywhere and waste two hours a day travelling back and forth. As if the city council couldn't provide you with a new state-owned apartment in the middle of town! I'll have a word to Promyslov, Now ... Take this file away with you. It contains one body of which we know the whereabouts, and another that we don't. That's all. It won't delay you very long. Only it *is* urgent . . .'

He handed me a grey-coloured file, bearing the following inscription: 'MVD USSR. Investigation No. SL-79-1542. Begun 26 May 1979.' Today was 4 June, so the case had been started nine days earlier. I knew that nothing good would come of this summons. There's nothing worse than taking over a case that someone else has already begun. They'll have messed it up for you. Their dirty marks will be everywhere: every lead will be broken, all the evidence jumbled; the witnesses plucked clean to no purpose, the criminals put on their guard . . . The Chief Public Prosecutor certainly knows how to do the dirty on you! Yet how gently he goes about it, even offering you an apartment in the centre of town! And not even a co-operative one, but one belonging to the state – and costing practically nothing. So what kind of priceless corpse is this that the prosecutor is talking about? Whose body is it? I hope not the son or daughter of some big government wheel who's got bumped off. In that case, it wouldn't be so much a question of an investigation as of making polite inquiries. You just try cross-examining Kosygin or Suslov! And if you go to see them, they'll soon tell you where to get off – and you'll only have yourself to blame. The whole game isn't worth a toss, and yet it has to be you, a special investigator, who carries out the inquiries. They wouldn't entrust the case to anyone lower in the hierarchy. Can you imagine letting a simple investigator near any government corpse!

So there I was, holding this grey folder in my hands, not daring to open it. It might have been a dangerous landmine. 'So whose body was it?' I asked.

'You just go ahead and open the folder, and don't worry,' said the prosecutor with a laugh, as if he could read my thoughts. 'One of the bodies is that of a tramp, a drug-addict from somewhere in the Caucasus. And as for the other one, the one that hasn't been found yet, well . . . Do you read *Komsomolskaya Pravda*?'

'Well, yes . . .' I said, somewhat uncertainly.

'Have you ever come across the name of Belkin?'

'Yes, I have,' I replied. In fact, this was one of the three or four journalists' names that I really do know. It was Vadim Belkin, I think. Yes, I'd read some of his articles about the deserts of Central Asia, the fishermen of the Tyulkino fleet, and the border police. He always chose gripping subjects from everyday life to write about. His style was simple, conversational even, but what he wrote was always absorbing, as if he hadn't been infected by the usual run of journalistic clichés . . . I looked at the prosecutor and said: 'Has he really been murdered?'

But there was no time for him to reply. Vera Petelina's voice suddenly interrupted our conversation: 'Roman Andreyevich, it's the Kremlin on the line – Comrade Suslov.'

The prosecutor lifted the receiver off the red telephone, which was placed by itself on a separate table. I got up to leave, so as not to disturb their conversation, but he motioned me to stay where I was. He had turned

13

away from me slightly and I could see him in profile. Two stars indicating his marshal's rank were sewn on to the collar of his uniform and they were pressing against the folds of his somewhat flabby neck. Yes, I thought, the former scourge of the Nuremburg trials is getting on now. This fat, tired old man was the one who ought to be gathering mushrooms in the Izmailovsky Park, but here he is, a marshal, sitting in Stalin's former office and rising to the occasion, as ever.

'He's already dealing with it . . . Of course . . . The best we have available . . . The most energetic of our people . . . By the eleventh at the very latest, I understand . . . Of course, I'll keep an eye on it personally . . . Of course, alive if possible . . . No, I think we'll be able to manage without the KGB . . .'

I felt a sinking feeling in the pit of my stomach. Were they really discussing the case in hand? If that were so, then everything the prosecutor was saying referred to me . . . So I was really stuck with it. What was all this about – 'the most energetic', 'the best we have', and so on? What about Baklanov? He'd just come back from holiday and had more experience than me . . .

Meanwhile the prosecutor had replaced the receiver and turned to face me.

'Did you follow all that?'

'All what?' I said, pretending not to have heard, let alone to have understood anything.

He gave me a hard stare for a few seconds, as if making up his mind and then endorsing his decision.

'Look, Igor Iosifovich,' he said, 'I know that it's a difficult case. But there is no choice. Andropov and Shcholokov are just biding their time. If I refuse to take it on, they'll say to the Central Committee: "Look, here he is. He won't surrender responsibility for criminal investigation to us, and yet he refuses to take on the difficult ones." So listen to what I have to say. In ten days' time, on 15 June, Comrade Brezhnev will be flying to Vienna to meet Carter. He'll be accompanied by a press corps consisting of five of our best journalists.

14

Leonid Ilyich confirmed the selection of participants himself long ago, and this Belkin was his own personal choice. But two weeks ago Belkin disappeared at the Kursk railway station in Moscow. He was meeting some dubious acquaintance of his, a drug-addict from the Caucasus. The two of them were bundled into a car in the square directly in front of the station and driven off somewhere. Two days later the drug-addict's body was found underneath a bridge outside the city, with a broken skull. Meanwhile there was no trace of Belkin at all. Whether they've killed him or not, how are we supposed to tell Comrade Brezhnev that the journalist whom he chose personally to accompany him to Vienna has disappeared without trace?'

So that was what it was all about, I thought. Belkin didn't matter. Nobody was concerned with him, even if he was a really talented journalist. He'd disappeared, and that was that. What was really exercising the prosecutor and all the others was the question of how to tell Brezhnev. After all, just imagine, here is Brezhnev on the eve of his momentous meeting with Carter and someone is supposed to go up to him and say that they can't find his favourite journalist. 'What do you mean, you can't find him?' Brezhnev would reply. 'Where is he?' – 'We haven't the faintest idea, Leonid Ilyich' ... No, it was absolutely certain that no one would risk saying such a thing to Brezhnev, especially just before his departure abroad. And yet, on the other hand, somebody would have to tell him, if ...

'So, you see, Belkin must be found, dead or alive, by the eleventh,' said the prosecutor, appearing to read my thoughts yet again. 'Of course, it would be better if he were found alive,' he continued, 'but that doesn't depend on you. On the twelfth the journalists are due to be briefed by Zamyatin and Suslov. Two days later they're due to have lunch with Leonid Ilyich himself, and on the fifteenth they fly to Vienna. Now there's no question of sending a corpse along to lunch on the fourteenth, as you'll understand. Which means that the latest time for finding out what has happened to him is Monday, 11 June. You've got seven days at your disposal, just like God. If you can resurrect Belkin in that time, you'll have a chestful of medals, a flat in the centre of Moscow, and you'll be promoted to the rank of senior juridical counsellor, despite your ... er ... -youth.'

I think that he had some impediment other than my age in mind, but he thought better of it at the last moment and used a different word. And if I didn't suspect myself of oversensitivity, I should say that I knew what he'd been driving at. He'd had in mind my Jewish patronymic, or, to be more exact, my half-Jewish origins. People might hurry over my patronymic, but there was no doing away with my Jewish background. Certain persons have their careers halted for less.

So this Belkin might be my Waterloo, God damn him!

'But taking all in all, Roman Andreyevich, I've only just completed work on a very important case, and I'm more than due to take a holiday. And there's plenty of time for me to gain promotion to senior counsellor ... when I get a bit older,' I added with a certain air of defiance.

This attempt to get out of it was, of course, rather clumsy. The prosecutor made a wry face. He leant back in his chair and eyed me coldly from head to foot.

'Well, this is the position, Igor Iosifovich. The Central Committee has ordered us to find Belkin, dead or alive, by the eleventh. And I'm entrusting the case to you. If you feel that it is beyond your capabilities, then tell me so officially at 9 a.m. tomorrow, and I shall draw my own conclusions. And it's an interesting case, too. I've glanced through it myself. Drug-addicts, journalists, and all that. The only thing is, you'll get pestered from above. But then who isn't? Do you think I'm spared it myself? Now, why don't you just get on with it?'

He rose from his chair and reached across the table to shake my hand. 'And don't forget that you've got complete freedom of action in this affair, including the Petrovka. But then you know all this yourself. Consider yourself as working on behalf of the Central Committee and assume whatever powers you need. If you find Belkin alive, you'll be getting all of us out of an awkward situation, Zamyatin and Suslov included. Also . . . not that this really matters,' he added with a smile, as if suddenly remembering something, 'my grandniece is head over heels in love with him, this Belkin. He gave a couple of lectures at the Faculty of Journalism, or something, and they all lost their heads over him. Not that it's of any importance, of course. They didn't have an affair, don't worry.'

Ah! So that's how it stands! Brezhnev, Suslov, *Komsomolskaya Pravda*, my foot! Rudenko's grandniece is in love with him! To hell with the lot of you! . . . The fact is that a special investigator is to be used to find the Chief Prosecutor's grand-niece's boy-friend! They've certainly got enough people to do their bidding! And it wouldn't be so bad if these bosses were the only ones you had to serve; at least they hold important positions. But no! You're expected to serve their grandnieces as well! I remembered a rather striking, long-legged creature with a teenager's wanton gaze. I wondered whether she fell for Belkin *before* he became Brezhnev's favourite journalist, or after.

I went back to my own office and hurled Belkin's file into the corner of the room in vexation. As it flew by the table, it took a paperweight with it. The crash echoed so loudly down the corridor that Baklanov looked out of the adjacent office.

'What's wrong? Want to go and have a beer?'

'Yes, let's go,' I said angrily. 'They can all go and fuck themselves. Be a servant to them? I'd rather become a defence lawyer!'

'Be a servant to whom?' asked Baklanov with a show of curiosity.

I looked him in the eye and replied with great emphasis: 'The working people!'

If the walls of the Prosecutor's Department have ears (which assumption cannot be dismissed) – so much the better. Let them hear! Meanwhile Baklanov and I went off to sink a few jars.

Secret

To the Moscow Prosecutor
State Juridical Counsellor Second Class
Comrade Mikhail Grigoryevich Malkov

SPECIAL REPORT

In accordance with Secret Instruction No. 24 dated 5 August 1971, requiring that you be personally informed immediately of any cases of violent death occurring within the area of Greater Moscow, I have to inform you of the following:

On 26 May 1979, at 6.15 a.m., an unidentified corpse was found by a track maintenance man at the foot of a railway bridge, crossing the Moscow River in the area of Tsaritsyno Ponds about fifty yards from the Moscow River railway station on the line to Kursk. The body is that of a young man aged between seventeen and twenty years and bears the marks of a violent death.

The corpse has visible injuries such as scratches and contusions, which were inflicted while the victim was still alive and which indicate a measure of self-defence on the victim's part. In the opinion of the forensic expert, death was the result of damage to the skull inflicted by a heavy object or by being hit against a heavy object. The most likely thing to have happened is that the victim was hurled on to the railway track from a moving train. No papers were found on the corpse. The word 'Sultan' is tattooed on the back of his hand, and both forearms show the marks of injections from a hypodermic syringe.

A CID investigation team travelled to the spot

where the corpse was found. The murder investigation has been transferred to the Moscow River Prosecutor's Department, in whose area the crime took place. The murder inquiry is being led by Investigator V. N. Pshenichny.

At the same time I have given instructions for the Head of the Second Section of the CID Third Department, Lieutenant-Colonel M. A. Svetlov, to take active measures to uncover the perpetrators of this crime.

CID Head
Major-General P. Minayev

Moscow, 26 May 1979

It is a well-known fact that beer weakens the system and a beer-bar relaxes the nerves. After our third pint of *Zhigulyovskoye*, Baklanov and I decided to view life philosophically. If I saw that the case was a dead duck, then I would tell the prosecutor so first thing in the morning and go away on leave. And there wouldn't be a thing the Chief Public Prosecutor could do about it. You don't find investigators like us growing on trees. If the worst came to the worst, I could become a defence lawyer. And if I did come unstuck, so what? Fishing out logs of wood in the River Pechora was no worse than looking for the grand-niece's boy-friend. Although the latter would be more interesting: you were looking for a living person, after all. Only what was the connection between him and the corpse of this 'Sultan'?

Secret

To CID Head
Major-General P. A. Minayev

OFFICIAL TELEGRAM
Concerning the discovery of an unidentified corpse

on 26 May 1979 near Moscow River railway station, I have to report the following:

On 26 May at approximately 10.30 a.m. outside the wine and spirit shop in the village of Lenino-Dachnoye, a certain Aleksey Popov, a person who has been compulsorily dried out from alcohol in the past, sold a diamond necklace weighing one carat and worth 1,750 roubles to Citizen M. P. Korkoshko for 50 roubles. Drinking in the company of friends, Popov announced that earlier that day he had accidentally discovered a document case, containing jewellery, in a clump of bushes not very far from Tsaritsyno Ponds.

A CID agent nicknamed 'The Carthorse' was present at this conversation. At a signal from him we arrested Popov. The impounded document case was found to contain diamonds, jewellery, rings, earrings and pendants of great rarity. According to the preliminary estimates of experts, the valuables are worth no less than 100,000 roubles.

Since the document case was found not very far from the platform close to where the corpse was discovered, I took steps to have the case dusted for finger-prints. This revealed prints from the right hand of the man whose body was discovered near the railway platform on 26 May. This would indicate that the document case belonged to the deceased and was thrown from the train 850 yards from the spot where the body itself was ejected.

Head of Second Section
CID Third Department
Lieutenant-Colonel M. Svetlov
Moscow, 27 May 1979

You need to know how to read the official documents which form part of a criminal investigation. The important thing about this telegram was not that jewellery had been discovered, nor even that it belonged to 'Sultan', but that Lieutenant-Colonel Svetlov had taken the initiative himself, and, also, that his efforts and those of his agents had been successful. Nor had he lost any time in informing the head of Moscow CID of their success. This was the real reason for sending the telegram in the first place, I said to myself with a smile. After all, I knew Svetlov's character. He was clever, but boastful.

I leafed through some of the other documents in the file. Aha! Here was something which had more to do with Belkin himself.

REPORT OF EXAMINATION AND TRANSFER OF DOCUMENTS
28 May 1979, Moscow
. . . An examination of the incident book at the Kursk Station Militia Office in Moscow has revealed that on 24 May 1979, at 12.56 hours, the duty officer. Captain Abushakhmin, was approached by a woman called Aina Silinya, born in 1962, an inhabitant of Riga, who was passing through Moscow. She reported that she had seen four unknown criminals seize Yury Rybakov and Vadim Belkin at the taxi rank outside the Kursk railway station and forcibly bundle them into a car. In her account Silinya mentioned that she and her acquaintance, Yury Rybakov, had arrived in Moscow by train from Baku on 24 May. On the platform they were met by Yury's friend, the journalist Vadim Belkin. When the three of them walked up to the taxi rank on the square in front of the railway station, they were unexpectedly approached by an old *Rafik* ambulance, the registration number of which she had no time to memorize. Four men got out (two of them were dressed in white overalls) and rushed at Rybakov and Belkin from behind, shouting out as follows to the people standing in the queue: 'Comrades, help us to capture these mental patients!' Drowning out the protests of Rybakov and Belkin, they pushed them

21

into the ambulance. Then one of them, who was in his early fifties with metal teeth, grabbed Aina Silinya with one hand and tried to force her into the ambulance as well. She bit his arm and managed to escape. People standing in the queue tried to help the so-called medical orderlies by stopping her, but the former, seeing a militiaman approaching, hurriedly got into the ambulance and drove off.

Having made her statement, witness A. Silinya returned to her place of residence – No. 5 Artilerius Prospect, Apartment 7, Riga.

Comrade Silinya's statement has been removed from militia files and appended to the series of documents relating to the murder of the unidentified individual, found near the Moscow River railway station.

Investigator V. Pshenichny
Witnesses

TELEGRAM

To the Head of the Riga City Militia, Lieutenant-Colonel Robert Baron

GIVEN URGENCY OF INVESTIGATION REQUEST YOU SEND TO MOSCOW IMMEDIATELY COMRADE AINA SILINYA RESIDING 5 ARTILERIUS PROSPECT APARTMENT 7 STOP HER APPEARANCE AT MOSCOW RIVER PROSECUTOR'S OFFICE ESSENTIAL STOP INVESTIGATOR PSHENICHNY

28 May 1979

FORENSIC ANALYSIS REPORT

Moscow, 29 May 1979

At the request of Investigator Pshenichny, I, forensic expert S. Fradkina, have carried out a biological analysis of blood, saliva and urine samples from the unidentified corpse found near Moscow River railway station. Samples of tissue and part of the stomach of the deceased were also analysed.

Traces of chemical substances found in the blood and urine prove that between five and ten hours before death took place the victim had injected himself with powerful drugs – with morphine and also with derivatives of the tranquillizer phenothiazine (whether with triftazine, sanapax or aminazine has not been determined).

Forensic Medical Section
Moscow City Health Department
Senior Scientific Officer
Sofia Fradkina, MD

NOTE: The general diagnostic picture (based on organic changes occurring in the veins, brain, stomach and other organs) is of an organism which has become inured to drugs of the morphine type over a number of years. For this reason the presence in the body of phenothiazine derivatives, which are considered to be powerful drugs used in psychopharmacology, is unusual, but biological analysis is not able to explain the reason for this substitution.

S. Fradkina

So this 'Sultan', who was most probably Rybakov, was injecting himself with drugs. Nice company for one of the country's best journalists: a drug-addict and a jewel speculator! I wondered what part Belkin had played in this business with the diamonds.

Just then, I came across something about Belkin himself as I turned up the following letter from the chief editor of *Komsomolskaya Pravda* on a sheet of personalized notepaper:

Urgent, By Special Messenger

To the Moscow City Prosecutor
Comrade M. G. Malkov
Copy to the Head of CPSU Central Committee
Ideological Section
Comrade L. M. Zamyatin

Dear Mikhail Grigoryevich,

Yesterday and today, without any search warrant, V. Pshenichny, an investigator at the Moscow River Prosecutor's Office, conducted a series of illegal searches at the editorial offices of *Komsomolskaya Pravda* and at the apartment of our missing correspondent, V. Belkin.

Without wishing to interfere in the operations of our investigative organs, I should like to make the point that any attempts to locate the whereabouts of the missing journalist at his place of work or at his home in an apartment block belonging to the Komsomol Central Committee, are in our opinion quite senseless. The searches which have been carried out compromise the reputation not merely of the newspaper's editorial staff, but also of the Prosecutor's Department entrusted to your care.

Speaking on behalf of the entire editorial staff of *Komsomolskaya Pravda*, I beg you to transfer the responsibility for finding V. Belkin, a talented writer and one of the country's leading journalists, to an investigator who is both better qualified and politically more mature.

At the same time I have to inform you that, as a special correspondent representing *Komsomolskaya Pravda*, V. Belkin has been included in the press corps which will report on the meeting between Comrade L. I. Brezhnev and President J. Carter, due to take place in Vienna from 15 to 18 June.

The disappearance of Vadim Belkin and the absence of requisite action to discover his whereabouts is a source of concern both to the editorial staff of our newspaper and to the CPSU Central Committee's Ideological Department.

Yours sincerely,
Chief Editor of *Komsomolskaya Pravda*
Member of the CPSU Central Committee's Central Auditing Commission
Deputy of the RSFSR Supreme Soviet
Lev Korneshov

To the Moscow City Prosecutor
State Juridical Counsellor Second Class
M. G. Malkov

REPORT

In connection with the complaint received from the chief editor of *Komsomolskaya Pravda*, Comrade L. Korneshov, I have to report the following:

On 27 May I assumed responsibility for investigating the death of an unidentified person. Thereafter I took action to ascertain that the victim was one Yu. A. Rybakov, aged seventeen years, who had been kidnapped at the Kursk Station in Moscow on 24 May, together with *Komsomolskaya Pravda* correspondent, V. Belkin. (The corpse was positively identified by A. Silinya, an inhabitant of Riga, who also witnessed the said kidnapping.)

Since the document case belonging to Yu. Rybakov was found to include diamond jewellery to the value of not less than 100,000 roubles, it became necessary to examine the nature of the contacts which Yu. Rybakov had with the above-mentioned Belkin. In connection with this and in the presence of witnesses (employees of *Komsomolskaya Pravda*, living in the same apartment block as Belkin), on 31 May I conducted a search of Belkin's flat and removed for further examination certain of his personal effects and manuscripts connected with the case in hand. Among the former was one of the notebooks which V. Belkin had used during a recent assignment in the south. Marked 'Tashkent-Baku' No. 1, it contains information of crucial relevance to the investigation and is appended to the case-file. Apart from this, the search of Belkin's apartment also brought to light a number of books, proscribed by the censorship, including A. Solzhenitsyn's *Gulag Archipelago*, V. Voinovich's *Life and Adventures of Ivan Chonkin* and issue No. 3 of the journal *Kontinent*.

With a view to discovering notebook No. 2 or any other jottings written subsequently by V. Belkin, on 1 June 1979 I searched his room at the editorial offices of *Komsomolskaya Pravda*. This search revealed that his desk was nearly empty. All his manuscripts and notebooks had disappeared. Furthermore, I was informed by I. K. Tarasevich, a journalist who shares Belkin's office, and I. G. Uryvskaya, the office cleaner, that from the day Belkin disappeared until yesterday evening (31 May), the latter's desk had been filled with his papers and notebooks.

Thus it cannot be ruled out that documents of direct relevance to this investigation have been deliberately removed by a person or persons unknown.

At the same time, I would draw attention to the low level of professional discipline among Belkin's colleagues at *Komsomolskaya Pravda*. Despite the fact that his last visit to the editorial office took place on 24 May, for a whole week nobody at the office became worried by his absence. And it was only as a result of the search conducted by me that the editor, Comrade Korneshov, grew aware that this employee of his, this 'talented writer and one of the country's leading journalists', had disappeared at all.

In view of the fact that Comrade Belkin's name has been included in the press group due to accompany Comrade Brezhnev on his journey to Vienna, I consider that the process of discovering the whereabouts of Belkin and of the criminals who abducted him and Rybakov would be much accelerated by the formation of a special investigative team, including agents of the CID. For one investigator, in this case me, to co-ordinate all these actions will be extremely difficult, especially if it is borne in mind that at the present moment, apart from the case involving Rybakov and Belkin, I have eighteen investigations of various kinds on my hands – including five major embezzlements and three murders.

Investigator
Moscow River Prosecutor's Office
Legal Expert Second Class
V. Pshenichny

1 June 1979

The more I read of this Pshenichny, the more I like him! Not a mistake made, apart from one blunder – inviting as witnesses to the search of Belkin's apartment neighbours who subsequently turned out to be colleagues of his at work. I can easily conjure up an image of this suburban investigator, overwhelmed with work, tired, getting on in years and paid a mere 165 roubles a month. Five embezzlements, three murders and another ten cases of lesser importance – my God! What a weird world we live in! It's a round-the-clock succession of embezzlers and speculators, conning ordinary citizens with the help of the Great God Economic Shortage. Everywhere you go you meet men worn out by overwork, routine and alcohol, who beat their wives to within an inch of death; fights and squabbles in communal flats; the misbehaviour of hooligans hanging about in the doorways of apartment

27

blocks; the day-to-day wine and spirits existence of a country in which 90 per cent of criminal acts are committed by individuals under the influence of alcohol. Half a million criminal and civil actions are heard by the Moscow courts every year. There are tens of thousands of arrests, hundreds of thousands of people are held for questioning, and an unimaginable number of cases, perhaps a million, have been processed by People's Courts throughout the country in the past year. And all of it constitutes the exhausting daily routine of thousands of ordinary investigators, such as this Pshenichny. And he's clever, this one, too. It goes without saying that a special team will have to be assembled to investigate the Belkin affair, and first in line for inclusion in the team will be Investigator Pshenichny himself. And this despite the fact that the chief editor of *Komsomolskaya Pravda* has lodged a complaint against him and the case has been taken out of his hands. Still, we'll make sure it works out for you, Pshenichny. I'll take that responsibility on myself . . .

And the second member of the team should be Svetlov, I think. He's a first-class detective with a trained nose for these things. Of course, he's already lieutenant-colonel with a whole CID section at his command, a sleuth turned administrator. He's become one of the bosses. All the same, we'll have to have him with all his staff . . .

As all this was going through my mind, I opened a large grey envelope attached to the file and extracted from it that famous No. 1 notebook, marked 'Tashkent-Baku, April – May 1979', which, according to Pshenichny, contained 'information of crucial relevance to the investigation'. The writing had been rapidly scribbled and was difficult to follow. In fact, in places it was downright indecipherable.

As well as the notebook, the envelope also contained forty-eight numbered typewritten sheets, clipped together, which had also been found by Pshenichny at Belkin's flat. Obviously Belkin had been transferring the contents of his notebook to his 'Colibri' typewriter.

I lit up a cigarette, settled back in my chair and began to read.

I can't keep it to myself any longer. If I don't commit to paper an account of all the terrible things that have happened, I'll have to go and drown myself in the Caspian. But if I put over the *whole* horror of events, then who will read it – or rather: how shall I succeed in concealing it from potential readers? I shall have to mix fact with fiction, and vice versa, so that what I am about to write will bear the label 'adventure story' . . .

Chapter I

A Coffin without a Corpse

In May 1979, I, Andrey Garin, special correspondent for *Komsomolskaya Pravda*, the most popular youth newspaper in the Soviet Union, happened to be flying from Tashkent to Baku. To be perfectly honest, my assignment was only supposed to take me to Southern Uzbekistan, or more precisely, to the Surkhansk foothills of the Pamir and Altai mountains. There, a party of glaciologists from the Academy of Sciences was experimenting with a new method of melting glaciers by seeding them from the air with coaldust and soot. I spent part of the time climbing with the glaciologists, and the rest of it flying with the pilots of the Antonov agricultural planes used in the exercise.

Down beneath us was a green carpet of cotton plantations, criss-crossed with the bright-red patches of poppy fields. Early May is the time when poppies flower, and you could see streams of scarlet licking the mountains like flames, reaching to an altitude of 2,000 metres, with only the snow cover of the eternal white peaks surveying their depredations. I don't know which brought the local farms greater profit, the giant cotton plantations in the valleys or these mountainous fields of opium poppies, which are grown here for the pharmaceutical industry. Of course, I had heard a lot of fantastic stories about Afghan smugglers who were supposed to arrive here over secret mountain paths. If I hadn't myself had occasion in the past to write a series of articles about our border police, and if I didn't know how jealously they guard every inch of our own frontiers, then I might have been tempted to believe these wild stories myself. In any case, once I had had a fair bit to drink with Major Ryskulov, the head of the local border post, I asked him a point-blank question about these smugglers. He burst into laughter and said: 'That's one of those tall stories, old fellow! Not even a buzzard crosses the border around here without my permission!'

'And with your permission?'

'Somebody who crosses with my permission wouldn't be a smuggler,' he said with a laugh and changed the subject.

The day before my visit was due to end, some of the Charshanga helicopter pilots dropped me down without question into the neutral zone between frontiers, a mountain valley filled with edelweiss. Of course, the duty officer at the local air-control tower asked us for the password and then began to swear at us for landing in the neutral zone without special permission, but I took the head-set away from the pilot and began to serenade the anti-aircraft gunners with Vysotsky's song: 'And in the neutral zone flowers of unusual beauty . . .' And Vysotsky is absolutely right. These edelweiss were as soft as a kitten's paw: flowers as beautiful and downy as these I hadn't seen during the whole ten days of my visit, and I'd been all over the Surkhansk mountains with the glaciologists.

So now I was carrying back to Moscow a whole pot of magnificent edelweiss – well, the pot was actually one of those black mess-tins that scientists take into the field with them. All the members of the expedition had scratched their names on it, and the glaciologists had made a present of it for our newspaper museum. I didn't know which lucky lady I would present the flowers to in Moscow (I was between love affairs at the time), but knowing my amorous nature, I didn't think the edelweiss would stay in the smoke-blackened mess-tin very long. Could I even have imagined then that my next affair would have such fateful consequences for me? But I won't leap on ahead. I'll merely mention that I was returning with a whole bunch of edelweiss, a nose peeling from the sun, a black mess-tin, and passes to enter the frontier zone and the tiny Charshanga agricultural airport, both signed by the Head of Anti-Aircraft Defences, Central Asian Military District, General Fedoseyev. I also had a few notebooks filled with jottings for a future article, and what was more, a healthy feeling of tiredness, caused by all that walking up and down mountains. Of course, I should have surrendered both special passes at the Chief Border Police Authority in Tashkent, but after the exhausting flight from Charshanga to Tashkent via Samarkand, was it really worth travelling from the airport right into the centre of town merely to hand in a couple of documents at Anti-Aircraft Defence Headquarters, and then rush back to the airport to catch the flight to Moscow? Anyway, they could manage without those two passes, I decided, and you'd have to be a first-class idiot not to keep two such unusual souvenirs for yourself.

So I found myself sitting in the office of the director of Tashkent airport, who had summoned his chief ticket-clerk to write me out a ticket to Moscow, to save me the bother of waiting in the monstrous queue to the booking office. I was listening to a voice on Radio Moscow announcing: 'The temperature in Moscow is plus four degrees, with low cloud and drizzle . . .', when I had a sudden idea: Why not first visit my grandmother in Baku, spend a few nights sleeping on her divan, do a bit of fishing in the Caspian with my old

31

friends and make a start on my article about the glaciologists? After all, it didn't make any difference whether I wrote it at the office in damp old Moscow or at my grandmother's flat in Baku!

'Look here,' I said to the grey-haired ticket-clerk, who was only too willing to ingratiate himself with a famous correspondent from the capital. 'Make me out a ticket for Tashkent – Moscow via Baku, will you? I've just remembered that I've some business to transact in Azerbaidzhan. When's the next flight to Baku?'

The ticket-clerk looked inquiringly at his boss, but the latter couldn't have cared less where he sent the Moscow journalist off to. Just let him get out of the airport as quickly as possible so as not to notice the enormous crush for tickets in the departure hall and write a critical article about it in his newspaper.

'So you want to fly to Baku first?' said the airport director.

'That's right.' I answered decisively.

And while the clerk was writing out the ticket, I could almost feel the cool, green waves of the Caspian flowing into my soul, enveloping me in a weightless and translucent cocoon. It seemed more and more a good idea to go from wandering the sunbaked Uzbek mountains and dirty, soot-covered glaciers straight to my native Caspian where I would dive, swim and harpoon deep in the limpid waters.

I could already taste the sea salt on my lips, the cool green Caspian waves and the unique combination of tiredness and languor that the sea calls forth. I passed through the crowd waiting to get their tickets endorsed, handed my rucksack in at the check-in desk and went out to the tarmac towards the plane, carrying nothing but a small travelling bag. It was an old TU-104 airliner, standing close to the glass building of the air terminal, but passengers weren't allowed on yet, as the baggage was still being loaded. The latter consisted mainly of huge, unwieldy wooden boxes, which were technically forbidden to be transported by plane, and large, mock-leather suitcases, bound with string and peppered with little holes to prevent the fruit and vegetables within from perishing during the flight. Amid all these cumbersome objects the baggage loaders handled my rucksack as if it were a beach ball. Then I watched them tense their muscles and lift an amazingly heavy, zinc coffin towards the plane.

Go on a journey with a corpse! Now I'm a modern, enlightened and educated man, but all the same: an omen is an omen, and I immediately remembered all the signs connected with a coffin. If a coffin is being carried towards you, that's a good omen, because it means that unpleasantness and misfortune are no longer lying in wait for you but have been removed from your path. But if a coffin accompanies you on your journey, that's a sure sign that fate is bound to play some nasty trick on you.

The sods! I thought indignantly. After all, there was a rule against transporting dead bodies in passenger planes. They have to be taken in freight aircraft. I know the rules of Aeroflot. After all, I've been flying about the country for nine years without a break. Someone must have been bribed, without a doubt . . .

To distract myself from the sight of the coffin, I ran my eyes over the passengers who were assembling at the turnstile before walking out on to the airfield. There was a whole crowd of speculators with their great Caucasian peaked caps, their faces badly shaven or not shaven at all, and wearing dark, creased jackets, and taking green vegetables to the Baltic States. There was a round-faced major from the border police, as proud as a turkey-cock, a couple of elderly women dressed in silken Uzbek dresses, and some individual or other, dressed in mourning and wearing a small, black-framed photograph of his dead relative on his chest . . . But wait a minute! I lookd more closely at the face of this 'individual'. Why! It was Ziyalov, Oleg Ziyalov, who had been in the same class as me at school in Baku. We'd been in the sixth form together. We'd cut classes to go off to the cinema together. I'd copy out his assessment work for chemistry, and he'd do the same for me for literature.

'Oleg!' I said, as I stepped towards him.

It seemed to me that he froze for a split second, without turning to face in my direction (this is a natural reaction, after all, when somebody suddenly calls your name). Then I thought that he had to make a conscious effort to turn towards me. After all, he had just lost a relation, I thought, and it was obviously him transporting the coffin. In such a state of mind, it is difficult to switch on to a different wavelength . . .

'Hello! It's me, Garin. Don't you recognize me?' I said, seeing full well that he had recognized me, of course. 'Accept my condolences. Who is it you are burying?'

'My uncle,' he replied very slowly indeed, looking at me suspiciously all the while, as if asking himself: did he know me or not?

'Ziyalov, we were at school together! What are you looking at me like that for? It's me, Garin, you used to sit at a desk behind me at the back of the classroom. Remember?'

'Er, yes . . .' he said reluctantly, as if finding it difficult to remember. 'That's right . . .'

These words of his didn't betray any of the enthusiasm or the friendliness customary on such occasions. I even regretted going up to him. After all, I hadn't altered so much over these eleven or twelve years that he shouldn't recognize me. In fact, he'd become fatter and somewhat flabbier than me. It wasn't that he'd aged, but, after all, there's no need to have folds of fat round your neck at twenty-seven. However, at this point they announced that passengers could board the plane, and started to let people through the turnstile towards the embarkation steps. I wandered off after Ziyalov in the strange position of an old school-friend who hadn't exactly been spurned, but who, none the less, had scarcely been acknowledged.

Well, I don't know, I thought. Perhaps this uncle of his was closer to him than a father, and that was possibly why he was in this trance-like state. I hadn't buried any of my close relatives yet, neither my parents in the Ukraine, nor my grandmother in Baku, so I wouldn't take offence.

'Listen,' I said, when the queue of people came to a halt in front of the steps. 'If you ever need my help in Baku or in Moscow . . . Are you ever in Moscow?'

He gave me a long, hard look once again and took longer than was needed to remember whether he ever visited Moscow or not.

'I was asking you whether you ever go to Moscow,' I said again, thinking to shake him out of this funereal trance. 'I've got a job there with *Komsomolskaya Pravda*, so in case you ever need my help, write down my address. Or give me a ring. The number of the editorial office is printed in every issue. You only need to mention my name . . .'

'Uh-huh,' he said. 'OK.' And walked up the steps, showing the air hostess his ticket.

I was offended. Go to hell then, after all that, I thought. I was a well-known journalist, one of the best feature-writers in the country, whose articles were translated by newspapers and magazines all over Europe, Africa and South America. Why, even Brezhnev himself had included me in his own personal press corps! Yet here was this Ziyalov who didn't want to exchange two words with me! I couldn't give a damn! He was burying his uncle: let him get buried himself, I couldn't care less! Only it was pity he'd had to spoil my good mood. Just as I was beginning to look forward to scuba diving and shashlyks of grey mullet – grilled on a skewer kebab-style – by the seashore, this idiot Ziyalov had to come along with his coffin. Still, I'm exaggerating a little. One thing Ziyalov never was was an idiot. Chemistry, physics and geography were his really strong subjects, and the veranda at his house was always strewn with ancient tomes on palmistry and black magic. I remembered descending on his place with some friends of ours from school and coming upon a strange scene. His ten-year-old sister, an incredibly skinny little creature with huge eyes and a black pigtail, was playing with a skipping-rope and had a completely blank expression on her face. Her eyes were staring straight ahead, while she muttered automatically: 'Five hundred and one, five hundred and two, five hundred and three . . .' Meanwhile Oleg, looking pale and tense, with dilated pupils and sweating intensely, was standing opposite her, his eyes glued to hers, so that we couldn't work out whether he was training her to be a gymnastics champion or whether he'd got her hypnotized.

As I thought about this my feeling of indignation gradually faded and I began to doze off in my seat.

And in all probability I wouldn't even have gone up to Oleg Ziyalov at Baku airport. I would have collected my rucksack at the baggage desk, taken a taxi and – farewell, former school-friend! I haven't seen you for twelve years, and I probably won't see you for another twenty, but still . . .

However, those of us in the third cabin were the last to leave the plane, and when I stepped down on to the hot and dusty airfield at Baku airport, I realized that I wouldn't be able to avoid Ziyalov. There he was, waiting for the coffin at the baggage section, but he wasn't the one who caught my attention. Standing next to him were two other people, one of them a man of about fifty, featureless apart from having a mouthful of metal teeth, and to his right . . .

Forgive me, but the girl standing to his right deserves a fresh paragraph. I know that from the point of view of classical literature this may sound hackneyed, banal or even stupid, and . . . Call it what you like, if a person falls in love the first time he sees someone, it is hackneyed, banal and stupid, of course, but . . .

She was about twenty-two, with deep blue eyes and black hair tied up in a tight bun. She was wearing a blue-grey summer dress and her whole figure exuded grace and harmony. That's all, my friends. I've nothing further to add, except to say that the vision of this figure outlined against a background of Ilyushin and Tupolev airliners, like some cheap Aeroflot advertising poster, was impressed on my soul for ever, despite all the fateful events which were to occur during the days that followed.

Obviously not all my rational faculties had deserted me, because I suddenly remembered from somewhere deep in my memory that skinny ten-year-old girl with the big, staring eyes who had been jumping over a skipping-rope and intoning. 'Five hundred and two, five hundred and three . . .'

And then I went straight up to face those deadly blue eyes. I strode right across the tarmac, despite the obvious displeasure of Oleg Ziyalov, who was standing next to me and eyeing me in an almost hostile manner. He could go to hell! I walked right up to her, to those eyes of hers. It was too late for her to turn away, as I looked into them and said to her: 'I know you. You're Oleg's sister. Hello. My name's Andrey' – and I offered her my hand.

She looked at her brother anxiously, but he said nothing, so she took my hand. 'I'm called Anya,' she said.

Her grip was light and cool.

'Oleg and I were in the same class together at school,' I said. 'I saw you once at your house. You were playing with a skipping-rope and saying, "Five hundred and one, five hundred and two, five hundred and three." Remember?'

She smiled and shrugged her shoulders. 'I don't remember,' she replied. 'But if somebody was skipping there, then it was me.'

Nodding in the direction of the aeroplane, where I could see baggage handlers unloading the coffin from the hold, I offered her my condolences. Meanwhile I noticed that all three of them, including the older man, who was twisting a set of car keys around his fingers, had become very tense and had their eyes glued on the coffin. However, at a sign from Ziyalov, the man walked over to the baggage handlers. At that moment I registered the fact that Anya had come to the airport to meet her uncle's coffin wearing a light summer dress, not the dark clothes usually worn by somebody in mourning. This gave me the moral right to open my bag, extract the pot of edelweiss and offer her the entire bunch of downy, beautiful flowers.

'Anya, these are from the Pamirs. I realize that this is neither the time nor place, but . . . I hope I'll see you again.'

Then I turned towards Ziyalov. 'May I phone you some time?'

'Uh-huh,' he mutterd, none too certainly, and took his sister by the hand. Good heavens! How unalike they were! He led her out of the baggage area, following in the footsteps of the porters, who were carrying the coffin towards the exit, assisted by the fifty-year-old man. The four of them were obviously finding the coffin a heavy burden. You might have thought that the Ziyalovs' uncle weighed fifteen or sixteen stone. I tapped Oleg's elbow. 'Come on, let's give them a hand,' I said. 'Here, Anya, hold this,' and I passed her my bag.

'Stop!' said Ziyalov rather rudely.

'What do you mean? Let's give them a hand.'

He shook his head. 'No, I'm not allowed to.' And I suddenly remembered that he was quite right. According to custom, close relatives are not supposed to touch the deceased's coffin. But this didn't apply to me, so I almost forcibly thrust my light travelling bag into Anya's hands, caught up with the baggage handlers and put my shoulder to the heavy zinc coffin. Of course, this was done not so much to help the porters, as from a desire to busy myself in front of the girl with whom I had fallen in love and to whose house I might get invited, or at least to the funeral . . .

Whatever the reason, I put my shoulder to the coffin

and we carried it through the turnstile, past the crowd of people waiting to meet the other passengers, and headed on outside, towards a car that was waiting on the station square. Suddenly, some six-year-old boy, with his arms outspread and making a humming noise like a plane, ran into one of the baggage handlers, the one on the left at the front.

It wasn't so much the boy's weight as his impetus that pushed the man from under the coffin, as if somebody had pulled away a support, and the heavy zinc box lurched sharply forward. The other man left on his own at the front, let go of the coffin as he moved his shoulder to one side, and the enormous object hurtled to the ground in an almost upright position.

The crowd of passengers were suddenly hushed. 'Good God!' said someone, as the coffin hit the ground, fell forward once again and finally landed sideways on the asphalt, breaking open a line of soldering as it did so. Nobody moved, neither me, the porters, nor the crowd. Everybody expected the body of the dead man suddenly to fall out of the coffin. It appeared unavoidable, but it didn't happen. What did fall out were dozens of paper packages. Some of them had broken open with the impact, scattering all over the ground tiny pieces of polythene film, packed in bundles. Each piece was about the size of a postage stamp and stained with some brownish oily mark!

We were stupefied! One of the baggage handlers bent down cautiously, picked up a whole bundle and turned it over in his hands: 'What's this then, naphthalene?' he said with a Caucasian accent.

I saw Ziyalov's male companion silently back away behind the crowd, his metallic teeth clenched tightly, his eyes firmly fixed on the shattered coffin, which was still spewing forth tiny pieces of polythene film all over the roadway. Then one of the passengers bent down, picked up a polythene bundle, rubbed one of the brownish grease-marks with his finger, put it to his nose, gave a sniff and suddenly said with a loud laugh:

'Naphthalene, my foot! It's opium!' – and grabbing a whole armful of the bundles, began to stuff all his pockets with them.

My God! You should have seen what happened next! The people who had just been standing in muted sorrow before the coffin all at once rushed towards it, snatching up bundles of opium was they did so. One of them forced the lid of the coffin up a little further, grabbing more packets from inside. It was pandemonium! Those who had managed to fill their pockets or clutch great piles to their chests weren't able to get back through the hordes of people behind them. Taxi drivers, flower-sellers, speculators – all joined in the fray, and were getting crushed. If it hadn't been for the sound of a police whistle, I don't know whether or not I would have come out of it alive. The militia didn't yet know what it was all about, of course, and supposing that somebody might be getting murdered at the epicentre of this swarming rabble, they rushed in towards us, hitting out with fists to left and right and blowing their whistles all the time. It was this sound rather than the fists which finally brought the crowd to its senses. People picked up what opium they could and rushed off in all directions. The baggage handlers ran off too, and only I remained, at the centre of events, not yet understanding what had happened and looking around all the while for Ziyalov, his sister and the fifty-year-old relative. But there was no sign of them anywhere. I thought I could see a minibus disappearing off the edge of the square, the same one that we'd been carrying the coffin towards. But I was wrong. There was a different, cloth-capped moustachioed Azerbaidzhani sitting at the wheel. I looked around me in panic. After all, Anya had been carrying my bag containing all my notebooks, papers, passport . . . And at that very moment a black-moustached Azerbaidzhani militiaman put his hand on my shoulder and said, with a strong accent: 'You are under arrest.'

'One p.m., Moscow time!' came a voice from behind the wall in Baklanov's office, reminding me that it was time to go for lunch.

'*What* time is it?' I said to myself in panic, automatically looking at my watch. I'd become absorbed in all these documents when I should have been getting an investigation team together as a matter of urgency.

'No. I'm not going to lunch, I'm sorry,' I shouted through to Baklanov. Then I picked up the telephone. The people I needed most urgently now were this Investigator Pshenichny, whom I didn't know, and that old bloodhound, Lieutenant-Colonel Marat Svetlov. They both already knew the details of the case. If only I could get them. There wouldn't be any problem about Pshenichny, but as for Svetlov . . .

I dialled the number of Moscow River Prosecutor's Office and said: 'This is the USSR Prosecutor's Office speaking, Special Investigator Shamrayev here. I need to talk to Investigator Pshenichny.'

This was enough to make whoever was on the other end of the line pause a moment and then say in an obliging rush: 'Shall I get him to come to the phone?'

People always make fools of themselves when they're talking to anybody of higher rank. I've caught myself doing it. What else would I wish him to do, if I was phoning him up? But I didn't want to exchange witticisms with the Moscow River Prosecutor, so I waited while the distant voice at the other end of the phone shouted out: 'Quiet! Where's Pshenichny? Tell him to come quickly! There's a call for him from the USSR Prosecutor's Office!'

Half a minute went by, and just as I was beginning to lose patience a voice said: 'Hello, Investigator Pshenichny here.'

'Hello,' I said. 'My name's Shamrayev, Special Investigator at the Chief Public Prosecutor's Office. I need to see you urgently.'

'About the Belkin case?'

'That's right. What time suits you?'

'When do you want to see me?'

'When? To be quite honest, right away.' I tried to make it sound not so much like an order from above as an ordinary request from a colleague. I don't know whether he detected this or not, but at least he didn't start making awkward objections. Instead, he replied quite simply: 'I can be there in forty minutes. Where's your office?'

'Fourth floor, Room 418. Thanks. I'll be expecting you.'

Yes, he certainly appeals to me so far, this Pshenichny! And I was already happily dialling '02', the Moscow Militia number.

'Operator, get me CID Department 3, Head of Section 2.'

'Svetlov? Just one moment.'

And a few seconds later I could hear another female voice saying: 'Kulagin's Department. Secretary speaking.'

'Get me Svetlov, please.'

'And who is this calling?'

'Tell him it's Shamrayev.'

I didn't have long to wait. Svetlov lifted the receiver immediately. 'Hello! What brings you to the phone?' he said in his usual cheerful patter.

'Hello, colonel,' I replied, to make him realize that I knew all about his rapid promotion. 'How are things? Are you buried in paperwork, or are you still alive?'

'Well ... Do you want to go out and get some women?'

The sod, I thought, down to basics straight away, as usual.

'Well, we can go and get some women, too ...' I replied. I wasn't sure yet how to broach the subject so I thought I'd draw things out a bit.

'But you don't need detectives to help you get women, eh?' he said. 'Don't forget that I'm not a detective any more, but a bureaucrat, an office

42

drudge,' he went on airily. He still prattled on in the same way, despite his promotion.

'OK, drudge! But couldn't you abandon your papers for a couple of hours, get into your special colonel's police car, set your sirens blazing and tear over here to see me at Pushkin Street?'

'Oho! With sirens blazing, no less! What's this – an order? An instruction? What's happened?'

'Nothing terrible, but I do need to see you.'

'All right,' he said in a businesslike way. 'I'll be over there right away.'

People like Svetlov thrive on intrigue and excitement – even in their ordinary everyday lives. I was certain that he'd arrive within ten minutes.

Then Baklanov's inquisitive face appeared at the door.

'So what was that about serving people?'

'What?' I said, uncomprehendingly.

'You know, I was asking you about being fed up with being other people's servant.'

He was quite right. I'd completely forgotten about our earlier conversation. That's what's known as getting into the swing of a case.

'Well,' said Baklanov again. 'Shall we sink a few more jars, as a mark of protest?'

'No,' I replied, 'I can't any longer. People will be here any minute.'

'So you've taken the plunge?'

'Yes, I have.'

'OK. In that case I'd better go and ask for some work to do, too. Here I am, back from vacation, and people seem to have forgotten all about me.'

BELKIN'S MANUSCRIPT
(continued)

Chapter 2
The Baku Drug-Addicts

Sashka Shakh was keeping an eye open for the militia or vigilantes, while Sickly Simon was on the lookout for somebody, preferably a woman, wearing a gold watch or carrying a purse. If he found a likely victim he'd give the signal to Rafik Gaikazyan and help make a commotion near the victim, while Rafik grabbed the spoils.

This was their ordinary 'work'. It had a certain element of risk about it, to say the least, and they were all three of them experts at their trade. But that day they were out of luck. What they'd taken that morning turned out not to be a gold watch at all, but just an ordinary gold-plated watch-case, and Tolik Khachmas, the sod, wasn't born yesterday. They were long-standing customers of his, and Tolik wouldn't even give them enough hash for a single joint. Meanwhile, the morning rush-hour had passed and by now, after 10 a.m., only housewives would be in the trams, travelling back from market, with their bags full of green vegetables, aubergines, chickens and radishes. And it's not worth thieving a radish!

Shakh could feel the first stiffening in his joints. It was tolerable at the moment, but in half an hour's time, unless he could get a fix, this aching feeling would begin to flatten him and even cause pain in his eyes. He had to steal something as quickly as possible and buy a fix, one of those life-saving, greasy brown drops of opium on a piece of polythene film.

Ah! At last! There was a No. 7 tram with a trailer turning out of Basin Street into Lenin Street, with Sickly Simon hanging off the platform of the first door in the trailer. Nobody has shut the door of a Baku tram for as long as anyone can remember – in the first place, to keep the air cool by letting in a bit of ventilation, and in the second, for the convenience of the passengers. Anybody can jump on or off a tram while it's in motion, if he can. This is the done thing, and even quite elderly Azerbaidzhanis sometimes jump off as a tram slows down to turn a corner.

Sickly Simon was hanging off the platform of the

trailer and nodded his head slightly in the direction of a man in glasses, who was hanging on beyond him. Shakh noticed the gesture and could see even from a long way off the Seiko watch the man was wearing. He moved stealthily forward and with a series of long strides caught up with the tram. There was no question of undoing the watch-strap and letting the Seiko simply fall into his outstretched palm. It was one of those bracelet jobs, so getting hold of it wouldn't be so easy. Grabbing the hand-rail, Shakh jumped on to the platform and roughly shoved Simon forwards and upwards, so that he pushed the man in spectacles back towards Rafik, who was waiting further inside.

'What are you shoving for?' shouted Simon, spoiling for a fight.

'Fuck off,' said Shakh, pushing him once again.

'You son of a bitch!' snapped Simon, moving his hand down threateningly towards him.

The man in glasses, of course, moved on further into the tram, to get as far away as possible from these hooligans, but Rafik pushed against him from behind, while Simon shouted from the platform: 'Rafik, they're attacking us!'

And now the two of them. Rafik over the head of the man in glasses, who was getting in his way, and Simon, began to belabour Shakh around the head and shoulders, while Shakh, with all the appearance of mounting rage, grabbed hold of Simon and began to push him off the moving tram.

'Let's get off and fight it out, you bastard!' shouted Shakh.

The main aim of the scuffle was to create the maximum crush around the man in glasses, and then, the moment he tried to extricate himself from the three brawlers, one of them would grab the arm with the watch for a moment and press it under his own arm, so that when the victim finally pushed himself away from the fight, the watch would no longer be around his wrist.

And everything went beautifully, without a hitch. The General hadn't spent a month training them for nothing. He was as good a professional as you'd find in the best theatrical schools. He was the king of the Baku criminal fraternity. I don't mean that he was the leader of all those thousands of layabouts, hooligans, tramps and other uncontrollable ruffians who swarm over this enormous city with its million inhabitants. I have in mind the gang of professional, hash-smoking thieves that he himself created. As recently as three or four years ago, when Shakh was in the sixth form at school, he was still filching Bulgarian cigarettes from his father, who, as a colonel in the border police, could get them at the officers' stores. He and his mates would go and smoke these cigarettes behind the Sabunchinsky railway station on a small hillock which was the quiet, inconspicuous scene of their teenage tomfoolery. They could play truant from school there, and the wild mass of bushes which concealed this hillock from the rest of the world was an ideal place for them to play about in and smoke. They could daydream, swear as much as they liked or read the dog-eared pages of books like *One Hundred and Forty Ways of Indian Love-making*. Beyond the fence, at the foot of the hill, was a marshalling-yard with freight trains constantly coming and going. If you had nothing else to do, you could spend hours watching the loading and unloading of goods trucks, listen to the loaders exchanging foul language with their traffic controllers, or follow all the customers as they fussed about, looking for their boxes and containers . . .

But one day the General turned up on the hill. Of course, nobody knew his nickname then. As far as Shakh and his friends knew, this was simply some old fogy coming up to them to talk. (Anybody aged over forty was an 'old fogy' to them.) Anyway, here he was, and he told them that he was a trainer in unarmed combat and looking for lads to join his youth class. He had a look at all of them, but didn't choose anybody in particular. Instead, he saw that somebody had a pack of cards and offered to teach them how to play the Russian gambling game called *sekka*. The boys had played cards for money before, just to amuse themselves, but the stakes had never been more than thirty or forty kopecks. But after the General's first appearance, things began to change, slowly but surely. The stakes grew larger, and they took more and more risks. At first the General always used to lose. He was easily and even cheerfully parted from his money, and after playing for an hour he might leave the lads with eight or nine roubles. He would then go off, saying he had some business or other to attend to, and they would continue to play against each other, redistributing the money which he had contributed to the game in the first place. The next day, the one who ended up winning would reappear, showing off a new pocket-knife or Cuban cigar which he had bought with the money. A couple of years later, when Sashka had become one of the General's close assistants and had been given his nickname, Shakh, or the Shah, he realized that these regular losses on the General's part of eight or nine roubles a day were in fact the opening moves in a carefully calculated psychological game. First of all, the General would begin by getting them used to handling money, and not only the lads who gathered together on this particular hill, but the denizens of twenty or thirty similar places elsewhere in Baku. Adding them all together, he would probably lose 200 or 300 roubles a day, but this didn't last very long. Once he'd got them used to taking risks for higher stakes, he would gradually begin to win his money back, and soon the whole macro-gang, consisting of boys in their last year or two of school all over Baku, was in debt to him. Moreover, it would somehow turn out that the boys in greatest debt were the strongest ones, the leaders of their group. And although the General didn't demand repayment at the beginning, the feeling that they were in debt none the less made them dependent on him, and unable to break away. After that the General began just as imperceptibly to get them used to taking drugs, hashish for the most part.

At first they were afraid to inject themselves with morphine and limited themselves to hash. But once they had got to like the latter, and they had no money to buy it with, the General would start to bring them pharmaceutically produced morphine or drops of opium on polythene strips. Gradually he got them accustomed to it. He also showed them how to use a hypodermic syringe, and then they'd inject morphine and opium into their veins, getting high in the little public garden next to their hill.

And so it went on. The General was in no hurry. He would observe and sometimes, for a joke, show them how to filch a watch off someone's wrist without their noticing, use a razor blade to cut away someone's back pocket with a wallet, and other such tricks of the sneak-thief's trade. But he would always sternly forbid them to try anything like it themselves in real life. But there was no stopping the boys. They had a great need for money now, not just to play cards with or repay debts to the General and to each other, but also to buy hash, opium and morphine. There's no stopping the hardened addict, especially if he's young and not yet out of his teens.

So it was that, as if yielding to their pressure, the General split them up into groups of three and began to teach them to become professional thieves. As a result of what he taught them and the money they owed him, they became his debtors for life, and hence his permanent assistants, obliged to share part of their spoils with him on every occasion. The General spent a month training them, and this amounted to nothing less than a whole course of instruction in the art and science of being a thief. It included both theory (thieves' law) and initiation ritual. Shortly after, the whole town, and especially its tram routes, was strictly divided up between the groups of three. According to Shakh's

48

arithmetic, there were about thirty such trios beholden to the General. His boys were at work along practically the whole tram network. And it was an exciting, vital life, meeting your friends at an agreed street corner in the early hours, checking out two or three trams in the morning rush-hour, whipping a couple of watches and a wallet or two, and then heading straight to the Drama Theatre in the middle of town. There in his usual place, you'd find Tolik Khachmas, a pusher of hash and opium.

The lads would never hoard very much of their loot, they hadn't the patience. They would just take as much as would buy them enough drugs for a couple of fixes or two or three joints. In the morning the hardened smoker doesn't think about a packet of cigarettes to last him the whole day. His mind is fixed on a single cigarette, or even on one long puff of one. And what happens later, when the high begins to pass, doesn't matter. It'll be lunch-time by then, the trams will already be filled with people during the midday rush-hour, and there'll be pickings enough to buy a new fix . . . And so it goes on, till evening. Only once did they steal, not for money or drugs, but for the sheer hell of doing so. That was a real art for art's sake occasion, when each of them exerted himself to the limit of his professional ability. It had happened the previous summer, during the Neftyannik–Ararat football match. This game was bound to be nothing less than a historic battle between Azerbaidzhan and Armenia, with political, cultural and nationalist overtones. Indeed, it was one of the only legal expressions of the ancient tribal enmity between the Azerbaidzhanis and the Armenians. It couldn't be ruled out that, were Ararat to win, the whole city of Baku might have been witness to an Armenian massacre. That's obviously what the authorities thought too, because troops were drafted into the town the day before the match, and there were reinforced military patrols with six men apiece openly walking the streets.

It was obvious that, on the day of the match, the trams going to and from the stadium would be fantastically full, and it would have been a crime not to take advantage of such an opportunity. So the General organized a competition between all thirty of his 'trios' to see who could steal most watches on that one day. As they say in the newspapers, the lads took up the challenge with animation and fervour, especially since the General had promised the victors a unique reward – a real Browning automatic.

They were due to count up who'd stolen what at 9 p.m. in the Malakansky Gardens in the centre of town. Once all the groups had gathered together, each trio began to unload its takings on to a park bench. One lot had filched eighteen pairs of watches, another twenty-three, and a third group twenty-seven. This was the work of Shakh's team, but even they were outclassed by Arif, nicknamed Mosol, whose trio had taken two pairs more. So those were the ones to whom the General presented the revolver. It was a tiny, lady's version without any bullets. 'That doesn't matter,' said Mosol. 'It's a Browning, and that's the most important thing. We'll soon get some bullets!' Then the General, with a quiet chuckle, opened his own briefcase and emptied his takings into the general pile. Without anybody's help he'd managed to take sixty-nine watches in one day. There's work for you!

But on the day I am describing, the routine on the tram went as smoothly as clockwork. In a short scuffle lasting perhaps twenty or thirty seconds, Simon and Rafik managed to crowd in on the man in glasses so that he pushed his way further down the tram out of fright. However, the wrist on which he wore his watch seemed to get accidentally stuck under Rafik's elbow, and as the man attempted to dislodge it, Shakh deftly undid the bracelet with a fingernail. Nothing else was necessary. As he moved his arm, the victim in glasses himself slipped his wrist out of the bracelet, and the watch fell, like a ripe fruit, into Shakh's waiting palm.

'Got it!' Shakh whispered to Simon, before shouting, 'You son of a bitch!' at him and pulling him off the platform, as if dragging him away for a fight. Rafik jumped off after them, and in full sight of the passengers in the departing tram, they carried on the scuffle with Rafik trying to keep them apart – but only for as long as it took for the tram to disappear round the corner. Then Shakh took the watch out of his pocket and all three of them admired their prize – a real Japanese Seiko. If they were to queue up at the State Commission shop, they'd make a hundred roubles in half an hour. But they wouldn't bother, of course. They needed some opium and hash right away, and although Tolik Khachmas wouldn't give them more than fifty roubles for the watch, it wouldn't make any difference. If only he was still in his usual spot and hadn't slipped off anywhere yet. It was already eleven o'clock, after all.

Without a word, all three of them set off by their usual route, across Station Square towards the Drama Theatre in the centre of town, when suddenly . . .

Shakh froze. The others stopped too.

There on the pavement in front of them, leaning against a street lamp and crying bitterly, like Snow White in the fairytale, was a seventeen-year-old girl of exceptional beauty, with light-blue eyes and obviously not from Baku. At her feet was a small suitcase, and she had an open travelling bag in her hand. The Baku sun was beating down on her ash-blonde hair, its rays shimmering in a faint rainbow – an effect they had never seen before, as if each hair were able to refract the sun's light into marvellous colours. And, just like a child, she was trying to use her fist to wipe away the tears of an uncontrollable crying fit.

'What's the matter?' asked Shakh as he strode resolutely towards her.

'N-n-nothing . . .' she said through her tears.

'What are you bawling for then?'

She raised her blue eyes to look at him, and Shakh's heart missed a beat.

51

'I've ... I've ... lost my money ... and the ... address ...' she said.

'What address? And how did you lose it? Where do you come from?'

'I've ... I've ... just got off the train ... from Vilnius ... I've come to visit my aunt ... I just got off this minute ... I had a purse ...' and she showed him the bag which she was carrying. 'My money was in it, and my passport, and my aunt's address ...' And then she started wailing again.

'Wait a minute,' said Shakh, taking her by the arm. 'Did somebody approach you?'

'No,' she said. 'Although one lad did help me carry my things at the railway station ...'

'What was he like?'

'Nothing much. He was tall with black hair ... So what?'

'Was he wearing a peaked cap?'

'Yes, he was. So what?' she asked, looking at him once again with those great blue eyes of hers. The boys looked at each other.

'It must have been Mosol,' said Rafik confidently. The station was Arif Mosol's patch, and all three of them realized that it must have been his doing. Shakh looked down at the stolen Seiko. It was a quarter to twelve.

'What time did the train arrive?' he asked.

'At eleven o'clock ... So what?'

'It doesn't matter. Let's go.' And, taking her suitcase, he moved resolutely towards the taxi-rank.

'Where are we going?' she asked in amazement.

'Let's move!' he said to Rafik and Simon. 'How much money was there in the purse?' he asked her.

'Eighty roubles for the return ticket,' she replied. 'But where are we going to?'

'Get in,' he said, opening the door of an empty taxi. There was no time to lose. After filching the purse, Mosol would have taken out the money straight away and thrown the purse itself and the other contents

52

aside somewhere, in a rubbish bin, or under some gate or other. But where? He looked round the square from where he was standing, imagining what he would have done with the purse, to get rid of the evidence as quickly as possible. But how was he to know where and at what precise moment Mosol had lifted the purse? He might have done it on the platform. No, there was nothing for it. He'd have to find him immediately, and with eighty roubles, there was only one place where Mosol would have gone, of course – to Tolik Khachmas.

'Drama Theatre,' he said to the driver, and almost pushed his flabbergasted accomplices and this blue-eyed cry-baby into the taxi. 'What's your name?'

'Lina.'

'And your surname?'

'Braknite.'

'What?' he asked again.

'Braknite, Lina Braknite.'

'I see. OK,' he said, committing it to memory. 'My name's Sasha, Sasha Romanov. Don't forget. And I'm your cousin.'

'Cousin?' she repeated in amazement.

'Yes. We'll have to play it like that. And if anybody asks, you're my cousin.' Then he turned towards Rafik and Simon: 'Understood?'

'OK,' they replied, already guessing what he was intending to do. Then he added for their benefit, and in Azerbaidzhani, so that Lina wouldn't understand, 'And if anybody gives me away, I'll . . . I'll . . .' But he couldn't bring himself to swear in her presence, even in Azerbaidzhani. His tongue simply wouldn't form the usual word. In any case, it didn't matter, as Rafik and Simon understood perfectly well what he meant.

'So why didn't your aunt come to meet you at the railway station?'

'I don't know . . .'

'Can you remember her address?'

'No . . .'

'What about her surname?'

53

'Of course, I can remember that. Her name is Nora Gustavovna Braknite,' she said, looking at him with the trusting gaze of a child who has found the firm hand of an adult to hang on to.

And it was this expression of hers, this trusting belief that he, Sashka Shakh, would help her in this strange and unknown city which made him feel, perhaps for the first time, that a woman had faith in him as a man, as someone who would protect her. It filled him with such resolution that even if Mosol were to meet him with a loaded gun, nothing would have stopped Sashka.

The taxi drew up at the Drama Theatre.

'Stay here,' he said to Lina, and he almost ran down the narrow alleyway between the buildings towards the half-hidden shady courtyard behind the theatre, where Tolik Khachmas usually hung out. Thank God, there he was in his usual place! Sashka silently offered him the Seiko and saw Tolik's eyes gleam. 'How much will you give?' he asked.

'Made in Odessa, I suppose?' said Tolik in a drawling voice, trying to lower the price.

'Khachmas, don't mess about. I'm in a hurry. It's not rubbish, you can see that for yourself. It's the real Japanese make. Have you seen Mosol?'

'What if I have?' replied Tolik, examining the watch, or rather admiring it.

'I need to see him. Has he been here today? With bread?'

'Yes, he's been . . .'

'How long ago?'

'I'm not sure . . . Ten minutes ago . . . I'll give you forty roubles for it.' he said, naming his price.

'Give it back,' replied Shakh, making a decisive grab for the watch.

'Not so fast. What's up?'

'Nothing. I'm going to Mamed, I need bread.'

'Don't you want any hash or anything?'

'I need bread, money, get it?' said Sashka angrily and impatiently.

'How much?'

'Fifty. And if you let me have it, I'll take enough for two joints from you, or even three.' He was remembering about himself too. He had in mind enough each for Rafik and Simon, whom he had to get rid of as quickly as possible, to stop them blurting out anything in Lina's presence that she didn't need to hear. The third pellet he would hide somewhere for himself and smoke it when Lina wasn't around. After all, he couldn't smoke hash in front of her, but he couldn't *not* smoke it either. His bones and joints would start to ache terribly.

'I'll give you forty,' said Khachmas.

'Fuck off!' shouted Sashka, and tore the Seiko out of Tolik's hand.

'Wait a minute. Have you lost your marbles today, or what?' asked Khachmas in amazement. He'd really never seen Sashka in such an excited state. 'Here, take hold of these,' he said, producing three tiny pieces of hashish from the lining of his jacket and handing over thirty-five roubles as well.

'Who gave you this bread? Was it Mosol?' asked Sashka, pointing towards the rouble notes.

'Well, what if it was?'

'Was it eighty roubles he gave you?'

'None of your business. However much he gave me, it's my money now,' said Tolik, just in case. 'You've got your bread. Now push off!'

He was quite correct. Nobody has the right to look in somebody's pocket, especially if there's stolen money in it! Sashka stuffed the notes into his own pocket, closed his fist over the pellets and went back to the car, gesturing to Simon and Rafik as he did so. They immediately scrambled out of the taxi, and Sashka deftly slipped the two portions of hash into Rafik's hand, without being noticed. Then he said: 'Push off somewhere, only don't go up the hill. You haven't seen me today at all, OK? Right! That's that.' And he dived into the car, saying to the driver as he did so: 'Drive us to Armenikend, the Stalin Palace of Culture.'

The palace was in the Armenian quarter of Baku, and although it had long ago been renamed after Yury Gagarin, nobody in the city called the palace by its new name. Behind it was another public garden with a hill – only this time it was the domain of Arif Mosol.

When the car moved off, Sashka took Lina by the hand and said: 'Don't worry. It'll all turn out all right. Look, there's the Malakansky Gardens, and now we're coming into the centre of town. Over there is the Nizami Museum . . .'

The taxi hurtled along the main streets up towards the hilly area of old Baku. As they reached the top of steeply ascending Lenin Street, Lina looked around and gave a gasp of admiration. There was the enormous greenish-blue saucer of the Caspian beneath them, and all round it the city dipping down to the very water's edge in narrow terraces with green, flat roofs, dotted here and there with modern, whitewashed houses, public gardens and parks. The sails of boats from the Yacht Club gleamed white in the middle of the sea . . .

'How beautiful!' said Lina. 'And everybody told me that the sea was a black colour, polluted with oil. Just look – it's perfectly green!'

The car braked to a halt outside the Stalin Palace of Culture. Sashka left Lina sitting in the taxi once again, crossed the street and entered the public garden. Mosol and his band were there in their usual place. They were sitting back on a park bench, enjoying a high after injecting themselves with opium. When Sashka went up to them, Mosol opened one eye very slightly, and then, just as lazily, a second. They had never been enemies, but then they'd never been friends either. Each had his own area, and each observed the rules, never interfering in one another's patch. Of course, there was scarcely any love lost between these lads from Armenikend and the boys from the city centre, but there was no open enmity between them either. There had never been an opportunity, I suppose.

This was the reason for Mosol's surprised and expectant expression.

'Hello,' said Sashka, looking at them all and feeling his knees go weak with envy. There they were, all of them high on drugs, having smoked or injected their fill and now experiencing that indescribably airy, fluid feeling of euphoria and buoyancy, that carefree feeling of joy and well-being which no words are able to convey.

'Salaam,' replied Mosol.

'I've got some business to discuss with you,' said Shakh.

'Carry on,' came the reply.

Sashka looked at the two lads sitting on either side of their chief. They had also opened their eyes suspiciously and Sashka could see the torpid gaze of their drugged pupils. All right, there was nothing else for it. He'd have to speak in their presence, too. After all, Mosol hadn't come to him. He'd visited them in their garden.

'OK. An hour ago you took my young cousin's identity papers from her at the railway station. Makhanya was supposed to meet her but she couldn't as she's ill, and I was ten minutes late in arriving. There was some bread in her purse, too, but the money's yours now, and I'm not asking for it back. But I do want the purse back, or for you to let me know where you chucked it.'

Mosol stared at him for a long time and one could see that native wit of his stirring in the depths of his black, Armenian eyes. Sashka could read in them the way Mosol was willing himself out of his drug-induced state, freeing his brain from it and coming out with the only response of which he was capable: 'And what if she isn't your cousin? Then what?'

'I tell you, she is. She's sitting outside in a taxi. You can go and ask her, if you like.'

'Huh, why bring the girl into it?' said Mosol with a laugh. 'It's you I'm asking. If she's your cousin, that's one thing, but if she's not, that's another. Am I right?' he asked his two cronies, who burst into helpless fits of laughter.

Sashka stood there, calmly waiting. Of course, Mosol wouldn't do anything for anybody for nothing. At the very least he'd boast to people that Shakh had stood before him asking for a favour.

'OK, that's enough. Shut up, you two!' Mosol suddenly said to his companions in Armenian. Then he addressed Sashka: 'I chucked away the papers and the purse, you know yourself . . .'

'Where did you chuck them?' asked Sashka impatiently.

'In the courtyard where they used to sell kebabs. Do you know where I mean?'

Shakh knew. Mosol meant the yard next to the station. Only which rubbish skip had he thrown them into? There were nine or ten there at least. It was a huge courtyard, and as many as a hundred families use those skips for their rubbish.

'I know the place,' he replied. 'Only which skip did you chuck them in?'

Mosol laughed slyly and spread out his hands in a gesture of helplessness.

'I don't remember, old lad. You know, I was in a hurry. Perhaps it was the third one, or the fourth . . . Eh?' he said, turning towards his companions.

Those blockheads started to laugh, like hyenas, at the thought of Sashka Shakh rummaging about in rubbish skips looking for his little cousin's passport.

'OK, that's enough,' said Sashka. 'Thank you, Mosol.' And he was about to go when Mosol stopped him.

'Wait a minute, Shakh.' He thrust his hand into his pocket and pulled out some crumpled rouble notes. Then he did the same with the other pocket, slowly, as if to make a point and to show that he was producing all the money which he had on him. Spreading them out on the park bench, he smoothed out each note, counting aloud as he did so. 'Twenty, twenty-one, twenty-two roubles – and forty kopecks. Here you are. Take it, Shakh.'

This was what Sashka had feared, that Mosol would give him all the money left over from Lina's purse. And he'd done that very thing.

'No, didn't I say the money was yours? You didn't know she was my cousin,' said Shakh, resisting the offer.

'When I didn't know, I took it. When I found out, I gave it all back. Can you all see?' he said to his companions.

They nodded. They could all see that Mosol had dug deep into his pocket and given every last kopeck to Shakh, because Shakh had said that the money belonged to his cousin.

'Take it. If it's your cousin's money, that's enough for me. I believe you. Take it.'

There was nothing else to do. Sashka took the money, and the moment he had it in his hand, Mosol said softly but firmly: 'You've accepted it. Everybody saw you. But if she turns out not to be your cousin, then I've got a claim on you, right?'

'OK, Mosol,' said Sashka as lightheartedly as he could. 'OK. Goodbye.'

And he went off towards the taxi. Those unlucky twenty roubles were burning a hole in his hand. Because of the money, Mosol now had a claim on him. In any place, at any time of day or night, in front of any person, Mosol could now do what he liked with him – beat him up, cut him with a razor blade, stab him or even kill him, and according to the rules of the criminal fraternity, Sashka would have no right to offer resistance. He'd taken the money, he'd put his seal to the fact that Lina was his cousin, and if Mosol could prove this was rubbish, then he would have a claim on Sashka.

Shakh went up to the car, saw Lina's anxious eyes – they were like snowdrops, or like the eyes of a child's doll – and, aware suddenly of gentle emotion, overcame these dark thoughts. She had faith in him and was anxious on his behalf, so what did some jerk like Mosol matter? Let him go to hell with all those 'claims' of his!

Sashka sat in the taxi and said to the driver: 'Take us to the station, the courtyard where they used to sell kebabs.'

'Let me see the money first,' came the sudden reply. 'There's already twenty-five roubles on the clock. Are you going to be able to pay?'

'Don't worry, I'll pay. Here, take this,' he said, emptying all the money he'd got from Mosol on to the front seat along with the twenty roubles from the cash he'd received from Tolik Khachmas. 'Is that enough for you? Let's go!'

'Have you given him all your money?' said Lina in alarm.

'What if I have?' asked Shakh.

'I want something to eat . . .'

Damn it! That soft Baltic accent of hers, those eyes, that hair, that trustfulness! God knows what was making his head spin, Lina or the fact that he'd not only not had a fix all day, but that he hadn't even taken a drag of hash!

'But we've got to find your passport.'

'Yes, I know . . .' She spoke so softly that he really did begin to think that she was related to him, a cousin or something.

The car came to a sudden halt by the yard next to the kebab house. Lina wanted to go with him, but he left her in the cab again. Having her rummage about in the rubbish skips with him was all he needed! He nipped in quickly behind the gate to the place where the rubbish was stowed.

Dozens of bright blue and green flies were buzzing around the piles of old food and refuse. Nearly an hour and a half had passed since Mosol had tossed Lina's purse and passport into one of the skips, along with her aunt's address. The latter wasn't very important, it was true. You could always find somebody's address from the local information office, but getting a new passport wasn't easy at all.

Sashka walked firmly up to the first skip, frightened away a cat that was sniffing around it and overturned it with a single jerk. The refuse came tumbling out along with a second filthy cat that had been digging around in the middle of the skip. It ran off like greased lightning. Then Sashka overturned a second skip and a third. Then he turned to those on the other side of the entrance. He had to hurry. If he were seen by one of the people who lived in the block, they'd cause an enormous stir, there'd be no end to it. Thank God! There it was! He could see the red corner of a Komsomol membership card sticking out from under some pieces of bread. He bent down, raked through the rubbish and extracted the Komsomol card, a new passport and a piece of paper folded in four – her aunt's address. Written in large, almost childlike letters was the following: 'Aunt Nora, No. 6 Agayev Street, Buzovny, Baku.'

When he had read the address, Sashka held the piece of paper in his hands for a few moments, then screwed it up and threw it back into the rubbish.

Armed with the passport and the Komsomol card, he walked out on to the street and watched Lina's eyes light up with gratitude.

'Here they are,' he said, handing her the documents. Then he told the driver to take them to his own address – No. 8 Melnichnaya Street.

He didn't yet know what his mother would say, but there was no alternative. As far as Mosol and the whole gang were concerned, she would have to live in his family for a few days as a cousin.

He could feel how long it was since he'd last had a joint – the day before! He desperately wanted to smoke some hash. He remembered that he had some in his pocket and mentally he slapped his forehead. What a fool he was! He could have had a drag behind the gateway, when he had been searching for her passport! But how could he do it now? Certainly not with her present. She'd be sure to smell it.

His mother was at home, and she stared at Lina and her suitcase in amazement. But Sashka led her off to the kitchen, and they had a short business discussion. His mother had known for a long time what her son was getting up to, and it was a source of great sorrow to her. She would cry and beseech Sasha to give up drugs, while doing her best to keep it secret from his father. The last twenty-four months had seen her age ten years, and she could only pray to God that Sasha wouldn't get arrested before he was called up for the army. The army she saw as the only thing that would save her son. Then suddenly this blue-eyed girl, this seaside doll, makes an appearance. You only had to look at her son to see that he was head over heels in love with her. And his mother realized that God had sent her this one opportunity to save her son. She scarcely inquired who or what she was. It was enough for Sasha to mention a few preliminary details, like the railway station and her aunt's lost address, for the mother to say: 'All right, she can live with us for a whole month if she likes, but on one condition, Sasha – that you don't leave her alone for a moment.'

'But Mum, I've got things to do . . .'

'Do them with her, then,' said the mother. 'Go wherever you like, only take her with you. Show her the town, take her to the pictures, the beach. But remember one thing. A girl like that mustn't be left by herself in the town for a moment. You know better than I do what could happen to her.'

He did. Only Azerbaidzhani girls could walk the streets of Baku freely without encountering any problems. All the others knew very well that at every street corner, on every tram or in every shop, somebody might lay hands upon them, grab them by the front, or pinch their bottom – even in broad daylight. And after dark it wasn't safe to enter the parks unless there were at least ten of you together. He could see how his mother was purposely capitalizing on this, but he accepted her conditon. What other choice did he have?

'Sasha, give me your word that you'll give up injecting yourself and smoking this rubbish. If you can do that, it'll be all right. She can stay here with us. All right?'

'OK, Mum.'

'No, not "OK". Give me your word, your simple word as a man.'

Sashka could feel the aching of his joints. His whole body was beginning to suffer from withdrawal symptoms, and in his pocket he had that saving pellet of hash. But looking his mother in the eye, he said: 'All right, I give you my word.'

An hour later he had locked himself in the bathroom and switched on the shower to make as much noise as he could. Trembling with impatience, he crumbled the tiny pellet of hashish in his hand, mixed it up with tobacco and stuffed it all into a Belomor cigarette. Then he stood by the open window and took several short puffs. The feeling of relief and relaxation spread through his muscles, and tears even came to his eyes. If only he could give himself a shot right away. Perhaps he should tell everyone to go to hell, go down the fire-escape to the street, and run along to the corner of Vurgun Prospect and Ketskhoveli Street, where Kerim would be hanging about. He would take the whole twenty roubles for a shot of opium, because it wasn't the local type. It was imported from Central Asia or even Vietnam. But that didn't matter. Sashka had the twenty roubles after all . . . He could slip into a near-by gateway and inject himself with Kerim's syringe – and everything would be all right. He'd get high . . .

No! Stop! That was enough! Was he a man or a spineless creep? He crushed the unfinished joint in his hand, threw it down the lavatory pan and pulled the chain. Then he spent a long time washing himself under the shower, and rinsing out his mouth, to get rid of the smell of hash.

An hour later, when he and Lina were entering the Nizami cinema, the best in Baku, to see a new comedy film, Sashka came face to face with the man in glasses, the owner of the Seiko which he had stolen earlier that day. He turned out to be the manager of the theatre, and Sashka could see very well, as he slipped into the office to fetch a militiaman or vigilante. Sashka had a few seconds to make up his mind whether to run away or not. But where could he run with Lina? And what explanation could be give her? Looking at the door of the office, he could already see out of the corner of his eye the ticket-collector lift the receiver of the internal phone which had started ringing. Sashka grinned. They were already blocking the entrances, it was too late to run away. He looked Lina in the eye and said: 'Listen. I'm about to get arrested. Not for anything serious, just for a fight which I got involved in. Stay at our flat as long as you like, and tell Mum that I'm keeping my word. They'll soon release me. And wait for me, do you hear?'

A militiaman on duty was already approaching them. They moved into the auditorium, but the militiaman grabbed him roughly by the elbow.

'Wait a minute! Stop! Come with me,' he said in an Azerbaidzhani accent.

'What's the matter?' asked Sashka, feigning surprise.

'Nothing. You'll find out.'

Lina froze to the spot, wide-eyed with fright. Sashka said to her, as he was being led away: 'Don't be afraid. Our address is No. 6 Melnichnaya Street. Go home.'

An hour later Sashka Romanov, nicknamed Shakh, was being held at Baku Police Headquarters in a preliminary detention cell. Twelve people were sharing the cell with him, all arrested that day for various reasons, or lack of them, and one of them was me, Andrey Garin, special correspondent of *Komsomolskaya Pravda*.

The same day, 13.15 hours

That was all. Belkin's manuscript broke off at that point. I placed a fresh sheet of paper on the desk in front of me and wrote the following: '1. A middle-aged man between fifty and fifty-five years old, with no distinguishing marks except a mouthful of metal teeth, was at Baku airport and at the Kursk railway station in Moscow. 2. Did the drug-filled coffin exist? Check it out. 3. Summon Aina Silinya from Riga . . .' Most probably Aina was that same Lina Braknite, I thought, Sashka Shakh's girl-friend. And Shakh himself was this 'Sultan'. As Belkin had called himself Garin in his manuscript, this meant that all the names were fictitious. Not so the factual details, however. These I found immediately convincing. Of course, one would have to be cautious and recheck each fact at least ten times. Writers aren't judicial investigators, after all. They are not obliged to make an exact record of reality. They can alter the facts, mix them up and even invent them. But the pages which I had read contained so many authentic, or at least probable, details that not to have checked them out would have been a sin. Stout fellow, that Pshenichny, to have found these notebooks of Belkin's. The only pity was that he hadn't found more of them. Then I wrote down on my sheet of paper: 'Belkin's notebooks – *Komsomolskaya Pravda* offices.' This wasn't a plan of investigation, or even the first outline of one, but merely a few notes to jog my memory.

At that moment Svetlov appeared.

'May I?' he said, before entering. He was dressed in shirtsleeve order with his new lieutenant-colonel's epaulets and a peaked cap. Although not tall, he was well built, a stocky bundle of energy with a cheerful mien and resolute, intelligent eyes. Taking off his cap, he rubbed the beads of sweat from his receding hairline and entered my office. 'How are you, boss?' he asked.

'Still alive,' I replied, shaking his hand and motioning him to sit down in the chair next to my desk. 'Have a seat. Do you recognize this?' I said, showing him the file of case No. SL–79–1542.

He opened the file and glanced at the first page. His face registered disappointment. 'Ah, that. I do recognize it. The diamonds are still in my safe.'

'Are they good quality?'

'Absolutely magnificent! I've never seen anything like them. Shall I hand them over to you? I'd advise you to find out from jewellers who they used to belong to. I haven't got round to doing it yet, but if you're taking the case over . . .'

'Wait a minute,' I said, interrupting him. 'You know about the corpse and the jewels, but do you know the identity of the other man who was abducted?'

'Another speculator, I suppose,' he replied with a shrug. 'But it's none of my business. I've got enough on my plate. The Moscow River Militia are dealing with it now, I think. But how did you get involved?'

'Sit down and read this,' I said, handing him back the file. 'Only read it carefully and right through, especially the manuscript . . .'

As I handed it over to him I noticed once again that the first page was typed carelessly with plenty of mistakes, while the remaining pages were flawless. It was as if they'd been taken straight from a typing pool, although Pshenichny had written in his report that he had removed them from Belkin's flat.

Svetlov began reading. After a few minutes he undid the top button of his shirt, loosened his tie, lit up a cigarette and asked, without interrupting his reading: 'Listen, you wouldn't have any cold beer, would you?'

'No, we don't keep any here,' I said, with a laugh. 'But we can always nip outside after you've finished reading. There's a bar next door.'

A knock sounded at the door. I said, 'Come in,' and looked at my watch. It was 1.30 p.m., almost forty minutes since I'd spoken on the phone to Pshenichny. He entered and introduced himself: 'Hello, I'm Pshenichny.'

He turned out to be younger than I had expected, a tall, lean, thirty-two-year-old with fair hair. He had rather aquiline features, like the poet Alexander Blok, with serious, light-blue eyes. As he entered the office I noticed that he limped slightly on his left leg. I got up to shake his hand and said: 'Igor Iosifovich Shamrayev. And may I introduce Lieutenant-Colonel Svetlov . . .'

'Hello, we know each other,' said Svetlov. Without interrupting his reading, he raised his hand. Pshenichny shook it and sat down on a spare chair. He'd examined my office the moment he walked in as if noting everything about it: me, Svetlov and Belkin's case-file on the desk. Yes, this was just the person I needed, and perhaps even better than I'd expected, since he was younger. Thirty is the best age for an investigator. He's already got experience, yet his enthusiasm for the job hasn't dried up. As strong as a horse, but as stubborn as a mule.

'Right! Everything understood!' said Marat Svetlov, as he banged the last page of Belkin's manuscript down on the table. 'You need to fly to Baku and start from there. The drug addicts are there, along with this General and Ziyalov. The names are all invented, of course, but there's enough to go on – who was in the same class as this Belkin, who used to copy whose essays, and so on. Nothing difficult there. And it has to be done! They're already transporting these drugs by plane in coffins! It's amazing!' Svetlov was so worked up that he'd risen and was even walking up and down the room. 'But what do you need me for? That's what I don't understand.'

'Well, you read it yourself in the file. Investigator Pshenichny thinks it important to set up a special team to investigate this case. And I agree with him. That's why I've included him in the team, along with myself and you and your section.'

'Me? You must be off your head! Shcholokov will never let you have me! You know how he gets on with your boss!'

'Even if I'm investigating this case on behalf of the Central Committee? I've got to find this Belkin before the eleventh, in time for him to accompany Brezhnev to Vienna. And the law says that I can request any member of the CID to become part of my team.'

'Well, you just try! "The law says" my foot!' he mimicked my words. 'They'll palm you off with some incompetent fool, and you won't be at all pleased.'

'All right, we'll talk about it later,' I replied. 'But what I'm interested in first of all is whether or not you *want* to work with me on this. Just look: drugs, diamonds, a murder and the kidnapping of a special correspondent. There's a full house for you. Right up the street of a sleuth like you, I'd have thought. And an extra promotion wouldn't go amiss either, would it?'

'Well, you're a caution!' said Svetlov with a laugh. 'You know how to get someone hooked. But there's one thing missing.'

'What?'

'There's no woman involved.'

'What do you mean? There are two of them, at least! Anya Ziyalova, whom Belkin fell in love with at the airport, and this Lina, that Sashka Shakh fell for.'

'I doubt it,' said Svetlov with a wry face. 'This one falls in love, so does that one. It sounds too much like fiction to me. Now, a coffin full of drugs – that's something different . . . No writer would think up that! Or the fact that he got arrested himself . . .'

'None of it happened,' said Pshenichny softly.

We both turned round to look at him. He'd already lifted up his briefcase and was removing some kind of document from it.

'In any case, here's the cable which I received from Baku Militia Headquarters,' he said, placing it before us. I picked it up and read it out loud:

'TELEGRAM

'To Investigator Pshenichny, Moscow Prosecutor's Office

'IN CONNECTION WITH YOUR REQUEST NO. 3341 DATED 1 JUNE 1979, WE HAVE TO INFORM YOU THAT A PAINSTAKING CHECK OF FREIGHT TRANSPORTATION DOCUMENTS FOR BAKU AIRPORT HAS ESTABLISHED THAT THE LOAD TO WHICH YOU REFER (A ZINC COFFIN CARRIED ON FLIGHT NO. 315 TASHKENT/BAKU ON 12 MAY) NEVER REACHED BAKU STOP FURTHER EXAMINATION OF THE DOCUMENTATION INVOLVED HAS REVEALED THAT NO SUCH LOAD REACHED BAKU ON ANY FLIGHT DURING THE WHOLE OF MAY STOP NOR DOES THE BAKU MILITIA HAVE ANY INFORMATION ABOUT ANY ILLEGAL PARTY TRANSPORTING NARCOTIC SUBSTANCES (OPIUM) FROM CITIES IN CENTRAL ASIA VIA BAKU AIRPORT STOP AN EXAMINATION OF THE RECORD OF PEOPLE DETAINED IN BAKU HAS REVEALED THAT THE *KOMSOMOLSKAYA PRAVDA* CORRESPONDENT VADIM BELKIN NAMED BY YOU WAS NOT ARRESTED IN THE CITY DURING MAY AND WAS NOT PLACED IN THE PRELIMINARY DETENTION CELL STOP THE SECOND PERSON MENTIONED CITIZEN YURY RYBAKOV WAS DETAINED FROM 12 TO 16 MAY ON SUSPICION OF BEING INVOLVED WITH OTHERS IN A CASE OF THEFT BUT WAS RELEASED THROUGH LACK OF EVIDENCE STOP CONCERNING THE WHEREABOUTS IN BAKU OF THE CRIMINALS NICKNAMED THE GENERAL AND MOSOL WE HAVE TO ADVISE YOU THAT THE BAKU CID HAS NO INFORMATION ABOUT INDIVIDUALS BEARING THOSE NAMES STOP FURTHERMORE A CHECK OF THE RECORDS OF SCHOOL NO. 171 FOR 1967/9 CARRIED OUT AT YOUR REQUEST HAS REVEALED THAT NO PUPIL WITH THE NAME OF OLEG ZIYALOV WAS REGISTERED IN THE SIXTH FORM OF THE SCHOOL OVER THAT PERIOD STOP HEAD OF THE BAKU CITY MILITIA STOP COLONEL N. MAMEDOV
4 JUNE 1979'

'So there you are . . .' said Svetlov slowly, narrowing his quick, intelligent eyes and lighting up a pipe, something which was completely out of keeping with his plumpish, round face. The match burnt his fingers, and he shook his hand up and down quickly, but carried on puffing away at the pipe regardless and blew out a large cloud of smoke. 'So there you are,' he said again. 'I don't like it. The further you venture into the wood, the murkier it gets. One side is lying – either Belkin or the Baku militia. Now, Belkin is a professional liar, like any journalist, but the incident with the coffin did take place, I'd lay money on it. And the fact that there's no mention of the coffin in any of the airport records doesn't surprise me. Why, even Belkin writes that coffins are not allowed to be transported on passenger flights, so someone was probably bribed to register it as a container or suitcase. And this Colonel Mamedov is trying to pull the wool over our eyes, of course. You can smell that drugs are involved half a mile off. And even if Belkin invented the whole lot from start to finish, you can't get away from the fact that this Rybakov *did* inject himself with drugs and that he *was* carrying a suitcase containing diamonds. You won't get jewels like those in exchange for a shot of opium, but for a whole coffin full of the stuff, now that's something different . . . OK!' he said, thumping the desk with the palm of his hand. 'There's one way I can start getting involved in this case, but we'll have to act right away.' He looked at his watch. 'It's already 2 p.m. Since one o'clock my boss, CID Chief Minayev, and our new deputy minister, Churbanov, have been inspecting the work done on getting the Moskva swimming pool ready for the Olympic Games. They do the same thing every day, it's become a ritual, because the baths have got a marvellous sauna. Now Churbanov is Brezhnev's son-in-law. In the five years since he got married to Galina Brezhneva. he's moved from being a lousy adviser to the Central Committee of the Komsomol to being Deputy Minister of Internal Affairs. And that's why he'll do anything if Belkin is really needed by Brezhnev. So let's go off to the sauna. The two of them should be nice and warm by now!'

Once he'd made up his mind, Svetlov moved into action on the spot, like a dog when it's unleashed. His idea about Churbanov was a pretty good one, though I was far from clear about how we should approach Brezhnev's son-in-law, or about how we could explain our sudden and unexpected visit to the sauna. But I was acquainted with Churbanov myself. He'd been an external student at the Moscow University Law Faculty about ten years before, and I'd been giving a series of seminars on the Soviet legal process there at the time. I began to get ready to go.

'And what about me?' asked Pshenichny.

I moved my typewriter forward on the desk, slipped in a piece of official Prosecutor's Office notepaper, and typed out the following:

TEMPORARY IDENTITY CERTIFICATE

This is to certify that Comrade Valentin Nikolayevich PSHENICHNY, Investigator for the Moscow River District Prosecutor's Office, has been seconded to the USSR Public Prosecutor's Department as member of an investigation team, and that he is carrying out the functions of Special Investigator.

USSR Chief Public Prosecutor
R. Rudenko

As I removed the paper from the typewriter, I said to Pshenichny: 'Slip downstairs to Vera Petelina's office and tell her that I'm asking for this to be signed as quickly as possible, either by Rudenko himself or by one of his deputies. Then go to see Prazdnikov in the Supply Office and tell him that we need a special car equipped with a radio-telephone link for the whole

71

week. After that, you can wait for us here and write up your ideas for a plan of investigation. When the identity certificate is ready, ring up your own office to tell them that Rudenko has seconded you for ten days. OK?'

The same day, 14.30 hours
At the Moskva swimming pool on Kropotkinskaya Street, there was the usual hubbub with a few dozen teenage girls and boys playing ball, racing against each other, picking each other up and flirting generally. Young girl swimmers from a special sports school were being trained on the paths around the edge of the pool. And, as usual, the place was surrounded by inquisitive visitors from the provinces. The Moskva swimming pool is one of the city's prime tourist sights.

But few people know that the real sight at this pool is the marvellous sauna, access to which is restricted to the party and government élite. It has dry steam, Finnish equipment, Czech beer, Volga crayfish, export vodka and Russian masseurs. Yury Churbanov was there, the husband of Galina Brezhneva, stepfather to her married daughter and step-uncle to her nephew. But he was young-looking for his forty-two years, and didn't at all have the appearance of someone's step-uncle. There he was, relaxing in the dressing-room with the hefty masseur, Stasik, toning up the muscles of his sun-tanned and ever so slightly flabby body. Next to him, and receiving the same treatment, was the head of Moscow CID, General Minayev. Through the window the two of them were watching the actions of the young swimmers from the sports school with obvious interest. The girls were fourteen or fifteen years old, a ripe age for admiration.

I had already explained my request to Churbanov and Minayev. Brezhnev's favourite journalist, Belkin, had to be found in the next four days, and this could only be done with the help of Svetlov – that is to say, if the CID would be so kind as to help out their colleagues in the Public Prosecutor's Department. Minayev immediately saw what I was aiming at, knitted his brows and said: 'In that case, why don't you let us take over the whole case, if you can't manage by yourselves? You see, Yury, they keep their own investigation branch. The Public Prosecutor's Office has got more than 30,000 investigators scattered throughout the country, but as soon as something serious turns up, they're immediately asking the CID for help!'

But Churbanov already seemed to have a good grounding in the nature of Soviet power. His father-in-law had doubtless told him of his principal strategy, that of maintaining the balance of power between the three main investigative organs in the country: the KGB, the Interior Ministry or MVD, and the Prosecutor's Office, allowing none of them to acquire absolute authority. While Rudenko, Shcholokov and Andropov are competing, they are a danger to each other, but not to Brezhnev. But as soon as one of them gains the upper hand ... Churbanov was the agent of the Brezhnev family in the Interior Ministry, somebody whose appointment as deputy minister Shcholokov was forced to accept. And Churbanov showed a lively interest in the Belkin case.

'Yes, I know Vadim Belkin! A good fellow! I got to know him in my days with the Komsomol Central Committee. Agh! That hurts, Stasik! Comrade Shamrayev, could you pass me some beer from over there? Have some yourself. It's German and tastes fantastic. I don't like Czech beer. It's terribly sweet, but German beer is just right. So what are these diamonds which you've found, Marat?' he said, turning to Svetlov.

Although I think I'd be right in saying that this was the first time Churbanov had met Svetlov, he was already calling him by his Christian name. I could see how it jarred upon Svetlov, and a tiny shadow of anger passed over his face. But this disappeared immediately and he said: 'They're marvellous diamonds, of great rarity. Pendants and ear-rings mainly, and

73

obviously very old. I think that if we were to show them to experienced jewellers, we'd be able to locate their former owners and through them find out . . .'

'And where are they now, these jewels?' said Churbanov, interrupting him.

'In a safe at my office on the Petrovka,' Svetlov replied. 'They're evidence in the case.'

'Well, why didn't you bring them along with you to show us?' asked Churbanov. 'You're an odd fellow! I know! Let's go into the steam-room once more, then we'll go and look at these jewels of yours and make up our minds.'

15.25 hours
The legendary Moscow CID is to be found in the left-hand wing of the no less legendary building at No. 38 Petrovka Street. The ground floor houses the canteen and an enormous hall with panelling down the whole of one wall, commemorating in gold letters the names of CID men who died in the war and in operations to neutralize the enemies of Soviet power. The first and second floors contain the CID itself, with all its departments and sections. The people that work there are simple, noisy folk, not at all like the types you'll find at our Prosecutor's Office or at the KGB, say. At the latter two they all give themselves intellectual airs and are very formal in the way they address each other, always talking in quiet, measured tones. It's quite the opposite in the CID, where everybody uses bad language at all levels, whether they are interrogating suspects or talking to each other. They're not bothered about literary style in the slightest and informality is the watchword. That's why Svetlov always talks about his section as the 'lads'.

We were sitting in Svetlov's office on the second floor, Minayev, Churbanov, Svetlov and me, as well as Pshenichny, who had been summoned from the Prosecutor's Department. Svetlov removed a black document-case from the safe and emptied the diamond

74

and gold jewellery which it contained on to his desk. It was certainly something to look at, all those pieces of the most delicate craftsmanship. I'd worked on several jewellery cases in the past, but it had been a long time since I'd seen such exquisite pale green chrysolite or such delicate gold settings for the diamonds, fashioned like a bunch of grapes or a sprig of roses. The only place I'd seen anything like them was in the Diamond Museum. There could be no doubt that the value put on this jewellery in the official report, 100,000 roubles, was a massive underestimate. This was, however, not an unusual precaution on the part of the CID valuers, since it meant there would be less rumpus about responsibility in any aftermath.

Churbanov looked up at Svetlov. 'Are you sure that these haven't been stolen from a museum?'

'No,' replied Svetlov. 'We've checked. Nothing like this has gone missing from any museum. But, as you can see, it's not a complete collection. There are no rings or necklaces.'

Churbanov was turning the most luxurious item round on his hands – a gilt brooch in the form of a rose, decorated with chrysolite and diamonds.

'My wife, Galina Brezhneva, likes these things very much,' he said. 'I'll hang on to this one until tomorrow to show her.'

Then he turned to Minayev. 'You can pick it up from me tomorrow. All in all, I think we ought to give them the chance to find this Belkin and the rest of the collection. Leonid Ilyich really does read some of Belkin's articles sometimes and after Vienna he intends to write another book, so he'll need people to help him with it. And if these baubles turn out to be part of a complete collection,' he continued, nodding in the direction of Svetlov's desk, 'then they'd make a suitable gift for the CID to give Galina Leonidovna on her birthday.'

'And when is that?' asked Minayev with a lively show of interest.

Up till then Major-General Pavel Sergeyevich Minayev, a tall man of fifty with fair hair and delicate, nervous features, had been listening to my explanations about the Belkin case rather sullenly. He would occasionally scowl at Svetlov, obviously preparing to carpet him for bringing Churbanov into it. But when the latter himself mentioned that the CID might be able to make a personal gift to Galina Brezhneva, Minayev's attitude changed on the spot. You don't need very great intelligence to realize that the father would be at the daughter's birthday celebrations too, and if Minayev were able to attend bearing such a gift . . .

'In October,' replied Churbanov, 'so there's still plenty of time . . .'

He stood up and slipped the gold brooch into the inside pocket of his new general's uniform.

Minayev turned towards me and said: 'Svetlov and the whole of his section are at your disposal. Only do write me an official request, signed by Rudenko.' Then he turned to Svetlov and added: 'Come directly to me for whatever you need, understand?'

'Understood, Comrade General.'

15.35 hours
The three of us were now alone together, Svetlov, Pshenichny and myself. At last we could get down to brass tacks. There was a great deal of painstaking work ahead of us, but the main fact was that one of the seven days we had at our disposal had already flown by. Yet I'd done nothing to advance the investigation, except to set up this team with Pshenichny, Svetlov and his section. Still, even that wasn't bad going.

'Igor Iosifovich,' announced Pshenichny, 'car, registration number MK 46–12, is down below and equipped with a radio telephone, as you requested. I've drawn up a plan of investigation,' he added, placing a standard-issue exercise book on the desk in front of him. 'May I read it out?'

'Wait a minute,' said Svetlov. 'There are a few

things which need to be done urgently first.' And he shouted to his secretary through the half-open door: 'Zoya! Tell Ozherelyev to come and see me!'

'Here I am,' said the imposing, dandyish figure of Major Ozherelyev.

'Now listen,' said Svetlov imperiously. 'Check the CID and MVD card indexes. We need a man who answers the following description: aged between fifty and fifty-five with no distinguishing features apart from a mouthful of metal teeth. Unfortunately, we've nothing else to go on.'

'But Marat Alekseyevich ...' said the major beseechingly. 'Half the Soviet Union has got metal teeth. My own father's got metal teeth.'

'That's the first thing,' Svetlov went on, not listening. 'The second thing is this. Look in our own card index to see whether we've got anything on this *Komsomolskaya Pravda* correspondent, Vadim Belkin.'

I looked at Svetlov in astonishment.

'It's just a precaution,' he explained. 'We ought to check up with the KGB as well, but I don't want to be beholden to them. They've probably got something on him, as he works for a newspaper, but it'll more likely be something political rather than criminal. And the third thing is this,' he said, addressing Ozherelyev once more. 'Choose somebody to go down to Baku for two or three days. In fact, send a couple of men, to be on the safe side. What they have to do is simple: get Aeroflot to supply lists of the passengers on flights between Tashkent and Baku on 12 May of this year and check them against the list of pupils at Baku School No. 171 for the years 1967 to 1969. If even a single name corresponds on both lists,' he explained to Pshenichny and myself, 'then that's our man. That's the lot. Report back in twenty minutes,' he said to Ozherelyev.

Then he turned to the two of us once again. 'Good, now we can carry on talking. I hope I haven't filched anything from your plan, Valentin.'

I realized that although Svetlov was to some extent putting on an act to show off his own quickness and efficiency, in fact everything he'd done was quite correct. Or so far at any rate. His idea of checking with Aeroflot was a good one, although not foolproof. There were thousands of people sharing the same surname in Baku and Tashkent. There were any number of Gasanovs, Mamedevs, Bagirovs and so on – as many as there were Ivanovs and Petrovs in Moscow. Thus a dozen names on the lists might match up, not one alone. Even so it was a line of approach that deserved to be followed up.

Pshenichny smiled at Svetlov, his left hand poised above his plan of investigation on the desk: 'I asked Aeroflot for details of the passengers between Tashkent and Baku on 1 June, as soon as I'd finished reading Belkin's manuscript. But I haven't received a reply yet.'

'There will be one now,' Svetlov replied. 'If someone from the CID gets on to them, they'll move pretty quickly.'

I could see that Svetlov wasn't in the least bit piqued by the fact that Pshenichny had had exactly the same idea. As a person who had ideas all the time, he didn't begrudge them in others or guard them jealously for himself.

'All right, Valentin, let's have it,' I said. 'We're listening.'

Pshenichny arranged his notes more conveniently and began: 'From the very beginning we need to establish why Belkin was abducted, or at least sketch in possible reasons. I think that either he knew something about the drug smuggling and diamonds, or that he was on the point of finding something out about it. And you can't rule out the possibility that they were kidnapped by a rival gang. After all, the people who abducted Rybakov and Belkin almost certainly murdered Rybakov . . .'

'That hasn't been proved,' interjected Svetlov. Up

till now he had been listening to Pshenichny silently but impatiently, since he was a person who preferred concrete action to discussion. Pshenichny, on the other hand, was the complete opposite – he was a pedant with a penchant for meticulousness and logic. Fate couldn't have presented me with a better combination of talents.

'It hasn't been proved,' said Svetlov once again. 'There's no guarantee that Rybakov was murdered. He lost the document case, jumped out of the train after it and hit his head against a stone – and it could all have happened under the influence of drugs.'

'I've had a talk with the forensic experts,' said Pshenichny. 'They think that somebody hit the lad over the head with something and stove in his temple. But he fell out of the train on to his chest. Whatever happened, we have to find the kidnapper of Belkin and Rybakov. And what clues have we got so far? An ambulance without a registration number, unfortunately. And a few medical orderlies, possibly in disguise or possibly the real thing. One of them had metallic teeth and was obviously not an ambulance man, if you assume that he was the same person who met the coffin at Baku airport.'

'And what about this Aina Silinya from Riga?' asked Svetlov, obviously following his own line of thought. 'Are she and the Lina Braknite mentioned in Belkin's manuscript one and the same person?'

'Unfortunately, Aina Silinya left Moscow on 30 May, immediately after identifying the corpse, and I didn't find Belkin's manuscript until the thirty-first. So I wasn't able to ask her any questions connected with it. Besides, after identifying the corpse she was in such a state . . . But Rybakov's parents, who arrived by plane to claim their son's body, confirmed that a girl by the name of Aina did live with them from 12 to 18 May.'

'I see,' said Svetlov. 'Then we need to bring this Silinya girl to Moscow once again, that's one thing. And make urgent inquiries at the Kursk railway station, that's another. The place is always full of riff-raff, thieves, alcoholics, pie-sellers and the like. I'll lay odds that we can come up with somebody who witnessed the kidnapping, and not just one person either.'

'All right, I'll make a note of it,' I replied. 'Summon Aina Silinya back from Riga. And – find people who witnessed the abduction at the Kursk railway station. We'll decide who does what in a moment. What else?'

'Third point,' Pshenichny continued in an even voice, thereby implying that the first two mentioned by Svetlov had already figured in his own plan. 'Apart from the main terminus itself, we need to go down the line 100 or 150 miles in each direction from Moscow River station questioning all those railway employees who were at work on the night Rybakov was murdered. Perhaps somebody saw him with some other people. At the same time, we ought to check what trains travelled through Moscow River station that night . . .'

'What are we to do then?' interrupted Svetlov. 'Question all the guards? It'll take us a year. What we need is to think of some lightning strikes in all directions. Make a note of this,' he said to me. 'Get some jewellery experts to examine the valuables. I'll see to that myself.'

'Is that the lot, Valentin?' I asked.

'No. We need to question the journalists at *Komsomolskaya Pravda*. Knowing that I'd seized some manuscripts and books at the flat, including Solzhenitsyn's *Gulag Archipelago*, one of Belkin's friends at work removed all his papers from the office, I think. And a continuation of Belkin's notebook may have been among them. It's no coincidence that the one we've got is marked No. 1. This means that there may be a notebook No. 2.'

'OK,' I said. 'We'll stop exchanging opinions now and divide up the work – in a comradely fashion. We've got as much time at our disposal as we would have in a lightning chess match, so let's take the juiciest bits first. One or two of your boys, Marat, can take care of Aeroflot by flying to Baku and also checking out School No. 171. You can put them in the picture and give them Belkin's manuscript to read. That's the first thing. I'll look after *Komsomolskaya Pravda* and the whereabouts of the remaining notebooks. Svetlov can get the jewellery and diamonds identified. And Valentin can deal with the Kursk railway station. That should give us enough to be getting on with today and tomorrow morning. Unless there's an emergency, we'll meet again tomorrow afternoon here in my office. Any questions?'

'Come in, Ozherelyev,' said Svetlov in the direction of my half-open door. Obviously, from his vantage point, he'd been able to see the figure of the major looming through the crack in the door.

Ozherelyev opened the door with his back and came in carrying an enormous pile of CID files in his arms. He banged them down heavily on to the sofa and shook the dust off his uniform.

'Phew!' he said. 'There are no less than seventy-two known criminals aged fifty and with metal teeth. Lieutenants Rogozin and Shmuglov are going to make the trip to Baku. And here's what information we've got on Vadim Borisovich Belkin, *Komsomolskaya Pravda* correspondent, born 1952.'

'Where does the information come from?' asked Svetlov. 'Us or the MVD?'

'The MVD, First Special Section,' replied Ozherelyev, holding a typewritten sheet in his hand.

'Read us what it says,' ordered Svetlov.

'It's a report by the Interior Minister of the Yakutian Autonomous Republic, Lieutenant-Colonel Khalzanov.

'To the Head of the USSR MVD First Special Section, Major-General Yegorov. I have to inform you that on 16 January 1979, while he was on an official visit to the town of Mirny in the Yakutian ASSR, *Komsomolskaya Pravda* correspondent, Citizen Vadim Borisovich Belkin, while under the influence of alcohol, took part in a brawl between workers of diamond factory No. 7 and the kitchen and waiting staff at a restaurant. When apprehended he used vulgar and abusive language. Further investigation was halted at the request of the editorial staff of *Komsomolskaya Pravda* in view of the inexpediency of bringing Citizen Belkin to trial. I am appending standard form No. 1 concerning crimes committed, for registration in the Central Card Index. Lieutenant-Colonel Khalzanov, Interior Minister, Yakutian ASSR.'

Svetlov and I exchanged glances. First drugs, then diamonds, and now this – fun and games in Yakutia. Never a dull moment with this Belkin! But what makes him visit such places?

16.20 hours
'It is twelve days since your colleague, Vadim Belkin, was kidnapped. Either he has already been murdered, or he is in the hands of the criminals . . .'

I was seated in the office of the chief editor of *Komsomolskaya Pravda*, Lev Aleksandrovich Korneshov. The chief administrator, Stanislav Granov, was there, too. Korneshov's vast writing desk was strewn with piles of manuscripts, galley-proofs and the pages, as I realized, of tomorrow's edition. Similar printed pages were pinned to the wall. Korneshov was a small man with auburn hair and gentle, brown eyes. He was about forty or even a little less, while Stanislav Granov was no more than thirty at most.

'On instructions from the Central Committee,' I continued, 'the USSR Public Prosecutor's Office has set up a special investigation team to discover the whereabouts of Belkin as quickly as possible. One of our best detectives, CID Section Head, Lieutenant-Colonel Svetlov, is a member of the team, along with several experienced investigators and CID operatives. I am in command of the team. We know that as a result of his particular employment, Belkin had access to such things as drugs and Yakutian diamonds as well as border crossing-points. I want you to understand me correctly. The interests of the state compel us to consider every possible version of events. Might Belkin, of his own free will or otherwise, have got involved with dealings involving drugs, cut and uncut diamonds, or whatever? The youth kidnapped at the same time as Belkin and murdered two days later was patently a member of the underworld. He was a drug addict, and next to his body we found a document case containing jewellery of extreme rarity and value. We might be able to find the solution from the notebooks which Belkin kept during his assignments around the country. Here is the first of them, which we removed from his apartment. Look at it. "If I don't commit to paper an account of all the terrible things that have happened, I'll have to go and drown myself in the Caspian." It is possible that he himself has described everything that happened to him. But the second notebook, which could be a continuation of this one, has disappeared. And we believe that it went astray here, in your editorial offices . . .'

Korneshov picked up Belkin's notebook and began to read it with the speed of a professional, whose eyes metaphorically peeled the words from the page. He passed the sheets over to Granov, one by one.

Meanwhile he said to me: 'Carry on, please. I'm listening.'

'We must find the remaining notebooks,' I said.

'Do you share the opinion of the investigator who carried out the search of Belkin's flat, that one of our employees removed the documents in question?' he asked, without looking up from Belkin's notebook.

'I didn't put it like that. But work it out for yourself. On 31 May Investigator Pshenichny found a copy of Solzhenitsyn's *Gulag Archipelago* at Belkin's flat, as well as manuscripts written by Belkin himself, the tone and content of which was occasionally far removed from what you find in the newspapers. The neighbours of his, who were called upon to act as witnesses at the search, were also employees of your newspaper – that is to say, friends of Belkin. There is no doubt that at least half the staff of *Komsomolskaya Pravda* could have known about it within the hour, including one or more colleagues of his who may have decided to remove Belkin's other notebooks from the investigator's attentions, just in case. You never know what might have been written in them, after all. What if they contained something anti-Soviet? You can follow their line of reasoning. But although the motive may have been friendship towards Belkin, the actual result has been to hinder our search for him.'

At this point the two of them finished leafing through Belkin's manuscript together and then exchanged a short glance. Granov said: 'I'll be back in a moment,' and went out of the room.

'Do you want to question Loktyova and Zharov?' asked Korneshov. 'They were the witnesses.'

'No, that would lead nowhere. Let's assume that they told four friends of theirs, who then told four others, and so on. You'd have a geometrical progression, and before you knew where you were, the whole of my team wouldn't be enough to question all those in the know. No, there's no point in following up that line of inquiry. The notebooks could either have been taken by friends of his, or . . . did he have friends in the office?'

'Half the editorial staff, if not more.'

'Or else taken by enemies, so as to cast suspicion on him. Neither can we rule out the possibility that somebody doesn't like the investigative organizations and wants to put a spoke in our wheels. It sometimes happens. But we are carrying out the instructions of the Central Committee, and I am relying on your assistance.'

'Put in a nutshell, what you're saying is that you need to cross-examine the whole staff. All right, why don't you start with me?' he suggested mildly, but with a hint of challenge in his voice.

'OK,' I said with a smile, realizing full well, of course, that he had been expecting a different response, something on the lines of 'What on earth do you mean? You're above suspicion!' and so forth. 'Tell me, Belkin hadn't been into the office for a whole week, and yet nobody noticed his absence. Why? Doesn't he have to attend work every day?'

'Technically, yes, of course. But you know, with journalists like Belkin . . . He'd only just returned from an assignment and was supposed to be writing it up . . . And it's not easy to do that at the office. So . . . you understand, we turn a blind eye.'

'Lev Aleksandrovich, if it weren't for these lapses in discipline, if somebody had noticed that Belkin was missing on the day he was kidnapped, or at least the day after, we shouldn't now be in this terrible hurry. Meanwhile, Brezhnev is going to Vienna on the fifteenth, and it was only on the fourth that we started to look for this member of his press corps. In my opinion it would be in both our interests not to waste any more on inter-departmental sniping, but to co-operate with each other. I don't need to cross-examine the whole staff, as you put it, but simply to have a chat with them. Talk to them all at the same time – and as quickly as possible.'

He waited a moment before replying, as if weighing up in his mind all the pros and cons.

'All right, I see what you're driving at.' Then he bent down and pressed a button on his intercom. 'Zhenya, I want an emergency meeting of all the staff in the Blue Room in ten minutes. And I mean *all* the staff, without exception.'

He looked up at me. 'What else?'

'Belkin's personal file,' I replied.

'Zhenya, fetch Belkin's personal file from First Section,' he said into the intercom. 'What else?' he said again to me.

'That's all for the time being,' I replied. I'd got what I was after. The editor understood full well that, whether we found Belkin or not, whether the latter turned out to be a victim or an accomplice in the crime, it was better for him, Korneshov, to co-operate with my team now, and not defend the honour of his profession. At that moment Granov, the chief administrator, came back into the room. He was carrying some long, narrow sheets filled with fresh newspaper print.

Korneshov looked at Granov in amazement. Meanwhile the latter began to explain.

'I had to go to the printing department to get a fresh copy made. There's no copy of the article anywhere in the editorial office. They're all with the censor.' And he set the galley-proof before me. 'This is Belkin's last article, dictated over the phone from Baku. It reproduces word for word what he wrote in the second chapter of the manuscript, except that it lacks the final paragraph. That's why we didn't know that Vadim had been arrested and was being held in a preliminary detention cell.'

'The Baku Militia have informed us that they never arrested Belkin,' I said. 'But tell me, did he usually make things up in his articles?'

It was Korneshov who replied. 'Well,' he said, 'it's difficult to say. Probably not. It's a moot point. A journalist's choice of actual detail is a subjective affair. This article most likely errs on the side of generalization, perhaps even exaggeration. Did you talk to him about it?' he asked Granov.

'Yes. He said that it was all true, apart from the names of the people involved. He also reckoned that he'd most likely be bringing this Shakh to the office in a few days' time. And that was all. The next day he disappeared.'

'Shakh was the lad who was kidnapped at the same time as Belkin and found dead two days later,' I said. 'But I'll explain all this in more detail at the emergency meeting.'

I looked at my watch. A further ten minutes had passed. A secretary with pink varnished nails, about forty but trying to look younger, appeared at the door of Korneshov's office. She had Belkin's personal file in her hands.

'In about a minute everybody will be assembled, Lev Aleksandrovich,' she said softly, placing Belkin's file in front of me.

Without opening it, I said: 'Tell me, what was it that happened to him at Mirny in Yakutia? Something to do with a fight in a restaurant, wasn't it?'

'Yes, I know,' replied Korneshov. 'But Belkin's no drunkard, that's for sure. Sooner or later every journalist comes back from an assignment with a charge like this hanging over him. I dare say it happens to investigators too. The correspondent catches somebody fiddling the books or thieving merchandise, and before you know where you are, before he even has time to return from his trip, there's an anonymous or collective letter on your desk denouncing him. And do you know the funny thing? None of these letters ever comes from an individual. People usually tell the truth when they write in their own name. But this doesn't happen. People always write collective letters in these instances. They always get together, so as to make it more credible.'

'But a fight did take place in this case. It's registered in MVD files,' I said.

'Well, of course it did. A few diamond workers gave some cook a going over because he'd served them with rotten venison. In my opinion, they were right to do so – though that's between ourselves, of course. And Belkin was present when it took place. He even wrote an article entitled "A Brawl" – that was its name. And it wasn't at all bad. A shame the censorship wouldn't pass it. So, you see, Mirny's got its own mafia, too, and they cooked up the whole story, as far as it concerned Belkin. That's our opinion anyway. If we acted otherwise, nobody would be able to work in our profession any more. And until you prove that Belkin was really mixed up in some criminal dealings there ... We're willing to help you, but as for getting Belkin accused of something – I'm sorry, you'll have to go elsewhere.'

I didn't know whether he was saying all this exclusively for my benefit, or whether he was relying on Granov telling the whole staff about how the editor-in-chief defended his employees and so on. All the same, I felt some sympathy for him.

'Let's go,' he said, as he got up from his chair. 'They'll all be in the Blue conference hall by now. Please remember that we've interrupted production of the newspaper, and that even the typesetters have been dragged away from the printing-room . . .'

'I understand,' I said.

In the Blue conference hall, the famous room where *Komsomolskaya Pravda* arranges meetings with distinguished astronauts, composers, performers and travellers, I found myself confronting about fifty people, the entire staff of the newspaper at work that day, including typists, stenographers and messengers. Men and women, girls and youths, many of them tanned young journalists who had travelled thousands of miles in the course of their work – and all of them looking at me with the mixture of irony and interest typical of old hands who have seen everything in their time.

I explained to them as succinctly as I could what I knew of the affair. I didn't show off about being a 'special investigator' or try to portray myself as a Sherlock Holmes, but simply explained, in as few words as possible, the facts about the kidnapping of Belkin and Rybakov, the latter's death, the reasons for the search of Belkin's flat and what it had revealed – his manuscript describing the Baku drug-addicts and the disappearance of the remaining notebooks. I said that I wasn't interested in who had taken the notebooks or for what reasons. It was simply that they were absolutely essential to the investigation, if we were going to find Belkin's kidnappers and Belkin himself while there was still some hope of him still being alive.

'If the person who removed these notebooks doesn't

want to declare himself,' I continued, 'then I suggest the following simple solution. I see that there is a telephone in front of me. I shall sit by it for half an hour. During that time the person who took the notebooks can ring me up anonymously and tell me when and where I can find them. I give you my word of honour, as a party member, that I will not carry out any investigation into who it was who removed the notebooks. If only because there is no reason for me to do so,' I said with a smile. 'I have been instructed to find Belkin, and I don't want to waste time on extraneous matters.'

Nobody uttered a word. One was smoking, another was looking absentmindedly out of the window, while yet another had already got up and was impatiently asking the Chief Editor: 'Is that all? Can we go?'

'One moment,' I said. 'There is another thing. If anybody can add to my knowledge about Belkin, about his enemies – if he had any – his links with any suspicious individuals, or simply about what he was doing the day before he disappeared or anything like that, then even the most insignificant detail could be of great assistance to the investigation. For this reason, I ask anybody who knows anything at all to approach me during the next half-hour or ring me in my office at the Public Prosecutor's Department.'

With obvious relief they all started to move their chairs and to crowd towards the exit, laughing sceptically and talking among themselves as they did so. It seemed they were all preparing to leave the hall, down to the very last person. Even so one lanky girl, who couldn't have been older than seventeen, wasn't able to resist asking the following question. 'Look,' she said with a blush, 'everybody knows that you found a copy of *Gulag Archipelago* at Vadim Belkin's flat. And everybody knows that for keeping *samizdat* publications, books by Solzhenitsyn, Avtorkhanov and all the others you can get a gaol sentence of at least three years. Isn't that so? So if you do find Belkin, you'll send him to gaol all the same, won't you?'

It was a question I had been expecting. Indeed, I had been hoping that somebody would ask it, and now they had, thank God! Everybody stopped in the doorway, waiting for the answer. This was obviously the main obstacle in their opinion.

'No,' I said. 'You're wrong. I base my argument on the fact that you, as workers on the ideological front, need to know the weapons of your opponents, that is, the methods of Western propaganda. This is why I can see nothing criminal in the fact that Belkin had a copy of Solzhenitsyn's work at his apartment. Those whose job it is to know these things are allowed to do so. He wouldn't read Solzhenitsyn aloud in the Moscow underground, I hope.' This caused a few people to smile. 'In any case, we're not talking about abstract points of law at the moment. What's at stake is the life or death of one of your colleagues. Even if his manuscripts do contain something ideologically unsound or unprintable, I promise you, indeed give you my word of honour, that this will not affect his future.'

'If he has one,' said the girl.

'Yes, that's right,' I replied. 'Provided we take urgent steps to ensure that he does have one.'

It looked as if I had lost. I could see sceptical smiles everywhere. Their eyes reflected patent mistrust and derision. With scarcely a word, the staff went out of the conference hall, leaving the chief editor, the administrator and myself standing alone together. I could read an unspoken question in Korneshov's eyes: 'Well, what next? What else can I do for you?'

'Do you need us now?' asked the administrator.

'No. Thank you very much. I'll sit here by the phone, as I said.'

'We'll go back to our offices then,' said Korneshov. 'If you need anything . . .'

'Yes, of course. Thank you,' I replied.

And they left, closing the door behind them. I lifted the receiver to make sure the phone was working, then replaced it and began to wait. I didn't feel like reading

90

Belkin's file. The meticulous Pshenichny had read it before me, and if there was anything in it, he would have extracted it.

Time passed. There was no sound, either of a phone ringing or of a door being opened. There were three minutes left to go before the half-hour was up, then two, then one. I decided to stay on for another five minutes, but it was obvious my experiment had failed. People's aversion to the organs of justice, ingrained during the long years of Stalin's rule, went deep, and there was no way investigators could dissipate or overcome their distrust of the militia and the Public Prosecutor's Department by simple heart-to-heart talks or by offering their word of honour, as I had done. These newspaper workers were afraid of compromising their friend and of becoming undercover agents and informers themselves. They were afraid that their own homes might be descended upon the next day, their apartments searched and their manuscripts taken away. And we could do it, too. What's the point of denying it? You can twist the law any way you like, after all, and you can always find a reason for entering anybody's home. Not that you really need one! My God! Find me something that isn't rotten in *this* state of Denmark! Still, what is to be done? Throw in your job?

As I followed my bitter train of thought I was watching the orange-yellow sun slip silently behind the rooftops and still waiting for a miracle to happen, for the sound of footsteps outside and for someone to knock at the door. But the miracle didn't occur. I could hear telephones ringing somewhere in the distance, and the sound of people tapping away at typewriters in the typing pool. I started to gather my papers together, including Belkin's manuscript with its scrappily printed first page and its immaculately typed continuation, when suddenly I had a vague idea.

I got up, leafed through Belkin's notebook, tore out the dirtiest and least decipherable page from somewhere in the middle and walked along to the typing pool, past rooms marked 'News Department' and 'Students' Office', past journalists who eyed me with cold curiosity.

The door to the typing pool opened easily, at the touch of a hand. The room was bathed in light from the setting sun as well as by fluorescent lighting from above. In it were eight typists, all tapping away at their electric typewriters as if they were machine-guns. Scarcely had I entered than the noise came to a halt and everybody looked at me questioningly. The women were of different ages, but all took equal pains over their make-up. There they were, sitting at their humming machines, like so many tailor's dummies, their hands poised above the keyboards.

Raising the sheet of paper which I had torn from Belkin's notebook into the air, I addressed them in the lively, almost familiar tone of voice that I use with the typists back at the Public Prosecutor's Office: 'Girls! Who knows Belkin's handwriting? I'd like to get half a page typed out . . .'

Nobody said anything, but somebody automatically looked in the direction of a well-proportioned, dark-haired woman dressed in a green summer dress, who was sitting over by the window. That was enough for me. As I walked towards her, I could see she was already beginning to blush.

'Be so good as to type out this page for me. What's your name?'

'Inna,' she said softly, suddenly turning pale as she did so.

I pretended not to have noticed anything and laid the sheet of paper on the desk in front to her. 'Here you are. You won't find it difficult, I hope.'

Without a word she removed what she had been typing from the typewriter, inserted a new sheet and moved Belkin's page a bit closer. The room was once again filled with the sound of the secretaries typing away diligently – I would have said too diligently. A moment later Inna's typewriter joined in. Without looking at the keys, Inna's eyes were focused solely on the flow of Belkin's script, while her fingers flew over the keyboard without hesitation. It was the place where Belkin describes how he fell in love with Anya Ziyalova the first time he met her at Baku airport. Looking at Inna out of the side of my eye, I could see her face darken and her teeth clench as she typed out the text. When she had finished, she tore the sheet from the typewriter and handed it back to me.

'Thank you very much,' I said, in as off-hand a way as I could manage. 'I was quite concerned, as I couldn't decipher all of it. Thank you once again.'

And with that – I left.

Of course, I could have cross-examined Inna on the spot. But I didn't want to hurry, and I particularly didn't want to question her at her office. It was six o'clock and the two hours remaining until the end of her working day were hardly crucial. A quick look at the list of internal telephones revealed that there was only one Inna among the typists – Inna Vitalyevna Kulagina – but that was all I needed. Outside the building my black Volga was waiting for me.

In it, reading *Anna Karenina*, was Seryozha, my driver. I'd known him for some time, as he'd been employed by the Prosecutor's Office for upwards of three years. I picked up the radio telephone, dialled CID Headquarters on the Petrovka, and by way of them got through to the Moscow Address Office. 'Kulagina, Inna Vitalyevna, aged twenty-five or twenty-six, an employee of *Komsomolskaya Pravda*,' I said to the voice at the other end of the line, and a moment later was told her address: '12 Parkovaya Street, House 17, Apartment 73.'

'Listen,' I said to Seryozha, 'I don't need you until eight o'clock. Go and have something to eat or do what you like. I'll take a walk around here, as I need to be here at 8 p.m. anyway.'

'Do you mind if I earn a bit of money on the side?' asked Seryozha.

'That's your business,' I replied. What Moscow driver doesn't earn a bit of money on the side by giving lifts to passengers in his spare time? And what department doesn't turn a blind eye to it?

'Get in touch with me by radio through CID Headquarters if you need me,' he said, switching on the engine. Now that he had some time to earn some money on his own behalf, he hadn't a moment to lose.

I had walked as far as the news-stand at the corner, wondering where to head next, and whether or not simply to have a shashlyk at the kiosk on Leningrad Prospect, when suddenly someone spoke behind me.

'Excuse me. May I talk to you for a moment?'

I looked around at the sound of this quiet, female voice. There before me, in her green summer dress and with her black hair cut short over her dark eyes, was Inna Kulagina. And I had been intending to phone her in an hour's time so as to arrange a meeting after eight o'clock!

'I need to tell you something. I have those notebooks.'

'I know you do, Inna, but where do you have them? At the office?'

'No, at my apartment. Only . . .' she mumbled, suddenly stopping short.

'Only what?'

'I don't know . . . There are some phrases in them, you see . . . I'm afraid that . . .'

'Inna, let's go round the corner. Your office windows are above us here, and perhaps you don't want anybody to see you.'

'It doesn't matter now,' she said, almost in despair. 'The other girls in the typing office have guessed everything by now.'

'You've nothing to fear,' I said, taking her by the arm and moving her round the corner in the direction of the Circus Training School. A group of cheerful young circus artistes was heading towards us. They were in high spirits, gesticulating and laughing excitedly as one of them gave an imitation of somebody. 'And they

94

nearly failed him for doing it,' we heard him say as we walked past them. I suddenly thought how it was June and the final examinations would be taking place in the Training School at that very moment. Somewhere in the building there had to be a former 'client' of mine, Vasily Kozhdayev, once known as the Gipsy, the Professor, Blackie and the King of the Bird Market, and now head of the illusionist and trick department of the Circus School.

'Listen to me, Inna. Is there anything anti-Soviet in Belkin's papers?'

'Well, I'm not sure . . .' she replied helplessly.

'OK. I promise you that anything not relating to this case won't appear in the account of the investigation. When can I get these notebooks?'

'Perhaps I could bring them to you tomorrow?' She seemed to be already regretting talking to me.

'No. I need them today. Do you want us to find him?' I asked her point-blank. 'I mean – find him alive, if he is alive?'

'Yes, of course I do!' she replied softly. 'He's always getting into scrapes like this . . . I used to tell him . . .' Her voice already sounded tearful, and it would have been awkward if she had burst into tears on the spot, in front of all the passers-by. I quickly altered my tone of voice.

'Now, now. Everything will be all right. OK, so we'll meet here on this corner at eight o'clock, and then we'll go to your apartment to pick up the notebooks. Agreed?'

'It would be better to meet near the metro station,' she said. 'Everybody from the office will be around at eight o'clock. Let's say we'll meet outside the Belorusskaya metro at 8.15, by the entrance to the Circle Line. All right?'

'Suits me,' I replied. 'I live near the Izmailovsky Park, not very far from you.'

'Do you? And how did you find out that it was me . . .?'

95

'Because he typed out the first page of his notebook himself. It was done hurriedly and with lots of mistakes. But as for the rest ... Somebody was at his apartment and typed the rest out for him – somebody who knew his handwriting very well and was a good typist into the bargain. Did you type it while he was there? Did he tell you anything about this Shakh?'

'No,' she said, shaking her head. 'I didn't see Vadim at all this time. He flew in from Baku and didn't even look in at the typing pool. He never even rang me up. And after that he wasn't around at all – not for one day, then for two, then three. I couldn't wait any longer, so I went round to his apartment. I've got the key ... I've had it since ... well, you know ... I arrived there quite late and stayed up all night to finish typing what he had begun ...'

I pictured this young girl sitting up all night in Belkin's bachelor flat, waiting for the person she loved to return, as she thought, from somebody else's apartment or wherever, and instead of jealousy, hysterical scenes, throwing furniture and crockery about the place and all that other nonsense that you see on the cinema screen, there she was, quietly and submissively typing away at his diary, at his description of how he'd been away on an assignment and had fallen in love yet again with a local beauty, following her around all over the place. The loyalty of Russian women!

'Then his apartment was searched,' she continued, 'and the book by Solzhenitsyn was confiscated. When I was told, I was so afraid ...'

'That the next day you removed all the notebooks from his office?'

'No, on the same day. I work until eight o'clock after all, and the search took place at six or seven. Half an hour later the whole office knew about it. I stayed in after everybody else and ... listen, he won't get into trouble for having a copy of Solzhenitsyn at his place, will he?' she asked, almost beseechingly.

'I promise you! Word of honour!' I said, beginning to lose my patience.

'All right,' she said. 'I'll see you later.'

And she went back into the newspaper building. I imagined how she would feel during the next two hours. Wondering how to kill the time myself, I wandered along to the Circus Training School. Something was egging me on (curiosity and the lack of anything else to do, most likely) and so I strode into the building. The trained eye of the janitor immediately picked me out of the stream of young people wandering in and out of the school.

'Where are you going then?'

I had to produce my red Public Prosecutor's Office identity card.

'I want to see Vasily Nikolayevich Kozhdayev.'

The brick-red features of this obvious boozer immediately altered. 'Go on in, please. He's in the arena, supervising the exam. Go down this staircase.' And then he started obsequiously showing me the way.

'Did you work in the circus once yourself?' I asked, as we went.

'Who? Me? Once I did . . . I used to fight in the ring with Korolyov, when I was young. I used to win medals. And after that I started throwing weights about – empty ones, of course . . .'

'Did you begin to hit the bottle?' I asked, unintentionally holding on to him as we descended a dark spiral staircase leading to a passageway under the training arena, specially constructed for various trick performances.

'Well,' explained the janitor. 'You know how it starts. First you take a small one to dope yourself up, then you take another, then another . . . There weren't any of these drugs around in those days. There's Vasily Nikolayevich . . .' And he raised his hand to tug at the trouser-leg of somebody sitting directly above us. I lifted my head a little and could see that this trap-door was situated immediately below the desk at which the members of the examination panel were sitting. And there, swaying on a rope over the arena, high above their heads, was a young lad, playing the violin with his feet and juggling firebrands of some sort in his hands.

'Vasily Nikolayevich!' shouted the janitor, pulling once again at the leg of a light-coloured and well-ironed pair of trousers. Kozhdayev's familiar gipsy features looked down from above, and he saw who I was.

'What brings you here, old lad?' he said, raising his black eyebrows in amazement.

A moment later I was sitting at the desk with the rest of the panel, made up of famous stars of yesteryear who had now become teachers at the Circus School. It was funny to hear these former clowns, riders and jugglers, whose names were familiar to me from the circus posters of my youth, now addressed as 'professor'. And it was particularly funny in the case of Kozhdayev. He'd reacquired the title which he used to carry in the Bird Market, I thought, as he gave me a humorous, sideways glance with those fiery black eyes of his.

After the young juggler-violinist Shimansky, it was the turn of the teenaged twins, Nadya and Olya Tsuryupa, to perform, and then that of the young clown Ivan Urema. After him came Boris Nezhdanny, a conjuror equipped with playing cards and tennis balls. The names of Urema and Tsuryupa sounded somehow familiar, and I looked at Professor Kozhdayev in puzzlement. He literally started laughing in my face.

'Can't you remember?' he said, slapping me on the back.

And then I really did remember. Fifteen years earlier the names of Urema and Tsuryupa had been on the tongues of the entire Moscow CID. Urema had been a talented trainer of bears, as well as being an expert safe-breaker, while Tsuryupa was a handsome gigolo, able to pick up, soft-talk and seduce even the most upright lady in less than two minutes. The next morning the victim would phone the militia and explain in horror that all her jewellery, money, household silver and gold had disappeared. Yet never would a single victim testify that she herself had brought a strange man to her apartment the previous night.

'You've got it!' said Kozhdayev with a laugh, when we were talking in his office afterwards. 'It's the same Tsuryupa and Urema, except that it's their children, of course. I transferred them from their world to this. I write to all my talented friends, former friends, that is, and ask them to let me have their children. And often they don't know where their children are, so I have to search them out myself. Just take a look over here . . .'

He opened up a safe and extracted a long, narrow drawer.

'This is my card index,' he said proudly. 'Just like at the CID, filed according to names and nicknames.'

'You wouldn't have a general in there, I suppose?'

'A general? I know one person nicknamed the General, only he died six years ago in the mines of Temir-Tau and didn't have any children. Kravtsov was his surname. I only file the names of people with children.'

'No,' I said, 'this is somebody else. Here, take a look at this.'

And I placed the first two chapters of Belkin's manuscript on his desk. While he was reading them I flicked through his card index with interest. Some of the Christian names, surnames, and nicknames I knew or half-knew. The others were completely unfamiliar to me. But each card was complete with names, addresses and ages of the children, along with details of their talents and the dates when letters to them were dispatched and answers received. I looked at the former Gipsy and Professor of the Bird Market with respect. This was a valuable task which he was performing secretly and without self-advertisement or affectation. Some Belkin or other should write a ringing article about it in *Komsomolskaya Pravda* or *Yunost*.

Kozhdayev read the last page of Belkin's manuscript and looked at me.

'Is there any more?'

'No, but there will be.'

'You know that all the names in it are invented? I've never been to Baku myself, so it's beyond me. On the whole it contains a fair bit of nonsense, like a cinema film. But the bit about competing to see who could steal the most watches, that rings true . . . I think that could be Salo, otherwise known as the Chief. Nobody could filch watches like him, and nobody could be as mean, either. Getting these lads in a tight spot, so that they had to start working for him sounds just his style. I wouldn't be surprised if he turns out to be the one who is behind the drug-peddling there, so as to get rich twice over using the same gang.'

'What does he look like?'

'Difficult to say, really. Nothing out of the ordinary, just like the guy described in this story. On the other hand, that one's got metal teeth, and I don't remember Salo having any. Still, perhaps he has them now. I haven't seen him for twelve years. The bastard! Here I am battling over every kid, and there he is, ruining them by the dozen!'

'So you think that the General and this guy with the metal teeth are one and the same person?'

'Of course they are!'

Twenty minutes later I was in Svetlov's office at No. 38 Petrovka. Captain Laskin and I were going through the pile of CID files that Ozherelyev had thrown down on the sofa. By the time we'd waded through twenty of them we finally came across the following entry under the column headed 'Names Used when Committing Crimes'. There it was: 'The Chief, Salo, The Godfather, Kurevo.' Then we looked at the record card which was pinned to the file:

Gridasov, Semyon Yakovlevich, born 1926, sentenced four times for robbery and theft under Articles 144 and 166 of the RSFSR Criminal Code. Height 5″8′. Light-blue eyes, whitish hair, medium build. Distinguishing marks – metal crowned front teeth. 17 May 1973, escaped from Strict Regime Colony No. 402–77, Irkutsk Region. Present whereabouts – unknown.

The same day, Monday, 4 July (after 21.00 hours)

(continued)

Chapter 3
The Preliminary Detention Cell

So, I was arrested at Baku airport because of that crazy coffin filled with opium.

What does a person feel the first moment he's under arrest? The first thing you want to do is to twist your shoulder free from the militiaman's grip and shout out: 'Have you gone mad? Do you know who I am?' At the same time, you want to thrust your hand into your pocket and get your red *Komsomolskaya Pravda* identity card, with the initials of the All-Union Leninist Komsomol Central Committee embossed in gold letters upon it. Any policeman would change his expression and would give you a salute the moment he saw it. A powerful weapon! It opens the door to exclusive restaurants and beaches, directors' offices, special supply stores, booking offices, hotels, warehouses and even – women's hearts! Armed with such a document, you can do anything. Invite a girl to see a closed performance of a foreign film at the House of Journalists or at the House of the Cinema, arrange a holiday at a hotel reserved for the élite, get meat at Yeliseyev's shop, buy imported clothes at a special department in the GUM store, order a table at any restaurant, smoke Marlboro cigarettes and drink Scotch whisky bought at the editorial canteen, break the driving regulations and even tell the traffic cop where to get off! You can do whatever you like under the protection of the good old red card! But just as the Baku militiaman was taking me by the arm and saying: 'You are under arrest,' I suddenly remembered in horror that this particular magic wand of mine, which I had used to get out of many a scrape, was in the hands of Anya Ziyalova and her brother. So were the rest of my papers, the notebooks which I had kept during my trip to the Pamirs, my electric razor and a few other items besides. And the Ziyalovs' trail was cold, as they say. And there was I, dressed in an old, threadbare cowboy shirt, unwashed jeans and dirty tennis shoes – one of your ordinary plebs, a nobody.

I looked over towards the baggage section.

'Listen, my rucksack is over there with all the luggage . . .' I said to the militiaman, trying to make him see reason.

'Never mind that! Get a move on!' he shouted, pushing me roughly into the Black Maria. It was one of those which they move suspects and prisoners about in, with all the windows curtained off.

'Now you just wait a minute!' I said in a rush. 'I'm a journalist from Moscow! I work for *Komsomolskaya Pravda!*'

'Have you got any papers with you to prove it?'

'They were in my travelling bag, and that's disappeared. But perhaps they've been dropped somewhere . . .'

'Disappeared!' he said, mimicking my accent. 'You just watch yourself! Correspondent, my foot! You're a speculator! And you were carrying opium! A smuggler even! Come on, come on, get into the van! And let's have less yapping.'

Deprived of my red card, and my passport, I suddenly felt naked and weaponless. I'd become an ordinary person, just like that, a cipher, a nobody. And when he simply heaved me into the van like an animal, I had a sudden, sharp awareness of how terrifying, how dangerous it can be to be just an ordinary person . . .

But a few minutes later, when the bus was on its way and I could see out through the bars of the tiny rear window, I grew a little calmer and even began to take stock of my position with a certain interested detachment. I was being taken from the airport into town. Everything would get sorted out in the end, and meanwhile I had got caught up in an unusual adventure. It would make a marvellous newspaper article. I immediately thought of a number of possible titles. 'Coffin without a Corpse', 'The Flying Drugpedlars', 'Report from a Prison Cell' . . . The office would throb with excitement, and *Izvestiya* and *Literaturnaya Gazeta* would be green with envy!

Still, these militiamen were blockheads all the same, I thought. Instead of setting up roadblocks and apprehending Ziyalov and his beautiful sister – God! could she really be mixed up in this drug-running too? – instead of blocking off all the rail and sea links, questioning the baggage handlers, impounding the documentation relating to the coffin and so on, instead of taking urgent measures like these, which even I, a forensic ignoramus, could see were essential in such circumstances, they'd arrested the first person who had crossed their path. And here they were, wasting time by taking him off somewhere. Although my rucksack was lost, the police would probably seize it eventually, and the baggage office was hardly likely to give it to anybody else in the meantime. On the other hand, my travelling bag with all my papers was a goner . . .

Well, I'd never entered Baku under arrest before . . . We were already passing through Chorny Gorod, a suburb of the city filled with low-roofed houses and rows of oleanders lining the streets. We'd soon be at the Sabunchinsky railway station about three blocks away from where my grandmother lives. It was a good job that I hadn't sent her a telegram about my arrival, or else she would have been in a state of total panic by now. We turned to the right, so that meant they were taking me to Militia Headquarters right opposite my old school on Ketskhoveli Street. Amazing! Here was I, former top sixth-former, pride of the school, now working in Moscow for *Komsomolskaya Pravda*, arriving at the school gates in a Black Maria and being escorted into Militia Headquarters to be interrogated by a half-literate, Azerbaidzhani police captain.

'Name?' he asked, poised to fill in the preliminary report.

'Andrey Garin.'

'Where do you live?'

'Moscow,' I said, making a slight attempt at imitating his accent.

'So you live in Moscow, but you spend your time smuggling drugs between Tashkent and Baku? Don't you think we've got enough drugs here already?'

Not bad! He's got a sense of humour, this captain!

'So there's a lot of drugs in Baku, eh?' I asked.

He looked at me, pretended not to have heard the question, and went on, in a lazy drawl: 'Let me see your papers.'

'They were in my travelling bag, which got lost at the airport. I asked the militiaman to search for them, but . . .'

I hadn't yet worked out what to do. Should I give away the Ziyalovs, or not? He was an old school-friend of mine, after all, and I'd fallen in love with his sister. On the other hand, how would I get myself out of this mess over the coffin if I didn't tell him that it was the property of my friend and why I'd offered to carry it?

But while I was wondering whether to ask to see the officer in charge and prove that I was the person I said I was, or whether to play along with them for the time being so as to get better material for my future article, the decision was taken out of my hands.

'Where do you work?' asked the captain.

'*Komsomolskaya Pravda*.'

'What's that? A co-operative association?' he asked uncomprehendingly.

'It's a newspaper!' I said indignantly. 'You *can* read newspapers, I suppose?'

The captain got up slowly, in an almost idle way, came up to me and suddenly, without hesitation, dealt me such a blow to the ear that I fell down on to the filthy office floor, which was covered with cigarette ends. What had he done? And why? What right did he have? . . . Stunned, and grasping my head, I managed to get to my feet again, as he returned to his seat.

'If you talk to me like that again,' he said, 'I'll tear your head off. Understand? You go and sell your drugs in Moscow, not around here!'

I stared at him silently, trying to remember every detail about him – that arrogant face of his with its protruding, Caucasian eyes and the receding line of his black hair. You'll grovel at my feet yet, you bastard!

'Well,' he said, 'so where do you work?'

Now it was time for me to call a halt.

'I want to talk with the Chief of Militia,' I said as calmly as I could.

'In a moment,' he said with a laugh. 'As a matter of fact he's waiting for you! So, you don't work anywhere, you're just a speculator. Which address are you registered at?'

'I will give further information only in the presence of the Chief of Militia. Or the Public Prosecutor.'

He looked me in the eye, waited for a moment, then pressed some button or other on his desk. I could hear a buzzer outside, and immediately a duty sergeant appeared at the door. The captain nodded in my direction: 'Take him to the Preliminary Detention Cell! You stupid Moscow prick!' he shouted at me with contempt. '*Gyotveran!*'

Ever since I was a child I have known that the Azerbaidzhanis now hate the Russians more than they hate the Jews and the Armenians, regarding them as the agents of an occupying power. But for somebody in a government institution, and the militia at that, to call someone by an Azerbaidzhani obscenity denoting

105

'homosexual', and to display anti-Russian prejudice quite so plainly and openly, well . . . I'd never encountered that before. On the other hand, he had no reason to watch what he said. Who was I, after all? A drug-trafficker! As he told me himself, they had enough drug-pedlars of their own. I am certain that if he had arrested some Azerbaidzhani trafficker, it would have been quite a different story. At least he wouldn't have hit his fellow-countryman as he did me, that's for sure. He had a Muscovite in his clutches . . . So even if I really was a journalist, why not bash me up anyway? There were no witnesses, so the law didn't enter into it. Now, if I'd had my *Komsomolka* identity card with me, it would have been another matter. But without it I could even be killed, and nobody would be called to account.

I was led down a brown-painted corridor, lined with barred basement windows so that all you could see were the feet of passers-by. In the distance I could hear the shouts of boys playing football in the yard of my former school. The duty sergeant led me up to a door, pushed me through it, and waited outside himself.

I was already expected. The usual rough hands rummaged in the pockets of my jeans, and only after that was over did a burly Russian sergeant-major order me to take off my shoes and trousers and untie my belt and shoe-laces.

I did as I was told, and waited. Painstakingly and calmly, almost phlegmatically, one might say, the sergeant felt the elastic of my pants and then emptied the contents of my pockets all over the table. There was a half-empty packet of cigarettes, a handkerchief, and eight roubles (the rest of the money from the Pamir assignment was in Anya Ziyalova's hands, along with all my papers). Then, just as assiduously, he felt the seams of my jeans. After that he gave me back the rest of my clothing, apart from my belt and shoe-laces. He counted up the number of cigarettes in the packet –

there were six of them left – thought for a moment, and then said: 'OK, you can hang on to these. You'll want to smoke!'

I got dressed and took the cigarettes.

'Off we go,' he said.

The corridor seemed to continue endlessly, but now the office doors were replaced by metal ones with spy-holes and bolts. I counted six of them. The sergeant-major tiptoed up to the fourth door, looked through the spy-hole and uttered some silent obscenity. Then he shot the bolt with one sudden movement and opened the door.

'Fulevy!' the sergeant shouted into the cell. 'Give me those cards at once!'

'What cards?' came the reply from the cell.

'Go on in,' said the sergeant, nodding towards the cell, and I entered. It was covered in dust, with rows of double bunks along the walls and a dirty, barred window high up on one side. In one corner, not far from the window, was a latrine, and in the other a small cistern filled with water, with a mug attached to it by a chain. This was the sum total of the 'furniture' in the cell. Somebody was asleep on one of the upper bunks, while the other occupants, eleven in all, were lying or sitting on the lower beds. One of them, a skinny fellow, aged about forty with Tartar eyes and wearing a sweater of some kind, tried to argue with the sergeant.

'What cards, sergeant? What are you taking about?'

'Stop playing the fool with me,' said the sergeant-major quietly. 'Let me have the cards or I'll call Bagirov.'

I realized that Bagirov was the captain who had just landed me one on the ear. I could already feel the bruise above my temple.

'I'll call Bagirov, I'll call Bagirov,' said the Tartar mockingly, passing a pile of tiny pieces of paper, about the size of a matchbox, to the man sitting next to him. These were the 'cards', nothing but pieces of paper torn from a notebook. 'Shakh, you give them to him. He can go to hell!'

Shakh took the cards and went up to the door, eyeing me for a short moment as he did so.

'You might give me a book to read or something . . .' he said to the sergeant.

'Let me have them, Sashka, come on,' came the reply. 'So you're a reader, eh?'

He took the cards and asked: 'Are they all here?'

'They are, apart from the Queen of Diamonds.'

'So, where's that?' asked the sergeant.

'I screwed her,' said Fulevy from the other end of the cell. 'And now she's sucking off the cripple.' He started laughing at his own joke. Then the whole cell joined in, apart from the cripple in question on the top bunk. The lower part of his leg had once been severed and sewn back on.

Sashka Shakh smiled too.

The sergeant smiled good-naturedly, looking first at Fulevy, who was laughing away, then at the others, and finally at Sashka. He was not allowed to enter the cell except in the company of at least one other guard. Sashka was still standing by the doorway smiling. Suddenly the sergeant kneed him in the groin so hard that he bent double and immediately caught a premeditated blow to the chin from the same knee. This second blow was not a hard one, but it was enough to lay Sashka out flat on his back. At the same time the sergeant slammed the door shut, bolted it noisily and walked away, without even peering through the spy-hole. We could hear his unhurried footsteps recede down the corridor.

So, he'd got his own back on Fulevy through Sashka. What a bastard!

I looked at the prisoners. None of them, not even Fulevy, got up to help their seventeen-year-old fellow-inmate. He was writhing around on the floor, pressing both hands to his groin and gasping for breath. His bloody mouth was twisted in a noiseless scream. The others simply stared at him, as if they were watching a circus act. Amid the tedium of prison life here was a fine entertainment!

I pulled the end of my shirt out of my jeans, tore a piece off it, went up to the water-cistern and tried to moisten it. But the cistern turned out to be empty. I went up to Sashka and started to wipe the blood off his face with the dry piece of shirt.

'Get away, you son of a bitch!' snarled Fulevy suddenly.

I hadn't expected this, of course, so I turned towards him in surprise.

'Get away from him! Take your hands away, you stool-pigeon!'

'Have you gone mad or something?' I asked.

Fulevy raised himself from the bunk and walked right up to me. I could see that he was chewing away at something in his mouth, but I couldn't understand why he was moving his cheek muscles so vigorously. By the time I realized that he was simply gathering saliva, it was already too late – he suddenly spat a loud and juicy gob right into my face.

Well, I'd never had that happen to me before! Forgetting that I was a famous journalist and all that, I lost all self-control. Using the same trick as the sergeant, I kneed him in the groin, and then, when he was staggering from the blow, hammered both fists into his neck. As he fell, the bastard caught me by the legs, and we rolled round the floor of the cell, covered in spit as it was. He tried to bite me, but I managed to twist his arm and wipe my face on his sweater. I don't know how it would have ended if, at that moment, the door hadn't opened. Two new militiamen rushed into the cell, grabbed the pair of us, and dragged us past the smirking sergeant-major, along the corridor into the interrogation room – a different room this time. There were no windows in this one. And beneath those thick, concrete walls decorated with portraits of Dzerzhinsky and Kalinin, these two policemen began

109

painstakingly and professionally to beat us up.

I immediately received three shattering blows – to the jaw, the liver and, once again, to the ear, so that I fell senseless to the floor. Fulevy lasted a little longer, I think, though I'm not sure. The only thing I know is that they doused us with water and then forced us to get to our feet and 'make up'. We stood opposite each other, still swaying, while the militiamen, who were having a fine old time, said: 'Tell him, "I won't hit you any more, I swear!"'

I said nothing, not because I didn't want to, but simply because my jaw was hurting so much that I couldn't utter a single word. I received another blow to the ear for my pains and fell down on to the cement floor once more. Again, they doused my face with water and lifted me up. Through my clouded brain I could hear Fulevy's voice whisper, 'I w-w-won't h-hit y-you any m-more . . .' His voice sounded very distant, as if under water.

'Swear on your mother's grave!' they ordered him.

'I swear . . .'

'Now you!' they said, poking me in the ribs.

I mumbled something through my swollen lips, but they still weren't satisfied and forced me to say it more clearly. And only then did they haul us back to the cell, and shove us, not even on to the bunks, but simply on to the floor.

We lay there next to each other. Now it was Sashka Shakh's turn to wash the blood from our faces with that torn-off piece of shirt. But I was lost to the world and had only the vaguest notion of what was going on. It was probably two or three hours before I regained consciousness properly. A light was burning, fixed behind the bars of the window just below the ceiling. I was lying on one of the bunks, though I didn't know who had placed me there. Sashka Shakh was sitting above me and arguing loudly with Fulevy. Through the drowsiness and aching that I could feel throughout my body, I could hear the vague murmur of their voices.

'Look, if he was an informer, they wouldn't have beaten him up like that . . .' Sashka was saying.

'They beat up their own stoolies, too, so that us prisoners will believe them more easily,' replied Fulevy.

'Perhaps they do, but not as much as that! What are you talking about, Fulevy? Just look what they've done to him.'

'Well, how the fuck should I know?' came the reply. 'Only why did he rush to wipe the blood off you? He even tore up his own shirt. What a performance! So I decided that he was a stool-pigeon. What did they arrest him for?'

'But you didn't even ask him . . .'

'Yeah, then this fucking mess happened. Have you got a snout?'

'Let's smoke his – there's one left.'

I realized that they'd taken the cigarettes out of my packet. I desperately needed a smoke, so I managed to croak in a hoarse whisper: 'Cigarette . . .'

Sashka put it in between my lips, and I took a long, greedy drag at it. And it was as if some great weight bearing down upon my shoulders was suddenly lifted from them. I opened my eyes.

'Who are you?' asked Sashka. 'What were you picked up for?'

I said nothing, but carried on smoking.

'Can you hear me?' asked Sashka, but I took no notice.

'Listen, friend,' said Fulevy, touching my shoulder. 'I thought you were a bloody plant. But they gave you a worse going-over than me. So I owe you one, OK? What did they take you in for? There are one or two in here for fifteen days, petty offences and all that. One of them could take a letter out with him. Any good to you?'

'Uh-huh,' I mumbled.

'Hey, you! Bookkeeper!' he shouted, giving the guy asleep in the next bunk a hefty poke in the ribs. He looked a typical middle-aged alcoholic. He woke up with a look of fear in his eyes, ready to do whatever he was asked.

'Write this down,' ordered Fulevy. 'Now tell him what you want to say,' he said to me. 'He's got a brain. He is a bookkeeper, after all, and he'll remember everything. He'll remember it now, and then tomorrow, when he's at work, he'll write it down and send it wherever you like. They take him to work straight from here. You dictate what you want him to write, and he'll remember.'

I realized that Fulevy wanted to test me once again, but I couldn't give a damn any longer. It was time for me to be getting out of here. Bloody idiot! I'd had enough of being immersed in real life!

Now which paper would publish an account of everything that had happened to me? I looked at the bookkeeper, who was wide-eyed with fear. I expect I looked the same myself.

'Get hold of a telephone directory. Look up two numbers. The first is that of *Komsomolskaya Pravda*'s journalist department, where you'll find Izya Kotovsky. The second is the Azerbaidzhani Central Committee's Propaganda Department, where you'll contact Kerim Rasulov. Tell them that I'm here. My surname is Garin.'

'So who *are* you?' asked Fulevy dumbfounded.

Instead of replying, I said to the bookkeeper: 'Have you understood?'

'Repeat it all!' said Fulevy, kicking his leg.

'Get hold of a telephone directory,' said the bookkeeper, 'and look up two numbers, the *Komsomolskaya Pravda* journalist department, where I'll find Izya Kotovsky, and the Azerbaidzhani Central Committee's Propaganda Department, where I'll contact Kerim Rasulov. Tell them both that you're here and that your name is Garin.'

'Well, has he got it right?' asked Fulevy, not without a hint of pride. 'So who are you then?'

'I work for *Komsomolskaya Pravda*,' I said.

'Are you a writer?' asked Fulevy in amazement.

My swollen lips started to grin, but I immediately groaned with pain.

112

'Well, I'll be damned!' he said. 'Give them a description of our life here. You could write a whole novel about what I've been through. Will you do it? I'm begging you – please write about it. Just look at this!' He opened his mouth and pressed down his lips to reveal a mouthful of metal teeth. 'See these? I had all my teeth knocked out when I was being transported, before I was even fifteen. And what for? For nothing! Now look here.' He showed me his arm. It was covered in injection marks. 'See that? I've been on drugs for fifteen years. Yes, I could tell you my life story, and you could write a novel about it as good as anything by Tolstoy. And what have they nabbed you for?'

I told them – about the drug-filled coffin and about Ziyalov. The only thing I left out was his sister. I didn't want to get her mixed up in it somehow.

'A whole coffin filled with opium! Not bad!' said Fulevy, who was completely flabbergasted. 'Do you see how they use us, Shakh? Why, it'll have been worth a million roubles at least! Christ knows, perhaps even two million! That's the kind of money they earn, those people! Listen, writer, are you going to tell them all about it? Are you going to write about the going-over they gave you? Eh? Christ, they've bitten off more than they can chew with you, the shits! As for you, bookkeeper, if you don't make the phone-calls he's told you to, then don't come back here, OK? And if you snitch, I'll get you, even if I have to do it from Kolyma, understand? I'll cut your throat, get me?'

'I get you . . .' said the bookkeeper, fearfully moving a little further away from us.

The whole night, while the other inmates were snoring away, Fulevy and Shakh told me their stories. As well as being a drug-addict, Fulevy was a housebreaker who moved about from city to city. The morning before he'd been caught 'red-handed', as they say, while robbing the apartment of the chief engineer of the local tube-rolling factory. He already knew that they'd pin ten years on him under Article 144, Section

113

3. The only thing that was in doubt was whether he'd be sent to the Baikal-Amur Railway Colony, Vorkuta or the Naryn Hydro-Electric Power Station.

Then we discussed Sashka's story. According to Fulevy, his case presented no problem at all. In fact, his only crime was that he'd jumped on to the platform of a moving tram. After that two guys, whom he didn't know, started to push and kick him off the platform. He'd tried to defend himself and pulled them off the platform too. There *was* a man in spectacles around, but as for a watch . . . What watch? Where did it come from? I was supposed to have taken your watch? What are you talking about? In any case, Citizen Investigator, how could I have taken his watch, if he says himself that he saw me being attacked by the other two? I'm supposed to have done it while I was being beaten up, is that it?

Fulevy gave such an accurate, lifelike and detailed description of how Sashka should defend himself during the investigation that, looking ahead for a moment, I could see that all Sashka would have to do at the cross-examination was repeat the answers his cellmate had prepared for him.

The next morning, after the three fifteen-day merchants had been taken off to work (including the bookkeeper), Sashka was summoned for cross examination. When he came back he had a great parcel in his hands, containing a round Caucasian loaf, some grapes and a short note saying: 'We'll be waiting for you. Mum and Lina.'

But we'd hardly got to work on the parcel when I was called for questioning myself. The very fact that the guard was now taking me straight to the first floor seemed to prophesy some change in my situation. The corridor was no longer painted that dull brown colour (I realized now why brown paint had been used on the floor below – so as to make the blood less obvious, if any of it splashed on to the walls). No, the corridor on the first floor was painted light green and there was a

114

carpet running right along it. It was obvious that they wouldn't beat anyone up here, if only to prevent the carpet getting stained with blood.

The furniture in the investigator's room was far better than the standard office issue. There was a good desk, bentwood chairs and even a refrigerator in the corner. Sitting at the desk was a youngish-looking man with light-blue eyes and dressed in an ordinary suit. He was writing something.

'Take a seat,' he said, motioning me towards a chair. I did as I was asked. Without raising his head, he carried on writing for another four or five minutes. Then he placed his signature at the bottom of it, raised his eyes and sat back in his chair.

'Hm . . . yes, so you're Garin? From *Komsomolskaya Pravda*? And how can you prove it?'

I decided to say nothing, pure and simple. To make my point.

'Well, why won't you say something?'

The fact that I had been brought to a normal office, where somebody was addressing me fairly politely, spoke for itself. The bookkeeper must already have phoned Izya Kotovsky or Rasulov at the Central Committee, or perhaps he'd phoned the two of them.

'Well, why won't you answer?' he persisted.

Without looking at him, and fixing my eyes on the wall, I said: 'I don't know who it is I'm talking to.'

'Ah . . .' He sat back in his chair once again and said in an off-hand way: 'And why should you? Let's assume that I'm the investigator. It doesn't matter very much for the moment. We'll just have a little chat, not for the report. Now look. Somebody helps the baggage handlers unload a coffin from a plane and carries it to the airport exit. Right? On the way the coffin accidentally falls and splits open. It turns out that it contains drugs. That person is naturally arrested and taken off to Militia Headquarters. But while being placed in a cell pending further investigation of the case, he insults a militia officer and threatens to have everybody locked in gaol. He says that he's a journalist working for *Komsomolskaya Pravda*, although he has no papers with him to prove it. You see, everything has been entered in the report.' He pointed to it. 'After that, the said person has scarcely entered the Preliminary Detention Cell when he picks a fight with some of the other criminals and attacks the prisoner nicknamed Fulevy. You see, Comrade Garin, ours is a democratic country, and you don't have the right to insult the militia and beat up prisoners, even if you really are a newspaper correspondent . . .

I said nothing. If they had the testimony of my fellow-inmates, it must mean that the fifteen-day merchants had given me away, or rather the bookkeeper had, the son of a bitch. He hadn't phoned anybody, but had simply reported our conversations the previous night to the militia. He would doubtless receive some reward for his information. They wouldn't send him back to the same cell again, that went without saying.

'Well, I'm waiting,' said my investigator.

'I will talk only to the Chief of Militia,' I replied.

'He's at it again!' he said with a wry face. 'Listen, what's your patronymic?'

'You know it already, I think.'

He grinned. 'Quite right, we do. Andrey Borisovich. More than that I've read some of your articles – about the Arctic zone. Siberian workers and geologists, and the like. And I must tell you that I'm a great admirer of your work. You write very well. But . . . nobody has the right to attack a member of the militia. You attacked a captain no less. Here's his report. What shall we do?'

'Let the courts decide,' I said, looking him in the eye.

'Let them decide what exactly?'

'My case,' I replied. 'Let's have it tried in open court, and then we'll see who laid hands on whom. Let's invite *Komsomolskaya Pravda* and the Central Committee Propaganda Department to send along some observers . . .'

He said nothing for a few moments, but simply

116

stared at me. Perhaps he was revising his opinion of me, or weighing up what to do next.

'Hm ... Yes ... You're a strange fellow, Andrey Borisovich. Don't you know that the militia are never brought to court in our country? Although, of course, we do make mistakes, too. We're only human, after all, aren't we? The only people not to make mistakes are those who never do anything. Even the newspapers make mistakes. You and I know, don't we? They might write about somebody one day, saying that he's a first-class worker, a hero of labour, and then he turns out to be a petty thief the next. He's been fiddling the books, or some such nonsense. The Anti-Fraud Squad have got a whole file on him. But the newspaper doesn't get taken to court, eh? You see, Andrey Borisovich, you and I know what we are about. Yet here you are, going on about court, open sessions, the Central Committee Propaganda Department! Besides, you have yet to prove that you and Ziyalov weren't in cahoots with each other. Why did you arrive in Baku with him? What is he to you?'

'I was at school with him,' I replied. 'That's all.'

'Well, that's yet to be proved.'

He got up and began to walk around the room, lighting up a pipe as he did so. I couldn't help smiling: he did so remind me of Stalin. His features were quite different, of course, but as far as his movements and manner of speaking were concerned, he was the image of the Great Leader.

'Listen. This is how it looks to us. Two former schoolmates are transporting a consignment of drugs from Tashkent to Baku (one of them is an employee of a national newspaper who happens to get caught). The other one manages to escape, present whereabouts unknown. But only for the time being. We'll find him, of course. What are you smiling at?'

'Nothing,' I replied. All the same, it was amusing. He sounded so much like Stalin.

'You're wrong to smile. Drugs offences are very

117

serious. According to the Decree of 25 April 1974 entitled "Intensifying the Struggle against Drug-Addiction", drug-trafficking is now considered an especially grave offence. We could keep you under arrest for up to nine months while the investigation is proceeding. And bear in mind that no editor would be able to help you then. You see, you'd have to spend nine months in cells similar to the one you've just been in – with criminals, murderers and homosexuals for company. Come night they could do anything they liked to you. Eventually, of course, it might turn out that you were innocent after all, but meanwhile . . . Take that Fulevy, for instance. Did he bother you last night? He's a queer, after all, and if you won't do the kind of things he tells you to, he'll strangle you. And if he doesn't, somebody else will. I can't give you a cell to yourself, even if you are a journalist. But . . .' and at this he turned his smiling eyes towards me: 'It's your choice in fact. We could let you go after all . . . eh? How about leaving here on the spot, going home, taking a shower, catching up on some sleep, lying on a beach for a few days – and then flying back to Moscow? How about it?'

The bastard! He knew just the approach to take with me! I could see the gentle green waves of the Caspian bearing down on me. After spending such a terrible night on a prison bunk, I could imagine myself at that every moment immersing my tortured body in the healing, salty waters of the warm sea, and then lounging on the sandy beach, roasting myself in the sun and drinking cold beer . . .

And, as if reading my thoughts, the sod opened up his refrigerator, which contained a few bottles of Czech beer. Can you imagine? I was dumb-founded at the coincidence. Meanwhile, he gave me a smile and took out a couple of bottles (I could see tiny droplets of icy water glistening on them). He placed them on the desk, and then opened them up by pressing their metal caps underneath the lid of the desk. He poured some out into two glasses.

'Here you are. It's Czech beer, just like you'd get at Sokolniki Park in Moscow.'

I admired his flawless psychological approach. I took the glass, emptied it at one gulp, and said: 'Listen. Who exactly are you? This isn't your office at all.'

'What makes you think that?'

'Well, you wouldn't have opened the bottle like that if the desk belonged to you.'

He smiled.

'Andrey, let's call each other by our Christian names. We're the same age, and we both work in the same system, albeit in different sectors. Look, we made a mistake in your case. Our boys were too hasty. And they'll apologize to you. I'll call them in straight away. The captain and his two sergeants will crawl about on their knees in front of you, if you like. Shall I call them?'

I said nothing and he pressed some button or other underneath his desk. The duty officer immediately appeared at the door.

'Send for Captain Bagirov – right away,' he ordered.

The guard disappeared, and my 'investigator' continued to look at me silently. Then he said: 'Look, finish your beer, or else it'll get warm . . .' He opened up another bottle and poured some into my glass.

I am not sure, but according to the laws of literary narrative, if this story were being written by Victor Hugo or even the detective-story writer Yulian Semyonov, the hero – that is to say, me – would now hurl the glass away or at least spit the beer out into the face of the 'investigator'. He would then be led away to the cells, to get beaten up once more, either by the militiamen or criminals. But I am not Victor Hugo, or Yulian Semyonov or Shtirlits, the famous detective, for that matter. Also, it was by no means clear what I would be kept in gaol for. So as not to betray Ziyalov? But they already knew his surname, it appeared. To write an article about prison life then? But they would hardly be likely to print it. Anyway, there I was, sitting in the room with the 'investigator' and waiting for Captain Bagirov to arrive. I hadn't said either 'yes' or 'no' yet. In fact, I didn't know what he wanted from me, or why he had become suddenly so polite . . .

The door opened and Captain Bagirov entered the room. I recognized the same slightly protruding, arrogant Azerbaidzhani eyes, the beads of sweat on his receding hairline, and the black moustache.

'Allow me, comrade . . .'

'As you were, captain!' barked the 'investigator' suddenly, obviously unwilling to have his name or rank revealed. 'Shut the door.' And when Bagirov had done as he was told, the 'investigator' went right up to him and said softly: 'You swine, you're a disgrace to your uniform! Why the fuck do you think you're paid your salary? Why have you got those stars on your epaulets? I could fucking well tear them off you this minute! You should be able to tell the difference between shit and a prominent worker, that's what you're paid for, do you understand me?'

'I understand you, comrade . . .' said Bagirov quickly.

'And leave out the "comrade" bit. Do you know who you raised your hand against yesterday?'

'I have no idea . . .' said Bagirov in a muck-sweat.

'Well, you just apologize now. Go on! Ask his forgiveness. And if he tells you to get on your knees, you'll do it, understand? Otherwise I'll have you drummed out of the force on the spot! Have you got any children?'

'Yes, two, comrade . . .'

'Shut your mouth! Well, either your children will go starving because you've been cashiered, or you beg Comrade Garin to forgive you. OK?'

Yes, it was a hideous scene. Without asking why, or even thinking, this great ox of a captain suddenly fell on to his knees and crawled over towards me, grasping his Adam's apple: 'I beg you, Comrade Garin! Forgive me. I promise I won't do it again! I swear by my mother's grave!'

I could see the 'investigator' looking at me out of the

side of his eye, waiting for my reaction. Meanwhile, there kneeling beside me was this supposedly repentant hypocrite of a captain. The whole scene was so repulsive that I turned to the 'investigator' and said with a feeling of disgust: 'OK, that's enough! Stop it!'

'Do you forgive him?'

'Yes.'

'Thank you, comrade,' Bagirov started mumbling away to the 'investigator'. 'Thank you . . .'

'That's enough!' said the other, apparently repelled by the spectacle himself. 'Leave us!'

When the door had closed behind him, the 'investigator' said: 'Shall we summon the two sergeants now?'

'There's no need,' I said. 'What do you want me to do?'

He offered me a Marlboro. 'Have a cigarette. What do I want? I want you to forget about this whole business. Nobody beat you up, and in fact you haven't been to Militia Headquarters at all. We'll find Ziyalov. He's a crook – but the whole case has nothing to do with you. So why should you get mixed up in it? You'd be dragged along to the investigation, you'd have to give evidence in court, and so on. Do you really want that? Look, I'll tear up all the reports of your cross-examination, as well as the testimony of your cellmates. You haven't been here at all, OK? Otherwise it'll drag on and on. How you got arrested, where you were taken, how and why you were released, and all that. OK. Shall I tear it up?'

'Wait a minute,' I replied. 'Ziyalov has got the bag containing all my papers, after all. How shall I get on, if I don't have any documents? I need to get my passport back, as well as my *Komsomolka* identity card. I'd better put in an official request, or else he'll get picked up carrying my passport . . .'

'Ah, quite correct! Well done! But how do you think I found out that you really are the journalist Andrey Garin?'

'From the bookkeeper,' I replied.

'Well, from him, too,' he grinned. 'You're quite right. But before that happened, some woman rang up last night and said that items belonging to a correspondent of *Komsomolskaya Pravda* were to be found at left-luggage locker No. 23 at the marine station.'

He opened one of the drawers of his desk, took out my travelling bag and passport, and pushed them across the table towards me. 'What do you think? Who was this woman?'

I looked at him in silence.

'I don't know either,' he said. 'Some anonymous person. The duty officer who spoke to her just had time to make a note of the number of the locker, when she hung up. But she did say one other thing – that you weren't mixed up in anything. But that doesn't matter now . . .'

Of course, I knew who it was that had phoned – Anya Ziyalova. But why tell *him* that? Apart from loathing and the desire to get away as quickly as possible, I felt completely empty. I checked the documents in my travelling bag. They were all there – passport, newspaper card, driving licence, my Union of Journalists membership pass and even my money! I got up from my chair.

'May I go now?'

'If we've reached an agreement, then of course you may! May I tear this lot up?'

He was still holding the transcripts of my cross-examination and the reports of my cellmates. I was convinced that they were only copies, but I didn't care.

'Yes, go ahead,' I replied.

He tore them up, first into four, then into eight, and made a great show of throwing the pieces into the wastepaper basket.

'Excellent. So you haven't been to Baku Militia Headquarters at all, about anything? Correct? You've forgotten all about the incident with the coffin and about Ziyalov, too. Right?

'Yes,' I said, forcing myself to agree.

'Thank you very much!' he replied, offering me his

hand. But suddenly he appeared to remember something. He opened the drawer of his desk and got out a file bearing the inscription: 'GARIN, A. B. Agent's Dossier.' He opened the faded, grey file and extracted a yellow sheet of paper from it. He passed it over to me. I looked at it and was thunderstruck. It was a parody of a famous poem by Lermontov, written in my handwriting and composed more than ten years ago, in reaction to the events in Czechoslovakia in 1968:

> And you, with flames and shrapnel, you common Kremlin rabble,
> Remembered for our fathers' agony and death,
> Have crushed the heart of freedom
> That was in Bohemia's cities, beating still.
> You gannets, greedy crowd, that cluster round the throne,
> Butchers of liberty, art and choice,
> Have forced your laws with tanks and fire,
> Stifling any voice of peace and human right.
> Now you, you base manipulators, listen to another law.
> The people's law that waits and speaks from history,
> Not to be corrupted by jingling sounds of gold.
> It has in mind your future mind, of action or intent,
> So resort to scorn or slander it in vain,
> No second chance.
> Nor ever will your own black blood be payment
> Fit to drown the blood of freedom drained from Prague.

Thank God the poem was unsigned.

He grinned as he took the sheet of paper back from me.

'I'm sure this isn't your poem. In your youthful enthusiasm you simply copied it down from someone else. Those were ardent times, I remember. So let it stay in our files. We haven't even passed it on to the KGB. But if you don't keep to your agreement . . . Remember, this sheet of paper could ruin your whole career. No Lermontov will be able to help you. Do we see eye to eye?'

A moment later I walked out of Baku Militia Headquarters on to the street outside. The bright midday sun blinded my eyes. I stopped and listened. I could hear the hum of traffic in the streets. I could hear teenagers kicking a football around in the yard of my old school, swearing away in Azerbaidzhani, Russian and Armenian. An old man selling ice-cream was dragging his barrow along the roadway, castors squeaking as he did so.

'Ice-cream for sale!' he was shouting. Meanwhile, outside Militia Headquarters, some valiant Azerbaidzhani militiamen were dozing away, ready to drive off in their Volgas at a moment's notice. As I wandered along Red Army Street, down towards the Esplanade and the sea, I felt violated and useless, like a woman who has just had an abortion. Not even when that bastard Bagirov struck me round the ear, or when Fulevy spat in my face, had I felt as humiliated and used as I did at the moment I was released into the sun.

Oleg Ziyalov was the one who must have given them that poem ten years ago. That was why they were shielding him today, I thought. Oleg Ziyalov was one of their agents probably . . .

The same evening, 22.30 hours
No, there was certainly never a dull moment with this Belkin!

I was at 12 Parkovaya Street, on the twelfth floor of a whitish-coloured tower-block, sitting in the one-room apartment of *Komsomolka* typist, Inna Kulagina. It had a tiny entrance-hall, a minute kitchen and balcony, and one room measuring seven and a half square yards. I had an identical flat myself in an identical white tower-block just by the Izmailovsky Park metro station. If it weren't for the signs of a woman's hand – the lace curtains in front of the wide-open windows, the comfortable sofa with Inna drowsily curled up on it, waiting for me to finish reading Belkin's manuscript – if it weren't for all these admittedly significant details, I could easily have imagined that I was at home, sitting at my own desk and thinking about some purely routine matter. The table lamp highlighted the pages of Belkin's neatly typed manuscript, a glass of strong, tepid tea and a small glass bowl containing my favourite savouries. This was all I had agreed to eat and drink when we arrived at Inna's apartment.

But I didn't chew away at any of the biscuits, because I didn't want to wake Inna up with the crunching noise. Above the sofa was a photograph of a laughing, eight-year-old girl, Inna's daughter by an unsuccessful or 'difficult' marriage, as she put it. At the moment her daughter was at a summer camp organized by *Komsomolskaya Pravda* at Bolshevo, near Moscow. There was a photo above the desk at my apartment too – it was of my twelve-year-old son, Anton . . . Still, we mustn't get distracted. Let's examine the 'pickings from the goose', as my Jewish grandmother used to say – or rather, what there was left from the third chapter of Belkin's manuscript. I had a few thoughts about what I had read so far. In the first place, he had definitely been arrested and held in a preliminary detention cell – despite what we had been told by the Chief of the Baku City Militia. Only somebody who has actually been in one could have described the cell and its inmates in such detail. I'm no literary critic, of course, but even an investigator like me could tell that in the first chapters Belkin was still attempting to maintain the journalistic tone, probably thinking that he would write a story which could get past the censorship. Some things he exaggerated, others he kept quiet about or played down, all with this in mind. However, when he started to describe the way he had been beaten up in the detention cell, there had been no holding him. He described everything in the order in which it occurred, with a mixture of bitterness and malice. That was why the third chapter contained much more in the way of exact detail and was much truer to life. But who was this so-called investigator? Someone the same age as Belkin, with light-blue eyes, who had the power to strip a militia captain of his rank. No, it wasn't just the Chief of Militia, it was somebody higher up. He smokes a pipe like Stalin and has the same intonation – so that means he can't be Russian. Stalin had a Caucasian intonation . . . Of course, he really clipped Belkin's wings with that Lermontov parody. It's true, nothing is ever forgotten about in this 'state of Denmark' of ours. A poem written years ago by a thoughtless youth lies in the archive of the Azerbaidzhani Interior Ministry, until finally its hour arrives. A brawl which took place at some restaurant in Yakutia is the subject of a secret report placed in a CID Special Department archive. I couldn't help wondering what they had on me, and where. The USSR Prosecutor's Department is charged with keeping an eye on the work of every organ of state, including the MVD and the KGB, and yet once a year the latter gets to work on us too. For a week or more they tap our telephones at the office and at home, they intercept our mail, check out the people we know, our friends, and the nature and content of all the conversations we hold. And all this information, along with reports provided by various special agents, are placed in my file at the KGB Fourth Special Department. Nobody knows precisely when he or she is going to be worked on, not even the Chief Prosecutor himself, but we all know that it happens, at the very minimum once a year . . .

I bent down cautiously, and extracted from my briefcase the bottle of *Chornye Glaza* wine which Baklanov had brought back with him from holiday. Of course, when you've had thoughts like those you really need to drink something a little stronger, but this would do for now. It was a good job that I'd been carrying it around with me in my case all day. I had a penknife-cum-corkscrew with me, too! So it was easy enough to open the bottle without making any noise. It wasn't difficult to get a glass out of the sideboard . . .

Chapter 4
The Sea-nymph

A quiet islet in the green Caspian Sea, forty feet long and two hundred feet wide. Or, if you don't like that, then imagine whatever you like. The island is forty minutes by car from Baku, if you follow the road to Bilgya. Just before you reach the village of Rybachy you turn right, drive down an old dirt-track for about a mile, and there you are! – by the sea, on an empty, sun-drenched beach. Before you is a chain of tiny islets, made of nothing but rock and sand, and quite deserted. There's nothing for miles around, apart from a few fishing boats and the tiny village of Rybachy – a cluster of simple wooden houses. If you look beyond them you see the sloping shore of the Caspian disappearing into the heat haze, with Bilgya and its complement of beaches, summer houses and sanatoria hidden somewhere beyond the horizon.

But in this spot there is nobody, only the sun, the sand and the sea. When I dive in, equipped with my harpoon, the water is cool and gentle. Oh, if I could only live for ever in this submarine world, with its emerald light, its coral, its yellow flowers and silver fish! Forget about newspapers, salaries and trips to Vienna! Just imagine disappearing under the water and returning to the life from which we came, a world without governments, militia, moral codes for builders of Communism and queues for smoked sausage! The land beneath the waves has gardens and a sun of its own, and life there is completely natural . . .

This was the fourth morning that our special

127

correspondent, Izya Kotovsky, had driven me here in his Zhiguli. He then went about his business and left me in the same place until evening. He would ask no questions. He didn't try delving into my soul, but simply returned every evening, and I fed him shashlyks of freshly caught grey mullet. We'd sit there quietly eating and discussing trifles like tomorrow's weather or the football match between Spartak and Dynamo. Izya was marvellous. He looked after me, as a doctor would a patient. Or rather, he'd bring me out on trips to the sea, like a nanny, and would then take me back to his bachelor apartment on the Esplanade, and we'd spend every evening drinking spirits or sitting in the little shashlyk house in the Baku fortress.

Of course, something of life's conversations, smells and noises succeeded in penetrating my protective shield, but I didn't really want anything from it. There was I, one of the best journalists in the country, the representative of one of the Soviet Union's greatest national dailies, and yet some lousy bastard of a militia captain had managed to hit me in the face, and some idiot policeman had kicked me in the heart and liver. Then the next day they'd sealed my tongue with their hypocritical apologies and a childish poem à la Lermontov. What use is your freedom if you have to keep your mouth shut like that? Is that freedom? Go to hell, all of you, with your articles, typewriters, editorial phone calls, telexes, prizes awarded by the Union of Journalists, and all that shit!

My god, why didn't I enter the Geography Faculty, like half of my class at school, and eighty per cent of our Geographical Society at the Pioneers' Palace? I could have found employment as a geologist or glaciologist, in the mountains, in the swampy forest lands, in the tundra, or wherever you like. What the hell use was it being a talented journalist if you had to be as silent as a fish? You'd do better to become a real fish, like this grey mullet here, or maybe a dolphin.

The green waves of the Caspian rocked and comforted me. My fits of rancour and impotent rage grew fewer and fewer, as the sea lulled and gradually healed me. Then, on the fifth day, She appeared. From the depths of the sea, from the silvery bubbles and the froth of the waves, I suddenly saw a tall, sun-tanned body moving, hair spread out in the water. I was dumbfounded and almost let the snorkel slip out of my mouth. She was virtually a mystical apparition, this sun-bronzed nymph armed with a small harpoon who dived to reach reefs and weeds where I would never have dared to follow, even for the tastiest-looking grey mullet. The quiet ripples from her flippers and the telltale silvery bubbles of air were all that I could see of her. So I swam around the surface, waiting for her to reappear.

And reappear she did, but not where I was expecting her. She surfaced much further away, almost by my island. I saw her emerge on to the shore, take off her flippers and sit down at the bonfire which I had made. I swam to the shore myself. When I caught up with her, she was already roasting lumps of fresh mullet over the fire, and there were another three large fish lying next to her harpoon. She was sixteen. I can see her now, with her strong, shapely figure, grown used to the sea, and her firm breasts and thighs beneath her narrow, tight bikini. I can see her damp, sun-bleached hair, and her round face with its snub nose and brown eyes, following me closely, as I emerged on to the beach, took off my flippers and diving mask and wandered exhaustedly towards the fire. My skin had begun to peel from sunburn, and I felt awkward. I quickly donned my shirt, so that my pampered, city-dweller's body shouldn't get completely burnt up by the midday sun. But she said nothing. She just looked.

Ater I had put on my shirt and shorts, I lay down by the fire and recovered my customary, slightly ironic journalist's aplomb.

'Where are you from?' I asked.

'Over there,' she said, nodding towards the tiny

village. 'Here, take this.' And she offered me a piece of grilled mullet on a skewer.

What more can I tell you? The two of us were alone on the island, and within an hour our bodies had entwined on the sand, our mouths joined in long, deep kisses. She gripped me with her strong, firm thighs, the brown of her eyes melting behind closed eyelids and her half-open lips breathing in short, loud gasps. Then, when we tired of making love, we lay naked in the water, lazily moving our flippers and just touching each other with the tips of our fingers. We were like two fish, two dolphins, two sea creatures who had met in the water and surrendered to each other, silently and according to nature's law. That's all. And once we'd rested, we tackled the grilled fish, tomatoes and black bread which Izya Kotovsky had left me that morning. Then we embraced once again.

An hour before Izya arrived, she swam off to her village. She appeared again the next day, and so it continued for four or five days. I think I am right in saying that, in all that time, we didn't spend more than twenty minutes in conversation with one another. The rest of the time was spent with the sea, the sand, the hot stones beneath our backs, sex – and then once again the sea, that warm, green font of ours!

But, by the fifth day, I began to get tired of it all.

Nature is somehow generous with women. A single woman can go without men for years on end, seeming to maintain an even temper, mental composure and even a sincere cheerfulness of spirit. But it's not like that with men. Only a woman can cleanse the dross from our minds and dissipate our feelings of tiredness, irritation and anger. And so it was that this mistress of mine succeeded in purging my body and spirit. She restored me to life by dissolving all the bitterness I felt at being humiliated by the Baku Militia. Everything else, my sober realization of how powerless I was when confronted by the system, and my feelings of aversion both for myself and my profession – all this disappeared. By the third day of our love and games I was once again the witty, ironic, metropolitan super-journalist, and by the fifth I was like an impatient race-horse, champing at the bit. Neither the sea, nor underwater harpooning, nor my sixteen-year-old mistress were able to satisfy this new urge of mine – the need to act, to drive or fly somewhere, to write something and get it published. In short, to make my mark on the world. Lying next to her or diving into the cold, dark depths beneath the rocks, I was no longer thinking about her or about the next shoal of silvery mullet, moving hither and thither in the distance. Instead, I was thinking of the one form of vengeance open to me, if I were to get my own back on the Baku Militia. I would go among the Baku drug-addicts myself, using all my journalistic experience, and through them I'd get at the drug-traffickers. Then I'd write a detective novel about it, in which everything would be fact apart from the actual names used and a few odd details. And the first chapter of it would be my article for *Komsomolskaya Pravda* about the everyday life of addicts in Baku. I'd give a detailed description of their lives, from morning till night, and it would cover Sashka Shakh and Co., Mosol, Fulevy and others like them. I could already see the article in my mind's eye, as a bloodhound can scent its quarry. All I needed to do was to see with my own eyes what Sashka Shakh and Fulevy had described to me that night in prison. I needed to see and describe the way in which these fifteen-year-old lads set about their work every morn-ing, on the trams, at the railway stations, and in the shops and markets; stealing purses, filching watches and cutting holes in bags, and in the evenings how they set upon lone pedestrians in darkened streets – all with one purpose in mind: to obtain drugs in exchange for the money which they steal. I had to describe how they get high by smoking hash or shooting opium.

Nobody in the whole history of Soviet journalism has ever described such a thing! I'd be the first, and I'd do it! It would suit our newspaper right down to the ground. It was aimed at Soviet youth, after all, and this article about fifteen-year-old drug-addicts would cause a sensation, an explosion among all the newspapers.

On the sixth day I simply failed to turn up at the island. I felt young, self-confident and obstinate once again as I returned to 'normal' life. And this time I plumbed the depths in another sense, for it was an easy matter to discover Sasha Romanov's address and telephone number from the Central Inquiry Office. I phoned his mother, kicking myself for not doing so earlier. I didn't know where he was, whether he was still in the prison or at large.

Sasha came to the phone himself. His case had gone just as Fulevy had said it would. He'd been freed because of 'lack of evidence'. After a couple of minutes we agreed to meet at the main entrance to the Esplanade.

And then Sasha asked: 'Perhaps I can come along with Lina?'

I hadn't reckoned on including a girl in my journalistic plans, but I was interested in seeing the person who had succeeded in curing Sashka of his drug-addiction in sixty seconds flat. In any case, she could figure in my story in her own right.

They appeared on the Esplanade, holding each other's hand, like children, or rather, like two creatures who had discovered a whole new world in each other. There was Sashka Shakh, strong, sun-tanned and dressed in a sports shirt and a pair of Odessa jeans. And there was Lina, a skinny girl with deep-blue eyes, legs like skittles and wild, flaxen hair falling down to her shoulders. Whether they were walking down the Esplanade with me, surrounded by people and prams, or sitting squashed together under a canvas awning at an ice-cream parlour, they were always together and only together, as if their love cut them off from the rest of the world.

When they were in such a state, what was there for us to talk about? Sashka could neither hear nor understand anything. Indeed, he was scarcely capable of it. I kept trying to engineer situations which would allow me to spend a minute or two with him by himself. I talked Lina into going on a children's roundabout, and while she was spinning round with the five-year-olds, explained my idea to Sashka as quick as a flash – how I wanted to be introduced to the drug-addicts, spend a few days with them, smoke, play cards and even take part in a robbery, so as to write an article about it all in *Komsomolskaya Pravda* later. But this made no impression on him at all. He seemed to be in another dimension. He'd said farewell to the underground world and had entered another, and all I could get out of him was a promise to help me with my plan, but only after Lina had gone away.

'And when will that be?'

'In three days' time.'

'And where is she living? Is she still at your place?'

'No, at her aunt's.'

'So you're not spending all your time with her? When she's at her aunt's, you could help me.'

'No, I'm sorry, I go to see her first thing every morning . . .'

Throughout this whole conversation, he'd done nothing but follow her with his eyes, as she'd been spinning on the roundabout, and wave to her each time she came round. I realized there was nothing to be done. It was useless talking to the love-stricken Shakh. I must say, love does make people stupid!

'OK,' I said, changing the subject. 'So where's Fulevy now?'

'He was due to be transported somewhere in Siberia a couple of days ago. They've raised his old case again.'

'Where?'

'I don't know.'

'Sasha,' I said, 'what do you mean? You were in the same cell as he was, you used to share cigarettes – and yet now you don't know where he is. Perhaps he's still there, and I could get something through to him . . .'

'And what about you?' said Sashka, suddenly turning towards me and forgetting about his beloved Lina for a moment. 'Didn't you share a cell with him, too?' he asked point-blank. 'Didn't you get beaten up with him? And where did you disappear to, when they let you go? You might at least have smuggled him in a packet of cigarettes. Whereas now . . . You need me in order to write your article, so you've remembered him too!'

He was right.

I looked him in the eye: how could I explain to him? Even if I were to recount every detail of my conversation with the 'investigator' on the first floor of Militia headquarters, it still wouldn't justify my behaviour. And why had I forgotten about my fellow-prisoners as soon as I was released? Why didn't I arrange for something like fruit, cigarettes or books to be sent into them, through Izya Kotovsky, say? I looked at Sashka and said: 'You're right!'

'There you are, you see. It's the same thing . . .' And he took hold of Lina's hand as she ran up to him. 'See you later.'

'Goodbye!' said Lina, eyes sparkling. And with that, holding each other's hand, they walked away down the tree-lined Esplanade, without looking round. They had forgotten about me the moment they said goodbye.

Chapter 5
Shots at Sandy Beach
What can stop a journalist – I mean, forgive me if this sounds immodest, a professional – once he has got his teeth into an assignment? I borrowed some old brushed-denim trousers, a faded T-shirt and some plimsolls from Izya and changed into them. Dressed in this workaday garb, I took the tram bound for Armenikend and the Gagarin Palace of Culture. Once off the tram I easily found the overgrown, shady gardens where Sashka Shakh visited Mosol on the day Lina arrived in Baku.

The gardens were empty apart from a handful of five-year-old Russian urchins who were playing about with a couple of slightly older ragamuffins. But I didn't lose heart. I looked around. On the other side of the gardens I could see some so-called 'Khrushchev slums' – four-floor apartment buildings with balconies that had at one time been different colours, but which were now all reduced to the same unidentifiable hue. The clothes I was wearing meant that I could pass myself off as one of the locals, so I went up to one of the older kids and said: 'What's your name? Seryozha?'

'No, I'm called Alik,' he said in surprise.

'What's your surname?'

'Krasavin . . .'

'Which block do you live in?'

'That one over there,' he said, pointing towards one of the buildings.

'Do you get teenagers mucking around here too?'

'You mean the ones who smoke hash?' said one of the other youngsters in a businesslike voice.

'Yes.'

'They come here a bit later, after lunch.'

'And where do they live? In these flats too?'

'No, They don't come from our buildings,' said Alik Krasavin.

That was enough. I didn't think that Mosol and Co. could live in these flats, so close to the place where they smoked hash and shot opium. Otherwise, any one of them could have been seen by his parents. Sashka Shakh lived on Melnichnaya Street, and it wasn't an accident that he'd chosen a spot near the Sabunchinsky railway station for his patch, five tram stops away from home. So that meant that they were hardly likely to know all those who lived hereabouts . . .

I sat down on a bench in the shade and began to wait. I can't say that I found it tiring. It was a marvellous summer's day, a little on the hot side, but there in the shade of the trees and the luxuriant oleander bushes,

135

some of them more than six feet high, it wasn't hot at all. It was actually reassuring and peaceful. I think that I had even begun to doze off when I heard voices in the bushes behind me.

'Let me have the syringe. Give it here!'

'Wait a minute, there's some sod sitting over there . . .'

'To hell with him! Stop messing about! Give me a light!'

I didn't move, but carried on sitting, as if I were really asleep.

I heard a match strike behind me, and then, after a short pause, the sound of voices again.

'For Christ's sake, what are you doing? I'll do it myself . . . Give me the joint!'

The heady, heavy, honey-like smell of hashish wafted over from the bushes, and without any prior warning even to myself, I suddenly gave a loud, indeed thunderous, sneeze.

I could hear people laughing behind the bushes. I turned around. The thick oleanders hid whoever was laughing from my sight, but it was certainly me and my gigantic sneeze that they were laughing about. So, come what may, I strode through the bushes towards them. In a tiny clearing about three yards square, completely surrounded by shrubbery, five lads, aged between thirteen and sixteen, were sitting together in a circle. They were of Azerbaidzhani, Armenian and Russian stock. One very skinny boy of about fourteen had rolled up his shirt-sleeve. He was holding his thin arm out in front of him with fist clenched and swollen veins showing, while the other hand was clutching a syringe filled with a cloudy-white opium solution. He was trying to inject the large needle into his vein just below the elbow. But the vein had become hardened and glassy through over-use. Try as he would, he couldn't inject the needle into his body, and it kept on slipping off. As a result a stream of blood was slowly trickling down his arm and dripped past his elbow down on to the ground. But neither the lad himself nor any of his companions paid any attention to it. They hardly even noticed me. Only one of them got up as I approached, while the others kept their eyes fixed on their comrade's efforts to inject himself and took greedy puffs at the one joint of hash that they had between them.

'Let me have a drag!' shouted the lad with the syringe, pursing his lips. They gave it to him, and he inhaled deeply. This seemed to calm him down, as he suddenly managed to penetrate the vein. He drew some of his own blood up into the syringe, threw his head back, closed his eyes and then started slowly to squeeze the mixture of blood and opium into his vein. I could see that he wasn't the only one to experience a feeling of relief. The others did too. The feeling was almost palpable. It was as if they also were ingesting the drug at that moment.

'What do you want?' asked the youth who had got up when I appeared. He was a strong-looking Azerbaidzhani lad of sixteen with a shock of wiry hair.

'Can I have a drag?' I asked.

'And where are you from?'

'From Moscow, give or take a mile or two. I'm here on holiday at my cousin's, Krasavin. Do you know him? He lives in that block over there. Does anybody need any jeans, American ones?'

'Are you a speculator or what?'

'Well . . .' I said evasively.

Meanwhile the syringe had been passed on to one of the others, and he got a 'shot' out of his pocket – a piece of polythene film with a greasy spot of opium on it. He removed the opium with the blade of his knife, stuck it on the end of a matchstick, scraped it into the mouth of the syringe and dissolved it with ordinary water from a mug. Then he violently clenched his left fist a few times, forced blood into the vein, and raised the needle above his forearm, just below the elbow. I could see that his skin was covered with red injection

137

marks, just as Fulevy's had been.

'So, what about the jeans?' I asked the boys. But, of course, they weren't bothered about jeans at that moment.

'You'll have to ask Mosol,' said one of them lazily.

Then they lost interest in me, and Ramiz, the one I had been talking to, took the syringe and also started preparing to inject himself. I sat down on a rock next to them. I probably looked a little tense, as one of them said to me: 'What wrong? Haven't you ever seen it before?'

'Don't people shoot opium in Moscow?' asked another.

'I should say they do!' somebody answered on my behalf. Then he said to me: 'Do you want to have a game of *sekka*? Do you have any bread?'

I had only ever played the game once in my life, on the Yamal peninsula in the tiny Nenets fishing village of Novy Port, about 125 miles from Dikson Island. I had to spend six days with airmen in the tundra, waiting for a blizzard to end so we could fly on. We cooked some fish soup out of white salmon and sturgeon caught in the Ob, we drank spirits and played all the card games which any of us knew. Now this knowledge came in handy. I had eight roubles on me, so I sat down to play with the ones who weren't on opium, but were only smoking hash. I decided that my article about drug addiction in Baku would begin like this: 'To the Chief Accountant of *Komsomolskaya Pravda*. I request payment for the following expenses incurred in connection with my recent assignment: (a) 8 roubles 40 kopecks – lost at cards; (b) 6 roubles 12 kopecks – spent on drink; (c) 23 roubles – spent on drugs; (d) 16 roubles – cost of a pair of trousers torn as I was trying to get away from a police inspector.' I would follow this with a detailed, almost hour-by-hour account of how I spent my time. I was with these boys for almost ten days, playing *sekka*, smoking hash, hanging around the streets, running away from the militia, forcing money out of automatic lemonade dispensers, selling my jeans to somebody for 30 roubles ... I saw them inject themselves, filch watches on crowded trams and cut away the back pockets of shoppers queueing up for butter and buckwheat. Hanging around with these boys, I soon got a picture of their everyday lives and habits. Because they needed to save their money up for drugs, most of them would go without eating practically anything for days on end, relieving their pangs of hunger by chewing a cheap piece of halva or some sherbet. But it wasn't only their everyday life which interested me. I wanted to discover who was behind the pushers, how all these Tolik Khachmases, Arif Zelyonys, Magomed Gogols, who sold hashish and opium almost openly all over Baku, were supplied. But, however strange it may seem, none of the addicts themselves ever asked themselves exactly how the sale of drugs was organized. Obviously there was a professional supply network behind it, but the boys were so conditioned and stupefied by the actual drugs, that they never looked further ahead than the next pellet of hash or shot of opium.

I consoled myself with the thought that I would be able to contact Ziyalov through these drug-pedlars (I had been informed by the Baku Address Office that Oleg and Anya Ziyalov had officially left Baku six years earlier and that their present whereabouts were unknown). But none of my attempts to get in with Tolik Khachmas, Magomed Gogol or any of the other pushers had any success. They would coldly and sharply interrupt my every question, and any attempt I made to get into conversation with them, or even to stand near them for more than a few moments, ended the same way: You've got your shot or joint – now push off! They would even start moving their feet impatiently, as if they hadn't been able to go to the toilet for an hour and a half or more, so anxious were they to be rid of their importunate customer as quickly as possible ...

But I still had hopes of meeting Mosol, and, of course, the General, who hadn't been mentioned by the boys at all. When I succeeded in moving conversation in this direction, it turned out that they hadn't seen him recently at all. There was even a rumour going around that he'd been clapped in gaol. But Mosol had told them that that was nonsense, and that the General simply had other business on his hands. Mosol himself was also busy, they told me. He'd fallen for some girl and had been following her about all over the place. He hadn't been seen at the usual place for the last week or so . . .

Mosol finally put in an appearance on the third day, towards evening. He was no older than seventeen, a thin fellow, but strong and wiry with sharp, intelligent eyes. Despite the hot weather, he was dressed in Soviet-made jacket, jeans and tennis shoes. He stepped through the bushes, where we were playing *sekka*, and cast his eye over all of us. Suddenly he pointed to me and said: 'Who's this?'

'One of us,' replied Ramiz, shuffling the cards. 'He's a speculator from Moscow. He's been hanging around with us for the last few days.'

'OK. Give me a joint and finish the game,' he said to Ramiz authoritatively. 'I need you. And you too, Sikun.'

Ramiz and Sikun were probably the strongest members of the gang. Mosol took several drags at the joint himself, threw himself down on to the grass, and said in a dreamy, boastful voice: 'I've had enough! Today we're really going to get that Shakh!'

I was all ears, but gave no outward sign of it, merely continuing to play that stupid game. Mosol finished the joint, and then looked at his watch. Ramiz and Sikun stared at him in silence, waiting for his orders.

'It's early yet . . .' Mosol said to them with obvious dissatisfaction. 'At seven we'll take the tram to Sandy Beach. That's where they hang out, I've found. They're going away tomorrow. Up theirs!' he said, making an obscene gesture. 'Cousin, my eye! I'll give him cousin!'

He was lying on the ground, eyes narrowed and lips pressed tightly together. Suddenly he jumped up and gave the order.

'Let's go!' he said. 'And let's get hold of a bit of wine! It'll make this girl of his go with more of a bang!'

And he went off with Ramiz and Sikun.

A few minutes later I gave a yawn, pushed away the cards with a bored expression and said: 'OK, that's enough. I'm fed up with playing . . . I'm going to go and have a sleep . . .'

Out on the street I shouted to the first driver who came along. It was a private Moskvich. It was the same here as in Moscow. Any driver was willing to drive you around for money.

'Take me to the Esplanade!'

'Have you got any cash?' asked the driver.

'Yes, I've got some. Come on, get a move on!'

'Is there a fire somewhere or what?'

'Almost.'

Five minutes later we were outside Izya Kotovsky's apartment block.

I could see that his blue Zhiguli was parked outside, so I ran up to the third floor. Izya wasn't at home, but there, under the mat as always, was the key to the apartment. I rushed into the flat and ran to the telephone. It was already a quarter to seven by my watch. Sashka wasn't at home, of course! The phone just kept on ringing.

I went up to Izya's writing desk and rummaged about in the drawer. Car drivers usually have a second set of keys and keep them in some 'secret' place. With Izya it was his desk that was the repository for everything, from medicines to screwdrivers and pliers. Emptying the entire contents of the drawer on to the floor, I managed to find the keys. I quickly changed into an ordinary shirt and trousers, grabbed some money and my identity papers and tore out of the apartment. It was ten to seven.

A moment later, without a driving licence or anything, I was rushing down the Esplanade towards Sandy Beach. I remembered that Mosol had won a Browning automatic in the General's competition, so

141

that meant I had to get to Sashka before he did. Under the front seat, beneath my feet, was a car repair kit, the only weapon that the prudent Izya always carried around with him.

Now that I had my *Komsomolka* identity card with me again I felt at ease, even driving somebody else's car. I'd show these cloth-capped Azerbaidzhani roadhogs a bit of Moscow class! I approached every set of traffic-lights just as it was turning green, so that I was able to accelerate away in second gear towards the next set of lights without stopping. I went down 26 April Street, past the Nizami cinema and the familiar offices of the *Bakinsky Rabochy* newspaper, where I worked for three years before joining the *Komsomolka*. If only they knew – Artur Gurevich, Alyoshka Kapabyan, Nina Krylova and all the rest in the office – if only they knew who was zooming past outside! It was quite possible that Izya Kotovsky was there at that very moment too, chatting idly in the photographic laboratory . . .

26 April Street led me into Chorny Gorod. It was a route I knew well, as it led towards the airport. About three miles before Bilgya I had to turn right, towards the sea. I was doing seventy-five miles an hour, easily overtaking cars and Aeroflot buses, with the electric railway embankment running along beside me. I could already see that I was ahead of Mosol's seven o'clock train, and I even slowed down a little, when suddenly . . .

The noise of the engine stopped. The car carried on moving down the roadway, losing speed as it did so. In dismay I looked at the instrument panel. Hell! There was no petrol. The hand on the gauge was pointing towards zero and the red warning light was flashing. What an idiot I was not to have looked and filled her up in town!

Cursing my stupidity, I moved to the side of the road, got out and rushed to the petrol tank. I unscrewed the lid and looked inside – there might have been a bit of petrol left by some miracle after all. No! It was empty. In desperation I started to wave down the passing motorists – you never know, one of them might have been able to give me some petrol by siphoning it out of his own tank. But now, of course, I was being passed by the same drivers whom I had just so insolently overtaken myself. And they sped by, wearing smiles of sweet revenge. One of them stuck out his tongue at me, another made a V-sign . . .

At that moment the electric train flew by too. And Mosol was in it, I had no doubt, accompanied by Ramiz and Sikun. Rattling over the joins in the rails, the carriages rushed along the embankment and disappeared into the distance.

I sat back helplessly in the driver's seat. Then I tried hailing a car once again – but it was no good. The main road to the airport is a government highway, and vehicles are not allowed to stop on it. So even if somebody could have given me some petrol, he wouldn't have done anyway. Why risk losing your driving licence? I sat in the car dumbly. Should I run to Sandy Beach? Don't be stupid! It would take you half an hour to get there. There were oil derricks stuck along the road and everywhere else, as far as the eye could see. With their great cross-bars pecking away monotonously at the bore-holes, they seemed to be echoing my own thoughts: 'I-di-ot! I-di-ot!'

I am not sure, but possibly some twenty minutes had passed when a police car suddenly screeched to a halt. It carried the marking of the State Automobile Inspection. A young Azerbaidzhani police lieutenant got slowly out. He was already smiling broadly at the thought of the large fine he would extract from me for halting on a government highway.

'What's wrong?' he drawled, as he came up to me. 'Show me your papers . . .'

I looked at him, realizing that only he could save me now. But I had to choose the right tone of voice when dealing with him. Without saying a word, I got the red

Komsomolka pass out of my pocket, with the magical words 'Central Committee of the All-Union Leninist Komsomol' emblazoned in gold on the front. I showed it to him, and he immediately changed his tone.

'Are you waiting for someone?'

'Look, lieutenant, this is what's happened,' I replied. 'A really stupid thing. I've run out of petrol. Siphon me off a couple of litres, will you?' I continued, nodding towards his police Volga. 'I'll pay you for it.'

The lieutenant shook his head sorrowfully.

'Don't insult me. *Komsomolskaya Pravda* can have a couple of litres from the militia without paying! Have you got a siphon?'

How did I know whether Izya carried a siphon with him or not? I opened the boot. It turned out that he didn't even have a spare wheel, let alone siphon. The lieutenant looked at me reproachfully.

'OK,' he said, and using his police baton, waved down a passing car. A few moments later our cars were positioned back to back, with his petrol tank next to mine, and a siphon, borrowed from the third car, connecting the two. We were blocking the traffic, of course, but it didn't matter. I must have got half a tank's worth of petrol out of the police Volga.

Despite what he'd said, I was about to reach into my pocket to pay him, but he stopped me with a look of disapproval. I realized that he would take offence if I offered him money again. I shook his hand, jumped into the car and roared off down the highway. Now that I had the blessing of the militia, I could jam my foot on the accelerator as hard as I liked. The speedometer lurched to the right: 75, 80, 85 m.p.h. . . . The car was light, without any ballast even in the boot, and I thought its wheels would suddenly leave the asphalt and fly up into the air. Yet at the factory testing track the makers had told me that a Zhiguli would hug the ground even at very high speeds, the sods!

It was getting dark very quickly, so I switched on my headlights and swung smoothly across on to the old dirt

144

road which disappeared in the direction of Sandy Beach. The railway line ran alongside, and in the distance I could see the dotted lights of the train standing at the terminus. Without sparing a thought for Izya's car, I pressed my foot down hard on the accelerator yet again. I had to keep both hands on the steering wheel and keep my back firmly pressed against the seat so as not to hit my head against the roof of the car with all the jolting it was making.

I was sure that I knew the place where Sashka and Lina would be. Sandy Beach was a spit of land leading into the sea, and it ended in two cliffs called the Stone Saddle. Beyond them was the tiny Lovers' Bay. Hidden from the gaze of others, generations of sweethearts had gone there to kiss and make love. I kissed my first girl there, as a matter of fact . . .

The train moved out of the station and headed towards me. That was it! Would I really be too late?

A few moments later I was already driving up to the empty station, which had just said farewell to its last day-trippers. All was deserted, station as well as beach. The dirt road came to an end there too, and from now on, as far as the Stone Saddle, were only dunes and wet sand. I turned left towards the water's edge and, raising whole fountains of water with my wheels, headed towards Lovers' Bay. When I emerged past the Stone Saddle, I saw what I had most been afraid of: there, on the deserted beach, Ramiz and Sikun had Sashka Shakh pinned to the ground. He'd already been beaten up and Ramiz was holding a knife to his neck, to stop him interfering, while Mosol was trying to rape Lina by the water's edge. She was biting him and twisting and turning like a snake, with her knees tucked tightly to her chest. But Mosol was forcing open her arms and striking her with his fist, which was clutching the revolver.

'I'll kill you!' he was shouting. 'You're mine! I've won you! I'll kill you!'

With his free hand he kept on trying to get his trousers down . . .

145

I switched on my headlights again, sounded the horn, and drove the car straight towards this pair of bodies, struggling together on the wet sand. In the gloom they couldn't tell who was at the wheel. Was it the police, a private motorist, vigilantes? Out of the corner of my eye, I could see Ramiz and Sikun abandon Sashka and take to their heels past the Stone Saddle. But as for Mosol . . .

He wasn't one to lose his head at crucial moments. Blinded by the headlights hurtling towards him, he jumped up, pressed Lina to his body and put the Browning up against her head, slowly and clearly, so that whoever was in the car could see what he was doing.

I slammed on the brakes. The car swerved to a halt in the sand two yards from where Mosol and Lina were standing. The blinding light of the head-lamps still prevented him from seeing who was in the car. From the driver's seat I could see the two of them very clearly. There was Lina, bruised and almost naked, dressed in a torn bathing costume. I could make out her childish breasts, her shapely legs and her downy forehead. And there was Mosol, badly bitten and with his trousers half hanging down, gripping Lina tenaciously with one hand while pressing the revolver against her face with the other. Seeing that the car had stopped and that the meaning of his gesture was perfectly well understood by whoever was inside, Mosol paused for a moment and then began moving slowly to one side, out of the headlights, dragging Lina behind him. I sat motionless in the car, my face pressed forward as hard as I could against the windscreen. If only he would take to his heels and leave her alive! But just as Mosol moved out of the light, a body rushed towards him in the darkness and knocked both Mosol and Lina to the ground. At the same moment I heard a shot ring out and suddenly felt the windscreen shatter into a thousand fragments, all over my face, my shirt, my trousers. Sashka Shakh had attacked him, and as he fell, Mosol had pulled the trigger. The bullet had hit the the windscreen and shattered it to smithereens. I don't know what reflex mechanism was at work, but I just managed to shut my eyes before the slivers of glass shot into my face. I'd most probably blinked out of fear at the sound of the gunshot, but it probably saved my sight.

I could hear a fight to the death going on outside on the sand, but couldn't open my eyes for the splinters of glass. Yet I managed to open the door and feel my way out of the car. When I got to Sashka, Mosol was already zig-zagging away over the sand-dunes and Sashka was firing at him with the Browning automatic. 'Don't Sasha! Don't!' shouted Lina. But he pushed her away with his free hand and took aim once again. In the heat of the moment I seemed to hit him harder than I had intended, as he suddenly groaned and dropped the revolver. He immediately picked it up again with his other hand, however, and started shooting into the darkness at random, in the general direction which Mosol had taken. Lina and I hung on to him, preventing him from running after him. He kept trying to break free from us, crying out hysterically: 'Let me go! I'll kill him! Let me go!'

I had him in a full nelson, while Lina was tearfully kissing him and trying to calm him down.

'Sasha, it's all over. No more, please ...'

Naked, her face wet with tears, she hung on to him, inadvertently pressing into my arms, which were locked around Sashka's neck. I could feel her breast, stomach and shoulders against my elbows.

Chapter 6
A Dangerous Decision

That night Izya Kotovsky's apartment was transformed into a veritable field hospital. I used iodine, witchhazel and sticking plaster to ease and cover the various cuts, bruises, scratches and other injuries that Sashka and Lina had acquired in such profusion, then saw to my own luckily superficial wounds. Meanwhile Izya, overwhelmed by the loss of his Zhiguli windscreen, was wandering up and down the flat with a cold compress applied to his head, wailing like a Jew at a funeral. 'Where on earth will I get another windscreen like that?' he said. Then he clicked his tongue and started all over again. 'Where, oh where will I get another windscreen? There aren't any to fit a Zhiguli *anywhere*! It would have been better if you'd burst all four tyres! Or broken the bumpers! On second thoughts, no! There aren't any bumpers to be got anywhere either! Oh, I don't know . . . It would have been better if you'd smashed the headlights! Oh where, oh where will I get another windscreen?'

'Izya, it wasn't me who broke it! We were being fired on, see? Somebody was taking a pot-shot at me! One or two inches to the right and I would have been killed. Look at these marks on my face. Understand? And all you can do is go on about the bloody windscreen! I promise I'll get you one!'

So I swore not to leave Baku until I had replaced his windscreen. We'd visit the garage manager the very next day. If we had no joy there, then we'd go on to the Ministry of Transport, and then to the Propaganda Department of the Azerbaidzhani Party Central Committee if need be. But come what may, we'd get his windscreen! Can you imagine?

'I don't know,' said Izya, shaking his head sorrowfully. 'I don't know at all. What I do know is that tomorrow I'm supposed to drive around the area taking photographs of leading cotton-growers, and that I've got nothing to travel in! In any case, there haven't been any windscreens like those in Azerbaidzhan for the last eight months! Gurevich, director of the Azerbaidzhani Telegraph Agency, smashed his Zhiguli up, and what happened? His car has been standing at the garage for the last six months! Or look at Orudzhev, the Rector of the University. He had a crash. They took him into hospital. By the time his fractured leg was just about healed, his car had been repaired and given a fresh spray of paint – but guess what? He couldn't drive it, because they had no windscreens! What am I going to do? What *am* I going to do?'

Sashka Shakh couldn't stand it any longer. He disappeared into the kitchen and came back with one of those rubber things – I don't know what they're called – one of those big rubber suckers with a wooden handle that you use for clearing blocked sinks.

'Izya,' said Sashka, 'go and ask your neighbours to lend you another one of these for a few minutes.'

'What for?' asked Izya in amazement.

'Look, do as I ask. I only want it for five minutes, but I need it urgently.'

Izya shrugged his shoulders and went next door. A few moments later he reappeared with another of the rubber suckers. Sashka took both of them and went out of the flat.

'Where are you going?' I asked in surprise . . .

'I won't be long. Look after Lina . . .'

Lina had a blanket over her and was fast asleep in Izya's bedroom, curled up on his bed. To calm her nerves and make her go to sleep, we'd had to persuade her to drink a double brandy. Now she was quivering in her sleep and mumbling something through her swollen lips. She was sweating and her hair was stuck to her forehead.

Sashka really did return at the end of five minutes, carrying a Zhiguli windscreen, held between the two rubber suckers.

'What's that?' asked Izya, absolutely flabbergasted.

'It's a windscreen for your car,' said Sashka, placing it on the floor and carefully prising up one of the suckers with the edge of his knife. After that, the whole sucker easily came away in his hand, and he passed it over to Izya. 'Will you give it back to your neighbours, please?'

Izya was looking alternately at me, then at Sashka, with a look of horror in his eyes.

'You mean that you've removed this windscreen from another car?!'

'Not from one of those on your street, so don't worry. I got it around the corner,' said Sashka. 'What's up with you? Nobody saw me. And the car wasn't from Baku, but from Kyurdamir. They're speculators, and they won't even try to get a new windscreen. They'll buy themselves a new car.'

'For Christ's sake!' said Izya, beginning to sway about once again. 'If I get arrested tomorrow . . .'

'For what?' asked Sashka Shakh.

'For stealing a windscreen.'

'But were you the one who stole it?' asked Sashka in total astonishment.

'Unbelievable!' said Izya. 'Absolutely unbelievable . . .!'

'Listen, Izya. A windscreen like this costs 200 roubles on the black market. I've never nicked them because that's the monopoly of the boys in Chorny Gorod. So if anybody at the garage asks you where you got it, say that you happened to buy it in Chorny Gorod. That's all – and stop getting worked up. You'd do better to give me a reward! Now take that sucker back to the neighbours!'

When Izya had gone out, Sashka said: 'I need to talk to you, but not when Izya's around. Shall we go for a walk?'

'All right. But why don't you ring your mother first, so she doesn't worry about you not coming home.'

'She'll survive,' said Sashka, brushing my suggestion aside with a total lack of sympathy.

Ten minutes later, as we were walking along the sea-front, I began to understand the reason for the cruel note that had sounded in his voice. The water in the fountains along the Esplanade, turned down at night, could still be heard murmuring away. On the other side of the granite embankment lay the silent Caspian, divided into two by the reflection of the moonlight. In the Esplanade gardens the oleander bushes

150

were giving off a heady scent, while the paths were strewn with ripe berries from the black and green mulberry bushes. Here and there in the darkness beneath decapitated street lights you could just about make out the brownish outlines of courting couples, sitting motionlessly on park benches. Sashka and I wandered from path to path as he told me his story.

'I've decided to leave Baku. For ever. I love Lina, and she loves me. We want to live together – for always. I told my mother that I wanted to move to Vilnius with Lina. I can't stay here. If I do, I'll start to shoot opium again tomorrow and go thieving on the trams. You come across it wherever you go, after all! I know everybody here, and everybody knows me. There's no getting away from it. Either I'll nail Mosol, or he'll nail me. I told my mother all this yesterday morning. That I had to go away with Lina – for ever. I want to rent a room or an apartment in Vilnius. Then we can marry, and I'll get some work and finish at night-school. Whether I then go on to college or join the army I'll decide later. To cut a long story short, I asked my mother to give me some money, or at least lend me a couple of thousand roubles. So as to get to Vilnius, find an apartment – and generally start a new life there. You should have seen what happened next. She called her all the names under the sun! "Baltic tart", "vicious prostitute" and anything else you can think of! She hadn't fed and clothed me for seventeen years, she said, in order to give me over to some whore! It would have been better if I'd stayed in prison! She reckoned she'd denounce me to the militia herself and get them to lock me up again before she'd surrender me to that "dirty bitch". And what was the reason for all this? Two thousand bloody roubles!'

'Wait a minute!' I said. 'I don't think it was because of the money. It's just that you're only seventeen, and that's young to get married . . .'

'That's our affair,' said Sashka harshly. 'Understand? We're not children. We're both seventeen, and already living with each other as husband and wife. But why should we have to do it in secret, hiding away in other people's apartments, or on the beach? We want to live like normal people, we've nothing to hide. Are we supposed to have stolen something? I love her, and she loves me. That's all. I asked my mother to lend me two thousand. I know how much she and Dad have got stashed away at the bank. What will they do with all that money? Who are they saving it up for?'

He stopped talking. We were just walking past the Yacht Club. The pointed masts of some yachts were outlined against the black and yellow patchwork of the moonlit sea, looking like the fins of some gigantic prehistoric fish. Our footsteps were gently swallowed up by the quiet warmth of the southern night. Sashka said nothing for a long time, and I didn't hurry him. I realized that he hadn't dragged me out on this long walk just to complain about his mother. At last he started talking again, only this time in a different, much calmer voice.

'So, in a nutshell, she didn't give me the money. Not even enough to buy me a ticket to Moscow. But I got the money from elsewhere – the General. Of course, he doesn't give money away for nothing, but this will be the last thing I do for him. I know that I oughtn't to be telling you this, that you're a newspaper correspondent and all that. But you did save my life, and Lina's, and I've no one else to ask. If something should happen to me, if I should get caught and locked up in prison, please help Lina wait for me. Will you do it? Will you help her?'

'What kind of job is it you're being asked to perform, Sasha?'

'I can't tell you.'

'As you like. But you're being stupid. You're willing to trust me with looking after the thing that means more to you than anything else, the girl you love, and yet you won't trust me with knowing about some shady deal between you and the General. As you like, but . . .'

'OK, I'll tell you. Although . . . although I oughtn't to, but still . . . There you are! Only you must give me your word that you will tell nobody else. Otherwise they'll get the two of us. Give me your word of honour!'

'OK. I give you my word of honour.'

'The General says to me: "Here's a thousand roubles in advance, and you'll get ten thousand more when you've done what I ask." And this is what it's all about. He wants me to take a case full of money to Moscow. When I get there, I'm to exchange it for a rucksack of drugs at a prearranged place. So I take the money to Moscow and get a rucksack of drugs in return. With a rucksack I'll look like any number of students. I then bring it back to Baku on the train, hand it over to the General, and fly back to Lina in Moscow. I'll only have to fix her up with a room in a hotel and think of an excuse for disappearing for three or four days. Can you help me?'

Here's a pretty kettle of fish! A *Komsomolka* correspondent helping drug-pedlars! Still, wasn't that the reason why I'd dived into the seamy side of life in the first place? But how could I be sure that things weren't closing in on Sashka Shakh? Taking part in this operation was an enticing prospect, of course. I'd then be able to describe it in my second article for the paper. But Sashka Shakh could get eight years in gaol for certain. Hang on a minute, Garin! You've already been clapped in a detention cell once . . . You'd do better to stop now, and stop Sashka . . .

'Sasha,' I said, after a short pause. 'Let's start from the beginning with the reason for all this. You need money to start a new life in Vilnius, right?'

'But I'm not going to borrow any from you!' he said immediately.

'And I'm not offering you any. I don't have that kind of money. Though if I did, why shouldn't you borrow it? But look, that's not the point. I've another suggestion. Let me get you a ticket to Moscow. The newspaper will pay. You can then give me an interview at the

Komsomolka office – you can tell me everything that you told me that night in detention. If you like, we can alter your surname. In the interview you can tell me that you're renouncing your past and starting life afresh.'

'No, I'm not going to inform on anybody!'

'Wait a minute,' I said in annoyance. 'Nobody's asking you to . . .'

'But if I'm supposed to name my mates, the ones I used to go thieving with, take drugs with . . .'

'You can change their names, too. It makes no difference to the reader whether Ashot was involved with you, or Rasim. It's the gist of the story that matters. After the interview the *Komsomolka* will be responsible for you *and* Lina. The Komsomol Central Committee in Lithuania will be able to get you an apartment and a job. We'll even arrange your wedding for you. All in all we'll make a hero of you, and for the first few months we should be able to help you out with a bit of money too – I mean, the newspaper and the Komsomol. I'll take responsibility for it. I can see the headlines now: former drug-addict falls in love with Vilnius girl and begins a new, honest, normal life. Another great coup for Andrey Garin! Of course, it won't be as sensational as it would have been if I'd written an article about secret drug-running, but all the same, it won't be bad. The Central Committee's Propaganda Department on Staraya Square much prefers positive material like that in any case. It wasn't a fluke that my last three articles earned me the personal thanks of Zamyatin, the head of the Central Committee's Ideological Section. And now that the battle against teenage crime and drug addiction has become almost a national problem, it's time for the newspapers to start talking about it. And something positive like the article I've been outlining might be just the thing to break the censorship taboo on the subject.'

But I'd let my imagination run ahead of me to no purpose.

'It's already too late,' said Sashka. 'He's already given me the money.'

'You can always give it back.'

'No, it's not a question of taking it or giving it back. I already know the background to the whole thing, you see. I worked for the General for two years, but I didn't know that he got us all addicted to drugs so as to sell the drugs to us. And it turns out that Tolik Khachmas, Magomed Gogol and all the other pedlars get all their merchandise from him, the General. I didn't know about this before, but I do now. Even if I were to give him all his money back right away, it wouldn't make any difference. In fact, it would make it even worse, because I wouldn't be properly involved in it, and yet I'd know all about it. They'd knife me right away if I tried to get out now. So I'm already mixed up in it, thanks to my mother,' he said with a sarcàstic grin. 'Andrey, I trust you. If you can help me, then do. If not, I haven't told you anything at all, OK? Otherwise they'll get the two of us, me and you. We're not talking about some petty Mosol with an old Browning, but about the real mafia – and don't you forget it!'

Chapter 7
(Untitled, unfinished)
The next day I flew to Moscow. On the General's orders Sasha and Lina took the train to avoid the baggage search which takes place at every airport these days.

The General accompanied Sasha and Lina to the station to hand over the case containing the money. He bought them two sleeper tickets on train No. 5 from Baku to Moscow and ordered them to place the case with the money inside the larger suitcase containing Sasha's belongings. This he was to stow beneath the lower bunk and not move away from it for the entire journey. On arriving in Moscow, they were to go straight from the station to the Hotel Tourist, just beyond the Exhibition of Economic Achievements in

155

the north of the city. They were to head for Block 5, place twenty-five roubles in each passport and be given two single rooms in exchange. After that they were to sit in one of the rooms and wait for a phone call. Only in an emergency, if there were no rooms in the hotel or something similar, were they to take a taxi at 6 p.m. and travel to the Circus box office next to the Central Market for collective farm produce.

I didn't like the sound of any of it and, in general, was fed up with the whole assignment. First, the Pamir mountains with coal dust and glaciers, glaciologists, poppies and edelweiss. Then the descent from those ethereal heights into the Baku detention cell and getting beaten up by the police. Then a spell of harpoon hunting, the brief encounter with the sixteen-year-old nymph, four days of uninterrupted sex. Then drug-addicts once again, thieving on the trams, the fight at Sandy Beach, the bullet that missed my temple by half an inch. All in all, wasn't this a little too much for a three-week newspaper assignment? Not to mention the effort of writing two articles over the same period and keeping a fictionalized diary!

Still, never mind! I've been digressing. It came about that the day after the fight and my nocturnal conversation with Sashka Shakh, I took the plane to Moscow. I hadn't even visited my grandmother on Bondarnaya Street, even though that was the reason why I had flown from Tashkent to Baku in the first place, to have a few days' relaxation at her apartment. Some relaxation!

In Moscow I went from the airport straight to the offices of *Komsomolskaya Pravda*. The chief editor's secretary, Zhenechka, was sitting at her desk in the room next to Korneshov's. She was over forty, but like all secretaries liked to be paid compliments and be given presents, however small. I got a ballpoint pen out of my pocket and gave it to her. It was one of those which has a top filled with some pinkish-coloured transparent liquid and a swan swimming in the middle of it. Made in Baku, it was the last word in artistic taste.

'Zhenechka, that'll go with your mother-of-pearl-coloured fingernails,' I said. 'You can only get them in Baku.'

'Thanks very much,' she replied, taking my hand and motioning me to come closer.

I went round the other side of the desk and stood right over her. From above, through the modest cut of her regulation grey dress, I could make out 'two hills with a hollow between them', as I had heard in a French film somewhere. Say what you like, but Zhenechka had a real secretary's bust! She read my thoughts and said in a reproachful voice: 'Andrey!'

'Amazing!' I replied impudently. 'A bust like yours, and yet you're still allowed to walk around! Unbelievable!'

'This trip of yours has turned you completely mad! But listen – only keep it to yourself. I ran through your article about the drug-addicts yesterday. Is it really all true? It sounds absolutely awful!'

Ah! So that meant the editor-in-chief already had the article.

'And did you really smoke hash with them? Tell me about it!' she went on in a pestering voice. 'Is it pleasant? Did you bring any back with you for us to try?'

'Zhenya!' I said. Now the reproachful tone was all on my side. 'What are these proclivities of yours? Ask around the foreign correspondents – they'll send you some LSD from New York!'

'OK,' she said, with a wave of the hand. 'Are you going to write any more?'

Well, if the chief editor's secretary was asking me about a continuation, then I could sleep easily. I nodded towards the boss's leather-clad door. 'Is he in?'

'No. He's gone to the Central Committee with your article. Only I haven't told you anything about it.'

'The Central Committee? Which one? On Khmelnitsky Street or Staraya Square?' I asked, meaning had he gone to the Komsomol Central Committee first, or straight to his patrons, Zamyatin and Suslov, in the Party Central Committee, who are in overall charge of ideology?

'To Khmelnitsky Street,' she replied. 'Did you know that you have finally been confirmed as a member of Brezhnev's press corps? There are three from *Pravda*, and two of ours, you and Agaryshev from the Foreign Section. You're to receive instructions from Zamyatin and Suslov on the twelfth. Then there'll be lunch with Brezhnev on the fourteenth, and you fly off on the next day.'

Suddenly the telephone rang and she lifted the receiver: 'Chief editor's office . . .'

I gave her a smacking kiss somewhere about the ear and went off to my own office, waving a copy of my article. It was all turning out marvellously. The piece about the glaciologists, 370 lines, was appearing in tomorrow's edition. What I'd written about the drug-addicts was already being given an airing in the Komsomol Central Committee, and on 15 June I was due to fly to Vienna to cover the Brezhnev–Carter talks. No! I'd show those Baku militiamen where to get off yet! Tomorrow I still had to go to the station, meet Sashka Shakh and persuade him to give an interview to the newspaper. After that I could fly off to Vienna . . .

The same evening, 23.50 hours
That was the point at which Belkin's manuscript broke off. I laid the final page to one side and began to think. Certain things had become more clear, but others were as confused as ever. Gridasov, alias the General in Belkin's version but the Chief in real life, had given Sashka Shakh (or rather, Yury Rybakov) a case full of money, which he was to exchange in Moscow for a rucksack filled with opium or some other drug. But why had that same Gridasov turned up in Moscow before Shakh and Lina and been waiting for them at the Kursk railway station at the very moment they arrived? It

couldn't be ruled out that the exchange was to take place there and then at the station, of course, instead of at the Hotel Tourist or at the Circus on Tsvetnoy Avenue. But what Gridasov hadn't envisaged was *Belkin's* arrival at the station. He'd already seen him at Baku airport, so he knew who he was and what he did. Belkin was getting in their way. He was messing up their arrangements and was generally dangerous. So they kidnapped the two of them. OK. Let's say that I've more or less reconstructed a logical version of events, but where does that get me? How are we going to find Belkin? And who are the other three who took part in the kidnapping? This Chief or General has already been on the run for six years. He could do the same for another six, but how would we find him? We have to get the other three kidnappers too, but how do we do it? How do we recognize them? We must interview Aina Silinya, damn it! In all the fuss and bother, I'd forgotten to get off a telegram to the militia in Riga, asking them to send her to Moscow as a matter of urgency . . .

Forgetting that I wasn't at home, I took out a cigarette and lit a match. Then I suddenly remembered and started to curse myself. Clumsy fool! It was too late. Inna had woken up and nimbly jumped up off the sofa.

'Oh, what time is it?'

'About midnight. Inna, what's the name of your Baku correspondent?'

'Rady Sverdlov. Or rather Rady Aukhman, but Sverdlov was his mother's name. Vadim calls him Kotovsky in his story.'

'Inna, may I phone from here?'

'Of course.'

I got through to the inter-city exchange, gave the password for the Prosecutor's Office, and asked them to connect me with the *Komsomolskaya Pravda* correspondent in Baku urgently.

'Inna,' I said, 'sit down and have a second glass of wine. It's a very good one. A friend of mine brought it back from holiday with him today. I've been dragging it

159

around with me and now it's come in handy.'

'Hello,' I said into the receiver. 'Comrade Sverdlov? This is Investigator Shamrayev speaking, from the USSR Public Prosecutor's Office. I'm sorry to be ringing so late. Vadim Belkin was living at your apartment from 12 to 23 May, I understand, and I'd like to know . . .'

'At my apartment?' said the voice in bewilderment. 'Belkin at my place? What are you talking about? I haven't seen him for a year or so. Last summer it was . . .'

'What do you mean?' I said, dumbfounded. 'He was in Baku from the twelfth.'

'Yes, I heard what you said. He was passing through, as it were. But he didn't get in touch with me. It may be that he tried to phone me, but I was travelling about the region all the time. Now that it's summer there's a lot of work on . . .' His voice sounded apologetic but firm.

Well, how do you like that?

'All right, I'm sorry to have bothered you.' With that I hung up. I looked at Inna.

She hadn't touched her wine. She was standing there in the middle of the room, her figure lit up only by the lamp on the desk. In the semi-darkness I could see those deep, black eyes of hers, full of anxiety for Belkin. He had abandoned her, and she obviously felt hurt by it, but she continued to love him all the same.

'What did he say?'

'He said he hadn't seen Belkin since last summer. Tell me, Inna, was he given to making things up, this Belkin of yours? Sit down and try some of the wine. Now, was he?'

'It tastes nice,' she said, sipping it. 'Did he make things up? I don't know. When he used to tell me stories about his various assignments, it always sounded very smooth and coherent, like in a book. And even if it wasn't true, you wanted it to be. But what do you think? Is he still alive?'

She asked the question quickly, point-blank. What could I say to her?

'Look, Inna, I'll be honest with you. I'd like to know

that myself.' I could see her eyes lose their sparkle on the spot, so I hastened to add: 'Inna, I've only been working on the case for one day. Or rather, since early this morning. And we already know that the General is a certain Semyon Gridasov, otherwise known as the Chief, aged fifty-three, height five feet eight inches, with pale-blue eyes, and so on. The CID are looking for him all over the country, and between ourselves, from tomorrow every prisoner in every gaol in the Soviet Union will be asked whether they know anything about this Gridasov. That's what we call investigating a case . . .'

A spark of hope reappeared in her eyes, and so did her respect for me as a person. I didn't tell her, of course, that the CID nationwide had been looking for this Gridasov for six years without any success. But I must confess that I did want to make a positive impression on her, as a detective who knew what he was about, the sort she might have seen in a TV series. I'd like to know what those 'experts' would say if it suddenly transpired that a manuscript describing a whole series of major crimes turned out to be a pack of lies. If Belkin hadn't been living at Sverdlov-Kotovsky's apartment, then there hadn't been any sixteen-year-old nymph at Rybachy Island.There hadn't been any of this masquerade with Belkin changing into a T-shirt and a pair of old jeans, or visiting the drug-addicts on that 'hill' of theirs. He hadn't chased after Mosol in a Zhiguli and there had been no shoot-out at Sandy Beach. He hadn't had that nocturnal chat with Sashka Shakh, so he couldn't have known that Rybakov and Aina Silinya were travelling to Moscow. The Baku Militia deny the story about the coffin or that Belkin was ever arrested, while Rady Sverdlov is supposed never to have seen Belkin in Baku at all. So was Belkin there, or not? If it weren't for the corpse of Rybakov, if it weren't for this General – Gridasov – abducting Belkin at the railway station, if it weren't for the fact that Belkin dictated his two articles over the phone to the *Komsomolka* office, and if it weren't for the anxious black eyes of this Inna, sitting in front of me, then one might well wonder whether this Belkin existed *at all* ...

Inna and I had another glass of wine. We agreed that I would keep her informed of what was happening, and that she would ring me if she discovered anything new. Picking up Belkin's manuscript, I left for home. The unfinished bottle of *Chornye glaza* was standing on the table, and Inna tried to insist I take it with me. But I refused.

'We'll finish the bottle when it's all over, and we've found Belkin,' I said. 'We're neighbours after all. I live next to the Izmailovsky Park ...'

Then I walked from 12 Parkovaya Street to Izmailovsky, thinking more about Inna than about Belkin ...

Part 2

Part 2

Tuesday, 5 June 1979. After midday
During the first half of the day nothing of interest happened. Having sent the Riga Militia an urgent telegram, requesting them to dispatch the witness Aina Silinya to Moscow as soon as possible, I gave detailed instructions to the two 'lads' of Svetlov's who were flying to Baku: first, they were to check the passenger list for the Aeroflot flight from Tashkent to Baku against the records of School No. 171, where Belkin had been a pupil; secondly, they were to carry out low-key, unofficial inquiries among the baggage handlers at Baku airport to ascertain whether this business with the coffin actually took place; thirdly, they were to make contact with the Baku underworld and find out what they could about Gridasov, alias the Chief. This was more than enough work for two men, especially if you took into account the fact that they would be operating in a foreign city and unable to call on the aid of the local police. The moment the door closed behind them, I made a start on all the boring paperwork which no investigation, however urgent, can do without.

Baklanov tried to drag me off to the beer-bar again. He obviously wanted to chat about this new case of his over a pint of ale, but I had no time. There was enough for me to do, devising the plan of my own investigation.

Baklanov went off by himself, somewhat offended, and I started tapping away at my typewriter again. At that moment the door opened with a bang, and Marat Svetlov crashed his way in.

'Damn, damn and damn again!' he shouted, as he stamped in through the door. He looked sweaty and dishevelled, and his shirt was unbuttoned. 'What the hell did we take on this work for? I just get to visit the old woman and she's kicked the bucket! It's fucking amazing!'

I didn't understand a word he was saying, so I merely looked at him, waiting for him to go off the boil. A minute or two later he'd calmed down, and I got to hear his really 'amazing' story.

After dispatching his two subordinates to Baku that morning, Marat Svetlov had assembled his remaining staff at ten o'clock sharp to give them instructions for the day. His section was basically concerned with unravelling particularly difficult murder cases and other dangerous crimes, so that those of his men who were following up important, fresh leads in other cases he didn't touch. This left him with five detectives at his disposal, and he gave each of them a pile of photographs. They were like snaps from a museum collection. A photographer from the CID Technical Department had taken shots of the brooches, pendants and ear-rings found in Sashka Shakh/Rybakov's document case. Svetlov ordered his men to pay a visit to all the shops in Moscow which buy and sell gold and diamonds, and also to question any black-market dealers, fences or other riff-raff of their acquaintance, in case somebody could identify the owner of the valuables. Each of them was assigned five or six shops on the outskirts, while Svetlov himself took the city centre.

When he reached the Sretenka, Svetlov stuck his car outside the Sports Bookshop. With a small case in his hand, he walked over to the doors of a gold and diamond merchant on the same street. He called the manager from behind the counter and was soon closeted with him in a back room. This was the first place Svetlov had visited, so he asked the manager to give his expert opinion on the merchandise he had brought with him. When he saw all those filigree brooches and pendants decorated with chrysolite, mother-of-pearl, garnet and diamonds, Giltburg clapped his hands in appreciation: 'Marat Alekseyevich, where did you get these from? They must come from a museum . . . No, I have never touched or even seen anything like it. We came across this kind of thing during the war, confiscated abroad, but even so – nothing of this calibre . . .'

In short, Svetlov was no further on after his visit than he had been before. But he didn't give up. He went round to one of Moscow's oldest jeweller's shops on the Stary Arbat, then he visited shops in the Krasnaya Presnya district and in Stoleshnikov Lane, and even looked in on the specialists at the State Diamond Museum. But apart from being told in very general terms that the jewellery was obviously the work of a single hand and probably no later than the nineteenth century, he discovered nothing. Not even Moscow's oldest and most experienced jewellers had ever seen these particular brooches and pendants before.

Svetlov interrupted his travels, and by midday was having lunch in the restaurant of the Union of Artists building. When he had finished and was walking back out on to Gogol Avenue, Svetlov suddenly clapped his hand to his balding head. 'By Christ! How could I have forgotten?!' He was standing near the famous Kropotkin bread shop. The same building was also inhabited by Emmanuel Isaakovich Sinaisky, one of Moscow's most experienced jewellers, who had lived in the same place since the Revolution.

Svetlov ran up the stairs to the first floor. The blackened copper name-plate was still there: 'E. I. Sinaisky, Jeweller'. He rang the bell impatiently.

'Marat Alekseyevich, old friend. To what do I owe this honour?'

Svetlov was embraced in a theatrical manner and ushered into the flat by an elderly man, smartly dressed and the image of the famous singer Alexander Vertinsky. A buxom young girl was quickly motioned to serve them snacks. These were washed down with brandy, vodka and kirsch.

'She's my niece from Vladikavkaz, Marat Alekseyevich,' Sinaisky whispered confidentially. 'You mustn't get the wrong idea.' (He had a slight stammer and pronounced his r's in the French manner.)

He then went on to examine the jewellery through a magnifying glass, while entertaining Svetlov all the while with a succession of stories drawn from his inexhaustible store of anecdotes.

'Now, where did you get these treasures from? Tell an old man.'

'You're asking me?' said Svetlov in the same jocular tone. 'Why do you think I've come to see you?'

'No, seriously. You must have caught a pretty big fish?'

'We don't bother with small ones, Emmanuel Isaakovich.'

'Yes, I can imagine! So what do you want from me?'

'Have you ever seen these pieces before?'

'Well, that's a pretty specific question, I must say! Listen, Marat Alekseyevich, I've retired from business now. I live a quiet life on my pension and the few shekels I managed to put together while I was at work. Of course, some people will tell you that Sinaisky is a crook, that he's rolling in money and has seen to it that his children are well provided for too, and his grandchildren and great-grandchildren. You'll always find there's someone around ready to tell tales about you. And then they'll start to harass an old man. But can I rely on you to protect me from such slander on this occasion, Marat Alekseyevich?'

'Absolutely,' said Svetlov with a smile. He was prepared for a trade-off. If the old man was making a few conditions, it meant he knew something.

'Well, let's drink to it then, old friend.' He beckoned to the girl. 'Be an angel, er . . . niece, and fill up our glasses, will you . . .?'

They drank a toast to 'friendship and mutual understanding'. Then Sinaisky began: 'Since you've already arrested the last person to own this jewellery, I see no harm in filling you in on its past history. The woman is honest in any case, and there can't be any charges to bring against her. She's been living on her family's jewels, which had been hidden for years. She leads a modest, quiet life. One of these things gives her enough to survive on for a whole year.'

'Who are you talking about?'

'My very oldest customer. Olga Petrovna Dolgo-Saburova. She's over ninety-two years of age and very lively. Longevity runs in the family. She comes from aristocratic stock. Her younger sisters got away from Petrograd in a naval cruiser in 1917 and are still alive and kicking somewhere in Rome. They run a guest-house there. She didn't go with them, but had the family valuables stashed away somewhere. These are some of them that you've brought along today. None of them are in museums. Do you know who made them? The master jeweller Aleksey Trofimov, a serf of theirs. And she's been living on the proceeds from them throughout all these years of proletarian rule. There was one break, of course – from '37 to '56. She was supported by the state then, so to speak. But after they'd let her out, she'd invite me to her room on Meshchanskaya Street about once a year. And I used to value the jewels for her. It might even have been a bit more often to begin with. After she'd been let out of the camps, she became very fond of men, you see, but that all came to an end – ten years ago or more. Not completely, I admit, but after all, being ninety-two years old is no joke! Pour us out another brandy, will you, angel?'

'So who used to sell these jewels for her, then? You?'

'Not me, old chap, please! She used to sell them herself. All I would do was name her a price and take my commission – three per cent, as laid down according to the law. The thing was that my valuation was reliable. The buyer would often rely on my judgement himself, or so she told me many times.'

'So who was the buyer? Do you know him?'

'Marat Alekseyevich! We seem to have misunderstood each other. I thought that you'd arrested him, and might even have been intending to show him to me. For years I've been wanting to meet the person who accepted my valuation for all these things without a quibble. The countess always kept his identity a secret from me, you see. And now it turns out that you're looking for him yourselves.'

'We are,' admitted Svetlov. 'Where does she live, this Dolgo-Saburova of yours?'

'Well, I can't get out of that one. Apart from the time she was in prison, the Countess Olga Petrovna Dolgo-Saburova has spent the last ninety years in her own former residence on First Meshchanskaya Street. These days it's called No. 17 Peace Prospect. Out of the whole three-storey house they left her one single apartment, if you can call it that – one room only, on the top floor. Would you like some more brandy?'

'Don't take offence, Emmanuel Isaakovich, but it's time for me to be going.'

'Are you going to call on the countess? I dare not delay you in that case. Angel, pour out Marat Alekseyevich one for the road . . .'

Twenty minutes later Svetlov was at the street in question, and ten minutes after that he discovered that the occupant of flat No. 47, Olga Petrovna Dolgo-Saburova, had died the week before and that the apartment was now occupied by one Rakov, a plumber-cum-locksmith who worked for the Housing Department.

Svetlov rushed off to the said department and burst into the director's office.

'Where are the belongings of old Dolgo-Saburova?' he asked. 'Who arranged her funeral? And where is the locksmith who moved into her flat?'

'We buried the old woman ourselves, at the Housing Department's expense,' replied the plump woman director. 'She's got a nephew somewhere or other. He works on the railways as a sleeping-car super-intendent or something. We did try to phone him, but he was away on duty. We had to transport her body to the Vostryakovskoye Cemetery at our own expense.'

'And where are her belongings? How can I get into the room? Where is your locksmith?'

'What belongings are you talking about? All she had was a filthy mattress and a load of old clothes. I'm not sure, but Rakov has probably thrown everything out already. I only just managed to persuade him to take the room, and temporarily at that. They won't sign on with you for anything less than a two-room apartment these days. He moved in yesterday . . .'

After searching out the locksmith, Svetlov and the director managed to enter Dolgo-Saburova's former room. It was empty apart from half a dozen bottles of vodka, got ready for the housewarming party.

'So where's her furniture? Where are all her belongings?'

'Furniture?' said the locksmith. 'It was a load of old lumber, not furniture! I took it all down to the rubbish dump this morning – photograph albums, a Bible, and a mattress, stinking of urine. I cleared everything out and opened the windows a bit, to get rid of the stench. The tip is over there. Come on, I'll show you.'

When Svetlov, the locksmith and the director arrived at the Housing Department rubbish tip, they could see the flames of the bonfire that was already consuming old Dolgo-Saburova's photograph albums, Bible, bed linen, clothing and mattress. The latter was dirty grey in colour, and the men standing around the fire poked it around a bit, to make it burn a little quicker. Then something strange happened. The mattress cover broke open and out burst a number of brooches, pendants and ear-rings, adorned with rubies, diamonds and chrysolites. There weren't very many of them – only seven pieces in all – but what they lacked in quantity they made up for in quality! They should have been in a museum!

'Look, here they are!' said Svetlov, pouring them out on to my desk. 'You see what an unlucky sod I am! The old countess might have lived another week, damn her! Then we would have known who she was selling these baubles to . . .'

I looked at him silently, and then asked: 'When did the old countess die?'

'On the twenty-eighth. So what?'

'Don't you find that a little strange? It seems a far-fetched coincidence! The old woman sells the jewellery to someone. On the twenty-sixth Sashka Shakh dies in possession of the same jewellery. Then, two days later, the old woman herself dies all of a sudden, with the rest of the jewels still in her mattress.'

'Well, she had to die sometime, I suppose,' said Svetlov, though he could already see the direction my thoughts were taking.

'Well, of course,' I replied. 'But why should it have happened straight after the death of the person who had part of her collection? And what sort of a fellow is this railway-employee nephew of hers, who didn't even attend the funeral? Have you found out?'

'Yes. His name is Herman Veniaminovich Dolgo-Saburov. He's a sleeping-car superintendent with the Kursk railway. I don't know anything else about him.'

'Well, that's something.'

Just then the telephone rang. It was Pshenichny.

'Igor Iosifovich, you couldn't drop in at the Kursk station, could you? I've found somebody who witnessed Belkin's abduction.'

I looked at Svetlov for a second.

'Yes, we'll be straight over,' I replied. 'And can you do something else for me, Valentin? Make a note of the following: Dolgo-Saburov, Herman Veniaminovich, a sleeping-car superintendent on the Kursk railway. Find our something about him – what trains he works on, his duty roster for this month, and anything else you can.'

The Kursk station is not only the most modern in Moscow, it vies with the main station in Bucharest for the title of largest railway terminus in Europe. Silent escalators, flashing signs, endless rows of left-luggage lockers and the longest ticket queues in the world! During the summer months the place looks more like an army camp on the move. Thousands of people are dashing around the halls and up and down the escalators. Everywhere you look, people are sitting or lying on seats and benches, on the floors and in the subways, and the queue outside the women's lavatory stretches a hundred yards at least.

Svetlov and I forced our way past all the suitcases, bags, pails, baskets, children, old men and other passengers aged somewhere in between, until we reached a door bearing the legend: 'Railway Militia'. The Kursk branch of this organization looked as beaten up as its sister offices at the Kazan, Pavelets and every other Moscow terminus. Still, there's nothing to be done about it. Turning even the most modern offices into a pigsty seems to be an unavoidable feature of militia work.

The duty office was filled with the customary oak benches, occupied as usual by any number of ruffians, petty thieves, drunks, prostitutes and speculators, as well as howling children and passengers who had got lost or who had had their belongings stolen. Some had been detained by the militia, others had come by themselves, or brought somebody along with them. And all these passengers were either shouting, cursing or demanding something, or else trying to justify themselves to the duty officer, a red-cheeked captain with a triple chin.

'Comrade Captain, it's three days since I lost track of my wife in the hubbub. We were standing in different queues and lost sight of each other. Perhaps she's been robbed, or perhaps something worse has happened . . . Help me find her, I beg you . . .'

'Listen, sir. I was carrying three sacks of dried apricots, mine, you understand, to sell at the market. I went up to this pretty, fair-haired girl, you see, and said: "Look after this for me, will you, my dear, I need to go to the toilet." And what do you think happened? When I came back ten minutes later – no girl, no sacks of apricots, no suitcase. How such a girl could even have lifted up three such heavy bags, I don't know . . .'

'So I said to them: "Look, I'm carrying Polish cosmetics to Odessa for my friends." I didn't want to, of course, but they kept on asking. "Our train is going any minute," they said. "You can always buy some more. You can get whatever you like in Odessa, but there's nothing to be had at all in Norilsk where we live . . ." Well, there you are. I felt sorry for them . . . And then this sergeant comes along and says: "Ah, selling goods on the black market, eh . . .?" '

Amid such confusion, with suitcases, children, fiancées, husbands and wives disappearing or getting lost all the time, I could imagine how Aina Silinya's story about the kidnapping of her fiancé and a newspaper correspondent had been received: 'Never mind, it's nothing terrible. Your fiancé will turn up. He's probably gone off to down some vodka somewhere . . .'

Svetlov and I had scarcely had time to introduce ourselves to the duty captain when Pshenichny suddenly appeared out of nowhere. He looked exhausted. His cheeks were sunken and his eyes were red from lack of sleep. But from the way he behaved, moved and answered questions, you could tell he was in his element.

'Have you been here long?' I asked.

'Almost twenty-four hours, since yesterday evening,' came the reply. 'Let's go.'

Dragging his left leg slightly, Pshenichny led us into a corner office. We each lit a cigarette, and he started to tell us what he had succeeded in discovering over the previous twenty hours.

To find witnesses to the attack on Belkin and Yury

Rybakov, he had needed to question the people who knock about the station square all day and every day. Porters, taxi drivers, militiamen, stall-holders, petty speculators, and so on: these were the people Pshenichny had moved among during the past twenty hours. He'd gone over every inch of the square as methodically as if he'd been ironing a shirt. He'd talked to literally dozens of people – from traffic controllers to ice-cream merchants and flower-sellers. Being firmly of the opinion that there exists somewhere in the world a pair of eyes which witnessed what nobody else seemed to see, and that someone would recall what nobody else remembered, Pshenichny had gone from person to person, as if he were following the links in a chain. After meeting scores of people who said: 'I don't know', 'I don't remember', 'I didn't see', 'I didn't hear', he finally encountered an old porter who said that, although he hadn't been on the square himself at the time it happened, he had nevertheless heard the fortune-teller, Zemfira, attempt to threaten her demanding children with the words: 'If you keep on asking for things, I'll hand you over to the ambulance men, and they'll take you off, like they did those loonies.'

Pshenichny arrived at the militia office just as citizeness Zemfira Sokolova was being transferred to the preliminary detention cell after a two-hour interrogation. This turned out to be more difficult than one might have imagined, however. As the duty officer's assistant was attempting to shove the gipsy woman into the cell, he was suddenly surrounded by her eight children, who started pulling him in all directions, rummaging through his pockets and perching on his shoulders. They pretended to cry and then started biting him.

Pshenichny conducted her into a room containing a picture of Lenin, and began to question her himself. Zemfira remembered the incident, and confirmed that there had been four ambulance men and that the car into which they had been dragged was indeed an ambulance. But she couldn't remember what the ambulance men looked like, however hard she tried. On the other hand, she did say the following:

'When the ambulance drove off, a drunk came up and said: "They're picking people up straight off the streets, just as they did in '37!" '

'Who was this drunk?'

'I don't know his name, but I see him every day. He visits Lidka's to get beer.'

Lidka, the woman who ran the beer-stall by the suburban ticket office, immediately recognized the drinker in question from Pshenichny's description of him, as provided by the fortune-teller.

'Lev Pavlovich is the one you're after, it's obvious. He comes every day at three, regular as clockwork. Hang about and you'll see him!' Pshenichny spent the next hour sitting near the beer-stall and waiting for a tall, elderly, fair-haired man to turn up, carrying his own metal tankard for beer. Lev Pavlovich Sinitsyn finally arrived. He was a teacher from the Surikov Art Institute and one of Lidka's regular customers.

When she'd filled his container and he'd ordered another mug of beer to boot, Sinitsyn, with great dignity, went off with Pshenichny to talk.

'How can I help you?' he asked.

Pshenichny explained what he wanted. Rubbing the palm of his hand up and down the side of his glass, Lev Pavlovich began to tell his tale in a thoughtful, unhurried way. Yes, he could remember that morning very well. His annual holiday had just begun, and he'd come for his beer at an unusual hour. He'd just finished queueing up for some anchovies at the fish shop. He was walking past the taxi queue on his way to the beer-stall, carrying his fish and his empty tankard, when he suddenly saw a very peculiar scene. An ambulance drove up to the end of the taxi queue and stopped. Then four men got out, two of them medical orderlies dressed in white coats, and another two in ordinary clothes. They fell upon two young men and a girl who were waiting in the queue. The girl either managed to get away from them, or they let her go themselves – Sinitsyn didn't remember. Neither did he recall the number of the car. On the other hand, he remembered very well what struck him most about the whole incident. He didn't have in mind the fact that here were people being seized in broad daylight, and that what happened reminded him of 1937. 'What's so surprising about that?' he asked with a sad smile. 'History's a tragedy when it first happens, but a farce when it repeats itself.' No, what struck him was the fact that one of the ambulance men was the former European middleweight boxing champion, Viktor Akeyev. On the other hand, as he later thought, why shouldn't a former boxer get work as an orderly in a mental asylum if he wanted to? . . .

Pshenichny kept Sinitsyn at the police station, and then phoned me. And now this same tall, fair-haired individual was seated in front of Svetlov and myself at the station.

'Are you certain that the man you saw really was Viktor Akeyev? How did you recognize him?' I asked, after Sinitsyn had repeated his story in our presence.

'Well, my dear fellow, I am an artist after all!' he replied. 'Four years ago, before he won the championship, this same Akeyev spent a whole semester posing for my students. I've sketched not only his face, but his every muscle at least a hundred times. Still . . .' He sounded a little uncertain. 'I *was* sure at the time. Even though he was wearing dark glasses and a cap, I *thought* that it was him. Still . . . How shall I put it?'

'Wait a minute, Lev Pavlovich!' said Pshenichny with a start. Up till that moment he'd been proud of his discovery. 'There wasn't any doubt in your mind at the time that it was Akeyev, was there?'

'No, and nor is there now, but . . .'

'But what?'

'Well, I don't know. There's something strange about it, of course – a boxing champion turning into a medical orderly...'

We let Sinitsyn go home, and Pshenichny gave me the information about sleeping-car superintendent Dolgo-Saburov, which he'd gathered from the Railway Personnel Department. Then I sent my persevering assistant home too, so that he could get some sleep. The last twenty hours had knocked him off his feet, although he wouldn't admit it and begged me to give him something else to do. I simply ordered him to go home. He lived in Mytishchi, a suburb of Moscow, and was intending to get there by train. I could just imagine what it would be like for him to traipse off now in a crowded compartment, so I ordered my driver Seryozha to take him home in the car.

Meanwhile, Svetlov was already on the phone to the Central Address Office to find out where Akeyev lived. A moment later his face changed: 'What do you mean, "He's in detention"?'

When he had a further reply, he put the receiver down and said: 'This Akeyev left Moscow a year ago after being convicted and sent to a prison camp.'

So much for our artist! It looked as if the results of Pshenichny's twenty-hour stint had gone up in smoke. It was just as well that he'd gone home to bed. But I didn't want to believe that this was true myself, so I rang up the CID First Special Department and received the following information: 'Akeyev, Viktor Mikhailovich, born 1942, last worked as a boxing instructor at a children's special sporting school in the Lenin district of Moscow. Former address: 70 Lenin Prospect, Block 11, Apartment 156. On 24 January 1978, convicted by the Lenin District People's Court under Article 191/1, Part 2, and Article 206, Part 2, of the RSFSR Criminal Code, and sentenced to three years' imprisonment. Serving his sentence at strict régime penal colony No. UU–121 at Kotlas, Archangel region.'

So, the old artist had been wrong. Akeyev couldn't

have been locked up at the strict régime prison camp in Kotlas and simultaneously wander around Moscow dressed as a medical orderly. And if he'd escaped from the camp, there would certainly have been a note about it in the information I had just received from the CID Special Department.

All the same, if you looked at what we'd gained rather than what we'd lost, we at least knew now that one of the 'orderlies' resembled the former boxing champion Akeyev, and that, of course, would help us to form an identikit picture of him. Svetlov looked at me rather sourly when I suggested that we wander round all the ambulance depots in Moscow to see if anybody recognized the picture. It wasn't much to go on – some kind of ambulance or other, and a person resembling the boxer Akeyev – but what else could we do? We had no other information to act on as yet.

Without any enthusiasm, and more downcast than hopeful, we started to examine the information received from the Railway Personnel Department regarding Citizen Dolgo-Saburov, superintendent of sleeping-car team No. 56, operating between Moscow and Central Asia. Reading through his duty roster, we suddenly came upon the following curious detail: '26 May, Train No. 37, Moscow–Tashkent, manned by team No. 56, departed on its regular trip from Moscow at 5.05 a.m.' We exchanged glances and then got a copy of the railway timetable from the officer in charge at the militia station. It certainly looked significant. Train No. 37 had passed through Moscow River station at 5.30 that morning. And at 6.15 a.m. the linesman had found the body of Rybakov near the platform!

Svetlov emitted a long whistle. Well, what were we to make of that! Furthermore, the same duty roster revealed to us that on 24 May, the day Belkin and Rybakov were attacked at the Kursk station, superintendent Dolgo-Saburov wasn't on his usual route. Instead, he was resting in Moscow between trips. This made Svetlov and myself exchange a further glance.

179

We hardly spoke. True, according to the same information, on the day of his old aunt's death, the nephew was already a long way from Moscow, approaching Aktyubinsk, and that curbed our imaginations a little.

'Well ...' said Svetlov, screwing up his eyes. We were already in the Personnel Department, leafing through Dolgo-Saburov's personal file. 'Look, it's like this ... He's a bachelor, living by himself, and he doesn't arrive from Tashkent until the day after tomorrow. I think we should search his apartment.'

We both understood that there were no legal grounds for conducting a search. The only things that Dolgo-Saburov was guilty of so far were that he was the old countess's nephew and that his train passed through Moscow River station on the night of 26 May. 'So what?' would be the response of the Public Prosecutor, and he'd put the search warrant to one side, without signing it.

On the other hand, what has legality got to do with it if a special investigator and a CID section head want to take a look in somebody's flat? You can twist the law any way you like, after all ...

17.30 hours and subsequently
At 5.30 in the afternoon, Svetlov and I were already at Smolenskaya-Sennaya Square, in the building which houses the Arrow cinema. Seven storeys above is the two-roomed apartment which Herman Dolgo-Saburov inherited from his parents when they died. We took the cinema manager and the ticket-collector as witnesses (they didn't have anything to do while the show was running, after all), and then we forced open the door to Dolgo-Saburov's apartment. A cursory glance was enough to tell you that this sleeping-car superintendent was living way beyond his means. The flat contained a Western radio set, a colour television and an expensive bedroom suite. There was the usual mess that you find in any bachelor apartment. A handful of Western magazines lying on the sofa with pictures of naked girls

as well as the general feel of the place indicated that this Dolgo-Saburov didn't waste his time between trips. A cupboard in the bathroom contained packets of Indian and German contraceptives (with 'ticklers' and without), and there was somebody's bra there too. There were more porno magazines in the kitchen, as well as some packs of erotic playing cards. The cocktail cabinet and the refrigerator contained Armenian cognac, Scotch whisky, Rigan balsam and export vodka – in other words, something for everybody. Apart from this, the refrigerator also contained fish, an open pot of caviare and an impressive birchwood bucket filled with a honeycomb weighing at least seven pounds. In a word, this fellow lived a pretty good life and was obviously spending far more than the 160 roubles a month he received as his salary. Still, what railway attendant ever lives on his official earnings? They're all involved in black-market dealings of some kind or other, as even a child knows. At a time when there is a scarcity of everything in a country as massive as the Soviet Union, railway attendants are not unlike general suppliers to the population at large, and as we could see from the example of Dolgo-Saburov, they didn't do at all badly out of it.

But even the most careful search of the apartment failed to reveal what we were after. There were no diamonds stashed away anywhere, no hard currency, nothing out of the ordinary at all, in fact, unless you counted those pornographic magazines and samizdat copies of Moscow – Petushki and Sex in a Hundred Easy Lessons.

An hour later our uneventful search of Dolgo-Saburov's apartment was coming to an end, to the accompaniment of deep sighs on the part of the impatient witnesses. We drew up a report of the search according to the rules, got the witnesses to sign it and came out on to the street empty-handed.

We felt done in. A whole day's work had been wasted. We two 'brilliant detectives' were bloody idiots, neither more nor less. We were like blind kittens, wandering about near the saucer of milk and with no way we could find it.

'He's got some pretty decent cognac up there, the sod!' said Svetlov hoarsely, putting his hand in his pocket to dig out some money. 'I've got fourteen roubles. How about you?'

'Ten,' I replied, not bothering to check. I always know exactly how much money I've got.

It is difficult to believe that a special investigator and a CID section head would only have twenty-four roubles between them. It seems ridiculous, especially these days, when there's bribery staring you in the face wherever you look, but . . . what can I say? It is growing less common all the time, it is true, but you can still come across honest people, though you feel a little embarrassed to talk about it, as if you were poverty-stricken or uneducated or something. It's as if you had something to apologize for.

At all events, we felt that we had to wash away the failures of the day with something stronger. When all's said and done, why should these railway attendants spend their time stuffing themselves with caviare and having a good time with girls (the porno magazines and the woman's bra in the bathroom weren't there by accident!), while two normal, virile forty-year-olds like us should live like monks? Like hell we would!

Egging each other on in this way, we drove off in Svetlov's CID Volga and rolled up outside the Prague Restaurant on Arbatskaya Square. As always, there was an enormous queue outside the front entrance with a sign saying 'No free places' behind the glass door. A commissionaire, dressed in braid, was standing behind it, like a great statue. But we pushed open the door in a proprietorial way, calmed down the commissionaire by showing him our identity papers and were led upstairs, like a couple of foreigners, by the obliging head waiter. We could have a separate room, sit down next to the band, or even have a table at the very top, in the so-called 'winter garden' with its fountains. In short, such honoured guests as ourselves could sit wherever we liked.

But we were modest in our requirements. We took a quiet table in the winter garden and, mindful of our limited resources, gave our order to the waiter.

'A bottle of vodka, roast beef and salad. Can we keep it down to twenty-four roubles?'

'Absolutely, Comrade Colonel,' the waiter replied with a smile. Svetlov looked up at him in surprise, but the waiter had already disappeared.

We looked around us. There was soft music coming from the main restaurant below. A group of girl students was sitting three tables from us. A little further away, at tables set along the wall, was a larger group, all men, dressed in sober business suits, no women. Either they were celebrating the passing of somebody's dissertation, or they were making a presentation.

The atmosphere of a restaurant always raises your spirits, especially the thought of having something to drink and, in this case, getting to know the students who were sitting near by. Sveltov and I both straightened our backs and looked like eagles! Of course, that miserable twenty-four roubles of ours wouldn't allow us to have a really good time and treat the girls, but all the same, we could ask them to dance, and we'd see how things turned out.

Suddenly – I don't remember what Svetlov and I were talking about, probably his men in Baku, and how if they didn't put their finger on anything, we might as well go on the scrapheap – suddenly I noticed something unexpected and stopped speaking: the waiter was placing a three-tiered dish of *hors d'oeuvre* on our table, like at a banquet when you simply help yourself. There were ripe Bulgarian tomatoes and Nezhin cucumbers, pickles and olives, pressed and unpressed caviare, fillet of sturgeon – more than I can describe. Then a bottle of vodka appeared in a silver ice-bucket, some three-star Armenian cognac and some Gurdzhuani wine.

'Wait a minute!' said Svetlov to the waiter. 'What are you doing? We only ordered vodka, salad and roast beef. This isn't our order.'

'Don't worry, Comrade Colonel,' replied the waiter, smiling as always. 'It's just that we want to give you a little treat.'

'But wait. I told you that we've only got twenty-four roubles.'

'Now, Comrade Colonel . . .' replied the waiter in a reproachful voice. 'What are you talking about? We know each other after all. Relax. In about twenty minutes I'll be serving you sweetbreads, mushrooms and shashlyks of fresh mutton à la Kara. It's all being cooked by our chef Stukozin just for the two of you, Comrade Investigator. Do you remember him?'

'Stukozin?' I repeated, trying hard to remember. I seemed to recall that he'd been mixed up in a case involving floating restaurants, plying up and down the Volga. Yes, that's right. Stukozin and a few other cooks had been quietly fiddling the books, without ever really overstepping the mark. At least they hadn't served people rotten meat, so I'd taken pity on them. They'd been treated separately from the rest of the group involved, dyed-in-the-wool criminals all of them, and 'transferred to a workers' collective for re-education'. Well, what do you know! I'd no objection to eating these mushrooms of his! Stukozin was in my debt, after all. If it had gone differently, he would have been completely finished. I could easily have got him five years in the place where ex-boxer Akeyev was serving his stretch even now.

'Of course! I remember Stukozin!' I replied, brightening up. 'Say hello to him for me!'

Now I was on equal terms with Svetlov. We'd both done a turn for each other – he through his reputation as a CID officer, I through my prestige as a special investigator. In any case, it cheers you up when people recognize you in restaurants and pay back old debts, especially when they do it in such splendid style . . . I'd have to visit the kitchen afterwards, I thought, and exchange a few pleasantries with the cook. Meanwhile, Svetlov and I set to on the feast. Half an hour later, after we'd made short work of the *hors d'oeuvre* with the aid of a bottle of vodka, Svetlov and I were on top form, chatting up the girls at the neighbouring table, dancing with them, and then persuading them to come and join us. They were very willing to get to know us, too. They were all external students at the Co-operative Institute, and they'd come to Moscow from Donetsk and Voronezh with the express intention of not wasting their time while they were here. I picked up a plump, dyed blonde, aged twenty-three, while Svetlov went for a provocative, flighty piece with brown hair, the 'little babe', as he called her. Every now and then she would pass her tiny pink tongue over her delicious, full lips, and I could see Svetlov's eyes glaze over dreamily.

Everything was going as it should – the dancing, the girls, the grilled mushrooms '*à la* Public Prosecutor', as Svetlov dubbed them, the piping-hot sweetbreads, the Caucasian shashlyks, all downed to the accompaniment of Armenian cognac and Georgian wine. The only jarring note was the succession of official toasts coming from the party across the way. 'To the health of our deputy minister!', 'To the achievements of our directorate!' was all we could hear coming from that direction.

Svetlov couldn't stand it any more, so he said to the waiter in some annoyance: 'Just who *are* those individuals over there?'

'They're from the Health Ministry, Comrade Colonel,' the waiter replied in almost military fashion. 'The one on the left is Petrovsky's deputy – Eduard Sarkisovich Balayan. He used to work in the KGB before he went to Health. He knows a thing or two. They're celebrating receiving some official prize for making a new drug to be used by astronauts.'

'OK,' said Svetlov with a magnanimous wave of his hand. 'Let them carry on celebrating then. Only I wish that Balayan wouldn't keep on ogling our girls.'

It was quite true. Balayan was about forty-five with a broad, grey streak running through his thick black hair. His dark-brown, velvety eyes came to rest too often on our table, examining us calmly, closely and at considerable length. I didn't like this at all. To get my own back on him, in full view of everyone, I grabbed my blonde around the waist with one hand, and placed my other in comradely fashion on the shoulders of Svetlov's 'little babe'.

'Isn't it about time we went back to my bachelor pad, colonel?' I said in a carefree, Don Juanish tone. 'We can dance there, and listen to some music. The night is young.'

Whatever we said, the girls wouldn't believe that Svetlov was a militia colonel and that I was a special investigator. Still, we didn't particularly press the point. Instead, we both made an 'honest confession' – that we were stomatologists from a local clinic, and I even promised to cure one of the 'little babe's' teeth when I got home.

All in all, it was the kind of conversation that you usually have in restaurants. At one point my blonde from Voronezh said it would have been better if we had been sportsmen: she 'adored' sportsmen and her fiancé was the third best boxer in Voronezh. He was a boxing instructor at a special children's sports school.

'Just like Akeyev,' I couldn't help saying. They didn't know who he was, so Svetlov explained.

'Viktor Akeyev is a good friend of ours. He was the former middleweight boxing champion of Europe. He's been touring abroad now for more than a year, and Igor misses him terribly,' he said, nodding towards me with a broad grin.

'I think you may be able to see him,' said the waiter suddenly, as he was serving us with ice-cream and iced coffee.

Svetlov and I fixed our gaze on him immediately.

'He's come back from abroad, obviously,' the waiter continued. 'He had lunch here on Thursday.'

'Who did?' I said, leaning forward as far as I could towards the waiter.

'Why, Viktor Akeyev, of course, the former boxing champion,' he replied.

'Are you sure?'

'Comrade Investigator, you're insulting me!' he said. He was smiling, but his eyes had narrowed, and he looked offended. 'He had lunch here – at the table over there. His hair was closely cropped. He was dressed in a new grey Hungarian suit and a light-blue shirt without a tie. What else? He had two girls with him. One was about twenty-three years old with dyed brown hair. She was about five foot seven inches tall and had a northern accent. The other was about twenty-two or twenty-three, too, with dark blue eyes, a bit like Natasha Rostova in Tolstoy's novel.'

Our 'girls' shut up straight away. They became very serious, looking now at Svetlov and me, now at the waiter. I must say that it didn't take the two of us very long to recover our composure.

'Where's the telephone?' I asked. He showed me directly into the head waiter's office. I quickly rang the duty officer at the Main Directorate of Corrective Labour Institutions and gave him urgent instructions. He was to contact the local office in Archangel by VHF radio and check whether this Akeyev was still at the camp or on the run. Three minutes later I received the following reply: 'Viktor Akeyev, prisoner No. 1533, at corrective labour institution No. UU–121 at Kotlas, was released for good behaviour and first-class work and transferred to a government building site in the same city until the expiration of his sentence. He is to be found there at the present time.'

'Thank you,' I replied – and immediately rang Aeroflot. 'When is the next flight to Kotlas?'

'At 10.40 in the morning.'

'Isn't there one before that?'

'It left an hour ago.'

I returned to the dining room fully convinced that our 'girls' would have already fled in fright. But nothing of the sort! On the contrary, they had both drawn very close to Marat, and their eyes were full of enthusiasm and curiosity. Just imagine! They'd got to know a real colonel from the CID!

'And we thought that you were pulling our legs,' said my blonde. 'We thought that you were a couple of store managers or speculators, and we wanted to lead you on a bit. Yet it turns out that . . .'

She looked at me enthusiastically and was much more respectful.

'You're flying to Kotlas tomorrow,' I said to Svetlov briefly in response to his questioning look. 'We can get on with the rest of it afterwards. Well, what now? Time to go home, girls. Where are you staying? We can drop you off . . .'

'What do you mean?' said my blonde indignantly. 'Who was it who said: "We can dance and listen to music. The night is young"?'

Meanwhile, the 'little babe' licked her lips and, looking Svetlov straight in the eye: 'This won't do, Comrade Colonel!' she said. 'It's leading girls on something rotten – only to disappoint them. You picked us up, bought us drinks, danced with us – and then what? And you're supposed to be a member of the Moscow CID. If you're not careful, I'll go off with that Balayan . . .'

So we had to answer for our Don Juan act after all. Svetlov's CID Volga was parked outside my flat at Izmailovsky Park all night. In the morning, Svetlov, looking rather the worse for wear, phoned his wife, spun her some tale about urgent CID business and rushed off to Petrovka headquarters to arrange his official trip to Kotlas.

'You and I haven't managed to catch any criminals yet,' he said, as he was leaving, 'but what about gonorrhoea . . .!'

REPORT OF THE EXHUMATION AND AUTOPSY CARRIED
OUT ON THE BODY OF CITIZENESS O.P. DOLGO-SABUROVA
On 6 June 1979, at the request of Comrade I. I.
Shamrayev, chief investigator at the USSR Public
Prosecutor's Office, I, A. B. Kogan, forensic expert
at Mortuary No. 3, Moscow City Health Depart-
ment, Forensic Section, carried out an exhumation
and autopsy on the body of Citizeness O. P. Dolgo-
Saburova at the Vostryakovskoye Cemetery, in the
presence of Comrade Shamrayev and witnesses.

The results of the autopsy are as follows:

The presence of vomit in the respiratory tract, of
colourless abrasions around the mouth, and of small
scratches and contusions around the nostrils, show
that death occurred as the result of asphyxiation
caused by the blocking of the mouth and nose.

The victim may have been smothered through
having an object like a pillow pressed tightly over
her face.

The conclusion of the autopsy is that the death of
Citizeness O. P. Dolgo-Saburova was caused by violent means and was *not* the result of natural pro-
cesses, as indicated in the medical report and death
certificate issued by the Dzerzhinsky Register
Office in Moscow.

> Forensic expert A. Kogan
> Signatures of the other persons
> present . . .

I sat staring at the report, thinking of all the effort I
had gone to to get it. But what the hell use was it to me,
now that I had it? Getting the body exhumed and forcing a forensic expert to carry out an autopsy usually
takes a week at least. The experts all turn out to be
busy a week in advance, you can't get hold of any

grave-diggers at the cemetery and so forth. But today I had managed to get it all done in three hours, at considerable cost to my nerves and my pocket (you had to give the grave-diggers enough money for a bottle of vodka, after all). But the main thing was that it had deprived me of a whole morning. And what was the result? Certainly, my supposition had proved correct. The old woman had been suffocated to death two days after the murder of Shakh/Rybakov. But who killed her? And what did it have to do with Belkin?

However I tried, I could make neither head nor tail of it. I could see very well that, apart from giving me extra work – here was one more crime to be solved – the investigation hadn't progressed at all. What else did we need to do to discover this journalist, damn him! This was the third day we'd been looking for him. In terms of the amount of time available to us, today and tomorrow should see the end of our preparatory work. We should then be able to use all the information accumulated to bring about some firm, qualitative results, but . . .

I urgently needed to see this Aina Silinya! I could then show her pictures of Akeyev, Gridasov and even the nephew Dolgo-Saburov, and if she so much as recognized even one of them as a kidnapper, I'd be able to pull all the threads together. But if she didn't, and none of the three turned out to have been at the Kursk station that day, then that meant that all of our work over the last seventy-two hours had been a waste of time and we'd have to start from scratch.

I lifted the receiver and ordered an urgent call to the Militia Chief in Riga. The password used by the USSR Prosecutor's Office never fails with the operator. Twenty seconds later I could already hear the soft voices of the Riga telephonists, and then the sing-song, Baltic accent of Lieutenant-Colonel Robert Baron's secretary. I don't understand a word of Latvian, but I could guess what was being said. The telephonist was explaining to the secretary that there was an urgent call from the Public Prosecutor's Office in Moscow.

At last, the lieutenant-colonel lifted the receiver, and I said to him without any more ado: 'Listen, colonel. What is it you want? Do you want Churbanov or Shcholokov to get in touch with you personally?'

'What's the problem?' he asked.

'Yesterday morning I sent you an urgent telegram, and sent another by phone last night. I urgently need to question the witness Aina Silinya. I asked you to ensure her appearance in Moscow this morning. But it's already twenty past twelve and I haven't heard a thing from you.'

'Unfortunately, Comrade Investigator, the person whom you wish to question is not in Riga at present.'

'Where is she?'

'Her neighbours reported to the local divisional inspector that she had gone away on holiday with her parents to the coast.'

'Where to exactly?'

'They didn't say, Comrade Investigator . . .' Baron spoke Russian with an accent, but there was a certain mocking tone in his voice, as if to say: All right, we carry out your requests, of course, and in general we do what you tell us, but on the other hand . . . It's no good your giving us orders, we've got our own republic, after all.

I had no time to play at being polite with him, however. 'Listen to me, colonel,' I said. 'The job I'm doing is connected with Comrade Brezhnev's imminent meeting with Carter in Vienna. You and I have a very limited amount of time at our disposal. This Aina Silinya must be here in Moscow today, even if you have to comb the whole coastline near Riga to find her. Do you understand?'

He said nothing. He needed time to think through the situation again. Would he really need to comb the whole Riga coastline, or was there a chance that he might get out of it?

'Tell me,' he said cautiously. 'Does Comrade

Shcholokov really know all about this case?'

'Not only Shcholokov,' I replied, 'but Rudenko, Suslov and Andropov too. Which one of them would you need to get a telegram from, if you're to find the girl?'

'Well, that's not necessary . . . I don't know . . .' murmured the colonel indecisively, realizing that it was better not to force me to go to Shcholokov or Suslov in order to get such a telegram. If every militia chief were to ask a minister to confirm the authority of his special assistants, it would lead to nothing but an explosion of anger on the part of the authorities. Especially if I were carrying out a task on the direct instructions of the Central Committee itself . . .

'And please don't forget, colonel,' I said, 'I am acting on the direct instructions of the Central Committee, and every hour could be crucial. Those who help to bring this case to a successful conclusion won't be forgotten, either. Do you get my meaning? I need her today. I'm not kidding!'

First show the big stick, then offer the carrot – it never fails.

'All right,' said the colonel, changing his tone. 'I'll see to it today, personally. Where can I ring you?'

Of course, once it was a question of early promotion to the rank of full colonel, Baron would see to the matter personally, that very day. I gave him the number of my own office and apartment, as well as that of Rudenko's secretary and CID Third Section, where one of Svetlov's men would always be on duty.

'Can I take her into custody, if she refuses to come of her own free will?' asked Baron.

'Of course. I'll prepare the necessary warrant. Formal niceties have to take second place in this investigation.'

From that moment Lieutenant-Colonel Baron and the Riga Militia would begin literally to dig over the whole surrounding coastline if necessary. I imagined that half an hour later the resort of Yurmala would be swarming with agents and informers of all descriptions, all of them employees of the Latvian MVD.

I replaced the receiver. Now it was just a question of waiting – of waiting for Baron to find this Aina Silinya, for Svetlov in Kotlas to find something out about the boxer Akeyev, for the CID men in Baku to come up with something too, for train No. 37 from Tashkent to arrive in Moscow tomorrow with Herman Dolgo-Saburov on board, and finally for Pshenichny's team at the Kursk railway station to come up with somebody who witnessed the murder of Yury Rybakov that night (or could it have been an accident?).

I was feeling sleepy – and I started absent-mindedly rolling up some papers that were lying on my desk. After a night on the tiles, you feel more like sleep than work. Of course, what would have livened me up on the spot would have been a call from Baku, Kotlas, or at the very least from the Kursk railway station. For some reason, I didn't believe that they would pin down this Ziyalov simply by comparing the lists of Belkin's former classmates with the list of passengers on the flight from Tashkent. Probably because it would have been just too simple, and I've never been given anything *just like that* in the whole of my life. There was another reason, too. I didn't believe what Belkin said any more, or what he wrote in his manuscript. If he had lied about Sverdlov, then why shouldn't he also have lied about Ziyalov being in his class at school . . .?

I don't know whether I was still awake or nodding off as I thought about all this, but some instinct suddenly made me lift my head and look towards the door. There, standing in the doorway, I saw the figure of Roman Andreyevich Rudenko, Chief Public Prosecutor of the USSR. Dressed in a marshal's uniform and with his hair smoothed down, there he was, staring at me silently with those lustreless blue eyes of his, as if he were listening to my thoughts or reading them from a distance. When he saw me look up, he started to smile.

'I don't detect much enthusiasm here,' he said.

About once a month, as part of the new trend towards greater democracy, the Chief Public Prosecutor would walk round all the offices himself, chatting about this and that with his employees, showing interest in their personal lives and working conditions, so to speak. But this obviously wasn't the only reason for his visit today.

'Hello, Roman Andreyevich,' I said, getting up from my chair.

'Hello,' he replied, walking up to my desk and staring at me very closely. 'Why are you looking so much under the weather today? There are bags under your eyes. It's the life bachelors lead, I suppose. Been having a riotous time?'

I tried not to breathe near him, so that he at least wouldn't catch a whiff of brandy and vodka.

'Now, what time would I have for riotous living, Roman Andreyevich? That's quite a case you've landed me with.'

'Well, and how's it going? What can I tell the Central Committee? Will we get Belkin back, or not?'

'Well, what can I say? We're still looking for him. We've found somebody who witnessed the kidnapping, and we think we know the identity of one of the kidnappers . . .'

' "We're still looking for him", "We think we know"!' he said, mimicking my voice. 'I don't detect any enthusiasm in your voice, Igor Iosifovich, or firmness of resolve. It's not good enough. And don't forget that you've only got four days left. Perhaps you need some more assistance? Where are the rest of your team – Svetlov and that . . . what's his name?'

'Pshenichny,' I prompted. 'Svetlov is in Kotlas at the moment, looking for a convict. And Pshenichny is combing the Kursk railway line. He's looking for anybody who might have witnessed the murder of Belkin's friend from Baku.'

'I don't know, I don't know . . .' he said, tapping his fingers on the desk. 'You're running the case, so you've

194

got a better idea of what's going on, but . . . here you are with one of your team-mates away in Kotlas, and the other one looking for witnesses to a murder. Look, the murder's not going to run away, you know. But Belkin we need *now*, and preferably alive. Otherwise, what am I to tell the Central Committee? That we can't find a person in our own country?'

I said nothing. All I could do in my position was keep silent and wait. And even if he were to give me more assistants that very day, what would I do with them?

He lifted the receiver and began to dial. Then, as though his thoughts were elsewhere, he rather abstractedly stuck his pencil into one of the holes and stopped the dial half-way round.

'How did you get hold of Svetlov, then?' he suddenly asked, staring me straight in the eye. 'Did Shcholokov say you could have him?'

Ah! So *that* was why he had come! And that was why he'd turned the dial on the phone and had stuck his pencil in it. What a funny scene! The Chief Prosecutor of the USSR is afraid that the KGB might be bugging the phones at his office, so he decides to disconnect one of them for a few seconds, just to be on the safe side! And at the same time, we both had to pretend that I hadn't understood or even noticed what he was doing.

I told him as quickly as I could what had happened with Brezhnev's son-in-law, Churbanov, and about the diamond brooch which he had taken away with him to show Galina Brezhneva. The Chief Prosecutor listened with obvious satisfaction. At the end, he even deemed me worthy of praise.

'Good fellow!' he said. 'Shcholokov won't go against Churbanov, of course, so they'll not take Svetlov away from you now. But bear it in mind that both Shcholokov and Andropov will be very pleased if we *don't* find Belkin. So one of them may try to put a spoke in your wheels. Be very careful, and don't make any mistakes!'

He let the dial on the phone return to its usual position, and then came out with a peremptory remark, addressed to me, but obviously said for the benefit of anybody else who might have been listening in.

'There's no point in you wearing out the seat of your trousers by sitting around in your office all day. You've got to get on with investigating the case in hand. I wish you every success.' And with that he left.

I lifted the receiver again and listened. There was the usual dialling-tone, but nothing special. That didn't prove anything, however. You can't tell whether a phone is being tapped or not just like that, of course. OK, that was enough pondering for one day. It was time to move into action. The Chief Prosecutor had given me a warning – and that was the most he could do. Svetlov was a long way away in Kotlas, but I did need to help Pshenichny out, it was true. I dialled the number of the head of Militia at the Kursk railway station. I got his number direct by looking it up in the MVD internal telephone directory. Somebody answered immediately.

'Colonel Maryamov speaking.'

'Good afternoon, colonel. This is Shamrayev from the Chief Prosecutor's Office. You don't happen to know where my assistant, Investigator Pshenichny, is at the moment?'

'He's in Podolsk, Comrade Shamrayev. Your team has set up a temporary headquarters there. We've had all our people working on it since early morning, down the line as far as Serpukhov. Everybody has been pressed into action, Comrade Shamrayev!'

'Good, colonel. You couldn't come over here, could you?'

'I'm ready to come if you need me. I'm at your disposal.'

'I'll come and pick you up in about ten minutes.'

At the same time, in Kotlas

'It's pure prostitution, Comrade Colonel! There's no doubt about it! Look at these girls. They've got the faces of angels. What would you say they were? Students and members of Komsomol? Not a bit of it!

They're nothing but whores, who do it for three roubles.'

Lieutenant-Colonel Svetlov had driven from Kotlas airport straight to camp No. UU–121, where he arrived right in the middle of a slanging-match taking place in the office of the camp commander, Major Smagin. Five pretty young girls, aged between fifteen and eighteen, and all with enticing lips, were huddled together on the major's sofa, listening to him heap abuse on their heads, but not the slightest bit afraid of him. They weren't prisoners, but students at the Kotlas Technical School who were free to come and go as they pleased.

'Well, what am I to do with them, colonel?' asked Smagin. 'Can you imagine what these creatures have been doing? We don't leave any guards on duty in the wood-felling area at night, as all the prisoners are inside the camp, you see. So these tarts come along and hide away in all kinds of nooks and crannies. And they just wait. Later on, at six in the morning, the area is cordoned off by soldiers, and an hour after that the prisoners are brought along to chop down the trees. These creatures set about their work at the same time, the filthy whores. They've fucking well learnt to suck them off the French way, and they can get through a hundred prisoners in a day, stinging them for three roubles a time. Komsomol members. I'll be damned! It probably takes a prisoner a whole month to save up the money, kopeck by kopeck, and they suck it out of him in two minutes . . . Well, what shall I do with them, Comrade Colonel?'

Svetlov, exhausted by his own adventures of the previous night, had barely managed to grab a couple of hours' sleep in the plane. He looked away and shrugged his shoulders impatiently. He had no time to worry about these students. All three of them – Major Smagin, Lieutenant-Colonel Svetlov, and the deputy camp commander, Captain Zharikov, an irritable-looking man with nicotine-stained buck teeth – all three knew perfectly well that there was nothing any-body could do about these girls. Since the Article about prostitution had been removed from the constitution in 1936 (there was no such thing as whoring in the USSR!), the worst thing that could happen to the girls was a fifteen-rouble fine for 'violation of public order'. And the girls knew this very well themselves. That was why they were listening so calmly to the major ranting on. They had no fear of threats. Finally, Major Smagin sent them packing. However, when he found out about the purpose of Svetlov's journey, his face changed.

'Akeyev, you say? He's been released from direct custody and is working on a building site. They're building a big chemical plant. He's been assigned to the site manager there, and doing work as a welder. What about him?'

'Are you certain that he's in Kotlas? Where's the site manager's office?'

'I'll get you a car and drive you there myself.'

But Svetlov declined the major's offer to accompany him. He took the car and drove across Kotlas in the direction of the building site. When he arrived, he avoided talking to the manager's secretary, a big-bosomed girl not quite twenty years of age, who was dressed in a mini-skirt. She was an ex-prisoner, released on parole too. He walked right past her and went straight into Captain Chabanov's office. A few minutes later it emerged that, although Akeyev was registered at the site as a welder, his real job there was to act as a 'fixer' or 'go-getter', someone who could get hold of spare parts for machinery and other items in short supply at the building site. It was in connection with this that he was sometimes sent on official busi-ness to Archangel, Kirov and even Moscow. Who could be better at hustling than a famous sportsman, a for-mer European boxing champion?! And it was with the site manager's knowledge that the chief engineer at the plant had just sent Akeyev to Moscow to negotiate purchases at the Ministry of Industrial Construction.

It took Svetlov another hour, no less, to get the salary office at the plant to do copies of all Viktor Akeyev's travel documents and thus to establish exactly when and where he had been away on business. It turned out that he spent more time in Moscow than in Kotlas, and that his trips were often extended by the Ministry itself while he was in the capital. He'd gone off on his last trip as long ago as the beginning of May . . . However, the chief engineer at the plant, one Kogan, was very satisfied with what Akeyev had managed to achieve.

'I don't know about him being a boxer or a welder, but what I do know is that if I had five or six fixers as good as Akeyev, I'd get this chemical plant built in a third of the time. He even managed to get Gosplan to waive the quotas on ferro-concrete reinforcements, can you imagine!'

When he'd got all the documentation he needed, Svetlov, hoping he'd be in time to catch the last flight to Moscow, rushed back to the airport.

Captain Zharikov was waiting for him. Svetlov looked at him in surprise.

'May I have a few words with you, colonel?' said Zharikov in a gloomy voice.

'Of course.'

'It's about Viktor Akeyev. I couldn't talk at the camp office, you see. Walls have ears. And it concerns Major Smagin, the camp commander . . .'

'Hang on a moment. I've just got to get my return ticket endorsed.'

The Pechora–Kotlas–Moscow flight was late as usual, so there was time to talk.

'Smagin wants his daughter to marry Akeyev,' said the captain. 'She's head over heels in love with him, and can twist her father round her little finger. That's why Akeyev has been released on parole and transferred to the chemical plant. And at the moment they're both in Moscow, at the Hotel Peking.'

'How do you know?' asked Svetlov in astonishment.

'As soon as you left the camp, Major Smagin tried

three times to book a call to the hotel, to talk to his daughter. I think he wants to warn them about your visit. Only he couldn't get any reply from her hotel room.'

'Thank you,' said Svetlov. 'Come along with me.' And the two of them hurried towards the airport post office. There was an inter-city telephone booth there, and Svetlov immediately dialled through to No. 38 Petrovka, and dictated the following message to his deputy, Major Ozherelyev: 'Place a tap on the phone of Yelena Vasilyevna Smagina at the Hotel Peking. Don't connect any inter-city calls. Have Smagina put under immediate observation, as she may be in touch with Akeyev.'

Akeyev himself wasn't entitled to stay at a hotel, as he had no passport. But a big enough bribe would enable him to spend any number of nights with his mistress, even at the Peking.

'Thank you very much, captain,' said Svetlov. 'The country will not forget you. I'll inform the Main Directorate of Corrective Labour Institutions of your scrupulous devotion to duty.'

'But I haven't told you everything,' replied Zharikov, as lugubriously as ever. 'Our camp is supposed to be a model of its kind and is always having official visits. Everywhere you go there are placards saying "Honest labour is the way to freedom" and "Support the moral code of builders of communism" and so on. But in fact it's all a fraud. Smagin is for ever making liberal overtures towards the prisoners. He's even set up an orchestra, and the result is . . . Look!' And he opened his fist to show what he had been clutching throughout the whole conversation: two ampoules of morphine.

'I seized them from the prisoners during our last search,' he said. 'And this is what they came in. I found it in the rubbish bin.'

Zharikov produced part of a small cardboard box from his pocket. On it was a factory label bearing the words: 'Chief Pharmaceutical Authority, Moscow'.

'As you can see, the goods come from Moscow. And I have no doubt that they were brought here by Major Smagin's future son-in-law, Viktor Akeyev.'

'Yes,' thought Svetlov, 'this Captain Zharikov wants to become a camp commander very badly indeed. He'll soon sort them all out!'

He thanked the captain once again, said that he'd inform the prison authority of his good work without fail, took the ampoules and the label and departed for Moscow.

At the same time, in Moscow

Secret

To Special Investigator
USSR Prosecutor's Office
Comrade I. I. Shamrayev

REPORT

Today, 6 June 1979, I, V. Pshenichny, acting Special Investigator at the USSR Public Prosecutor's Office, along with a group of police operatives from the Railway Militia, questioned all those railway employees who were at work on the night of 26 May 1979, when Citizen Yu. Rybakov was killed.

Thirty-two militia agents took part in the operation, and a total of 214 people were questioned, at stations and halts on the Kursk railway between Serpukhov and Moscow. Each person questioned was shown a photograph of the deceased, Yu. Rybakov, and identical pictures of the persons presumed to have kidnapped Rybakov and Belkin – Citizens S. Gridasov, V. Akeyev and H. Dolgo-Saburov.

The results of the operation were negative. None of those questioned was able to provide any additional information about the death of Yu. Rybakov . . .

A tank or a tractor would have envied Pshenichny his energy. Sitting in the headquarters of the Railway Militia at Podolsk, he was just about to finish writing the above report when he heard the voices of some railway personnel walking by outside his window.

'But why haven't they questioned the cleaners? They work nights, too, after all . . .'

'That's all we need!' said another voice.

By this time Pshenichny had already risen from his chair and jumped over to the window.

'Hey! Wait a minute! Which cleaners?'

Fortunately, all the cleaners at Podolsk lived 'on the wheels', as they say – that was, in carriages stabled in sidings not far from the station. It was late in the evening and the rest of us, including Colonel Maryamov, Pshenichny's assistants and myself, had long since gone home. But Pshenichny was a man of conscience, and he went off to question all the cleaners. When he was on almost his last interrogation, chance intervened in the form of a night-watchman called Sytin, the common-law husband of the cleaner whom Pshenichny was questioning at that moment. As he was listening to Pshenichny's insistent voice meticulously asking: 'Do you remember whether you were on duty on the night of 26 May?', Sytin, an unprepossessing dwarf of a man, suddenly said:

'Listen, chum, stop bothering her and hear what I've got to say. I remember that night very well, because it's my name-day. You can check it in my passport. Pelageya was ill in bed that night, women's trouble, you know. So I did her shift in Tsaritsyno instead, except that I wasn't at the station. I was wandering up and down the tracks, talking to the drivers of a goods train. It had stopped at the points. It was carrying new Zhiguli cars straight from Tolyatti. I can remember it well. That's why I was chatting to them. Then the signals changed to green, just as a clock was striking midnight or one o'clock somewhere. Just as the signal changed, this guy jumps on to the track carrying a briefcase or something in his hand. He was breathing hard, like he was running away from someone, and his shirt was sticking out of his trousers. "How can I get to Moscow?" he asks. And how *would* you get there when the last train for the night had already left? "Climb up on to the goods train," I says. "It'll be leaving any minute, and you can arrive there with the cars." And that's what he does. The train had just started to move when up drives a car and two men jump out. "Have you seen a young lad with a case?" they ask. "What do you want to know for?" I say. "He's escaped from hospital, you see. He's soft in the head." Well, right enough, the fellow hadn't looked quite right, I'd noticed it myself. Then they say to each other: "He must be in the goods train, there's nowhere else for him to go." And on they jumped too, as the train was beginning to pull away quite fast . . .'

INVESTIGATOR PSHENICHNY'S REPORT
(continued)

. . . Additional questioning of the cleaners at the Podolsk railway complex has revealed that on the night of 25–6 May the cleaner Pelageya Sinyukhina was away sick, and her co-habitee, the night-watchman Nikolay Nikolayevich Sytin, was deputizing for her at Tsaritsyno railway station. The latter testified that between midnight and one o'clock on 26 May he saw a young man, carrying a document case, climb on to a passing goods train, followed by two men in pursuit who also jumped up on to the same train. From the photographs which he was shown, N. Sytin recognizes the young man as Yury Rybakov and his pursuers as Semyon Gridasov and Viktor Akeyev. Their identification was categorical. Records of the cross-examination and the identification procedure are appended.

Acting Special Investigator
V. Pshenichny

6 June 1979

The same day, 21.45 hours

URGENT TELEGRAM

Moscow, USSR Public Prosecutor's Office
Investigator Shamrayev
(copy to Lieutenant-Colonel Svetlov, CID)
AFTER CHECKING LISTS OF PUPILS ATTENDING BAKU
SCHOOL NO. 171 BETWEEN 1967–9 WE HAVE NOT DISCOV-
ERED ANY SURNAMES CORRESPONDING TO THOSE OF PAS-
SENGERS ON TASHKENT FLIGHT STOP TOMORROW WE
WILL SEARCH FOR AND QUESTION BELKIN'S FELLOW-
PUPILS TO ASCERTAIN WHO HIS FRIENDS WERE STOP
ACCORDING TO HIS GRANDMOTHER, S. M. BELKINA, AND
HER NEIGHBOURS, VADIM BELKIN WAS NOT AT THEIR
APARTMENT BLOCK DURING MAY STOP YOURS. ROGOZIN,
SHMUGLOV

Thursday, 7 June 1979, 03.45 hours
As the poet said: 'This day witnessed what a hundred
more will not . . .'

During the night I was woken up by the phone. It was
Svetlov ringing from the Peking.

'The girl has come back drunk and has gone to
bed.'

'Which girl, where?' I asked, still half-asleep.

'Well, she's not come back to your place, of course!
Lena Smagina I mean, Akeyev's mistress. She arrived
back at the Hotel Peking so drunk that she couldn't get
the key into the door. Then she went to bed. Before this,
according to Central Telegraph, her dad tried to ring
her twice from Kotlas. But I've blocked all inter-city
calls to her room so they won't connect her to Kotlas.
As you're in charge of the investigation team, I want to
know whether to arrest her now and interrogate her,
or to lead her on and observe her.'

'What do you think yourself?'

'Well, in my opinion, we can always arrest her any
time. But if she really is in love with this Akeyev, she

may not confess and betray him. So I would rather we tried another line. I'll put Ozherelyev on to her, as soon as she wakes up. If you have no objection, that is. He can tell her something he shouldn't, and we'll wait to see the reaction. OK?'

I know that this is a favourite trick of Svetlov's. Sometimes he calls it 'forcing the issue', sometimes 'casting the bait'. In fact, it's the purest form of provocation: you incite the criminal to commit a series of actions whereby he incriminates himself. So what? Let him try. Our moral code (if you can call it that) allows us to adopt these tactics in the struggle against crime.

'All right,' I said. 'Only don't overplay your hand or let it drag on too long. We need Akeyev urgently.'

'And what shall we do about Dolgo-Saburov, the old woman's nephew? Are you going to follow up that angle?'

'Of course I am! I told you that somebody smothered the old woman to death. When the Tashkent train arrives at 5.50 a.m., Pshenichny and I will search Dolgo-Saburov's carriage.'

'Well, you'd better get up then. It's already 3.45.'

The same day, a few minutes after 07.00 hours
The search of carriage No. 5 on Moscow–Tashkent train No. 37 had already lasted more than an hour – with no tangible result. The passengers had gone home long ago, and the train itself had already left the Kursk station and was now standing in the Kalanchevskaya marshalling-yard. The attendants had taken the sheets off to the laundry, while Pshenichny and myself, accompanied by three inspectors from the Railway Militia, were busying ourselves with the sleeping car and Dolgo-Saburov. The inspectors were doing the search of the actual carriage, as there is no way a simple investigator could manage that by himself. You have to know the detailed layout of the carriage and its possible hiding places. Meanwhile,

Pshenichny and I were questioning Herman. Did he know that his aunt had the family jewels in her possession? What were his relations with her? When did he find out about her death? Herman Dolgo-Saburov was a lean thirty-year-old, with brown hair, sharp features and a prominent chin. He was irritated and angry, but he gave precise answers to all our questions and didn't appear to be concealing anything. Yes, he had known that his aunt possessed some old family jewels. He'd also known that she'd sold the occasional brooch and lived on the proceeds. Well, what would you expect an old woman to live on? No, he'd never laid any claim to these valuables. Why should he have done? He had enough to live on anyway. He'd known nothing about her death, and he was hearing about it from us for the first time. Whom did he suspect of the murder? He shrugged his shoulders . . . Nobody, he thought, though Heaven alone knows. The old woman had had a crowd of admirers in her time up to the age of seventy, if not later. She'd still been amusing herself with men, so possibly one of her former lovers had . . . But in any case, it wasn't him. He couldn't identify the jewellery from photographs, because he'd never seen it. His aunt had never shown him.

The inspectors removed various items of food from the refrigerator and from a hatch in the floor. These included two boxes of fruit and grapes, a side of mutton and a wooden bucket filled with an amber-yellow honeycomb.

'What are you carrying the fruit for?' I asked.

'What do you mean? To eat it, of course. Can you get grapes like that in Moscow?'

'And the mutton?'

'To make shashlyks, what else?'

'And the honey?'

'It's from the Altai. It's the best cure for any cold. Besides, real honey helps my liver. I've got inflammation of the gall-bladder.'

So there you were. What more could you get out of

him? I finished the cross-examination. Empty-handed, Pshenichny and I went off to the near-by Hotel Leningrad to have some breakfast. Seryozha, my driver, was still reading *Anna Karenina* and asked me yet another question.

'Igor Iosifovich, where in Mosocow was a hotel or restaurant called the England? Oblonsky had lunch there. I know more or less all the inns in Moscow, but as for the England . . .'

I didn't know where it was either. It was the Peking which interested me at that moment, not the England. I contacted Svetlov over the radio phone and discovered that Lena Smagina was still asleep, but that Major Ozherelyev had already moved into the room next door.

The same day, 09.30 hours

'Mercenary shits and ponces – that's who we've got looking after our interests in the Central Committee! A load of lecherous womanizers! I'll be goddamned if Shevtsov, Titov, Pavlov and the rest will ever tell the Politburo about the true state of affairs. For eight years I've been asking them to give us emergency powers to deal with drug-trafficking. And what happens? Not a fucking thing! The country is being torn apart by drug-addiction, prostitution and VD, but everybody acts as if the place is like a bloody convent! Of course, under Stalin and Khrushchev the place *was* clean, but now it seems, wherever you look, there's nothing but fucking immorality, alcoholism and drugs . . .'

Never before in a government office had I heard anybody make such frank observations, and certainly not from the lips of an attractive young woman and spiced with such vulgar language. But there she was. Nadezhda Malenina, a thirty-three-year-old former gymnastics champion with fair hair and a well-preserved figure. She now held the rank of major in the militia and was the head of the recently formed narco-

tics section of the Anti-Fraud Squad. She was married
to a professor at the General Staff Military Academy,
who was particularly close to Marshal Ustinov, the
Defence Minister, so she could say publicly what
we usually only utter in the privacy of our own homes
amid a small circle of close friends – and even then
only after we're on to our third or fourth bottle of
vodka . . .

'The country is being plundered from top to bottom,
the young people have no beliefs or principles, teenagers are shooting dope into themselves, yet the newspapers blather on about universal happiness and how
everything is flourishing. Strong government, that's
what we need! In Central Asia, the Caucasus, the
Crimea – whole fields are given over to the cultivation
of hemp and the opium poppy, and there are hordes of
organized criminals going about selling the stuff. In
Simferopol there's an opium poppy by every telegraph
pole. People grow them for profit. Just come here and
look at this!'

She had an easy, familiar way of talking to me, as if
she'd known me for a hundred years, although I'd
heard of her existence only an hour ago, when I
decided to bring the Anti-Fraud Squad in on the investigation. After all, Svetlov had brought two ampoules
of morphine back with him from the camp at Kotlas,
and they had a definite place of origin: Chief Pharmaceutical Authority, Moscow. It turned out that because
of the ominous growth of drug-addiction in the country,
a special narcotics investigation section had been set
up as part of the Anti-Fraud Squad.

Malenina turned to the wall and pointed to a map of
the USSR. It had a large number of tiny flags pinned to
it, all in the south of the country. 'Just look! These flags
indicate the whereabouts of opium-poppy fields in
Turkmenistan, Uzbekistan, the Caucasus, the Crimea
and the Amur basin. They're all on collective farms, of
course, run by the state for the pharmaceutical industry. But do you think I got this information through

official channels? Like hell I did! Both the Ministry of Health and the Ministry of Agriculture were as shifty as Jews at a market-place. And do you know the reason? Because they've all been bribed. If there are poppy fields belonging to collective farms, that must mean that there are private holdings in the same place, with the produce sold on the black market. There's thieving everywhere! Nobody works anywhere these days unless they can swindle the state out of something! I know what I'm talking about, believe me . . .!'

I smiled inwardly. I don't know about anywhere else, but the Anti-Fraud Squad really should know what's going on. They even take precautions against bribery in their own offices. Their investigators don't have individual rooms to work in. They have to sit two or three in an office to prevent each other from taking unofficial payments. As if there weren't other places where you could pocket a hefty bribe from some big noise in the underworld! If that weren't the case, then where did these Anti-Fraud Squad investigators get their imported suits from, their Italian shoes, their Bulgarian sheepskin coats and the various culinary delicacies that you can't get anywhere else? As they investigated all aspects of economic consumption in the country, the employees of the Anti-Fraud Squad had themselves become nothing other than an élite caste of well-heeled, elegantly dressed government inspectors, with the manner and appearance of respectable and prestigious guardians of the law. This made Nadezhda Malenina stand out all the more, of course, with her vulgar language and her links with the military group around Ustinov. It also meant that she was able to rise above bribery and corruption herself, thanks to the superior rations which her husband had access to as a general.

'Still, I've got somewhat carried away, and what you're interested in is what I can actually do for you in a concrete way. Two things, I think – and not so much for you as for myself. I've been sniffing around this

Pharmaceutical Authority myself. In the State Arbitration Department I found a whole load of complaints from the Defence Ministry's Medical Directorate, alleging that military hospitals were receiving consignments of drugs containing significant shortfalls in the number of ampoules. Four or five of them are found broken in each box. The thing to do is to go and check whether the damage occurred while the drugs were being transported, or whether the broken ampoules were substituted during the packaging process. So that's what I did. I planted some of my people at the pharmaceutical factories, who then reported that it was physically impossible for the women who did the packaging to substitute broken containers – they do everything in full view of everybody else. It turns out that what is needed is a full inspection of the main warehouses where the drugs are stored, but I'm not given permission to organize one. It's out of the question, they say. You can't interrupt the supply of medicines to the hospitals. But I've got them where I want them, now that you have given me these two ampoules. I'll get all the warehouses shut down right away for inspection. As for this coffin of yours, you'll soon know whether it was filled with narcotics or not. And if it was, I'll be able to turn the whole of Central Asia upside down to find the culprits!'

'Two CID men have been in Baku since yesterday, but they're not investigating the business with the coffin at the moment. They'll look into it in a day or two.'

'And I should think so too! What next, the scum! Soldering up drugs in a zinc coffin! What will they think of next!' said Malenina, not without a hint of admiration. 'By the way, I did achieve one thing at least. Every large airport is now equipped with dogs who are trained to sniff out drugs. Up till now they used to carry hashish and opium about quite openly, stuffing it in their suitcases. Even now they're finding ways around it, though – by sealing the hashish in wax, or stuffing opium into honeycombs! Bob's your uncle! There's not a dog alive that will sniff it out. Can you imagine?'

I suddenly turned cold. Only two hours before, in Dolgo-Saburov's coach at the Kursk railway station, I had seen a wooden bucket containing Altai mountain honey, and the day before yesterday I'd seen a similar birchwood bucket filled with the same stuff in the refrigerator at Dolgo-Saburov's flat. And I – damned fool that I was – had taken Dolgo-Saburov and his complaints about his bad liver at face value!

The colour had obviously drained from my cheeks as Malenina suddenly said: 'What's wrong with you?'

'Nothing,' I replied hoarsely. 'I'm all right. Only I've just remembered that there's something very urgent which I must attend to.'

10.20 hours

I rushed out of the building and almost ran across the pavement to where my Volga was parked. I pulled open the door and plumped down into the front seat right next to the driver.

'Smolenskaya-Sennaya Square, as quickly as you can! The Arrow cinema!'

'Well, to coin a phrase, I'd fallen for it hook, line and sinker. Fancy holding buckets full of opium and honey in your hands on two separate occasions and not even probing the honeycombs with a fork or something! And now all I could say was: 'Get a move on, Seryozha! Put your foot on it!' But what was the point? The old countess's nephew would no doubt be expecting me! . . .

All the same, I opened my briefcase and pulled out a pile of forms. There was one for practically every contingency – arrest warrants, search warrants, you name it! I hurriedly filled in one of the latter for Dolgo-Saburov's flat. Then I needed some witnesses, though this search, like the one which preceded it, was far from being legal, since we had no charges to bring against Dolgo-Saburov as yet. All the same, I couldn't be seen to break the law at every step. I had to observe due process in some respects at least.

211

'Stop over there by the Military Registration Office,' I said to Seryozha, nodding towards a brick building on the corner not far from the Arrow cinema. There was a group of close-cropped new recruits milling about outside the main entrance. I rushed past them, went up to the duty officer, stuck my Prosecutor's Office identity card in front of him and said: 'Quick, I need two witnesses urgently! Anybody will do!'

Whether it was my tone of voice that impressed him, or the identity card, I don't know, but he made no complaint. Instead, he suddenly shouted out: 'Zakharyev and Kupala, come here right away!'

Whereupon two young sergeants placed themselves at my disposal and got into the Volga.

'Let's go,' I said to Seryozha, and we sped off immediately.

The soldiers, who were obviously fresh from a sergeant's training course, looked around inquisitively and said: 'Where are we going? Is it far?'

But we'd hardly gone one hundred yards before the car came to a sudden halt.

'Follow me!' I said. 'And be quick about it!'

The lift *would* have to be in use, of course. Some delivery men were bringing a new suite of furniture for one of the tenants.

Swearing away, I started to run upstairs towards the seventh floor. By the time we reached the landing on the sixth, my heart felt fit to burst and I had to pause for breath while the two sergeants stared at me expectantly. Finally, we reached the door of Dolgo-Saburov's apartment on the seventh floor. I rang the bell, while the two sergeants, true to all rules of police behaviour, stood by the wall on either side of the door. But there was no reply, of course. I rang again and again, but it was a waste of time. I saw a light appear behind a peephole in the door of the next flat, but it only lasted a moment and then was turned off. I rummaged around in my briefcase and got out a penknife. I wasn't going to mess about now, so I shoved the knife around in the

212

lock as firmly as I could. Finally the lock gave. But one look at the apartment was enough to prove that Dolgo-Saburov had really got the wind up the last time I'd appeared. The hi-fi equipment and colour television were gone. There were no Western porno magazines and not even the *samizdat* copy of *Moscow – Petushki*.

I headed straight for the kitchen and opened the refrigerator. There was no honeycomb, of course, that was obvious. To the bewilderment of the sergeants, I irritably kicked the box of Uzbek grapes – they were the same ones we'd found in the train that morning – sat down at the table and started to drum my fingers. I needed to recover my composure. What in fact did it all amount to? Dolgo-Saburov was involved in illegal drug-trafficking. That still needed to be proved, but let's assume for the moment that it was true and that he really was carrying opium from Central Asia to Moscow. What did that have to do with Belkin? Or Akeyev? Or the General? Or the murder of the old countess? If he could prove that he was away from Moscow on duty at the time of her death, and if we'd missed the chance to catch him red-handed with the opium, then we had nothing on him. Still, he really had taken fright. He'd removed all his most valuable possessions, as if he were about to be arrested or flee the country. It stood to reason that the first thing he would do would be get rid of the narcotics. Even as I had urged Seryozha to drive faster along the Garden Ring Road, I'd been in no doubt about that. Still, I had at least hoped to find him at his flat and put him into the detention cell for a few days, just to be on the safe side. But now, as I looked around this half-empty apartment and saw Dolgo-Saburov's belongings thrown all over the place, I realized that his obvious haste could prove only one thing: that this nephew of hers had really taken me for a ride – and disappeared himself!

I rose from the chair and walked into the bedroom to make a phone call. Just as I was reaching for the receiver, the phone began to ring. I froze. Should I answer the call or not? Could it be Dolgo-Saburov himself at the other end of the line, ringing to check whether we'd appeared unexpectedly to carry out a second search? Or might it be somebody phoning Dolgo-Saburov? What should I do? Curiosity finally got the better of me and I lifted the receiver after the fourth ring.

'Yeah?' I mumbled, as if still half-asleep.

'Hello, Herman,' It was a young woman speaking.

'What?' I asked slowly.

'What's the matter, darling? Are you still asleep?'

'Uh-huh,' I muttered.

'Well, wake up and listen carefully to what I've got to say. Are you awake?'

There was a box of matches next to the phone. I got one out and ignited it right next to the receiver, so that the person at the other end would hear the sound. Then I started to cough, as if I'd just taken a drag at a cigarette.

The ruse seemed to work, as the woman gave a sarcastic laugh.

'Well, you might at least stop coughing into the phone, you sod,' she said. 'Now, listen to me. Katyukha says that the CID has circulated photos of the boxer and the old man all over Moscow. Police at all the railway stations and exit roads have been alerted. Can you hear me?'

'Uh-huh.'

'What do you mean, "Uh-huh"? What are you mumbling for?'

I could hear a note of caution creep into her voice. I realized that I'd have to say something properly.

I gave another cough. 'My throat hurts. Well?'

There was a suspicious silence at the other end of the line. I had nothing to lose. So as not to prolong the silence, I said: 'Well? What's happening about the journalist?'

The dialling-tone was the only answer I got. I carefully laid the receiver on the table next to the phone.

'Don't replace the receiver,' I said to the two sergeants who had been watching me all the while. Then I rushed out on to the landing and rang the bell to the flat next door. I held the button down until somebody came.

A light appeared at the peephole once again. 'Public Prosecutor's Department!' I shouted. 'Open the door! I need to use your phone! Quickly, it's urgent!'

I could hear the sound of locks being opened, and an ancient crone opened the door slightly. I pushed forward and literally tore into the flat.

'Sorry, missus, but where's the phone?'

Then I saw it myself, before she had a chance to reply. I dialled the number of the secret Central Telephone Surveillance Department at Zubovskaya Street. 'Hello – is that the duty officer? Password – "defence". Shamrayev speaking. Find out urgently which phone 244–12–90 is connected to. And for Christ's sake, get a move on!'

Until you replace the receiver you are still connected up to the phone which has originated the call. That's how the Moscow telephone system works. This meant that I might be able to trace the phone that had just been used to contact Dolgo-Saburov. It was a pity that I'd frightened her off, of course. If only I could have prolonged the conversation a little, I might have been able to find out a bit more and, at the very least, discovered whether Belkin was still alive or not. It was a pity, too, that the nephew had disappeared. But at least one thing had been proved: he was mixed up in this whole affair. Dolgo-Saburov, the boxer and the 'old man', whoever he might be: they all had something to do with it, and each of them must have known where Belkin was being held.

The Moscow Militia had three photos to work on: those of Belkin, Gridasov and Akeyev. The boxer was obviously the latter, so that meant that the 'old man' must be Gridasov. Yet another nickname! I tried to imagine who it might have been that was phoning just now. 'Katyukha says that the CID has circulated photos of the boxer and the old man all over Moscow.' That meant that the criminals had somebody called Katya working for them in the CID. Great! You couldn't move without them knowing about it! But in which department could this 'mole' of theirs be working . . .?

What are these telephone engineers doing, giving birth, or what?

As if replying to my thoughts. I suddenly heard a voice say: 'Are you listening? Number 244-12-90 is connected to a telephone booth at the Universitetskaya metro station. Shall we disconnect it?'

A telephone booth! Of course, the woman knew what she was doing! She wouldn't slip up by using a private number!

'OK. disconnect it,' I replied, 'but have number 244-12-90 tapped.'

This meant that all calls to Dolgo-Saburov's flat would be recorded and their origin traced.

'Have you got a warrant?' asked the duty officer at Surveillance.

'So far as you're concerned, yes,' I replied. 'I have full authority from the Chief Prosecutor. I'm acting on instructions from the Central Committee.'

I slammed down the receiver, without waiting to hear the reply. There was no point in wasting time with those idiots! I trudged back into Dolgo-Saburov's apartment. The sergeants were still standing by the telephone, staring at it hard, as if it might explode at any moment. I sat down next to it and rang Svetlov's section at the Petrovka.

'Duty officer Lieutenant Krasnovsky speaking.'

'This is Shamrayev. Where is Svetlov?'

'Colonel Svetlov is in the Incident Room talking to the Hotel Peking, Comrade Shamrayev. Is it urgent?'

'What's going on at the Peking, then?'

'The suspect appears to be waking up.'

'I see. And where's Pshenichny?'

'He's here with me questioning people who resemble the suspects.'

Poor old Pshenichny! He always gets the hack-work – and he's certainly got a lot of it from me on this job! Thousands of copies of photographs had been distributed to the Moscow Militia, the State Automobile Inspection and MVD secret agents – informers and stool-pigeons of all descriptions, the barmen at such doubtful places as the beer-bars at Sokolniki Park or on the corner of Pushkinskaya Street and Stoleshinikov Lane. All of them were now on the look-out for Belkin, Akeyev and Gridasov. I could just imagine how many so-called 'look-alikes' were now being stopped at every railway station and traffic inspection post – or simply on the street or in restaurants. And they were all being taken in to the Petrovka, where Pshenichny would be examining them and their identity papers. With any luck he was being assisted by Aina Silinya, the artist Sinitsyn, and the night-watchman Sytin.

'Any news from Baron in Riga?' I asked.

'We got a phone call to tell us that Baron had gone to Yurmala on the coast. They'd found the witness there, but she was unwilling to travel to Moscow.'

'I see. Take a note of this. All police stations in Moscow are to be circulated with photographs of Herman Dolgo-Saburov. I'm speaking from his flat now. Have some men sent over to relieve me right away, as I want to lay a trap for him. Get Minayev to issue instructions to have this phone tapped – number 244–12–90. Get a second squad to be in wait at his aunt's flat, as he may turn up there. The address is: 17 Peace Prospect, Apartment 47.'

'We haven't got enough men available, Comrade Shamrayev,' said the lieutenant beseechingly.

'Tell Minayev. He'll provide them. Tell him that it was me who asked. But you must send at least a couple of men here straight away!'

'All right. Will that be all?'

'Yes.'

I replaced the receiver and said to the two sergeants: 'Look, lads. I know that you're here as witnesses and that I don't have the right to use you in an

217

operation, but there's no choice. If anybody should turn up before the militia do, we'll all help grab him. OK?'

10.47 hours
Lena Smagina really had just woken up. She was lying luxuriously on one of the Hotel Peking's big double beds and smoking a Winston cigarette. The bright June sun was penetrating the closed venetian blinds, and there was the noise of traffic from the Garden Ring Road below. A cigarette first thing often does more to revive you than a cold shower, especially after spending a night as she just had. Lena thought what a shame it was that Viktor wasn't allowed to stay in the hotel with her yet. Instead of that, he had to spend his time hanging around somebody else's apartment, keeping an eye on the expensive Finnish furniture and other rubbish that belonged to his boss. What bastards they were in the Central Committee and the Council of Ministers! What harm would it do them to release Viktor once and for all, give him a passport and the right to live in Moscow? Still, one of these days it would all happen, and not so very long now – just as soon as Viktor's boss returned from his trip abroad. Then they'd be able to lead a proper life together – holidays by the sea, visits to the theatre and the best restaurants, a new car . . .

She looked at her Japanese watch and suddenly gave a start – the hotel buffet would be closing in ten minutes: it was time for her to get up. Lena forced herself to get out of bed, gave her face a quick cold-water rinse and slipped on an American dress which she had bought in the Beriozka shops for special foreign-currency certificates (she'd got those on the black market, of course). She ran a comb through her hair and then rushed along to the buffet. Fortunately, it was on the fifth floor, the same as her hotel room. As she was going along the corridor, she was nearly knocked over by a tall, good-looking officer, a major in the MVD. He'd come out of the room next door so fast that he'd simply bumped into her.

'What are you getting under my feet for?' she said in a rather insolent tone. The fact that he was an MVD officer didn't surprise her in the least. This wing of the hotel belonged to the Interior Ministry, and you were always coming across MVD personnel and their families there from all over the country.

'I'm ever so sorry,' he said. 'I was told the buffet was open until eleven. Is that right?'

'Yes, that's right. Come along with me. I'm going there too,' she said, immediately adopting the patronizing tone that she used when talking to officers in Kotlas. Apart from that, she'd been there many times before, and he was obviously a newcomer.

'I haven't seen you here before,' she said. 'There was a woman inspector from Krasnoyarsk living in your room.'

'I'm from Odessa. Major Smorodinsky. Edward is my first name, Eddie to you. What's yours?'

'Lena.'

'Glad to meet you, Lenochka. There you are, we know each other now!'

'Is this a great event in your life then?'

'Who knows?' he said with a smile. 'The ways of the Lord . . .'

He may be good-looking, thought Lena to herself, but he's soft, not like my manly Viktor.

Then they reached the buffet. Lena ordered herself an aristocratic breakfast – caviare with French toast, Turkish coffee and an almond pastry. You could tell immediately that the major was from the provinces, though. He ordered all kinds of pap – vinaigrette salad, four sausages, *kefir*, mashed potato and lemon tea.

Lena and the gallant major sat down at the same table. With both cheeks stuffed full of food, be began to spin her all sorts of yarns about himself, just like Khlestakov in Gogol's *Government Inspector*. And they all added up to the same thing: that there was nobody in the whole MVD more intelligent, courageous and resourceful than Major Smorodinsky. First he gave her a graphic account of how he managed to penetrate a band of speculators who were smuggling all kinds of foreign goods into the country by sea: sheepskin jackets, jeans, French perfume, you name it! Then he explained how he had risked his life uncovering an illegal woollen factory. Then he told her something else that sounded more like a scene from a detective film than anything else. He'd arrived at the Militia Academy yesterday to sit the summer exams as an external student, and everybody had been given photographs of three men. Two of them were of extremely dangerous criminals being sought by the police all over Moscow. The other was of a well-known journalist, much admired by Brezhnev. He was supposed to accompany the latter on his trip to Vienna in a few days' time, when suddenly – it's amazing what happens! – some men had abducted him in the centre of Moscow in broad daylight, and nobody knew where they had taken him. So now Major Smorodinsky had the chance to do a favour for Brezhnev himself by finding his favourite journalist. The day before, the Rector of the Academy, General Krylov, had gathered all the students together and told them that all examinations were postponed for a few days, so that they could join the Moscow Militia in hunting down the kidnappers and finding the journalist. The person who tracked him down would be sure of earning the personal thanks of the Central Committee and an early promotion. The major was convinced that it would be him.

'How will you set about finding them, that's what I'm curious to know?' said Lena, wondering how to get rid of this garrulous major.

'Very simple. Look at these.' He got the three photographs out of his pocket and laid them on the table in front of Lena. Staring up at her from one of them were the features of her own beloved Viktor, younger than he was now, and dressed in a track-suit.

'A nice-looking fellow, isn't he?' said Major Smorodinsky, interpreting her obvious interest in the photograph. 'That's the former boxing champion Akeyev. Together with this other one, an escaped criminal called Gridasov, they kidnapped the journalist and some other youth who they then proceeded to murder outside Moscow . . .'

Lena was no longer capable of coherent thought. Indeed, she could hardly even focus on what was in front of her. She felt a lump in her throat. All the time Smorodinsky was talking, she felt more and more shivery. Her Viktor was being hunted by the whole of the Moscow Militia! So that was why he was spending his time sitting in that flat and didn't want to go out on the street any more than he had to!

She managed to recover her composure for a moment, just as the talkative major happened to mention that, if the kidnappers were to hand over the journalist now, so that he could accompany Brezhnev to Vienna, they'd have half of their sentence commuted. But since they didn't know this, the major had the chance of earning himself another promotion. He'd been seconded direct to the CID. He'd soon teach them a thing or two . . .

Smorodinsky would have gone on and on like this if Lena hadn't interrupted him to say that she had some urgent business to attend to.

'Now, what sort of urgent business can you possibly have to attend to, Lenochka?' replied the major. 'I know. You've got to buy some clothes at the GUM Department Store! Do you think I don't know how pretty girls spend all their time?' After that he talked Lena into meeting him at seven o'clock that evening for dinner at the hotel restaurant.

'OK, I'll come,' said Lena, determined to promise anything, if it meant that she could get away from Smorodinsky. She had no intention of keeping her promise, of course.

221

When she finally said goodbye to the importunate major, she ran back to her own room. What should she do now? She had to inform Viktor, it went without saying! She had to save him! She grabbed the telephone and dialled the first three figures of his number–242. But then she remembered: Viktor didn't answer telephone calls. The apartment block was inhabited by high government officials, and probably all their phones were bugged. So his 'boss' had forbidden him to use it. Most probably her phone was being tapped too, she thought. After all, this was an MVD hotel. In fact, perhaps she was already being followed and that fool of a major had told her the story and shown her the photographs on purpose. She suddenly went cold. No, it couldn't be. Take your time, don't panic. After all, she was the one who'd started up the conversation in the corridor. And you could tell he was just a provincial bumpkin from all that rubbish which he ate in the buffet. All the same . . .

Lena cautiously went up to the window and looked outside. Everything seemed quiet on the Ring Road down below. There was nobody standing on the street looking up at her window. She went back and peeped outside the door of her room. There was only the chambermaid, Mariya Ivanovna, vacuuming the corridor. Everything seemed normal. Lena breathed a sigh of relief. It was just a question of going to see Viktor and telling him everything that had happened. But she'd have to be careful and check that she wasn't followed. She *was* the daughter of a prison camp commander, after all . . . It wasn't so easy to put one over on her. She knew all about the militia's little ruses . . .

REPORT

On your instructions, I, Major V. S. Ozherelyev, and a group of men under my command have been observing the movements of Citizeness E. V. Smagina, resident at the Hotel Peking, room number 626. I myself occupied the adjacent room, number 627, and pretended to be one Major Smorodinsky on study leave from Odessa, here to sit examinations at the Militia Academy. I made the suspect's acquaintance as she was about to have breakfast in the hotel buffet. There I appeared to show her by chance the photographs of Belkin, Gridasov and Akeyev. The first two were not recognized by the suspect, but when she saw the picture of Akeyev she displayed great emotional excitement. During the rest of the conversation I attempted to provoke her into getting in touch with Akeyev. I also suggested to her that those conducting the investigation would react favourably to Belkin's voluntary return.

Immediately after the end of the conversation, Smagina returned to her room, where she attempted to contact somebody by telephone. However, she abandoned the attempt after dialling the first three digits – 242. At 11.30 a.m. the suspect left the hotel and headed down Gorky Street in the direction of the Central Telegraph building . . .

11. 45 hours

I was sitting in Dolgo-Saburov's apartment waiting for the CID men to arrive. I had nothing else to do, so I began to leaf through the former's photograph album. Svetlov and I had noticed it during our first search, but hadn't taken much interest in it then. It contained mainly photos of girls in bathing costumes and various snaps taken at work: of the sleeping-car attendants from Moscow – Tashkent train No. 37, together with the restaurant-car staff from the same train. They were photographed in front of the carriages with Herman Dolgo-Saburov himself in the foreground embracing the chief steward from the dining-car. Inserted at the back of the album was a black envelope containing a handful of coloured photographs, all of a striking-looking, brown-haired girl on the Black Sea coast. One was of her standing in front of some palm trees, another showed her in a group of smiling holidaymakers, sunbathing. In yet another she was licking an Eskimo ice-cream, and in the last one she was cutting Dolgo-Saburov's hair on the beach. He was sitting in a chair, and her hands were poised above his head holding a pair of scissors and a comb. On the back was written the following: 'To Herman, I hope you won't forget! Zoya the Enchantress, Sochi, Hotel Zhemchuzhina, May 1979.'

Well, that was something to be working on, in any case! Now where the hell were those CID men? Every second was valuable, and there was I, hanging about like a dog on a lead.

I left the two sergeants by themselves in the apartment. They knew what they were doing, and I'd given them permission to eat as many of Dolgo-Saburov's Uzbek grapes as they wanted. Meanwhile, I nipped next door to talk to the old woman neighbour again. I showed her the photos of the girl.

'Listen, missus, do you know this girl?'

'I don't know anyone,' she said, pursing her lips and looking blank. You could understand her, I suppose. Why should she get involved with the police, and then have her neighbour take it out on her? She could have told me a great deal about Dolgo-Saburov's comings and goings, of course. After all, it was no accident that a light appeared at her peephole every time there was the slightest sound outside on the landing. Still, as far as I could see, she only *observed* what was going on. Most probably she wouldn't have known any surnames or Christian names.

I picked up her phone and dialled Colonel Maryamov of the Railway Militia.

'Colonel! This is Shamrayev speaking.'

'What can I do for you, Comrade Investigator?' said Maryamov in an obsequious voice.

'In May of this year Dolgo-Saburov was in the Caucasus, in Sochi. What I want to know is whether he was on leave, or not. Did he go by train on a free travel warrant, or did he fly?'

Once a year all employees on the Soviet railways are allowed to travel with their families to any point in the USSR free of charge. Most railwaymen use this facility for their annual holiday, of course, and this was what I wanted to find out in the case of Dolgo-Saburov.

'If you stay by the phone, I can let you have that information in a minute or two. I just need time to ring the Finance Office.'

'All right, colonel, I'll wait.'

In fact, it took less than a minute.

'Can you hear me, Comrade Investigator? According to the file, sleeping-car superintendent Herman Dolgo-Saburov was away on leave from 29 April to 6 May. Free travel warrants for Sochi and back were issued in his name and that of his wife, Zoya Kirilenko.'

'His wife? But he's a bachelor!' I exclaimed.

'There's something about that in Dolgo-Saburov's application: "Since I am intending to marry Citizeness Zoya Kirilenko in the near future, I request that she should be regarded as a member of my family for the purposes of issuing the warrants." '

'So who is this Zoya Kirilenko? Do you have any information?'

'Certainly. Her passport number is series XXIII – LS645217, and her home address is 27 Dybenko Street, Flat 8. She works as a men's hairdresser at the Enchantress beauty salon on the Novy Arbat.'

'Colonel, the Motherland won't forget you!' I said jubilantly. 'Hang on, I'll ring you back.' I pressed for the dialling-tone and immediately contacted Directory Inquiries.

'Operator, can you give me the number of the Enchantress beauty salon on the Novy Arbat?'

'247–28–82,' she said, rattling off the number.

Then I rang the salon. It was engaged, of course, but I carried on dialling again and again. Meanwhile, with the other ear, I listened out for any noise on the landing outside, in case the 'nephew' should appear. Finally I got a reply.

'Enchantress beauty salon.'

'May I speak to Zoya Kirilenko, please?'

'She's not here at the moment. She's at a customer's. She'll be back after four o'clock.'

'What do you mean: she's at a customer's? I thought she worked at a hairdresser's.'

'I mean that she's working at a client's flat. This isn't a hairdresser's, don't forget, but a beauty salon. Who is it calling?'

'The Kursk Railway Finance Office. In May she travelled to Sochi with an employee of ours, Herman Dolgo-Saburov. Do you know him? I need to ask them something in connection with the travel warrants they were given . . .'

'Have you got the auditors in, or something?' asked the voice at the other end of the phone impertinently.

'What if we have?' I replied, adopting the same tone.

'Well, ring after four anyway. They'll both be here then.'

'What do you mean, both?'

'Zoya and Herman, of course. He came back from work today and rang earlier to find out when she'd be around.'

'Thanks very much, poppet,' I said. 'You're worth your weight in gold!'

I was exultant. I looked at my watch. There was a long time to go until four o'clock, but I still had an enormous number of things to do. A minute earlier I'd been intending to arrest the fellow, if he came back home, but now my plans had altered. It was essential to remove all traces of the search in case he looked in at his flat before four o'clock.

I rushed back next door. My two sergeants had already consumed a fair proportion of the grapes, but there was still half a box left, thank God! So I performed a simple operation. I placed a pile of old newspapers at the bottom of the box, covered them up with the remainder of the grapes and – Bob's your uncle! The box was full again. I didn't think Dolgo-Saburov would be bothered about the grapes now, but it was essential that nothing in the flat should appear to have been tampered with, at least at first glance. The soldiers looked at me in astonishment, but I had no time to explain the reasons for what I was doing, especially as the CID men would appear at any moment to relieve me.

'Comrade Shamrayev, CID squad, three men at your disposal. I'm the senior officer – Lieutenant Kozlov.'

'Look, lieutenant, I asked Krasnovsky to get an urgent tap placed on this phone.'

'It's all been done, Comrade Shamrayev.'

'Good. This is what I want you to do. I want one of you to stay in the neighbour's flat next door. If Dolgo-Saburov shows up, make sure that the neighbour doesn't get in contact with him. If he rings, there's simply nobody at home, understand?'

'Yes, Comrade Investigator.'

'And I want the other two to keep a secret watch on the building from outside. I don't want him arrested, but simply followed. OK?'

'Yes, Comrade Shamrayev.'

'That's all. Let's leave the apartment now.'

I cast one final glance around. Everything seemed to be in the right place, and even if we had moved one or two things, was he likely to notice? After all, he'd left the flat in a pot-mess himself. I removed the photographs of Zoya the Enchantress from the album, along with a couple of others depicting the rest of his workmates, and walked hastily out of the flat.

The CID men disappeared. One of them was at the wheel of an unmarked Volga, parked next to the entrance in the middle of a whole group of cars. As for the other detective, I lost sight of him completely. I said goodbye to the sergeants ('Thanks a lot, lads! Be seeing you. And don't forget: you haven't been here. OK?') and walked quickly over to my own car.

'Seryozha, take me to the Kursk Station Militia Office, pronto!'

Before starting this game with the 'nephew', I still had to run through the various possibilities in my mind. If we were to arrest him now, what did we have on him that could make him confess? The drug-trafficking charge wasn't proved, and we hadn't managed to establish that he had anything to do with the murder of his aunt. The connection with Akeyev and Gridasov had emerged only twenty minutes earlier during a telephone call – and telephone calls effectively vanish into thin air: they are not admissible as evidence in a court of law. No, we'd have to crack Dolgo-Saburov by different means, using Svetlov's methods.

I lifted the receiver of the radio telephone and asked the Petrovka switchboard to put me through to Colonel Maryamov.

'Comrade Colonel, this is Shamrayev again. You've got some compromising material on the chief steward of Moscow – Tashkent train No. 37, I hope. Some black-market dealings he's been involved in, or cheating some passengers? . . .'

'I should say so! When was there ever a dining-car attendant who didn't dish out less food than he should, or something on those lines? We've got files on all the chief stewards . . . On train No. 37 the restaurant car is run by someone called Irakly Golub. We've got all kinds of things on him. Black-market dealings in caviare, smoked sausage, butter. Overcharging, substandard meat, serving spirits after hours. There's enough there to put him away for five years. He's about ready for it . . .'

'Wait a minute! I don't want him sent to gaol. He can provide us with some very useful information,' I said, smiling to myself. 'Stay where you are, and I'll come and collect you.'

Everything had gone smoothly so far. I lay back in the seat and switched on the car radio. It was time to listen in on the everyday goings on of the Moscow Militia. The loudspeaker immediately began to splutter out a stream of different police conversations.

'Central, Central! No. 8 here. At the northern exit to GUM there's a fight over women's boots!'

'Ostankino, Ostankino! A drunken driver in a dark, cherry-coloured Volga has knocked over a pedestrian outside the Botanical Gardens. Registration not known. Car now moving towards the Altuferskoye Highway!'

'Central, Central! This is patrolman No. 108. I have detained a person at the Riga railway station who looks suspiciously like the wanted prisoner Gridasov. He is carrying papers in the name of Heracles Isaakovich Shneyerson. What shall I do with him?'

'Hello, 108, take him straight away to Investigator Pshenichny at 38 Petrovka, Operations Room 10. Understood? Over and out.'

I grinned. Who'd believe a suspect could have a name like that? It was like something out of comic opera. Still, we could but see.

'Central! State Automobile Inspection post on the Mozhaisk Highway here. I have detained the owner of a Zhiguli named Yakov Alekseyevich Gridasov, aged thirty-four. He doesn't fit the description of the prisoner wanted by CID, but the surname is the same. Awaiting your instructions.'

'Central! A drunk named Viktor Mikhailovich Akeyev, born 1916, has been detained at the Pavelets railway terminus and brought to sobering-up station No. 31 . . .'

Moscow's multi-million population is hard at work. Or, if not, part of it is walking down the streets, travelling by metro, bus or trolley-bus, sunbathing on the beaches by the river or queueing up for ladies' boots or the first fresh tomatoes of the season. Meanwhile, at every railway or metro station and in every park, hundreds of informers, visible and invisible, secret agents, traffic police, ordinary militiamen or whatever, are staring closely at every passer-by, comparing their features with those of the photographs hidden in their pockets. And this is only the tip of the iceberg. Apart from this, inquiries are being made, about which the general public knows absolutely nothing. Early this morning the governors of every prison in Moscow and the surrounding district instructed their many stool-pigeons and informers to turn conversations in the cells around to the subject of Viktor Akeyev and Semyon Gridasov – in case one of the prisoners had seen them, or knew where they lived and the people they associated with. On top of this, hundreds, if not thousands, of public-order vigilantes were being given photographs and information about the wanted men at police stations and assembly points all over the capital.

This is one of the Soviet government's great strengths. Whenever it wants, it can issue a single order which will activate with the minimum of delay a huge army of informers, vigilantes, MVD agents, militiamen, the KGB and finally, in emergency situations, the regular army. Furthermore, it can isolate any city or even autonomous republic from the outside world in a matter of minutes, so that not even a bird can fly across the cordon without being noticed . . .

Today Svetlov and I had activated only the first layer of this system in the search for Akeyev and Gridasov, but even so, Moscow now resembled a gigantic filter, through which tens of thousands of people were passing.

Then I suddenly heard the following unexpected

announcement over the air: 'Attention all militia units and automobile inspection stations! Be on the look-out for the following person throughout Moscow and the Moscow region: name – Herman Veniaminovich Dolgo-Saburov, occupation – railway sleeping-car superintendent, year of birth – 1945. Photographs of the wanted man will be distributed later today. Physical description is as follows: height – five foot six . . .'

I grabbed the radio telephone.

'Central! Get me the Incident Room, Lieutenant-Colonel Svetlov! It's urgent!'

The reply came almost immediately: 'Svetlov here.'

'Marat, this is Shamrayev. Get it broadcast over the central network that Dolgo-Saburov isn't to be taken in! If he is found, he is to be left alone and secretly followed.'

'Why? It's only an hour since you asked us to put out a general alert for him!'

'Listen to me! At four o'clock he's due to appear at the Enchantress beauty salon on the Novy Arbat to meet a hairdresser called Zoya Kirilenko. He's almost bound to turn up, unless he gets scared. So will you have a tap put on the hair salon's phone as well? At four o'clock I'm going to try out one of your favourite tricks.'

'Ah, so you're taking a leaf out of my book!'

'That's right. And how are you getting on with this Smagina woman?'

'It almost worked first time. She rushed back to her hotel room and started to ring somebody up. But she only dialled the first three figures – 242 – and then hung up. Anyway, 242 is in the Lenin district of the city, so I've put the whole local CID network there on the alert. Now she's heading towards the centre, either because she thinks she's being followed, or simply out of fear. And she's not made any more phone calls. But she's heading in the direction of the Lenin district. Give it another hour, and I hope everything will have calmed down and it'll be all right. We'll get this Akeyev today, I promise you.'

'All right, but don't count your chickens . . .'

'Hang on, I've got Riga on the phone. It's Colonel Baron. Shall I pass him over to you?'

'OK, but don't hang up.'

After a few words from the operator, I could hear the soft Baltic accent of Lieutenant-Colonel Baron.

'Comrade Shamrayev? Hello. I'm speaking from Riga airport. I've got Aina Silinya and her parents with me. On no account did they want her to travel to Moscow, so I've had to use coercion. They're about to fly off with me now as long as you give your legal sanction.'

'I do. What time will you be arriving?'

'At 2.15 p.m. Moscow time. We'll be coming into Vnukovo airport.'

'Good. I'll have you met.'

'Thank you very much. See you shortly.'

I waited until he had rung off, and then I said to Svetlov: 'Did you hear all that?'

'Yes, I'll get one of the local CID lads to meet them at Vnukovo. In fact, I'll do it now. Turning out to be a busy day, eh?'

12.30 hours

Lena Smagina was walking towards the Central Telegraph Office. At half-past twelve she was due to meet Leva Novikov there, a masseur working for the Spartak football team and a drug-pedlar into the bargain. She'd been wandering around the centre of Moscow for the last hour, waiting to hand over the ill-fated packet of morphine which Viktor Akeyev had given her the day before. It was burning a hole in her pocket – or rather, in the bag which she had taken with her. But as she was afraid of being followed, she couldn't get rid of it by simply throwing it away in some rubbish bin. Of course, she should have flushed it away down the lavatory in her hotel bedroom, but she hadn't thought about the packet at all until her hand touched it, fumbling around in her bag for cigarettes as she was rushing out of the hotel. So, for the whole of the last hour, Lena had been trying to decide whether or not she was being followed. She'd been behaving just like a character in a detective novel, suddenly turning back as she was crossing the road, wandering in and out of shops, taking the odd ride on a trolley-bus and getting off when she felt like it, or simply sitting in Pushkin Square and watching the people around her.

She hadn't detected anybody following her, so she breathed a sigh of relief and decided to ask Novikov for his advice on what to do next. Perhaps he would call on Viktor instead of her, and tell him of the danger? At half-past twelve she ran up the steps of the Central Telegraph building on Gorky Street and turned left into the section dealing with inter-city calls. She was supposed to meet Novikov next to booth No. 3 – and there he was, alert and insolent-looking, like most masseurs. But what was this? As soon as he saw Lena coming, Novikov began to move towards the exit. As he walked past her, he muttered to her without looking: 'On your guard! There's somebody following you!' Lena didn't stop, but carried on walking up to the counter. Beginning to feel faint with fear, she asked the girl whether she could get through to Kotlas. 'You can dial direct from booth No. 16,' came the reply. But Lena didn't bother to phone. What could she say to her father now, after all? Almost on the point of passing out, she went out on to the street.

What was she to do? Feeling that she was about to start screaming there and then, Lena went into a ladies' lavatory. It was the one in Arts Theatre Street, and there was the usual petty black-marketing going on with women selling foreign cosmetics and contraceptive pills. Lena calmed down a little. The women were standing there offering eye-pencils and various other items of Polish and French make-up for sale, and nobody was arresting them. That at least meant that there were no militia around, and those who were following her had obviously stayed outside. She stood in the queue for the cubicles. Standing behind her, and

233

breathing heavily, was a fat, asthmatic woman carrying a couple of string bags, both filled with frozen chickens and salami. She'd obviously queued for three hours or so to get them at the Yeliseyev shop on Gorky Street. Then some prostitute ran in. Without looking at anybody, she went straight up to one of the black-marketeers and said in a loud voice, without a trace of embarrassment: 'Quick! Have you got any French ticklers? I've got a customer waiting for me.'

Lena went into the cubicle, sat down on the seat and burst into tears. Around her everything was going on as usual. People were buying and selling things on the black market, queueing up for chickens and salami, street-walking or making phone calls home and abroad – and only she was out in the cold! She was being followed and might be arrested at any moment. And why? All because of a paltry parcel of morphine and the 350 roubles she was supposed to get for it. What should she do? What? She undid the morphine. Inside were two smaller packets containing a hundred ampoules each. The simplest thing would be to wash them all down the pan, but would these glass containers actually get flushed away? She tore open the cardboard packaging with her teeth and emptied the entire contents into the waste bin next to the lavatory pan. (It wasn't very nice, rummaging about in a whole load of used sanitary towels and toilet paper, but Lena wanted to make sure that the ampoules dropped right down to the bottom of the bin.) She tore the cardboard packets into tiny shreds and threw them into the pan itself. By this time people were already beginning to hammer impatiently on the door. 'I'm coming right now,' said Lena, pulling the chain. Outside she gave her hands a thorough wash, rubbed away at her tear-stained face, applied a bit of eye-shadow, adjusted her hair and walked resolutely up the stairs to face, as she thought, her imminent arrest. Let them arrest her now, she mused. They could all go to hell! She had no drugs on her any longer, and who could prove that the ampoules lying in the rubbish bin had been left there by her, and not by the person ahead of her or behind her in the queue?

She walked out on to the street and looked around. Where were they then? They could arrest her now, if they liked.

Secret
To CID Third Department
Head of Second Section
Lieutenant-Colonel M. A. Svetlov

REPORT
(continued)

Changing direction more than once, the suspect spent the next hour visiting first the Central Telegraph building, where she inquired about making a phone call to Kotlas, and then the women's public lavatory on Arts Theatre Street. One member of the surveillance team, Militia Lieutenant M. Gorelkina, pretended to be a prostitute and entered the cubicle next to that occupied by the suspect. There she saw Smagina destroy two packets of morphine by emptying the ampoules into a rubbish bin next to the pan. When she left the lavatory, the suspect walked apparently aimlessly down Gorky Street, crossed the Manezh and Red Square, and was unexpectedly lost by Lieutenant V. Sveshnikova somewhere in the GUM Department Store. In order to rediscover Smagina's whereabouts, members of my team stood in wait at all the exits from the shop, but failed to find her . . .

12.52 hours
The chief steward, Irakly Kasyanovich Golub, didn't open his door for seventeen minutes. When Colonel Maryamov rang the bell at Flat No. 64, 25 Mariya Ulyanova Street, in the Cheryomushki district of Moscow, there was no reply at all. It really did seem as

if Irakly Golub had crashed out after his long trip from Central Asia. But we carried on ringing for ages, and then he most certainly did wake up. He spent the next ten minutes pretending that he couldn't quite bring himself round, however. He seemed to spend an inordinately long time looking for the key, his dressing gown, his slippers and so on. We could hear him rushing about on the other side of the door and found it easy to imagine what was going on. Having seen the Chief of the Railway Militia, Maryamov himself, through the spy-hole in his door, the chief steward was scared out of his wits and didn't know what to do – whether to hide the valuables, set fire to the money or throw the jars of black caviare down the rubbish chute. I suspect that he managed to do it all, considering the time he took to open the door! In any case, when we finally entered the apartment, there was still a strong smell of burning even though all the windows were wide open.

'It's not polite to keep visitors waiting outside the door for so long,' said Maryamov. 'This is my friend, Special Investigator Igor Iosifovich Shamrayev. And ask us into the living room, for Christ's sake! What are you keeping us out in the entrance-hall for?'

'Ah, of course. I'm sorry. Go on through, please . . .'

Apart from his Georgian Christian name and patronymic, Golub had a marked Caucasian accent as well. According to his file, which had been lent to us by the Anti-Fraud Squad's railway section, Golub had been his mother's maiden name. She was a Ukrainian. His father was a Georgian, however, who had died on the White Russian front in 1944. So Irakly Golub had been a love-child conceived in the midst of battle. It seems strange, but despite this, he was a terrible coward. We didn't even have to show him all the incriminating evidence which the Anti-Fraud Squad had on him, or open the secret agent's report on his particular restaurant car. All Maryamov had to say was this:

'Listen, Irakly, this is what it's all about. We've known for years about all the things you've been getting up to – speculating in smoked sausage, black caviare, butter, buckwheat, foreign cigarettes, the lot. You take items that are in short supply from Moscow to Central Asia and bring back fruit and vegetables and so on . . . Do you want to take a look at your file? Or shall we get down to the nub of the matter straight away, like old friends?'

Golub had probably decided that we were after a bribe, so he unbuttoned his shirt and asked, in a hoarse voice: 'How much do you want?'

'What do you mean, "How much"?' asked Maryamov uncomprehendingly.

I couldn't resist making a funny remark. 'How much we can *give* you, or how much we can take from you?'

'*Take* from me,' said Golub. You could tell just by looking at him that he was trying to work out in his head how much it would take to buy us off. He obviously couldn't make up his mind, however.

'Listen, Irakly,' I said. 'We're not going to *take* anything, but the court could certainly *give* you from eight to fifteen years under Section 3 of Article 92. The actual choice of camp would be the decision of the Corrective Labour Directorate, of course, but as you've spent all your time working in the south of the country, we would advise our colleagues on Bolshaya Bronnaya Street to send you up north – to Potma, Magadan, Norilsk or somewhere like that . . .'

I was overdoing it a little, of course. I'd got carried away by my own eloquence. But on the other hand, Maryamov and I had reckoned that Golub would take some breaking. Instead of this, he immediately said: 'I understand perfectly! Now what is it you want of me?'

'Something very simple. You've got a friend by the name of Herman Dolgo-Saburov. Later today we want you to pretend to meet him by chance on the street or at the Enchantress hair salon. One of our men will be with you. We want the two of you to invite Dolgo-Saburov to have a meal in a restaurant somewhere. That's all. All you have to do is talk him into going to a restaurant with you, nothing else.'

'Are you going to poison him?' asked Golub, showing a certain professional interest in the affair. I am certain that if I had said, 'Yes, he's got to be poisoned,' Golub wouldn't have refused to sprinkle the poison into some Kiev cutlets himself, if only he'd avoid going to prison by so doing.

Ten minutes later, after shaving and putting on a light summer suit, Irakly Golub was already sitting in my car, while I rang Svetlov on the radio telephone. 'I'm bringing the bait along now. What's happening with the girl?'

'At last!' replied Svetlov. 'I've got some important news for you. The railway police have tracked the nephew down at the Kalanchevskaya marshalling-yards. He's there at the moment – on track 34 where there's a group of old, condemned carriages. It looks as if he's got a secret compartment or store in one of them, I don't know what. He's busy dragging out some boxes and stowing them into his Zhiguli estate.'

'What sort of boxes?'

'I don't know. You can't get too close. There are railway employees wandering about all the time. It is a marshalling-yard, after all. But I'll think of something!'

'Just as long as they don't put the wind up him, OK?' I said. 'And what's happening about this Smagina girl?'

'My boys lost sight of her in GUM, can you imagine! But I ordered the manager to put some foreign goods for women on sale, and to make an announcement about it over the shop relay. You should have seen what happened next! They started selling French underwear and eye-shadow. There are 600 women queueing up already! Our Lena's number 403 in the queue. Good on her! She looked like a sleep-walker, but she's queueing all the same!'

'You won't lose her again, will you?'

'You must be joking! I've got four people shadowing her. If they lose her now, I'll wring their necks! Come on over, and we can decide what to do next – whether to let her buy the French knickers, or not.'

'OK. I'm on my way.'

Of course, I was very tempted to stop outside GUM *en route* to the Petrovka just to have a look at Lena Smagina myself, but there was no time. We headed straight for the Incident Room at CID headquarters. Svetlov was waiting for us there.

13.40 hours

The Operations Section of the Moscow CID is to be found in a three-storey building situated to the rear of the famous No. 38 Petrovka. Few people know that this building, the wing of an old former private house, hidden away on Sredne-Karetny Lane, is now the operational headquarters of the whole Moscow Militia.

On the ground floor are recreation rooms for the investigators, dog handlers and other expert personnel who are on duty sometimes for days on end. While waiting to be called out on a case, the officers can take a nap or play a game of chess or cards. Not that there is much time for relaxation. Something happens somewhere in Moscow every minute of the day – somebody will be stabbing his wife, robbing a savings bank or falling under a car. The loudspeaker down on the ground floor is never silent for long. No sooner has the message gone out: 'Duty Investigator to the car pound!' than a whole posse of new police Volgas or imported Mercedes, armed with the latest detection equipment, will be rushing through Moscow to the scene of any incident, headlamps full on and sirens blaring . . .

But the main office of the Operations Section, its brain, so to speak, is the Incident Room on the first floor. Here you'll find the duty officers for the City Militia and the CID, along with their deputies and the officers in charge of the various operational units. At their disposal is a huge, illuminated map of Moscow, mounted on one whole wall. There are smaller maps of the individual districts at a series of electronic consoles, as well as numerous items of communications equipment – telephones, televisions and radios. Every piece of urgent information about the life of the city is channelled through this room. It is from here that the various investigators and other experts are summoned from down below and dispatched to the scenes of incidents and crimes all over the capital. It is from here that covert surveillance teams are assembled and sent wherever they are needed. The officers put in charge of these aspects of militia and CID work are usually experienced detectives themselves, and their deputies – people of the rank and calibre of Marat Svetlov. You could have said that the work of the whole Operations Section required creative flair in a high degree if it hadn't been for the idiot put in overall charge of the set-up, Colonel Shubeiko, an absolute cretin and superannuated party hack, a former political instructor in the army . . .

As our car turned into Sredne-Karetny Lane, the sergeant of the guard obligingly opened the metal gates and we slid into the courtyard. On a bench outside the smoking room was the usual collection of drivers, dog handlers and other jokers, able to spend the whole of their twenty-four-hour shift blathering on about all the unbelievable rapes and *crimes passionels* with which they had had to deal. They were talking about the usual thing now. As we walked past them on our way into the building, I could hear one of them saying: 'First they raped her, then, blow me, if they didn't shove an empty champagne bottle up her . . .!'

As I headed towards the staircase, I came across someone whose face seemed amazingly familiar. I tried very hard to remember where I had seen him before, and suddenly it came to me: it was Belkin! The very same Belkin we were looking for at this moment! Yet this individual acted as if nothing were going on at all. He was simply heading for the exit . . . I was about to turn around and catch him up when suddenly a door opened next to me and a voice said sarcastically: 'Calm down, Comrade Shamrayev! That's not Belkin. He looks very like him, but he's not him all the same!'

I turned around and saw Pshenichny smiling at me. 'That's the third time he's been brought in today. I've had to give him a certificate to state that he's not Belkin. Don't look at me like that! It really isn't Belkin! I've seen eleven Gridasovs and six Akeyevs so far today. I've just had a phone call to say that they're about to bring three more of them in. It's a bit simpler with Akeyev, it's true. I've got Sinitsyn with me – you remember, the artist who witnessed the kidnapping at the Kursk station. He's the best Akeyev expert I've got! It's a pity that he doesn't remember what the other accomplices looked like . . .'

I stared at Pshenichny. Over the last four days an extraordinary change had come over him. From a tired, overwrought district investigator, weighed down by the enormous number of routine cases assigned to him, he had turned into a calm, reliable colleague, self-assured and fully aware of his value to the investigation. His light-blue eyes were attentive, but lacked that self-destructive streak which you see in so many Russians. You could see an immaculate white shirt-collar sticking out above his rather ancient jacket. Everything about him was clean and meticulous. Working for the Chief Prosecutor's Office was obviously a major event in his life. I wondered whether he had a wife and children. We'd been working together continuously for four days, but we hadn't even had time for a glass of beer together. There was something wrong about that – not the Russian way of doing things at all.

I looked at my watch: 'In about twenty minutes' time, Valya, Aina Silinya will be here. Show her photographs of all the principals – Akeyev, Gridasov and Dolgo-Saburov. We're about to get two of them now. If she can identify them, then the case is in the bag – touch wood! You do have some other photos ready for her to look at as well, I suppose?'

'Igor Iosifovich!' he said reproachfully, and I realized that my question had been superfluous, even tactless. The law requires that, for identification purposes, you show a witness not just a single photograph, but a number of them simultaneously, and certainly never less than three, so as not to influence the witness's reaction. Otherwise, the identification would be inadmissible as evidence in a court of law, and this sometimes happens with inexperienced investigators. But Pshenichny was no novice, of course.

'All right, Valentin. Here's the chief steward from train No. 37. Let him sit here with you, as he's not allowed up to the first floor. Which room is Svetlov in?'

'Incident Room, Igor Iosifovich . . .'

I left Irakly Golub in Pshenichny's hands and accompanied Maryamov up to the next floor. There was a great deal of activity there today. It seemed as if there were several covert surveillance teams at work besides our own. The first eight rooms looked more like dressing rooms in a theatre. One lot was dressed as a group of senior air-force officers, others as a band of bearded geologists from somewhere in the north, yet others as naval officers, and so on. To my amazement, I suddenly heard the familiar voice of my friend Baklanov coming from one of the neighbouring rooms: 'Unbelievable! Airmen, geologists, sailors – and they're all dressed in identical policemen's boots! There's a real conspiracy for you!'

I looked round the door. Baklanov saw the look of astonishment on my face.

'Greetings!' he said. 'I'm trying to nail a bunch of card-sharpers. They've been cheating our valiant officers when they return from service abroad, you see. They choose their victims more or less the moment they leave the station at Brest and pick them clean between there and Moscow. Still, never mind! We've got a few well-heeled clients all lined up for them! How are things with you?'

'I'll be in the Incident Room. Look in.'

As I entered I noticed at once the lively, restless figure of Marat Svetlov standing by an illuminated map of the centre of Moscow. I could hear voices of both surveillance teams coming across the air simultaneously.

'Comrade Colonel! The suspect is still standing in the queue. But the manager of GUM says that he's only got enough French bras to last another five minutes!'

'Attention, colonel! The suspect Dolgo-Saburov has left his car at the corner of Lermontov Square and the marshalling-yards. He's run over to a telephone box.'

Svetlov immediately turned to one of his assistants: 'What's the number of the phone booth at the corner of Lermontov Square and Kalanchevskaya Street?'

A series of diagrams appeared on one of the small screens, and we could already see an electronic map of the intersection in question. The map showed you clearly the entrance to every building, the name of every shop and the telephone box at the corner, with the relevant phone number: 754–214. The assistant immediately rang the Central Telephone Surveillance Department at Zubovskaya Street, ordering them to have a tap placed on phone number 754–214, and to have all conversations from it recorded.

A moment later we could already hear Dolgo-Saburov's excited voice: 'Hello, Tolik? This is Herman. Need any stuff today?'

'What's today – Friday?' said the second voice.

'No, it's Thursday. But I'm tied up tomorrow. How much will you take?'

'Uh-h-h, let's say 200 grammes . . . I've no bread today . . . Now, if it was tomorrow . . .'

'Well, how much have you got? Bear in mind that I'm selling at a reduced price today . . .'

'Two roubles, three at the maximum . . .'

In Moscow business slang, that meant 2,000 or 3,000 roubles. Meanwhile, Telephone Surveillance was already able to inform Svetlov's assistant on another line that the 'subscriber' was phoning the Zhiguli beer-bar on the Novy Arbat.

In the meantime, Dolgo-Saburov had already dialled another number, and we could hear his impatient voice once again: 'Robert, this is Herman.'

'Ah, how are you doing? Has something happened?'

'No. What makes you think that?'

'Well, today isn't Friday after all.'

'I know. That's why I'm ringing. I'll drop over right now with the goods. Will you be in?'

'And where would I get to? Come on over, that's all right. As a matter of fact, I've just run out . . .'

Suddenly we could hear the dialling-tone and the voice of the telephone engineer announcing: 'The subscriber was calling the Rioni shashlyk house on the Stary Arbat.'

Then we heard the covert surveillance group over the air again: 'Colonel, he's searching through his pockets. His money has obviously run out, and he's got nothing to dial with. Shall we let him have a couple of kopecks?'

'That's enough humour,' said Svetlov imperiously. 'Carry on watching him.'

'When shall we arrest him? At the beer-bar, with the goods?'

'You won't be arresting him at all. Shamrayev has brought the bait. Who is going to go along?'

'It ought to be Ozherelyev, colonel. He's the best at it. By the way, the suspect has got back into his car and is driving towards the Arbat.'

'Ozherelyev has already set one suspect up today, and that's enough,' said Svetlov. 'I don't like him to play the same part twice in one day, after all. He's not Sophia Loren.'

'Well, then you can do it yourself, colonel.'

'OK, I'll think about it. Hello, GUM, can you hear me?'

'Yes, Comrade Colonel.'

'Stop the sale of underwear now. Only don't let the

suspect out of your sight, or I'll have you all put back on point-duty, understand me?'

Then Svetlov turned to me and filled me in on what had been happening.

'It's like this. The nephew kept drugs in a secret hiding-place at the Kalanchevskaya marshalling-yards. It was very convenient – in one of those old carriages without wheels. You know, the ones that stand directly on the ground. There, in the middle of a load of old clothes and lumber, were boxes filled with packets of morphine ampoules. Why he decided to get rid of the store today I don't yet know. Perhaps those searches of the flat put the wind up him. Anyway, he loaded all this stuff into his estate car and drove off to the pharmaceutical ware-house on Lermontov Square. He was nearly arrested by the Anti-Fraud Squad when he arrived, but I managed to warn them just in time. Your Malenina is inspecting the whole building, and the warehouse is completely closed. The Anti-Fraud Squad boys are swarming everywhere. I got one of our girls to dress up as a cleaner, and she man-aged to tip him off at the office by the entrance-gate. So now he's rushing around Moscow trying to unload his goods. By the way, the car which he's travelling in is reg-istered in his aunt's name. He's got an official certificate to drive it, though. We got the automobile inspection to check his papers, after stopping him for overtaking on the right. Of course, what we really need now is a cine camera to photograph all his contacts, but where do we get one? There's only one such camera for the whole CID and Baklanov has grabbed that.'

'Comrade Colonel!' said a voice over the radio. 'The suspect has just left GUM and is standing in a queue for a taxi.'

'Is it a long queue?'

'She's ninth in line.'

'All right. Let her stand there for a couple of minutes, then get Fedotov to drive up. Is he available?'

'Of course, colonel. He's been on the job since morning.'

'Excellent. Put Fedotov in direct contact with me.'

Tension began to mount in the room as one of the decisive points of the whole operation approached. That old CID hand, Tikhon Yegorovich Fedotov, was about to drive up to the taxi-rank just outside GUM. In the twelve years I've known him, and over the thirty years that he's been working for the Moscow CID in fact, he has never once failed. There's something about that enormous moustache of his, his corpulent, good-natured appearance, his simple, peasant face, that always has a calming effect on even the most suspicious criminal. They might suspect anybody and everybody, but somehow it never occurs to them that this cheerful old man is a police agent. When they get into his taxi, they immediately relax, and even if they had intended to cover their tracks and change taxis three times before going to the right address, they lower their guard in Fedotov's car and tell him to drive to their real destination right away. His taxi contained a hidden radio transmitter, so that all conversations could immediately be monitored by the covert surveillance team and at the console in the Operations Section. So it was that after a few seconds we could hear Fedotov's good-natured, northern accent coming through over the loudspeaker.

'Central, this is Fedotov. I'm approaching the suspect now.'

Then his tone of voice changed completely. 'Wait a minute, comrades! Don't get into the car yet, please. Where are you going?'

'To Medvedkovo,' said a man's voice.

'No, I can't take you there, sorry. It's my lunch-break. And where are you going, love?'

'To Biryulovo.'

'No, I can't go there, either.'

By this time, Fedotov had obviously drawn level with the 'suspect', Lena Smagina, and he threw her the prepared bait: 'Lenin District, South-West metro station, Lenin Hills, Cheryomushki . . . any good to you?'

'I want the Frunze Embankment,' said a young woman's voice.

'He's got to her!' Svetlov couldn't help saying. 'Well done, Fedotov!'

They couldn't hear our remarks in the taxi, of course, but we could overhear everything that Fedotov was saying to Smagina and the other people in the queue.

'But comrade, can't you see? I've got somebody in the taxi already,' Fedotov was saying to another potential passenger. 'But I want to go to Cheryomushki, too,' she was saying.

'Did you hear that?' said Fedotov. 'She wants to go to Cheryomushki too! I don't know. Some people! Here I am, trying to get home for my beetroot soup, which will be getting cold on the table, and all they can do is try to push their way into the car! Now where is it on the Frunze Embankment that you want, love?'

'No. 48, one of the red buildings,' replied Lena Smagina. 'Do you know them?'

'I should say I do, my dear. I *have* been driving a taxi for twenty-five years, you know. It's all high government officials that live there, retired ministers and that sort of thing. I remember taking Bulganin there once. He'll be getting on now. I wonder if he's still alive? Did you ever meet him?'

This was the way Fedotov worked. He'd start chatting innocently enough, but then he'd gradually wheedle out whether the passenger knew the people who lived in the building, or whether he or she was going there for the first time. Meanwhile, the conversation would distract the passenger from noticing how slowly they were driving along. Fedotov needed to let the surveillance group get ahead of him, after all, so that they could place observers outside the building.

'No. I've never met Bulganin,' she replied.

'He'll have died by now, I expect,' said Fedotov. 'Perhaps not, though. They would have given him an obituary in *Pravda*, wouldn't they? He used to be our prime minister, after all. I always read the obituaries . . .'

'Could we go a little faster?' asked Lena.

'What for? We can if you like, only the traffic police don't approve of it very much. What do people say? More haste, less speed . . .?'

At that moment we heard a message from the second surveillance group following Dolgo-Saburov.

'Colonel, the suspect has parked his car outside the Zhiguli beer-bar. He has placed the box containing the morphine in a bag and gone into the bar. He's talking to the manager now. What are we to do?'

'How many have you got in the group?' asked Svetlov.

'There are eighteen of us.'

'The "nephew" is about to deliver to all his regular customers. You're not to arrest anybody until I give the word. Just observe what's going on, and who he talks to, OK?'

'When are you going to have lunch with him, Comrade Colonel?'

'Not for another hour or hour and a half at least,' said Svetlov irritably. 'We've got Akeyev on the go at the moment.'

'But, colonel! What if the nephew wants to eat a little earlier? Let's say he goes into a restaurant before you arrive – what am I to do?'

'I don't know. You'll think of something, that's what you're paid for. You could let the air out of his tyres, or something . . . Anyway, make up your own mind, it doesn't bother me. That's the lot. I've no time to talk now. See you later.'

Then Pshenichny entered the room and came over to me. 'Igor Iosifovich, Aina Silinya has arrived from Riga with her parents and Lieutenant-Colonel Baron.'

However much I wanted to stay in the Incident Room, I had no choice. I had to go downstairs and talk to the new arrivals. Lieutenant-Colonel Baron turned out to be a tall, hefty fellow, aged about forty. He listened to me give a few words of reassurance to Aina

Silinya's parents, and then rushed away 'to visit some of his friends'. That's why he'd insisted on accompanying the Silinya family to Moscow, I expect. I arranged for a car to take the parents off to the Hotel Minsk and Aina stayed with me. She was a quiet, somewhat phlegmatic girl with thin legs and big, greenish-blue eyes. It seems to me that eyes of that colour, which are fatally attractive for so many men, more often than not conceal a totally vacuous personality, although poetic, enthusiastic natures like Belkon or Yury Rybakov are inclined to attribute all kinds of fantastic qualities to them.

Once we'd seen off Aina's parents and Lieutenant-Colonel Baron, Pshenichny and I took Aina into a smaller room, which had been placed at our disposal for the day, and showed her a series of photographs to see if she would recognize Akeyev, Dolgo-Saburov and Gridasov among these. Akeyev she recognized straight away and without any hesitation, 'categorically', as we say, but she wasn't very certain about Gridasov and Dolgo-Saburov.

All the same, the fact that she had positively identified one of them meant that all the frantic to-ings and fro-ings on my part and on Svetlov's over the previous few days had been to some avail. We were about to pick up Belkin's trail, and were already hard on the heels of his kidnappers.

I turned to Aina Silinya and asked: 'Did you see the *Komsomolka* correspondent Rady Sverdlov while you were in Baku?'

'Yes,' she replied. 'He lives on the Esplanade. We spent one night at his flat, just before we left for Moscow. So what?'

'Valentin,' I said. 'Please make sure that that detail is entered in the report.'

Then I went upstairs to rejoin Svetlov. Things were moving at breakneck speed. We should have called in the cinema people from Mosfilm!

Lena Smagina was travelling directly to Vitya's. She was tired. It was stupid to spend the whole day dragging around Moscow, seeing a plain-clothes detective or secret agent in every passer-by. She still hadn't been arrested, after all. She started weeping again in the lavatory in GUM, but then she'd gone to a café on the first floor and had a cup of coffee and a sandwich. After that she spent two hours queueing up for some French underwear and felt very much more at ease. That idiot of a masseur must have been simply lying when he said she was being followed. If they really had been hoping that she would lead them to Viktor, then they would have stopped the people queueing up for underwear ages before. What good would it have done the militia to wait while she bought herself some French knickers? Lena considered herself to be an expert at recognizing detectives. She had studied the queue very carefully, and she hadn't been able to discover a single person who so much as resembled the types she knew from the camp at Kotlas. In any case, if she had been followed, it was probably either by some fancy man who wanted to get off with her, or by some stupid idiot like that major from Odessa, somebody to whom she'd given the slip long before, in GUM or even earlier. Anyway, Lena walked out of GUM towards the taxi-rank and got into the first cab that came along. She was intending to stop off at the Cheryomushki market and buy Viktor some grapes (he'd asked her to bring some when she was due to make her next visit in two days' time), but when a taxi turned up that was actually heading towards the Frunze Embankment, she'd given the market up as a bad job. Now was hardly the time to go buying grapes! Once in the car she'd begun to relax immediately. Indeed, she even began to doze off . . .

REPORT
(continued)

... After overtaking the taxi driven by Captain
Fedotov, our three special cars arrived at the
address given by Smagina: No. 48, Frunzenskaya
Embankment. The building had four entrances on
the ground floor, so each one was hurriedly covered
by members of the surveillance team. When the suspect arrived, she settled up with Captain Fedotov,
giving him a ten-rouble note and telling him to keep
the change. She then headed towards entrance No.
2, where she encountered Major Kuzmichova, who
was dressed as an old-age pensioner pretending to
take her own Tibetan terrier, Harry Truman, for a
walk. The two of them entered the lift together, and
Major Kuzmichova was able to see Smagina get out
at the sixth floor and ring the bell at flat No. 22.
Nobody came to the door for nine minutes. Only
when she began to disturb the neighbours by hammering at the door with her fists and shouting out:
'Vitya, open up, it's me,' did the door open and a
man's hand drag her inside.

Meanwhile, as soon as it became known which
apartment Smagina was heading for, Lieutenant I.
Z. Grinshtein from the Telephone Surveillance
Department managed to lower an EPU-5 electronic
microphone down to the window of the flat, with the
aid of the janitor who had been summoned for that
purpose. From 15.07 hours onwards our group was
able to overhear and record all sounds and conversations coming from the flat, as well as feed them
over the radio to the CID Incident Room. The relevant tape recordings are appended to this report.

Tape Recording

MAN'S VOICE: What! Have you gone mad, you little fool?! Who told you to come outside the prearranged times?

WOMAN'S VOICE: But Vitya, listen! Have you got anybody here?

MAN'S VOICE: Of course not, bonehead! Do you want to look around and check? You've raised the whole house with all this jealous ranting of yours! Did anybody see you on the staircase?

WOMAN'S VOICE: Vitya, wait a minute! I haven't come because I'm jealous! The whole Moscow CID is on the look-out for you!

MAN'S VOICE: Well, so what? That means that somebody at the camp in Kotlas has snitched and told them I've extended my visit illegally. So what? What the hell point is there in you causing so much panic?

WOMAN'S VOICE: Listen, Vitya, it's not like that at all . . .!

This was the point at which I returned to the Incident Room, where Major Ozherelyev's surveillance group was transmitting the monitored conversation. Until quite recently, two or three years ago, say, the CID, and indeed the militia as a whole, hadn't possessed such technology. It was the strictly secret preserve of the KGB. But now that we were on the eve of the Moscow Olympic Games, the KGB had purchased the latest American and Japanese listening equipment, and their old machines, which wouldn't work at distances greater than half a mile, had been passed on to the MVD. But thank the Lord for small mercies! Now, with the aid of a Soviet-made EPU–5 listening device, we were able to overhear a conversation of quite crucial importance for the investigation.

WOMAN'S VOICE: Listen! You're wrong! They're looking for some journalist or other, who you're supposed to have kidnapped. And they say that you've murdered some teenage youth! Vitya, is it true?

MAN'S VOICE: Shut your mouth, you fool! I haven't killed anybody! Who are 'they', anyway? Who have you been talking to?

WOMAN'S VOICE: At the hotel this morning some major in the Odessa police tried to pick me up. He's a student at the Militia Academy. They were all given three photographs – yours, and one of this journalist, and one of somebody else, who I think I remember seeing you with once. Vitya! Why have you got mixed up in this business? Why!

MAN'S VOICE: Wait a minute, and stop screaming! What else did he say?

WOMAN'S VOICE: I can't remember. I saw your photograph and I nearly went out of my mind!

MAN'S VOICE: Well, try to remember! What else did he say?

I bent down towards Svetlov and asked: 'Whose flat is it?'

'We've already found that out,' he replied. 'It belongs to one Viktor Vladimirovich Sysoyev, head of the Chief Pharmaceutical Authority. He's in Geneva at the moment, at the head of a medical delegation attending an international symposium. The whole of his family are on holiday in the south, at Pitsunda.'

Meanwhile, we could hear a woman sobbing violently over the radio: 'But Vitya, what's going to happen now? What's going to happen now!'

'Nothing. Everything is going to carry on just as normal,' said Akeyev, sounding angry but very self-assured. 'In the first place, I haven't killed anybody! And in the second place, the boss will be home in a week's time and he'll get me out of all this shit. I'm not working on my own, after all . . .'

'Vitya, why don't we go back nice and quietly to Kotlas, *now*! You can finish your time in Daddy's camp, and nobody will know that you've been to Moscow. How about it? Let's go?'

'Come on, come on!' said Svetlov impatiently. 'Just leave that flat . . .'

But Vitya Akeyev was not that stupid.

'You fool!' he said to Lena. 'If they're searching for me all over Moscow, it means that they'll be looking for me at the camp tomorrow. In any case, I can't leave here at all at the moment. What are you talking about? Are you sure you weren't followed? What's that car outside?'

'It was there when I arrived. Vitya, don't be afraid. My Dad was in the KGB. In any case, I wandered all round Moscow, checking to see whether I was being followed. I was so frightened at first that I emptied all the morphine away in the ladies' loo, two boxes of it, one hundred in each. Because I thought I could see people following me everywhere. Then I calmed down a bit, while I was queueing for French underwear in GUM. Can you imagine, they ran out when I was only twenty places away in the queue!'

'So how did you get here? By metro?'

'No, taxi. But don't worry. It was some clapped-out old duffer who drove me here. I chose him specially . . .!'

Everybody in the room suddenly collapsed with laughter. Despite his age, Captain Fedotov was a great one for women, and to hear him being called a 'clapped-out old duffer' meant that Lena Smagina had acquired a sworn enemy for life in the Moscow CID. As for Fedotov, he wouldn't shake off that description for a long time . . .

Meanwhile, the conversation in Sysoyev's flat continued:

'Vitya, but why did you kidnap the journalist?'

'That's enough, it's got nothing to do with you. It's just that the idiot poked his nose in once too often and persuaded the kid to snitch on us.'

'And did you kill *him*, too?'

'Idiot! I've already told you: I haven't killed anyone. And stop whining, or I'll fucking well throw you out of the flat! Let's have a drink, that'd be better! What do you want? Brandy, vodka? I asked you to buy me some grapes.'

'I know, Vitya. Only I was in such a state that I couldn't be bothered about grapes. Do you want me to take a taxi to the market and get you some now?'

'No, we'll sweat it out here until the boss arrives . . . What do you want to drink?'

Then we could hear Major Ozherelyev's voice over the air. 'We've missed our chance, colonel. She hasn't managed to get him out of the flat . . .'

'I know. I'm not deaf,' said Svetlov rudely. 'OK, let them have a drink and talk a bit more. Then we'll see . . .'

'You're a fool,' replied Akeyev. 'Here you are. Drink some brandy. There's nothing to be afraid of. What do you think I'm sitting here for? Guarding his wardrobe, or something? Listen! Out there in the kitchen, behind the slop-pail, is a safe full of diamonds, worth 3,000,000 roubles at least! As soon as the boss gets back, we'll be able to buy our way out of anything. Half the ministers are his friends, and the other half are mixed up in this business with him. Don't you understand the country you're living in? All you have to do is support those in power, and you're safe as houses. Nothing can get at you then, not the Anti-Fraud Squad, or anything . . .'

'Vitya, kiss me . . .'

'OK. Come here, then . . .'

Now all we could hear over the air was the sound of passionate kisses, the squeaking of springs in the sofa and breathing which got faster and faster. The CID men started to grin and smile. Everybody looked at Svetlov and myself. Then we heard Major Ozherelyev's voice, scarcely able to contain his merriment: 'This is where the porn show starts, colonel. What are your instructions?'

'Shut your mouth and wait!' snapped Svetlov.

'Yes, colonel,' said the major in an offended tone.

Meanwhile it really did seem as if a 'porn show' was about to begin on the Frunze Embankment!

'Take all my clothes off,' whispered the woman's voice. 'That's it . . . Take your time . . . Don't do it all at once! I want to be kissed . . . Don't move, don't move! God! How I love him! Look at him! Christ . . .'

'No, I'm sorry, but I can't work in these conditions!' said a middle-aged technician, Captain Shaginskaya, blushing deeply. And to shouts of derision from the rest of the officers, she left the room.

'Ozherelyev,' said Svetlov hoarsely. 'Take the strike group up on to the sixth floor, and don't forget that Akeyev was a European boxing champion and may be armed. So open the doors very quietly, and only when they finish, at my signal.'

'So they'll be finishing at your signal, will they?' asked Ozherelyev wickedly.

'You sod! I'll teach you to be witty with me! You just wait!' said Svetlov good-naturedly. 'And now get on with it.'

'Yes, sir. Only shall we listen in for a bit longer? It is interesting, after all . . .'

Not that Lena Smagina had been quiet all this time. As is well known, women can be divided into several categories – those who say nothing, those who chatter away and those who cry out. Lena Smagina turned out to be one of the chatterers.

'Take my breasts! My breasts, please,' she whispered, breathing hard. 'No, that hurts, Vitya. Let me go on top. Let me go on top! No, I'll do it myself . . . Oh! Ooh! That's marvellous! Oh God! How wonderful . . .!'

The shadowing of this particular suspect had turned into a full-scale porno show, make no mistake about it! The word soon passed around and people came flooding in to the Incident Room from all over the place. There were duty officers from along the corridor, engineers from the Technical Department on the second floor, officers from the recreation rooms on the ground floor, and a whole horde of investigators and inspectors from the CID and the Anti-Fraud Squad, as well as dog handlers, criminologists, forensic experts and chauffeurs – they were all there! The whole Operations Department was listening in to the case.

'Do it again, Vitya, again! Oh, that's wonderful, wonderful. Oh! . . . Do it again . . .!'

'Well, how long *can* they keep it up for?' asked Captain Pavlychko, one of the duty officers, indignantly. Then he looked at his watch. 'He *has* been screwing her for twenty-three minutes, after all!'

'The other way round, you mean,' somebody said. 'She's been screwing him!'

He was quite right. Lena did seem to be insatiable.

'Do it again, Vitya, do it again! Don't stop! Only . . . do it slowly. That's right. That's right, darling . . . oh, I'm dying! Oh, how marvellous! Go deeper, please, deeper . . . Again . . . Here, let me turn round. Let me turn round . . . Oh, what are you doing! Oh, oh! What are you doing?' She said the same thing, louder and louder, quicker and quicker. 'Oh, oh . . . I'm going to die . . . Oh . . .'

'What's going on here?' said an imperious voice. Everybody looked towards the door in surprise. There was a bewildered Colonel Shubeiko, the officer in charge of the whole Operations Department. All those not involved in our particular case rushed past him out of the room, leaving the rest of us and the pig-eyed Colonel Shubeiko to listen to Lena Smagina.

'Oh! What are you doing? I'm going to die . . . Oh . . .!'

'Is he strangling her, or what?' asked the colonel at last.

I must confess that neither Svetlov nor I could resist it any longer. We burst out laughing and tried to turn it into a cough.

'Comrade Colonel,' said Ozherelyev suddenly over the radio. 'The strike group with Sergeant Afanasyev is in position. What are your instructions?'

'He's fucking her, colonel, if you'll forgive the expression,' said Svetlov.

'Well, put a stop to it at once!' ordered Shubeiko.

'I'm sorry, colonel, but you mustn't interfere with our work,' replied Svetlov. 'Ozherelyev, can you hear me?'

'Yes, Marat Alekseyevich. Only how long is all this porn going to go on for? We'll all have to drink a pint of milk to restore our health!'

'That's enough idle chat. Who's going to open the door?'

'Technician Suzdaltsev.'

'Good. Prepare yourselves.'

To judge from what we could hear over the radio, it certainly seemed as if events in apartment No. 22 were about to reach their natural conclusion.

'Now, Ozherelyev, go! Open the door! Only I want him alive! I'm on my way!'

Svetlov got his assistant to take his place at the console, and motioned Vanya Korovin, formerly a bear-hunter and now a lieutenant in the Technical Department, to follow. The three of us rushed downstairs to the waiting CID Mercedes. We'd hardly time to slam the car doors behind us before the driver switched on the siren and we screeched out into Sredne-Karetny lane. The sound of our siren made the city traffic hug the side of the road in an effort to get out of the way, and we hurtled down the Garden Ring Road towards the Frunze Embankment.

Secret

To CID Third Department
Head of Second Section
Lieutenant-Colonel M. A. Svetlov

REPORT
(concluded)

... Acting on your instructions received by radio, technician Suzdaltsev managed to pick the lock of apartment No. 22 without any noise, and the strike group consisting of six men under my direct command entered the flat silently. From the bedroom we continued to hear noises emanating from V. Akeyev and E. Smagina. When these stopped, we heard the sound of a match being struck and a man's voice asking Smagina whether she wanted to smoke. She refused, saying that she needed to go to the bathroom. We allowed her to enter the bathroom without hindrance and then rushed into the bedroom where we arrested Citizen Akeyev after a short struggle. We managed to place handcuffs on him. He had no chance to use the revolver that was concealed under the mattress. At the same time we apprehended E. Smagina in the bathroom. Akeyev hurled abuse at her, accusing her of 'tipping us off'. When she recognized me as the 'major from Odessa', Smagina realized that our acquaintance earlier in the day at the Hotel Peking had been a put-up job and she fainted.

Special Investigator I. I. Shamrayev arrived on the scene and on his instructions the two prisoners were dressed in their own clothes. Lieutenant I. Korovin and Suzdaltsev then examined a cupboard in the kitchen. In it, behind a slop-pail, they discovered a well-concealed imported safe of quite new construction.

The prisoner V. Akeyev informed us that the combination to the safe was known only to the owner of the flat, Citizen Sysoyev, who was on official business abroad at that moment. According to the two technical experts, it was impossible to arrive at the correct combination any other way, so Special Investigator Shamrayev gave instructions that it should be opened by using an oxyacetylene torch. However, the safe turned out to be empty. A painstaking search of the apartment revealed no other secret hiding place, nor were any valuables, foreign currency, narcotics or any other similar items discovered on the premises.

Deputy Head of Second Section
CID Third Department
Major V. Ozherelyev

7 June 1971

The person most shaken by the sight of the empty safe was Akeyev himself. Neither his arrest, nor his having been 'betrayed' by his girl-friend ('that snitching bitch', as he called her), nor his own blunders ('I had a feeling that it was a police car outside!') – none of these things had as devastating an effect on him as when police technician Vanya Korovin burnt through the safe to reveal it as being absolutely empty.

Sitting in the kitchen, already dressed and hand-cuffed, Akeyev stared vacantly at the empty safe. Then he said, as if he couldn't believe his own eyes: 'But the diamonds were there! I saw them myself!'

'When?' asked Svetlov.

Akeyev looked at me, then at Svetlov, Ozherelyev and the CID men crowding around in the kitchen. His brain was working feverishly, I could see that. He screwed up his eyes and clenched his handcuffed fists together, like the boxer he was.

'OK,' he said. 'Which one of you is the investigator? I want to make a statement to protect the security of the Soviet Union!'

He'd probably seen a similar scene in a film or on the television. When I said, 'I'm an investigator from the Chief Public Prosecutor's Office,' he coughed into his fist and said with a great show of bombastic emotion: 'Today, 7 June, I, Viktor Akeyev, prisoner and former European boxing champion, wish to make the following statement in the interests of the country's security! I freely admit that over the last two years I have been involved with a gang of criminals. I would also like to inform you that the Head of the Chief Pharmaceutical Authority, Viktor Sysoyev, away at present on official business in the West, has taken with him diamonds to the value of 3,000,000 roubles or more, diamonds which belong to us!'

'Who is this "us"?' I asked.

'The Soviet State,' replied Akeyev solemnly.

'What do you mean? That you were guarding state property here?' I asked.

'He's a real bastard!' exclaimed Akeyev, forgetting his role as the saviour of state property for a moment. 'He got me to stand guard over valuables which belonged to the whole gang, whereas what was I really looking after? An empty hole in the wall! Meanwhile, he goes abroad with the whole bloody lot, the lousy swine! Anyway, I'm making a statement, Comrade Investigator! You ought to ring the KGB straight away to get them to arrest him in Geneva. And you can take my statement as proof of guilt.'

'But perhaps there never were any diamonds,' said Svetlov.

'Oh, yes there were, Comrade Colonel. I saw them myself. Before he left for abroad, I saw him insert the box into the safe with my own eyes. The box contained diamonds and hard currency, and we'd brought it over with us from the dacha. The next morning he left for the West.'

'Well, perhaps he hid them somewhere else?'

'Where? And leave me guarding an empty box? No, he took them away with him, Comrade Colonel. And they didn't belong only to him. They belonged to all of us, and I was supposed to be guarding them on everybody's behalf. Meanwhile he's having a whale of a time in the West, living on the proceeds, I tell you!'

'OK,' said Svetlov. 'We'll sort out the diamonds later. You tell me a few more things now you've got started. Where's Belkin? Is he alive?'

'Which Belkin?' asked Akeyev.

'The journalist, the one you forced into an ambulance at the Kursk station, along with Sultan from Baku.'

'Ah, that one!' said Akeyev, shrugging his shoulders.

'He was still alive while we were at the dacha. I don't know what happened to him after that.'

'Which dacha?'

'The one that belongs to the boss, Sysoyev, in Tsaritsyno.'

'What's the address?'

'Gagarin Lane, No. 72. Only you won't find him there now, of course. After Sultan escaped, they took the journalist away.'

'Where did they take him? And who did the taking?'

'Christ, I don't know, Comrade Colonel.'

Svetlov turned suddenly to Ozherelyev and said: 'Take a note of the address. Gagarin Lane, No. 72. Take some men and search the place right away!'

Then he turned back to Akeyev. 'Are there any secret hiding places at the dacha?'

'There's one. In the garage, beneath the sink. Only you'll find that empty now. We brought everything here, I tell you.'

Now that Akeyev had started to confess, he became really helpful and obliging, as often happens with criminals.

'Where might they have taken Belkin, and who took him?' asked Svetlov persistently. 'And don't forget that Belkin is more important to us today than the diamonds. If you can help us to find him, we'll reduce your sentence by half, I promise you!'

'But I wasn't one of those in charge, Comrade Colonel! They didn't report everything they did to me. When this boy Sultan from Baku managed to get away from the dacha, and the Old Man did him in on the railway, our boss told us to clear out of the dacha right away. I came here, but God knows what they did with the journalist. Most probably the doctor took him away. He had been carrying out experiments on him, after all.'

'Which doctor? What experiments?'

'You know, the doctor who caused the whole bloody mess. Him and the Old Man. The big bosses didn't know, but the two of them were dealing in a bit of opium on the side. They were taking a coffin full of the stuff from Mara to Baku via Tashkent, when the most stupid thing happened – the coffin burst open at the airport. It cost them 200,000 roubles to get the Baku Militia to hush the whole thing up. And everything would have been all right, if only this journalist hadn't got mixed up in it! Stupid bastard! He tried to get Sultan to spill the beans on everyone in *Komsomolskaya Pravda*. We arrived at the station with the goods to meet him, and there he is with a suitcase full of money. But guess who's waiting for him on the platform? That journalist again! So we had to push both of them into the ambulance, or else they would have gone to the newspaper offices right away. There was a girl with them as well, only she ran away . . .'

'Who else took part in the kidnapping? Don't try to conceal anything now. There were four of you, we've got witnesses. Quickly. Who's this doctor? What's his surname?'

'Honest, I don't know! They either called him Boris or doctor. He was from the same town as the journalist. I heard them say that a hundred times, when they were at the dacha.'

'So they were taken straight from the railway station to Sysoyev's dacha at Tsaritsyno, is that it?'

'Yes.'

'In the ambulance?'

'Yes.'

'What was its registration number?'

'The doctor had as many of them as you liked. He used to make them out of plastic, so you couldn't tell the difference between them and a metal one.'

'What were these experiments of his?'

'All sorts. He'd give you some gas to sniff, and it'd be great fun. You'd carry on laughing till your sides hurt. Or he'd give you an injection. Then you'd tell him everything you knew. You'd wake up an hour later unable to remember any of what you'd said. Or . . .'

'What did he do to Belkin?' I repeated impatiently.

'He wiped out his memory,' said Akeyev. 'He did the same thing to Sultan, too, only he escaped.'

'What do you mean, "wiped out his memory"?'

'Exactly what I say,' said Akeyev. 'By injecting them with something. I heard him swear to the boss that in three weeks the journalist wouldn't remember a thing, either about the coffin or about the dacha. He used to inject three lots of morphine a day into them, and some other drugs besides. I don't know which.'

Svetlov and I exchanged glances. Fifteen days had passed since Belkin had been abducted. The achievements of Soviet medicine have become well known from the accounts of open trials involving dissidents and those held in camera. Much secret research has also been conducted in psychiatric laboratories belonging to the military. I have no specialist knowledge in this sphere myself, but I have heard one or two things from the forensic experts I know. These days doctors have huge numbers of various psychotropic drugs at their disposal, and although they are most frequently employed in KGB investigations, what is there to stop somebody using such preparations for their own purposes? If we couldn't find Belkin by tomorrow or the next day, then we ran the risk of finding him with his memory totally erased. That would be a nice present for Brezhnev's press corps on the day he was due to meet Carter in Vienna!

'OK,' said Svetlov, going right up to Akeyev. 'What else do you know about this doctor? You'd better start remembering, and quick! What does he look like?'

'Well, he's fairly young, a bit on the fat side. He's got black hair and brown eyes, and wears a signet-ring on his right hand. That's all I can tell you about him.'

'Who else knows him?'

'Sysoyev, my boss.'

'I realize that, but he's out of the country. Who else? Herman Dolgo-Saburov?'

'He's out of town, too.'

Svetlov grinned. He'd caught Akeyev out. 'So how come you know Dolgo-Saburov?'

'Also through my boss. He works for him as well, bringing opium north and taking morphine down south. Only he won't tell you a thing about the doctor, never in a thousand years.'

'And why is that?'

'He's madly in love with the doctor's sister.'

'Have you seen her? Do you know her?'

'I should say so!' he replied, his eyes darting towards the silent Lena Smagina, who had her eyes closed and was slowly rocking from side to side in abject terror. 'She's another one like that whore! Good for nothing but screwing and going round all the night-bars! But she's good-looking, I'll grant you. You know what they say: pure in appearance but a whore underneath! That's all there is to her! But Herman comes from aristocratic stock. Once he'd fallen for her, all he could say was – Natasha Rostova! Natasha Rostova! But she's as much like Tolstoy's character as I'm like Tolstoy! She's a bitch, that's all there is to it!'

'What's her name? Where does she live? Does she work?'

'No, I don't know anything except that she's called Natasha. That's all. But this other bitch might know something, the two of them dragged me away to a restaurant a week ago.'

I went up to Smagina, but as soon as she opened her eyes, I could see that it would be a waste of time trying to get anything out of her. Her vacant eyes contained despair and nothing else.

'Don't waste your time,' said Svetlov, coming up to me. 'Let's go. We've got to deal with the nephew.'

Then he nodded towards Akeyev and Smagina. 'Take them away to Pshenichny, lads. He'll cross-examine them.'

16.42 hours
'Unbelievable! It's already five o'clock!' said Svetlov,

as he got into the police Mercedes waiting for us outside Sysoyev's flat on the Embankment. The car was a relatively new and unusual sight on the Moscow streets, and I need hardly add that it was surrounded by a swarm of inquisitive boys, peering in at all the windows, touching the bumpers and handles and asking the driver hundreds of questions. Svetlov shooed the most persistent of them away from the door and we climbed in. He sat back in the seat, exhausted. 'I haven't eaten all day!' he complained.

'Where to?' asked the driver cautiously.

'Just drive off, then we'll make up our minds.'

The radio telephone started to flash and bleep. It was obviously the Petrovka switchboard trying to get in touch.

'That's the fourth time they've tried to reach you,' said the driver, glancing down at the telephone as he started the motor.

Svetlov lifted the receiver and switched up the volume so that I could listen in as well.

'Lieutenant-Colonel Svetlov here. Hello?'

'Ah! At last we've got you, Comrade Colonel!' said the voice of Captain Laskin, in charge of the surveillance groups tailing the 'nephew'.

'All right, calm down,' said Svetlov. 'What's up?'

'This fellow's a maniac! He's distributed drugs to sixteen different places so far! Both Arbats. New and Old, the Hotels Belgrade and Ukraine, you name it! And everywhere he goes he picks up more money. I don't know, but he must have at least 100,000 by now!'

'OK, so where is he at the moment?'

'He's stuck in a lift, as you instructed.'

'What do you mean, "as I instructed"?'

'You told us to delay him for an hour or an hour and a half, until you were free. Well, he's been stuck in a lift for the past sixty-five minutes with the famous singer Slichenko.'

'Who did you say?' said Svetlov, visibly cheering up.

'It may seem funny to you, Comrade Colonel, but I've

got a major public disturbance on my hands. In order to delay him in the lift, I've had to cut off the electricity supply to the whole block, and it's an enormous place. There's a jeweller's on the ground floor, while the rest of it is filled with academicians, diplomats, famous singers and the like. And they've been without electric light for the last hour!'

'All right, I'll make sure you get a reward for inventiveness!' said Svetlov. 'Hang on a bit longer. I'm on my way. Where exactly are you?'

'Right outside the building, colonel. We've got an old electrical repair van drawn up, and we've cordoned off the area. I've got pneumatic drills tearing up the asphalt to make it look as if we're looking for an electric cable.'

'OK! Pneumatic drills, eh! And what was the nephew doing in the building?'

'He'd just called on the hockey player, Zhluptov. He left the last package of morphine with him. It's already five o'clock, and he needs to get to the hairdresser's . . .'

'All right. Switch off for now. I'll be with you in five minutes.'

Then Svetlov asked the operator to put him through to the Incident Room. 'They're trying to get through to you themselves,' she replied. Then we could hear the voice of Svetlov's assistant coming over the radio.

'Comrade Colonel! The Moscow Energy Department have really been getting on my nerves!'

'I know, I know! Tell them that we'll have the cable repaired in five minutes. And listen. Is Colonel Maryamov there?'

'Yes. He's taking a snooze in the corner.'

'Wake him up! Tell him to get the chief steward along to the Enchantress hair salon as quickly as possible. He's waiting downstairs. I'll come after them straight away. Any questions?'

'No, colonel! Everything's clear.'

Svetlov switched off the radio and looked at me.

'Well, let's go through everything once more. We've got two choices. Either we arrest the nephew now and bring him face to face with Akeyev and all those to whom he's just distributed drugs. Large-scale drug-trafficking is punishable under Article 224 and he'll get fifteen years. Do you think he'll give away the doctor?'

'Well, he might,' I replied, none too sure of the answer. In favour was the fact that we had incontrovertible evidence linking him with the illegal sale and distribution of narcotics. Against was Dolgo-Saburov's aristocratic background. He was the direct descendant of an ancient and noble family, after all, and yet the reality of life in the Soviet Union had turned him into a railway employee! This very fact might turn somebody like Dolgo-Saburov to crime, and it would have been a conscious decision on his part, too, without any feeling of guilt. He might well not betray his accomplices. And if you added the fact that he was in love with the doctor's sister, as Akeyev had just informed us, well ... It was quite possible that you wouldn't scare him by threatening him with Article 224.

I remembered the telephone conversation I had had in Dolgo-Saburov's flat with this anonymous woman. The tone had been intimate and there had been something enticing about her. I had no doubt now that I had been talking to Natasha and that she was the one with whom Belkin had fallen in love at the airport in Baku. *Cherchez la femme!* as they say ...

'The other possibility,' Svetlov was commenting meanwhile, 'is that I do the same thing with the nephew as Ozherelyev did with Smagina. The CID is after the whole gang, I could say, but the one who reveals the whereabouts of Belkin will get off scot-free.'

'I don't think he'd betray the others,' I said. 'He is a count, after all ...'

'OK. Let's say he didn't take the bait and didn't provide us with Belkin's address. He might take measures to get in touch with the doctor and his sister . . .'

'But they may well know what's going on already. I told you before that it was a woman who phoned up Dolgo-Saburov's flat. I had a few words with her, and I'm sure that it was this Natasha. And what she told me she will already have told her brother, it goes without saying.'

'Well, so what? Dolgo-Saburov doesn't know that! That's why he may well try to warn them!'

'All right,' I said. 'Do it that way if you must. After all, what have we got to lose?

We were already zooming down the Novy Arbat. In the distance we could see the 'electricity repair team' of Captain Laskin and his group standing outside the 'Agate' jeweller's. Meanwhile, a couple of real repair workers, called out by Laskin, were breaking up the asphalt with real pneumatic drills.

We arrived. Svetlov ordered them to finish the 'repair work' and went off to the hair salon to meet the chief steward. When Irakly Golub arrived a couple of minutes later, accompanied by Maryamov, Svetlov ordered Laskin to start up the lift again. Everything was ready for the 'nephew's' reception. The agents disguised as electricians and road repair men were hanging about outside the building, while Svetlov and Irakly Golub were walking up and down outside the Enchantress hair salon. I was sitting in Captain Laskin's car, waiting to see what would happen.

Finally, Herman Dolgo-Saburov walked out of the entrance, accompanied by the famous gipsy singer, Nikolay Slichenko. They said a friendly farewell to each other and then walked quickly towards their respective cars. That Slichenko should have been in a hurry to get to his Volga was understandable, but why should Dolgo-Saburov have been rushing towards his Zhiguli estate if all he had to do to reach the hair-dresser's was cross the road? Perhaps he needed to get something? No, there he was, sitting down in the driver's seat and slamming the door. A cloud of exhaust fumes came out of the back of the car and off he rushed, at top speed.

I looked at Laskin anxiously. Frowning deeply, he tried to move his repair van into the stream of traffic, but because nobody knew that it was a police vehicle, the other cars wouldn't let us out, as if on purpose. As we passed, some of the 'repair men' jumped into the van through the open door. I grabbed the microphone of the radio telephone, and called Svetlov.

'Marat, Shamrayev here! Something's gone wrong! He's driving past the hair salon. I can still see him, but he'll disappear before long!'

'He's not going to disappear anywhere!' said Laskin and flipped the switch on some instrument or other – the van was equipped with all kinds of apparatus, none of it having anything to do with electrical repairs of the ordinary kind. However, it had everything to do with periscopic vision and the long-distance monitoring and recording of conversations between suspects. The instrument which Laskin had switched on immediately began to bleep and a point of light suddenly began to flicker and move on the screen of a portable direction-finder.

'No, he won't disappear anywhere,' said Laskin. 'There's a homing device underneath the chassis and a microphone inside the car. He's been carrying them around since this morning. We managed to fix them on at the marshalling-yards. Now I suppose he'll begin driving all over Moscow again . . .'

The flickering light on the screen did a sudden U-turn to the right. 'He's turned on to the Dragomilov Embankment next to the Hotel Ukraine,' said Captain Laskin, as he accelerated. Travelling alongside us I could see a black, unmarked Volga carrying Marat Svetlov. He looked gloomy.

Dolgo-Saburov's car had stopped at the traffic-lights, and we came to a halt about five cars behind him. Svetlov quickly transferred to our repair van.

'Where's he going now?' he asked Laskin in a disgruntled voice.

'Shall I get out and ask him?' asked Laskin with a grin.

'A whole day's preparations turn out to be a total waste of time!' grumbled Svetlov on behalf of both of us. 'We set up the chief steward for him, we have one of his women waiting for him at the beauty salon, and what does he do . . .? Quick, off we go! Put your foot down!'

As soon as the lights changed to green, Dolgo-Saburov's car was away heading towards the Kiev railway station and doing far more than the official speed limit. We kept behind him at the same distance. Nobody said a word.

'Why can't I hear him?' asked Svetlov at last. 'Doesn't he even cough occasionally?'

'Well, he's got some English-language tapes that he switches on, whenever he goes anywhere,' said Laskin. 'It drives you mad, listening to them all day. Switch it on, Sasha,' he said to one of the technicians who was sitting somewhere in the depths of the van. And sure enough, we could immediately hear a metallic voice pronouncing English-language drills and then giving their Russian translation. 'He spends the whole day travelling around Moscow,' said Laskin, 'and listens to nothing else . . . *I have been, she has been* . . . Even I've managed to pick it up!'

Laskin suddenly brought the van to an unexpected halt. Dolgo-Saburov had stopped a little way ahead, right beneath the clock at the Kiev station, and the shapely figure of a woman dressed in a light summer raincoat slipped into the car. I looked up at the sky. It did look as if it was about to rain. What with running all over the place, you don't notice petty details like the weather. The English lesson was switched off. There came the sound of a quick kiss, followed by a voice which I had heard once before.

'Well, you're a real sod! I've been waiting there forty

271

minutes. I didn't know what to think. Couldn't you at least have rung?'

The car moved off and turned right, in the direction of the Lenin Hills. We listened to the rest of their conversation with increasing interest, while the technician made sure that every word was recorded on tape.

'I couldn't ring you or do anything!' said Dolgo-Saburov. 'I spent a whole hour stuck in a lift on the Arbat. But at least I had Slichenko to talk to, that was something!'

'Who?'

'Slichenko, the singer. Anyway, that's enough of that. What have you got to report?'

'I couldn't find out anything else. Katya came off her shift this morning. Still, you've got one thing to thank me for. When I rang through to your place this morning, I nearly fell into a trap. The fuzz was already there, waiting at your flat. "Come on, you sod," I said. 'Are you still asleep?" It was you I had in mind, of course . . .'

Svetlov looked at me and grinned. There aren't many women who can swear and get away with it, in my opinion. Usually only the most beautiful can pull it off, and not all of them possess the art. Here was obviously one of those cases, however . . .

'Well, what could they have on me?' said Dolgo-Saburov. 'There were no drugs left at the flat by then. Morphine, opium – I'd removed the lot, and they missed it first time round! I didn't kill my aunt, either. So I'm clean. The old man is a vicious sod, though! Why did he have to choke her to death? She would have given me everything herself, if I'd asked.'

'But he was only trying to frighten her . . .'

'Frighten her? I should say so! I can imagine what his "frightening" is like! Never mind! She'd lived her life . . . It's a pity, though, as it's thanks to her that we're in such an almighty hurry now with the police sniffing around everywhere.'

'Why do you say that? Nobody's panicking yet! It's

only the boxer and the old man they're looking for. The old man is a long way away, and it'll be some time before they run the boxer to ground. He's sitting in the flat guarding an empty safe and never goes outside. Even Lena he lets come to see him only every three days at prearranged times.'

'Listen, you're talking as if it's the most ordinary thing in the world,' said Dolgo-Saburov. 'But do you realize that we're driving through Moscow now for the last time?'

'So what? I couldn't care a fig. I know every last inch of the place anyway, and we've got the whole world before us!'

'But I love Moscow. If it wasn't for this Soviet government – may they rot in hell! – I wouldn't leave the place in a million years.'

'Not even with me?'

'You just wait, Natasha. As soon as you get your cut in the West, you'll want to get away from me as fast as you can.'

'Idiot! I love you! Don't get scared, count! I really do. Everything's going to turn out just fine.' She must have been smiling, and then we could hear the sound of another kiss. 'And what a life it's going to be, darling!'

'You know, I wouldn't be too sure about that!'

'Why are you being so horrible today?'

'You'd be horrible, too, if on a day like this you'd just had to spend an hour stuck in a lift! That cost me 5,000 roubles, you know! I had no time to call off at the hair salon.'

'Ah, so that's what's eating you! You didn't get to see that "enchantress" of yours! Well, you only have to say the word. We can always drive back there.'

'I can't. Boris told us to arrive no later than seven o'clock, or else we'd miss the plane. You haven't even brought a suitcase with you . . .'

'Boris has got all my things already. How much did you manage to collect today?'

'Ninety-two thousand. To hell with it! We've enough for the flight out, anyway!

'Let me look at the telegram.'

'Don't be daft! I managed to eat it up this morning, while the carriage was being searched.'

When I heard this, I could feel my cheeks turning red, although Svetlov didn't even glance in my direction. I had been searching for the aunt's jewels, after all, so what was the point in looking in his mouth?

'But can you at least remember what it said?' asked Natasha, to my extreme relief and satisfaction.

' "Dowry costs 200, wedding in a week. Fly out with money urgently. Dad," ' said Dolgo-Saburov. 'All clear?'

'Yes,' replied Natasha. 'It means that for 200,000 roubles he's managed to bribe the commander at the frontier post or somebody at the aerodrome. We'll be on our way in a week's time, but meanwhile he needs the money urgently.'

'He's got a hundred himself already. I managed to collect ninety today, and Boris has got another fifty. So we've got enough for the journey out, and the rest of it is no good to us, as we'll need hard currency after that. How much did Sysoyev have in the safe?'

'Didn't the old man tell you, or are you just checking?'

'How the hell should I know what you do? You may all have agreed to pocket some of my share for all I know!'

'You're impossible! I love you, you idiot, can't you see? Boris and the old man might have come to some private arrangement when they opened the safe, but can you really imagine Boris doing so behind my back?'

'Well, I've learnt to expect anything of your brother . . .'

'You'll get a black eye in a minute, count!' said Natasha in a serious voice. 'Boris is a genius! Can you imagine anybody else getting us out of that scrape with that stupid coffin of yours? Do you know what Sysoyev told Boris under hypnosis at the time?'

'I know. I heard about it. Only nobody else was

present, so perhaps your Boris invented it all. Perhaps Sysoyev was never under hypnosis at all.'

'Idiot! In that case, how did he discover the combination to the safe?'

'Well, I don't know . . .' said Dolgo-Saburov slowly. 'OK, let's assume that he did drag that out of him under hypnosis. There's no guarantee that he didn't simply invent the rest of it to drag the rest of us into the affair – you, me and the old man.'

'OK. You can get out now, if you like! Right away. We'll arrive at Boris's place, you get your cut, and off you go.'

'No, now that you're all about to make off with Sysoyev's diamonds, they're bound to nail me. So I'm going to see this one through with the rest of you – to the very end. It's just that it's so like the sort of thing you see in the cinema – fleeing across the border with a load of diamonds . . .'

'Keep your trap shut! In films, people who try to escape across the border always get caught. That's because the censorship won't have it any other way. A film director told me all about it once. Otherwise the film won't get a public showing . . .'

'Did you go to bed with him?'

'With whom?'

'This film director of yours.'

'Oh, God! What's that got to do with anything, count? Just remember this. Whether you like Moscow or not, whether you want to go abroad with me or not, we can't stay here any longer, any of us – and that's all your fault, not ours. It's all because of that stupid idea of yours about the coffin!'

'Why was it stupid?' asked Dolgo-Saburov, flaring up suddenly. 'In the end it was thanks to the coffin that we came across Belkin with those frontier passes of his. If it weren't for them, the old man wouldn't be on the border waiting already. It's an ill wind . . .'

Svetlov seemed to be taking in every word, and so was I. We were both sitting glued to the loudspeaker,

275

so as not to miss a single word, or intonation, or nuance. This was better than any cross-examination, and we only wished that it could go on for a bit longer. Suddenly we heard the woman's voice say: 'Don't go so fast! Just look at that rain!'

She was quite right. There was a regular June cloudburst thundering down on to the streets of south-west Moscow, whither Dolgo-Saburov's Zhiguli estate car and our own unmarked police Volgas and 'repair van' were bound.

'Don't worry, countess,' said Dolgo-Saburov. 'We're all going to come out of this alive.'

'Quite right,' said Natasha with a laugh. 'We ought to kiss my brother's feet. Sysoyev's band was ready to bump us all off, thanks to your conspiracy over the coffin.'

'They're bastards, all of them, of course!' said Dolgo-Saburov. 'They're able to get narcotics across the border, and hold Swiss bank accounts and use government money to make official trips abroad! Brezhnev's son even managed to hire a yacht and go elephant-hunting in Africa! Ah well! It doesn't matter. We'll meet them all soon enough. Sysoyev, Balayan and the rest are bound to travel abroad again some time. I'd give up any number of diamonds to get them when they do! They'll get what they deserve, those fucking "servants of the Soviet people"! I'll beat the living daylights out of them!'

'I don't think you've quite understood,' said the woman's voice slowly. She was obviously taking a long drag at a cigarette. 'Boris has a completely different idea. Listen! If somebody like Sysoyev or Balayan comes to the West on official business, we'll be able to find out where they are from the newspapers. Then we can kidnap them, as we did this Belkin, and force them to reveal the numbers of their Swiss bank accounts. They won't even be able to report it to the police. If they did, they wouldn't be able to return to the Soviet Union. It's a pity that we won't have time to get Sysoyev in

Geneva. while he's there at the moment . . .'

'Not bad!' said Svetlov, with a whistle. 'The cinema has got nothing on this crowd! This is a useful tape, I must say,' he added, nodding in the direction of the recorder.

Suddenly we could hear the sound of Dolgo-Saburov's own tape recorder being switched on. Here came the English lessons once again. They weren't on for long this time, however. We could soon hear Natasha saying: 'What's that?'

'It's English,' came the reply. 'I'm learning.'

'God, you gave me a fright!' said Natasha. 'I suddenly wondered whose voice it was. Listen, darling, I'll teach you English and French, don't worry. *Je veux traverser la frontière* . . . Haven't you got any music?'

'What did you say just now?' asked Dolgo-Saburov. He'd just switched on some jazz, but not very loudly, and we could still catch what he was saying. In fact, with the jazz playing softly in the background, the whole conversation sounded more like a movie sound-track than ever!

'I said: *Je veux traverser la frontière! Honte à vous, monsieur le comte!* I know French and English, Boris knows English, and even the old man, a convict and professional crook, knows Azerbaidzhani! But you . . . What about all your nannies and governesses?'

'But that's the point,' came the reply. 'My governesses first got bumped off in 1917 and then they had a second go at them in 1937 – before I was born!'

'*À propos, mon chéri*, at least Soviet power will have given me something. Without it I could only have been a nanny to your children, whereas now I have the chance of becoming a real countess . . .'

Now that they had begun to talk about less important things, we were able to think about something else and analyse the information received. So, the four of them – Dr Boris (we did not know his surname, but in Belkin's manuscript he figures as Ziyalov), his sister Natasha, the old man (alias the Chief or Semyon

Gridasov) and Herman Dolgo-Saburov – each had a place in the gang which was selling drugs on the black market. The head of the gang was Viktor Sysoyev, who was also the head of the Chief Pharmaceutical Authority. Above him was somebody else called Balayan, and the involvement of even higher-placed officials couldn't be ruled out. Sysoyev seemed to look after the money, however. The scale of their drug-trafficking organization was enormous, as were the sums of money involved. These were converted either into jewels or hard currency, which was then, somehow or other, transferred abroad. We would have to pass this information on to Malenina and the KGB, of course – it was really their department. Meanwhile, my characters seemed to have had a little game going on the side. Unbeknown to their bosses they had tried to move a coffin filled with drugs from Central Asia to Baku and had stood to make 1,000,000 roubles from the deal. Hence the risks which they had been willing to take. The bosses didn't look kindly on such private enterprise. In that, Natasha was absolutely correct. So was Dolgo-Saburov. If he stayed in Russia and was arrested, they would finish him off, no matter what camp he was sent to. 'Traitors', informers or people who simply know too much are all treated the same way sooner or later. The Main Directorate of Corrective Labour Institutions is always receiving short messages such as, 'Prisoner so-and-so died while felling trees through the misuse of mechanical equipment,' or words to that effect.

So, I thought, if they really had found out from Sysoyev, while he was under hypnosis, that the big bosses had decided on their liquidation, then there was no hope for them inside the Soviet Union. In that case, we'd have to give special thought to the future of Akeyev. Whether we arrested the whole gang, or whether once again we wouldn't be allowed to touch the people right at the top and they would be given special treatment, we would have to fix Akeyev up, come what may, in a special camp for high party workers. At least he'd have a quiet life there. Two such camps were set up ten years ago. Although it isn't customary to talk about them, they do exist. After all, there has to be somewhere where you can lock up erring party workers, city council presidents and secretaries, militia chiefs, prosecutors and so on, when their misdemeanours become so obvious to the public at large that the CPSU Central Committee itself sanctions their arrest. To put them in ordinary prison camps would be tantamount to condemning them to death, because the other prisoners would finish them off sooner or later. So it is that the privileged caste in our country even has its own privileged camps and prisons . . .

As far as Dolgo-Saburov and company were concerned, their part in the gang's activities seemed more or less clear. Dolgo-Saburov was one of the people who transported the drugs around the country. Gridasov organized a market for selling the merchandise in Baku. And Akeyev was the person used by Sysoyev to keep an eye on the criminal proceeds and on the drugs themselves as they were stolen from the pharmaceutical warehouses or brought up from the south. At the same time, he had involved his mistress, Lena Smagina, in the drug-peddling, just as Dolgo-Saburov had involved the girl Zoya from the Enchantress beauty salon. As far as the doctor and his sister were concerned, though, it still remained to work out their part in the whole affair. What was certain was that the frontier passes, which Belkin had so light-heartedly neglected to return to the Chief Border Police Authority in Tashkent, had fallen into their hands, most probably in Baku, when they had disappeared from the airport carrying his identity papers. By the way, it was interesting that Belkin hadn't mentioned the disappearance of the frontier passes in his manuscript. Fine fellow he was! But when their scheme to import extra opium in a coffin literally fell apart and the gang

279

leaders had decided to deal with the infringement in their own way, then those border passes of Belkin's came in very handy. That was when they came up with the idea of stealing the diamonds belonging to the whole gang from the safe and escaping abroad with them. With this in mind, they enticed Akeyev out of the flat for a couple of hours and got him to go to the Prague restaurant. Meanwhile, they cleaned out the safe. One thief stealing from another! Apart from that – you might as well make hay while the sun shines! – Gridasov smothered the nephew's aunt to death so as to lay hands on the last (or rather, next to last) diamonds belonging to the Dolgo-Saburov family. After this, Gridasov flew to Uzbekistan where he made use of Belkin's passes to get to the airport at Charshanga. He'd probably altered the surname. The important thing was to have the pass itself, duly signed by the commander of the Border Regiment, Central Asia Military Region. For 200,000 roubles he'd also managed to bribe the chief officer at the frontier post or one of the helicopter pilots.

Perhaps he'd bribed them all. After all, 200,000 is a lot of money. The telegram reached Dolgo-Saburov while he was travelling with his train from Tashkent to Moscow. He could have been given it at any of the stations en route. And that was why he had spent all day rushing round Moscow, putting together 100,000 roubles. He'd sold all the stocks of drugs that he'd had available and had probably wanted to get some more from the pharmaceutical warehouse to make some more cash that day. He'd managed to collect 90,000, the doctor had 40,000 more, and he was supposed to arrive at his place no later than seven o'clock that evening, so as to rejoin Gridasov by air in Central Asia. They wouldn't be travelling anywhere now, of course. When a detective is pitting his wits against a criminal, the most important thing is to keep at least one step ahead of your opponent. Over the last four days, apart from a few details, we'd learnt practically all that we needed to know about this particular criminal gang, and in some respects we had more information than they did. For example, they didn't know anything about Akeyev's arrest so far, or that he had confessed everything. Nor did they realize that we were following Dolgo-Saburov's every step or that we were tailing him at that very moment. Through him we would finally get to this 'genius' of a doctor who was trying to erase Belkin's memory.

Of course, we'd made a fair number of mistakes ourselves during the investigation, and we'd wasted a large amount of time with those stupid searches of Dolgo-Saburov's flat and railway carriage. The way I'd missed the drugs concealed in the honeycombs was simply shameful, as was the way we'd slipped up over the telegram that the old man had managed to send Dolgo-Saburov. The whole business with Irakly Golub had been a waste of time, too, and there were other things besides ... Still, nothing ventured, nothing gained! And to make up for it we had some of Belkin's kidnappers before us. We could see them and hear what they were saying. We were following them at about half a mile's distance. We didn't want to get any closer in case they became alarmed. And there they were, leading us to their hideout. Soon we'd know the one thing of which we were still in ignorance – whether Belkin was alive, and, if so, where and in what condition. Still, don't be in too much of a hurry, Chief Prosecutor, you'll get them all in good time ...

The rain was easing up as we sped down Sevastopol Prospect towards the outskirts of Moscow and the Outer Ring Road. Dolgo-Saburov and Natasha were seated comfortably in their car, listening to jazz music and making plans for their future life together in France. I soon realized that what they were most afraid of was not the actual crossing of the border, but what might happen to them during their first day in Afghanistan. They could easily get robbed, and, according to Natasha, the only thing that would save them was the fact that Gridasov and Boris had a knowledge of Azerbaidzhani, which to all intents and purposes was the same as Turkish. Even Natasha knew a little. She and her brother had grown up in Baku, after all.

'Well, that's not the only thing,' said Dolgo-Saburov. 'Look! I've got this nine-cylinder automatic with me, and that's no toy!'

'And what about me?' Natasha immediately exclaimed.

'You don't need one. The old man's got a Kalashnikov and Boris has got a Tokaryov revolver, so we'll manage to protect you somehow or other.'

Svetlov looked at Captain Laskin and then at me. Frowning, he grabbed the radio telephone and said to the two police Volgas that were following us: 'Attention! All men are to put on bullet-proof jackets and to have their weapons at the ready. There may be some shooting.'

'Perhaps we ought to wait until they start making love, Comrade Colonel,' came a voice from one of the cars.

'No jokes, thank you very much!' replied Svetlov.

Then he contacted the chief duty officer at Petrovka Operations. 'Colonel Serebryannikov, I am in pursuit of two armed criminals. I am about to drive out of Moscow on the Kaluga Highway. It's not clear yet when and where we will arrest the gang. I'm sitting on their tail at present, waiting for them to lead us to their hideout. There may be gunfire during the actual arrest. Please have an ambulance sent right away.'

'Do you need any more men?' asked the colonel, who was one of the old guard at CID headquarters.

'No, thank you. We'll manage. There are eight of us and only two of them. We should be able to do it.'

'All the same, it would be better if you could avoid using firearms.'

'I know.'

'I'll have a helicopter flying overhead, just in case.'

'There's no point, colonel. It may frighten them.'

'It'll be one of those belonging to the Transport Police. They've been circling over the Ring Road for years. Drivers are used to them.'

'All right, only tell the pilot not to fly low, unless I give the order.'

'Keep in direct contact from now on. Report back every minute.'

The operation was now approaching its climax, and I could imagine the scene at Operations. All those who had nothing else to do would be standing around the main radio console, listening to what was going on. Meanwhile, an ambulance was almost certainly on its way from the nearest hospital and a helicopter manned by armed CID men would be about to leave from Domodedovo airport. Svetlov was now supposed to report on the progress of the operation every sixty seconds. The four men sitting at the back of the 'repair van' had already donned their bullet-proof jackets and had released the safety catches on their revolvers. One of them offered a couple of jackets to Svetlov and myself, and without saying a word, we began to put them on.

It was all very businesslike, one might almost say routine, even though the next few minutes might see any or all of us blasted into the next world or, at the very least, into casualty at the Sklifosovsky hospital. And in the background all the time we could hear cheerful jazz music coming from Dolgo-Saburov's blue Zhiguli estate, which we could see travelling along way ahead of us down the Kaluga Highway. I looked at my watch. It was twenty past six. I could hear the voice of Captain Serebryannikov saying: 'Marat, an ambulance is on its way to you from the nearest hospital. It should be at your disposal in three of four minutes. The helicopter will arrive in about one minute. I have radio contact with both of them. Report on your situation.'

'Everything is normal at the moment, Comrade Colonel. I am continuing to follow the suspects. We are now approaching the Ring Road, and the suspects are about to pass the State Automobile Inspection post at the exit to the city.'

But Svetlov's tone of voice suddenly changed: 'Fuck it! What the hell's he doing?'

'What's wrong, Marat?' asked Serebryannikov anxiously.

'A bloody militiaman has stopped the suspects' car!' shouted Svetlov. 'Quick, colonel, get on to the Transport Police and tell them to stop him! Put the brakes on, Laskin!'

Laskin signalled to the drivers of the two following Volgas, and we all pulled in to the side of the road to await developments. Ahead of us something was happening that we could not have foreseen. The militiaman had been standing by the side of the road, waving Dolgo-Saburov's car down with his baton. Now he walked idly over to the Zhiguli and the usual policeman-driver exchange got under way.

'You were speeding, comrade.'

'Oh no I wasn't, captain,' replied Dolgo-Saburov, trying to put on a jocular tone.

'Give him the three roubles,' whispered Natasha.

'You just look at this,' said the captain, showing him the speed-trap. 'You were doing thirty-three miles an hour and the speed limit is thirty. Are you going to pay the fine right away, or shall I have to draw up a summons?'

'I'll pay it now,' said Dolgo-Saburov, without hesitating.

'Give him a ten-rouble note,' whispered Natasha once again.

'I will, I will, don't worry,' said Dolgo-Saburov, just as softly. 'Here you are, Comrade Captain.'

'Let me see your papers,' said the officer.

'Surely there's no need for that, captain. We're in a hurry, honestly! Here's a ten. There's no need to bother with a receipt, and I don't want the change.'

'I want to see your papers – now,' said the captain more harshly.

'Fuck it!' shouted Svetlov, hammering his fist against the car seat. 'For Christ's sake, take the bribe, you son of a bitch! Take the bribe!'

Then he grabbed the microphone and shouted: 'Colonel! What on earth is this traffic policeman doing? Get someone to order him to take the bribe and let the Zhiguli go!'

'They're ringing him now,' replied Colonel Serebryannikov. 'We'll soon get it sorted out.'

'Like hell they are! If they were ringing him, he would have heard!'

'Come on, be quick about it!' said the officer. 'I can hear my phone ringing. Or don't you have any papers?'

'What do you mean, captain? Of course I do! Here they are. It's just that we're in a hurry. I wish you'd taken the ten roubles.'

'We'll take the money, all in good time, Comrade er . . . What's your surname? Ah yes . . . Dolgo-Saburov. That's interesting. Herman Veniaminovich Dolgo-Saburov. A fellow-officer of mine will be along in a moment. I'd like you to go with him to headquarters. They want to have a word with you . . . OK, I'm coming, I'm coming,' he said, in the direction of the telephone. 'As for you,' he said to Dolgo-Saburov, 'drive off the roadway and pull up in front of the booth, as quickly as you can.'

'All right . . .!'

We saw the Zhiguli slowly move off the roadway to where the captain had directed. He, meanwhile, was heading towards his booth.

'That's that then,' said Natasha. 'We're caught.'

'Don't worry,' replied Dolgo-Saburov. 'Don't look back. I can see him in the front mirror.'

'What are you going to do? Go to his headquarters? He didn't say that by accident, you know . . .'

'I'm not going anywhere,' he said. 'Don't worry . . .'

Everybody's eyes were now fixed on the movements

of the militiaman, ours from a distance, Dolgo-Saburov's from close to. There was nothing we could do about it. This over-efficient traffic cop had obviously remembered the signal that went out that morning about keeping an eye open for Dolgo-Saburov. It was an unusual name which must have stuck in his memory. As for the rest of the message, however – that the suspect was not to be apprehended, but merely have his whereabouts reported to CID Operations – it had completely evaporated during the course of a long and busy working day. It had been swallowed up in the routine mass of orders and instructions with which a militiaman has to deal. Who was there to complain to? The matter was in the hands of God – and Dolgo-Saburov. The moment the captain reached his booth and his back was turned to the Zhiguli, Dolgo-Saburov drove off as silently as he could. But the officer obviously felt or heard something suspicious, because he turned around and shouted something in the direction of the disappearing car. Given another few seconds, he would have had time to answer the telephone and then let Dolgo-Saburov go, after extracting the relevant fine. In that event, things would have turned out differently for everybody, but there it was . . .

'There you are! You'll get nothing out of us!' Dolgo-Saburov shouted exultantly, as his car flew on to the roadway and hurtled away at top speed. The militia officer immediately jumped on his motor-bike and took off in hot pursuit.

'That's that then!' said Svetlov in a fit of temper. 'The whole operation's fucked up!' Then he ordered Laskin to follow Dolgo-Saburov and the militiaman.

'Svetlov, give us a report on what's happening,' said a voice over the radio. 'The traffic inspection post isn't replying!'

'Well, what is there to tell you?' said Svetlov angrily. 'It's all cocked up! That idiot of a transport cop has left his post and has gone after the suspects on his motor-bike. They are armed and may take a potshot at him any moment. The whole operation's been a waste of time. We'll have to reveal our presence so the criminals know it's useless to shoot. Where's this helicopter of yours?'

'It should be almost with you. Give me your bearings and a description of the suspects' car.'

'We're on the Kaluga Highway, south of the Ring Road. Right out front is a dark-blue Zhiguli estate. Then there's the motor-bike, then our repair van, and finally two black Volgas. Only tell the men in the helicopter not to take aim at the driver and his passenger. We need them alive!'

'OK. Can you see the chopper yet?'

Approaching at low altitude from the south we could indeed see a MIL–6 helicopter heading towards us. 'Yes.'

Meanwhile, the gap between the Zhiguli and the motor-bike was closing. From inside Dolgo-Saburov's car we could hear the sound of a verbal struggle.

'Don't shoot him!'

'Don't interfere!' said Dolgo-Saburov grimly.

'Don't shoot, Herman!'

'Don't interfere, I said! Keep your hands away!'

Laskin had his foot planted firmly on the accelerator, and we were doing well over 85 m.p.h. as Svetlov switched on the siren. The two police Volgas had supercharged engines, so they had already overtaken us and drawn level with the motor-bike. The captain looked round in amazement. He probably realized that he had an important customer on his hands, so he redoubled his efforts and increased his speed.

Dolgo-Saburov's estate car had also reached its top speed of 90 m.p.h. The other cars on the highway kept well out of the way of the chase. The vehicles involved drew closer and closer together, and there was the helicopter flying right overhead to help, if need be.

Suddenly, we heard Dolgo-Saburov speaking again:

'Turn off that bloody jazz, for Christ's sake!'

The music suddenly stopped and then we could hear Natasha's voice: 'Look! Just look how many of them there are! Don't shoot, you fool!'

Suddenly there was the sound of a shot. The noise of Dolgo-Saburov firing came over the radio. But he missed his target. He was simply shooting over the shoulder at random, simultaneously keeping one hand on the steering wheel and his foot on the accelerator. Natasha was in hysterics.

'Herman, Herman! What are you doing? We'll be killed! Stop!'

'Shut up, you whore!'

'Herman! I'm begging you! Darling, please! Look, there's a helicopter above us too. We're surrounded ... Stop!!'

'Like hell I will! Did you sleep with Balayan? I bet you did! And with Sysoyev? And with Vekilov in Baku! You'd go to bed with the bloody pigs to save your brother! It's too late now! We're going to die, the two of us!'

Between us, the Volgas and the motor-bike, we had Dolgo-Saburov's car hemmed in, with the chopper thundering along just over our heads. Over the radio Svetlov kept shouting: 'Don't shoot! Don't shoot!' The Zhiguli suddenly lurched sharply to the left and was heading towards a tip-up lorry coming along on the opposite side of the highway. By some miracle the terrified lorry driver managed to avoid a head-on collision at the last moment. The lorry crashed through the ditch by the side of the road and turned over on its side. The helicopter immediately flew ahead, one of the CID men in it using a loudspeaker to try to halt all traffic along the highway. We could hear Natasha's heart-rending scream of terror as Dolgo-Saburov drove full speed into the next vehicle coming along the road, a cement-carrier crawling slowly in the outer lane.

We were travelling at such a speed ourselves that we shot right past the place where the accident happened, but Laskin slammed on the brakes and we swung back in a U-turn. The cement-carrier was leaning to one side and under its wheels we could see all that was left of the Zhiguli estate car and its two passengers – part of the back section, which had concertinaed on impact, and a heap of twisted metal, bits of body and human intestine. There was blood everywhere. A few drops of petrol were dripping out on to the roadway from the shattered petrol tank.

The helicopter landed a few yards away, and the CID men who had been flying in it bounded towards us. Inquisitive drivers and passengers, halted by the accident, came running up from all sides. Some distance away the ambulance had arrived and the medical orderlies were busying themselves with the driver of the overturned tip-up lorry. The terrified young driver of the cement-carrier meanwhile slowly picked his way out of his cab. When he saw the mish-mash of mangled bodies and metal under his lorry, he rushed to the side of the road to be sick.

The militia captain had tried to do an about turn but had driven his motor-bike into a ditch. He lifted himself off the ground, switched off his engine and slowly limped towards us. He was as white as a sheet, and his lips looked grey without a trace of blood in them. As he looked at the remains of the Zhiguli estate he couldn't help saying: 'What a bastard!'

'You're a fool, captain,' said Svetlov quietly.

Then he turned to Laskin and myself. 'There's nothing else for us to do here. Let's go. We must arrest all those who bought drugs off him today, and as quickly as possible. One of them may know who the doctor is. Am I right?' he asked, addressing himself to me.

I nodded in agreement. I wanted to get away as quickly as possible anyway. I've seen some things in my time. I've been in any number of morgues, and visiting the scenes of fires, accidents and catastrophes in general is part of my job. All the same, to hear two people talking to each other one minute – about their love, their jealousy, their plans for the future – and to see a shapeless mass of twisted metal and mangled human remains the next ... I can hear the girl's final, despairing scream ringing in my ears to this day.

20.42 hours

Major Ozherelyev would be waiting for us in the Incident Room, but I left for there alone. Svetlov, Laskin and the others went off directly to the Arbat and all the other addresses which Dolgo-Saburov had visited during the day to sell drugs. There were at least seventeen people for them to arrest, including Zoya the Enchantress, and if any one of them were to confess right away and start naming names, there would be even more pushers to nab as well. If they had known Dolgo-Saburov, it was difficult to believe they wouldn't also know this 'Dr' Boris, and at least be able to tell us his surname, where he lived, where he worked.

It had been quite a day! It had started at five in the morning with the search of Dolgo-Saburov's sleeping-car. Then I had visited Anti-Fraud Squad headquarters, and gone on to search Dolgo-Saburov's flat for the second time. After that there had been the whole business with the arrest of Akeyev and his mistress, Lena Smagina. And just when we thought that we were on the point of arresting the doctor and discovering the actual whereabouts of Belkin, everything had gone wrong. Dolgo-Saburov had killed both himself and Natasha. So where did that leave us? We were going to have to start afresh, beginning with the cross-examination of Dolgo-Saburov's erstwhile customers in the hope of building up a verbal picture of the doctor. Then we'd need to show the resulting identikit picture around every hospital and clinic in Moscow and the surrounding region. He was twenty-seven years old (the same as Belkin) and trained as either a psychiatrist, a psychotherapist or an anaesthetist. It was enough to go on, but not if you needed to find your suspect within the next twenty-four hours!

And one day was practically all we had at our disposal – two days at the most.

Dolgo-Saburov had said to Natasha that Boris had warned them not to arrive later than seven o'clock or they'd miss the plane. He would hardly be likely to fly off now without the other two. But on the other hand, if he had anybody else like this 'Katyukha'to tip him off, then he'd be certain to find out about the car accident by either tomorrow or the next day. In that case, he wouldn't show up at any of the airports in Moscow. He'd be certain to fly to Central Asia, from Kiev, Leningrad, Rostov, Perm or somewhere like that – and just try to find him then! All the same, while Svetlov was on his way back from the scene of the accident, he had used the radio telephone to contact the airport police at Vnukovo, Domodedovo and Bykovo. He had asked them to place a check on all flights to Central Asia and had given them as much information about our Dr Boris as he could while also mentioning he would most probably be travelling under an assumed name.

Arresting all Dolgo-Saburov's drug contacts and placing a check on flights to Central Asia was all well and good, but ... *we were running out of time!* We couldn't wait for the mountain to travel to Muhammad. We had to come up with a new approach. But what?

I arrived at the Incident Room feeling irritable and depressed by what I had just witnessed on the Kaluga Highway. Ozherelyev and Malenina were waiting for me. Malenina seemed quite elated. The first day of her search at the pharmaceutical warehouses had revealed that ten per cent of the morphine ampoules awaiting dispatch in cases to various military and civilian hospitals were missing. One of the warehousemen had already confessed that ampoules were removed and the cases repacked at the stores themselves. She had been looking for me during the past hour to tell me of her success. Pshenichny had let her know that we had arrested Akeyev, and she couldn't wait any longer. She wanted to cross-examine the boxer straight away concerning dealings arranged by his boss, the director of the Chief Pharmaceutical Authority.

Meanwhile, Major Ozherelyev, having just returned from searching Sysoyev's dacha, was able to tell us the following:

'The dacha was empty, Comrade Shamrayev, empty of people, that is. It was full of clothes, Persian carpets and expensive furniture. There was a stereo record-player, a colour television, a cassette tape recorder and piles of records and tapes. The refrigerator was full to overflowing, and there was enough drink in the cocktail cabinet to keep a party going for days. To judge from the amount of dirty washing-up left about in the kitchen, they must have held a party for about twenty people before the owner left. There was lip-stick on the glasses, and all the sheets in the bedroom showed signs of a wild orgy. I've had all the glasses and crockery sent away to be tested for finger-prints, of course. Meanwhile, I found the hiding place in the garage, as mentioned by Akeyev, but it was empty. There were two mattresses in the garage as well, and I would guess that they had been slept on by Belkin and Rybakov. I found some rope, too. It looks as if they were tied up. The garage is made of brick and is some distance from the dacha itself. You could hold someone prisoner there for a month and nobody would know. All you'd have to do would be to stuff something in his mouth to stop him screaming. But the most interesting discovery was this cassette. We spent more than three hours searching the place, and had the tape recorder going all the while. It was a shame not to listen to such good equipment, you see . . . When suddenly we found this. Listen to it yourself.'

Ozherelyev inserted the cassette into a portable tape recorder and switched it on, while Pshenichny, Malenina, myself and Baklanov (he had finished his own case and had been hanging about waiting for me to turn up) listened to the energetic voice of a young man:

'... sixteen glaciologists plus workers. Any of them can go down into Charshanga or Dzharkurgan. Why shouldn't they? There's nobody to stop them. The frontier zone is like anywhere else. People live there, and there's a market and shops. The only thing is that you need a pass to get into the area in the first place.'

'Is the aerodrome very far?' asked the voice of another man.

'No, it's right in Charshanga itself. The street comes to an end, and the aerodrome starts. It's just an ordinary airfield with poppies growing around...'

'Is it protected in any way? Are there any guards?'

'Not really. It is an agricultural airfield after all. There's an old man on crutches who hangs about. He's from the collective farm. And the Border Regiment have one soldier on duty there. There are planes about, you see, and somebody could always hop off over the border. In theory, at any rate.'

'And in practice?'

'Well, that's not so easy. You'd need to know the password. There are electronic detection devices all along the border. Before you knew where you were, they'd have sent up a ground-to-air missile, and that'd be the end of you!'

'But do the pilots know the passwords?'

'Well, the military pilots do, of course.'

'And how far away is the military airfield?'

'It's quite close. About two miles. Though I've never been to it myself...'

'You say that there are electronic detectors all along the border. Where do the men who operate them and the missiles go when they're off duty?'

'What do you mean? There's nowhere for them to go. There's a cinema and the occasional dance, but nothing else.'

'How about the officers?'

'It's the same for them. Ah, I see. You want to skip

abroad and you're wondering how to do it! Well, it's quite simple, really. There are plenty of Koreans living near the border with Afghanistan. There are whole state farms run by them, producing practically nothing else apart from opium poppies. But then you know that yourself, I suppose. After all, you brought a coffin filled with the stuff back to Baku! These Koreans are always popping over the border into Afghanistan, taking their opium with them. And the border guards shut their eyes to it. I got blind drunk with the chief officer at the frontier post one night, and he told me all about it. The Koreans flog their opium in Afghanistan for hard currency. They then bring the money home and get it converted into roubles. That way everybody makes a profit – the state and the drug-smugglers. They've got their own weapons and everything! I could have written a fantastic article about it, only it would never have got through the censorship. So there you are. Crossing the frontier is a piece of cake! All you need do is slit your eyes like the Koreans! Ha-ha-ha!' The speaker couldn't help laughing at his own joke. But his laughter seemed overdone somehow, over-excited like the rest of his conversation.

'And what's the name of this officer?'

'Major Ryskulov. Only don't think that you'll be able to bribe *him*! He's amazing! He can toss a coin in the air and shoot a hole right through it with his revolver. He gave me one of their sheepdogs as a present, but what was I going to do with a dog? I spend all my time flying around the country, after all. Listen, do you think I could have another little injection? Only I can feel the high already beginning to go . . .'

Ozherelyev stopped the cassette recorder.

'Unfortunately, that's all there is, Igor Iosifovich,' he said. 'We turned the place upside down to see if there wasn't some more of it somewhere, but there wasn't. Akeyev has identified the voices as those of Belkin, of course, and of the doctor they call Boris.'

A few hours earlier, I thought, and this cassette

would have been really useful. Now it could tell us practically nothing that we didn't know already. In fact, we knew a good deal more. We knew that Gridasov had already entered the frontier zone, for example, and that he had succeeded in bribing somebody for 200,000 roubles – possibly some of the helicopter pilots, possibly some of the border guards and perhaps even Major Ryskulov. Belkin's voice had sounded spontaneous and relaxed, if a little over-excited. But even that wasn't of any great interest now. The tape was quite old, after all. It must have been made before 26 May, the day Rybakov was murdered, because after that the criminals had quit the dacha, taking Belkin with them. But where was he now and what had happened to him? Was he alive? Did he have any memory left? The one thing which Ozherelyev's tape proved was that this Boris, the leader of the pack, knew how to loosen somebody's tongue through hypnosis or drugs, or perhaps a combination of the two. After all, Belkin was hardly likely to have told him all that about the border if he'd been in his right mind, just as Sysoyev would scarcely have told the doctor the combination of his own safe of his own free will.

I wondered whether there was any news from Baku. (There wasn't.) Then I nipped into the buffet to eat some sausages and yogurt and made my way to the Petrovka's cell-block to cross-examine Akeyev. Malenina insisted on coming with me.

Secret

TRANSCRIPT OF THE INTERROGATION OF SUSPECT AKEYEV

7 June 1979
Moscow

I, V. M. Akeyev, have been informed that I am held on suspicion of kidnapping Citizens V. B. Belkin and

Yu. A. Rybakov, of murdering Citizen Yu. A. Rybakov and of acquiring and selling narcotic substances without special permission.

(Signed) V. Akeyev

INVESTIGATOR'S QUESTION: You are being shown three photographs.

Tell me whether you recognize any of these men?

ANSWER: I recognize the man in photograph number two. It's Vadim Belkin. He was the one we kidnapped at the Kursk railway station.

Q: Are you certain?

A: Yes.

Q: Now look at these other four photographs. Do you recognize any of the people?

A: Yes. Number seven is the Old Man, and number nine is Herman Dolgo-Saburov.

Q: I am now going to show you some ordinary snaps. Do you recognize anybody in them? And where do you think these photos were taken?

A: I recognize Herman Dolgo-Saburov and his former mistress, Zoya, who works in the Enchantress hair salon. The photographs were taken at the very beginning of May – 1 May, I think – on the Black Sea coast at Sochi. Dolgo-Saburov showed me them himself.

Q: Do you recognize anybody else in these photographs?

A: No, nobody else.

Q: What do you know about the events that took place on 24 May at the Kursk railway station in Moscow? Give us a detailed description of the kidnapping of Belkin and Rybakov.

A: On 24 May I was on duty at Sysoyev's dacha. I've been working for him for more than three years, since before I got sent to prison. I used to guard the drugs and valuables which he had in his possession, and sometimes I used to transport them around for him. He started off by paying me twenty-five roubles a day, then this went up to fifty. He first employed me in 1976 after I had knocked out my opponent in the European boxing championship. He wanted a personal bodyguard. When I got sentenced for starting a fight in the Sokolniki beer-bar, he was very upset about it. If it hadn't been for a report in *Komsomolskaya Pravda* headlined 'Boxing Champion Flies into a Rage', he would have managed to get the whole thing hushed up and I wouldn't have been sent to prison. The Sports Committee petitioned on my behalf, too . . .

Q: Come back to the events of 24 May, please. Why were you in Moscow and what part did you play in kidnapping Belkin? Let me remind you that your direct participation in the crime has been corroborated by the witnesses Sinitsyn and Silinya, both of whom recognized you.

A: I understand. I was sent to Moscow by the company building a new chemical plant in Kotlas. They employed me as a 'fixer'. I was supposed to get the ministry to provide spare parts for bulldozers, concrete-mixers and various other items of heavy equipment. As a well-known boxer, it was an easy matter for me to soft-talk the various women who work in the accounting and planning departments. My former boss, Sysoyev, found out that I was in Moscow and suggested that I start working for him again. I said yes, of course, and he managed to get my trip to Moscow officially extended there and then at the Ministry of Industrial Construction. So it was all quite legal. On 24 May, as I've already said, I was on duty at Sysoyev's dacha, looking after the place and especially the drugs, which he'd removed from the warehouse and brought along in his own car. At ten o'clock that morning he'd rung me up from town to tell me that two men, Herman and another person, would be arriving soon to pick me up. I was to get the two suitcases with the drugs out of the secret hiding place and go along with them wherever they went. Sure enough, an ambulance arrived, driven by Herman Dolgo-Saburov, whom I'd known for a long time. Travelling with him was this Boris.

Q: Describe his appearance.

A: He's about medium height, pampered-looking somehow, and even a bit on the fat side. He's got a heavy, round face with dark, penetrating eyes and black hair. He dresses well in imported clothes, and wears a gold signet-ring.

Q: Is he Russian or Azerbaidzhani?

A: Russian.

Q: Where did you go when you left the dacha?

A: They told me that we had to go to the Kursk station to meet the train from Baku. Someone called the Old Man was supposed to be arriving with 100,000 roubles in a suitcase. We'd give him the merchandise, and he'd give us the cash. As usual, I was supposed to do the actual handing over.

Q: What happened at the railway station?

A: When we arrived, I stayed in the ambulance with the goods, while Herman and the doctor went off to meet the Baku train. Then, according to their story, the following happened. The money wasn't being carried from Baku to Moscow by the Old Man himself, but by this young lad, nicknamed Sultan, and his girl, who knew nothing about the whole operation. But the old Man had travelled up by the same train, only in a different compartment. It would have been dangerous for him to carry the loot himself as the police were on the look-out for him across the whole country. So, without telling

Sultan, the Old Man had secretly followed him the whole way from Baku and was meant to meet him on the platform. Then we were supposed to exchange the goods and Sultan was to take the whole lot back to Baku, with the Old Man keeping an eye on him once again from a distance. But when the Old Man, the doctor and Herman went up to Sultan's carriage, they could see that he was being met by this journalist, Belkin. Herman overheard Belkin trying to persuade Sultan to go along with him to the newspaper office and spill the beans about the drugs operation, the Old Man and everything.

Q: How did Sultan, that is Yury Rybakov, react to Belkin's suggestion?

A: I don't know, and it really didn't matter. If he'd already let the cat out of the bag to Belkin, that meant that he could do the same to somebody else. So they left Herman standing near Sultan, Belkin and the girl, while the Old Man and the doctor rushed back to the ambulance. They told me that we'd have to grab all three of them now: Sultan, his girl and the journalist. I said that we couldn't do it, not in broad daylight and with so many people around. We'd have to wait for the right moment. They reckoned we wouldn't get another chance, though, as the journalist would probably drive Sultan straight to the newspaper office. And that would be the end of everything. In any case, the doctor said that he had some other things to talk over with the journalist. So he and I both put on white jackets. We had to pretend to be medical orderlies from a mental hospital, trying to pick up three inmates who had escaped. We drove right up to the taxi-rank where Sultan, Belkin and the girl were waiting. Then Herman and I threw ourselves on top of Belkin and held his arms, while the Old Man and the doctor grabbed Sultan and the girl. The two men were so surprised at what was happening that they made no attempt at resisting. We simply bundled them into the ambulance. But the girl bit the doctor in the arm and managed to run off. I wanted to go after her, but a traffic policeman appeared at that moment, and we drove away as quickly as we could. On the way the doctor changed the number plates just in case, though nobody was following us.

Q: Where did you take the two men?

A: Straight to Sysoyev's dacha. I forgot to tell you that we also grabbed Sultan's suitcase with the money, and it was all there. That evening the boss arrived, and they decided what to do with Sultan and the correspondent. The boss said we had no choice. Since we'd been so stupid as to bring them straight to his dacha, they'd have to be bumped off. But the doctor reckoned that was all so much nonsense. In three weeks he'd be able to erase whatever he wanted from their memories. The boss didn't like the idea. But he said he'd take advice and let them know what he had decided at his party on the Saturday.

Q: What party was this?

A: The boss always has a party before his trips abroad. On 28 May he was due to head a delegation to Geneva, so he'd arranged a big party for the Saturday – orgy, more like. The doctor brought some nurses along from his hospital . . .

Q: Which hospital?

A: I don't know, honest!

Q: All right, carry on. Who was present at this 'orgy'?

A: The boss, this Dr Boris, the Old Man and five guests of Sysoyev's whom I didn't know.

Q: Describe them.

A: I didn't see them myself. I was in the garage, you see, guarding Belkin and Sultan. But the

Old Man was at the party. He told me that two of the guests were from Baku. They'd come for the diamonds which they'd been promised as a pay-off for hushing up the incident with the coffin. So right at the beginning of the party Sysoyev and the doctor came into the garage, got the diamonds out of the hiding place and put them in the document case that they'd got ready for the two Azerbaidzhanis. Meanwhile, the boss was really swearing away at the doctor, while Boris was begging Sysoyev not to be in too great a hurry to hand over the diamonds. He reckoned that he might be able to persuade them to take the money instead. So off they went with the document case. They took the suitcase with the 200,000 roubles with them as well, just in case. Then the Old Man told me what a good time everybody was having across the way. The party was going very well, it seemed. The doctor hadn't just brought a few nurses with him. He'd brought some laughing-gas as well. You know, the sort the people are given when they're having an operation or in labour. When they'd all had a skinful of brandy, the doctor had tried out the gas and they had an orgy of group sex, such as the Azerbaidzhanis had never seen before! Then, at about ten o'clock, the two visitors left with the money instead of the diamonds. They had to get to the airport to catch the last flight to Baku.

Meanwhile the boss was having a really good time with two of the nurses. The doctor arranged a hypnosis session with the others trying to guess each other's thoughts and telling things about themselves that they would never have revealed in normal circumstances. I was able to see some of that for myself, because the Old Man had come to relieve me by this time. When I walked into the dacha, the nurses were sitting there stark naked, smoking hash and telling the others things I've never heard in my life before. By this time the boss was completely drunk and he wanted to unburden himself too. But the doctor took him into a separate room in case something were to slip out that wasn't for the nurses' ears. Sysoyev was very grateful to the doctor for saving the diamonds and palming the two Azerbaidzhanis off with paper money. Round about eleven o'clock, the doctor drove off with three of the nurses, leaving another two to spend the night with the boss. The three of them went off to the summer-house, completely naked, while I started to clear up the mess in the dacha. I could hear them singing bawdy songs through the window. Then they all started making love together, after which the boss insisted on showing them the diamonds and taking the two of them out for a joy-ride in the car. The nurses were very young, I must say, no more than eighteen years old. But that's how Sysoyev likes them. He's fifty-seven himself. All three of them turned up at the garage, Sysoyev carrying the document case with the diamonds and wanting to drive off in the car. But the Old Man tried to persuade him not to. Sysoyev hit him in the face and opened the garage doors himself, leaving the document case lying on the bonnet of the Volga. Then Sultan managed to untie the rope somehow and jumped up out of the pit . . .

Q: So Belkin and Rybakov were tied up in a pit. What kind of a pit was it?

A: An inspection pit. Just for repairs, you know, so that you can get to see the underneath of the car. The two of them were lying there bound and gagged. Usually they were pretty quiet, though, because the doctor used to calm them down with an injection.

Q: What sort of injection?

A: He used various powerful drugs. So I don't understand how Sultan managed to untie the rope and jump up out of the pit. Perhaps because the doctor hadn't given him an injection that evening. Either he'd forgotten, or he'd been too busy at the party. Anyway, by the end of the evening he looked pretty irritable and depressed . . .

Q: When did he become 'irritable and depressed', as you put it – before the hypnotism session with Sysoyev or after?

A: After. Why do you ask?

Q: What form did this irritability take?

A: After Sysoyev had had his heart-to-heart talk, the doctor rushed out of the room into the kitchen and swigged down half a tumbler of brandy all at one go. I told him that we ought to make the boss get dressed now, but he started to swear at me and him.

Q: Please return to your description of how Rybakov managed to escape.

A: When the boss had opened the garage and had this row with the Old Man, Sultan suddenly jumped up out of the pit and tore off into the bushes. The Old Man rushed after him, but how was he going to catch somebody like Sultan? Then the boss noticed that the lad had also grabbed the document case which had been lying on the bonnet of the Volga. I started up the car and drove off in pursuit, with the Old Man sitting beside me. It was already midnight and the boy had nowhere else to run to, except the railway station. He managed to take a short cut there, though – past the Tsaritsyno Ponds and the ruins of Catherine the Great's palace. We had to drive the long way round so he reached the station before we did. There was some old night-watchman hanging about there. We gave

303

him a tip, and he told us that the boy had climbed into a goods train carrying new Zhiguli cars. The train had just begun to move out of the station towards Moscow. We jumped on to it ourselves, and began to run up and down the trucks, looking for Sultan. I headed towards the back of the train, while the Old Man took the front. But I couldn't find anything, and I was just about to walk back when I suddenly saw the two of them fighting in the front truck. I started running towards them. The train happened to be crossing a bridge over the Moscow River at that point, and I was afraid the two of them might fall down into the river. But by the time I got there, the train had crossed the bridge and the Old Man had hit Sultan on the head with a knuckle-duster and hurled him off the truck. About a mile or so further down the line the train stopped at the signals. The two of us were able to slip off and make our way back up the track to look for the document case with the diamonds. We walked back as far as Tsaritsyno station, but found nothing, apart from Sultan's corpse. The Old Man had a good look at it to make sure that he was really dead and checked through all his pockets. Then we left the body where it was lying. We thought about hiding it or dragging it back to our car. But that was parked a couple of miles away and it would have been dangerous to do so. We decided it was better to leave it where it was. Let people think that he had fallen out of the train. At least a hundred trains go by that spot every night, after all.

Q: Tell me when and where Belkin was taken after being at the dacha.

A: He was taken away the same day, or rather the next morning. Sysoyev went mad when the Old Man and I arrived back without Sultan and

without the document case. He was already
dressed, and there were no nurses left by then.
I don't know where they got to. Perhaps they
went home by train. The point is that he was
now at the dacha by himself, and he blamed the
Old Man for the whole business. The Old Man
reckoned that the boss was to blame for it himself, though. It was bloody stupid of him to have
opened the garage and left the diamonds on top
of the car bonnet. Anyway, they had a real
set-to. In the end, the boss said he had no time to
sort it out now, but as soon as he got back from
his foreign trip he'd settle up with the Old Man
and the doctor. Meanwhile, the money and
valuables still at the dacha – including everybody's share – were to be taken back to his
Moscow flat as quickly as possible and the
dacha vacated. So' he rang the doctor and told
him to come over as quickly as he could to pick
up the Old Man and the correspondent. He
wasn't bothered about where they were taken.
Then we emptied the secret hiding place in the
garage of everything in it, including the iron
box of diamonds and a couple of sacks of
money – one filled with dollars, the other with
roubles. We placed everything in the boot of the
Volga, and the boss ordered me not to take my
eyes off it for one second. An hour later the
doctor arrived. He and the Old Man put the
correspondent into a car and drove off. Sysoyev
and I shut up the dacha, and then we left as
well.
Q: Where did you go?
A: To the boss's flat in Moscow, where you
   arrested me today.
Q: Did you see the doctor and the Old Man again?
A: No.
Q: Why did you agree to go to a restaurant with
   the doctor's sister and your girl-friend, if

305

Sysoyev had ordered you to stay in his flat and guard the safe containing the valuables?

A: Because I was fed up with sitting in the flat. It was like being in prison again, or even worse. At least you've got some people to talk to in the camp, whereas there I was completely on my own without even a screw to talk to. Apart from that, I wasn't afraid of leaving the apartment for two or three hours. The whole building is occupied by high government officials, so who's going to rob it? In any case, you'd need to know the combination of the safe. There's no other way of opening it. So I'm telling you once again that Sysoyev took the diamonds himself and has run off abroad with them. You mark my words, he won't come back. Meanwhile, he left me behind guarding an empty safe so the rest of the gang wouldn't smell a rat.

Q: Did this doctor visit the dacha when Sysoyev wasn't there, to interrogate Belkin?

A: Yes, the doctor called in at the place every other day after we'd kidnapped Belkin and Sultan. He used to inject them with drugs and they'd sing all day, from morning till night.

Q: What do you mean 'sing'?

A: I'm sorry. I mean that they'd tell him everything he wanted to know. There are special injections to make people do it, but I've forgotten what it's called. Inhibition, or something . . .

Q: [MAJOR MALENINA]: Amytal-caffeine disinhibition?

A: Yes, that's right.

Q: Were you present at any of the conversations or interrogations?

A: No, I wasn't. The doctor wouldn't allow anybody else to attend. He'd record everything on cassette and then let the Old Man listen to a few extracts. They wanted to find out what Sultan had blabbed to Belkin, and what Belkin had told

306

others or written for his newspaper.

Q: How do you know that this was what they were trying to find out?

A: They told me so themselves.

Q: Did the doctor's sister, Natasha, have a sexual relationship with your boss, Sysoyev?

A: I can't say for certain, although the boss did tell me once that he'd had her. That was why he'd got her brother a residence permit in Moscow.

Q: Who is Balayan?

A: Balayan is the USSR Deputy Minister of Health.

Q: What connection does he have with the criminal actions of Sysoyev and others? How is he connected with the theft and illegal sale of narcotics?

A: I can't answer these questions.

Q: You can't answer them, or you don't want to?

A: I know that I have the right to refuse to give evidence. For this reason I refuse to answer that question.

Q: During your last meeting with your mistress Smagina at Sysoyev's apartment, a few minutes before your arrest, you were heard to tell her that your boss had connections with some extremely influential people, if not with government ministers and members of the CPSU Central Committee. Whom did you have in mind?

A: I refuse to answer that question as well!

Q: Can you tell us why you refuse to answer these particular questions?

A: Because if I were to name names, your hair would stand on end, and I'd be dead before I reached camp.

Q: After your trial it would be possible to send you to a special camp for former government and party officials. Ordinary criminals wouldn't be able to get you there . . .

A: That's as may be, but the former government

and party officials could! No, I've already told you more than I should – out of spite, because Sysoyev left me guarding an empty safe. I can't understand why you don't get the KGB in on it. They could catch him while he's in the West. Please have this request of mine entered in the report.

Q: Very well, that will be done. Can you tell us whether Balayan had a sexual relationship with the doctor's sister?

A: I can't answer that question, either. I simply don't know.

Q: Did Natasha visit Sysoyev's dacha while Belkin and Rybakov were there?

A: No.

Q: [MAJOR MALENINA]: How long has the theft of drugs at the Central Pharmacuetical warehouse been going on?

A: I've been working for my boss for three years, and I know that we've been receiving drugs from the warehouse during all that time. What used to happen before I started working for him, I don't know . . .

The duty guard officer suddenly looked in at the door. 'Comrade Investigator, you're wanted on the phone at the Incident Room.'

We had to interrupt the interrogation. Besides, it was nearly 10.45 p.m. and you're not allowed to prolong the cross-examination of suspects and prisoners past eleven o'clock. Malenina and I left the prison block and walked across the dark, inner courtyard. She then headed for the exit and I walked towards the Incident Room.

I could see the tiny red pin-points of cigarettes as I walked past the smoking room, and I could hear a voice saying: 'He's been screwing her for an hour and twenty minutes with the whole CID listening in over the radio. Then Shcholokov walks in, the Interior Minister . . .'

I grinned and thought to myself: So that's how legends are created! Then I entered the Operations Section.

The corridor on the ground floor was full of people. More than forty people were sitting or standing around waiting to enter the cross-examination rooms, like patients at a dental clinic. I asked the guard what was going on. It turned out that these were the drug-pedlars arrested in connection with the Dolgo-Saburov affair. They'd been brought in from all over the centre of Moscow.

I walked up to the Incident Room on the first floor. An exhausted Colonel Serebryannikov nodded towards the telephone receiver lying on a table next to his desk.

'Some woman has been trying reach you. She says it's urgent.'

'Who is she?

'Someone from *Komsomolskaya Pravda*. She won't give her surname.'

I picked up the receiver.

'Hello, Shamrayev here.'

'Igor Iosifovich?'

'Yes.'

'Good evening. Sorry to have disturbed you. This is Inna, the typist from *Komsomolskaya Pravda*. Do you remember?'

'Of course I do. Has something happened?'

'I've got some important news about Vadim.'

'I'm listening.'

'I can't tell you over the phone. You've got to come here, so I can talk to you in private. Can you come right away? Or else he'll have to fly back.'

'Do I have to come on my own?'

'Well, I'm not sure,' she replied hesitantly. 'I'll ask. Who do you want to come with?'

'Some friends of mine.'

There was a moment's silence. She had obviously placed her hand over the mouthpiece so I could hear nothing of what was said at the other end of the line.

Then I heard Inna's voice again.

'Igor Iosifovich, he'd rather talk to you by yourself. But if you insist . . .'

'No, of course not. I was simply checking to make sure you weren't being threatened.'

'Good heavens, no! I can trust him. It's just that he's afraid . . . I can't tell you over the phone. Please, come – now! It's important, word of honour.'

'I'm already on my way. What's your address again?'

'No. 17, 12 Parkovaya Street, Flat 73, and in case you need it, the phone number is . . .'

I left the number with Colonel Serebryannikov and told him I would be there for about half an hour. Then I went downstairs to my car. As I was walking down the corridor on the ground floor, I suddenly stopped. Svetlov was addressing the assembled company of drug-pedlars in the following highly original manner:

'Today each of you received a consignment of drugs from Herman Dolgo-Saburov. That is why you have been detained and you will be charged under Article 224 of the Criminal Code. However, we are not allowed to question you after 11 p.m. It is now 10.56. That is to say, in three or four minutes you will all be taken to cells in the Petrovka prison-block and the cross-examinations will continue tomorrow. However, we need to get certain information now, urgently. We are looking for a dangerous criminal, and anybody who helps us catch him will be able to leave here very quickly with no charges preferred. This criminal is a friend of Dolgo-Saburov's called Boris. He is a doctor, twenty-seven years of age, who arrived in Moscow from Baku a couple of years ago and has been working since then either as a psychiatrist, or as a psychotherapist, or as an anaesthetist. I give you my word as an officer that anybody who can tell me his present whereabouts, or at least give me his surname and place of work, will be able to leave here a free man. I'll even get a police car to take him back to where he lives.'

Yes, that sounds like Svetlov! He's not allowed to cross-examine prisoners after eleven o'clock, you see, but doing a deal with them is a different matter. There was no time for us to stand on ceremony, of course. The week the Chief Prosecutor had given us was ticking away, and there was still no sign of Belkin . . .

Svetlov waited for an answer, but none of the suspects said a word. Some of them shrugged their shoulders, or exchanged glances, while others did nothing and simply carried on staring gloomily down at their feet.

'All right,' said Svetlov. 'Let's do it another way, just in case somebody knows something but is afraid of telling me in front of the others. Each of you will have one chance to go from his cell to the latrines. On the way there, you can let the guard know and he will summon the duty investigator, Comrade Pshenichny, and tell him. And don't forget: it's a good offer. We really need to find this doctor. Anybody who can truly help us will have much to be grateful for, I promise you. That's all. Guards, take them away.'

The guards started to lead the prisoners away to the prison-block where Malenina and I had just been quetioning Akeyev. Svetlov sat down on a chair in the corridor there and then and said: 'That's my lot! I'm done for! I need someone to take me to my cot, or I'll go to sleep on the spot.'

'There is something else you could do,' I said. 'You could come along with me to visit one of Vadim Belkin's female acquaintances. She has some news for us.'

Svetlov gave me a questioning look, but I didn't try to explain.

'Get up,' I said, 'and let's go. You can grab forty winks in the car.'

The same day – Thursday, 23.37 hours
Inna's other guest turned out to be Rady Sverdlov, grandson of our country's first president and the *Komsomolka*'s special correspondent in Azerbaidzhan.

On the table there was a bottle of export vodka, a few snacks and the familiar bottle of *Chornye Glaza*. God, had three days really gone by since the Monday evening when I first read Belkin's story at Inna's flat? The other thing on the table was a second copy of Belkin's famous manuscript. It turned out that Inna had made two copies. The top copy she had given to me, the carbon to this Sverdlov.

The lovelorn creature had been carrying out her own, private investigation, so to speak. She had persuaded Granov, the chief administrator at *Komsomolskaya Pravda*, to have Rady Sverdlov summoned from Baku to Moscow. When he'd arrived, she'd given him a copy of Belkin's diary to read. This rather portly, thirty-five-year-old descendant of our first president then downed half a glass of vodka to give himself courage and told me the following story in confidence and with great vehemence.

'Listen, Igor Iosifovich, I tell you this as one half-Jew to another, it's a real mafia we're dealing with. They're everywhere . . .! *Of course* Vadim was arrested and kept in the detention cell at Baku. And *of course* everything written in this manuscript is the truth. In fact, Belkin has left some parts out! And he did stay at my place – I was lying to you when I spoke to you over the phone before. Why did I lie? I'll tell you! On 22 May Vadim flew off to Moscow, and five days later, on the Sunday, I was suddenly invited to call on Vekilov at MVD headquarters. Do you know who he is? He's the same blue-eyed son of a bitch who interviewed Belkin. He also happens to be chief personal assistant to the Azerbaidzhani Minister of Internal Affairs. The things he gets up to, you can't imagine! My grandfather certainly helped to give us a stick to beat ourselves with, I must say! Anyway, this Vekilov invites me to visit him at his office and he says to me, as openly as I'm talking to you now: "Rady Moiseyevich, do you want to carry on leading a quiet, enjoyable life in Azerbaidzhan?" Well, what am I supposed to reply:

"No, I don't"? I say yes, of course. Everybody likes to have a good life, don't they? "In that case," he says, "remember one thing: Vadim Belkin did not stay at your place a week ago." "What do you mean," I say, "he didn't stay at my place? He even dictated an article over the phone to Moscow from my flat!" "Well," he says, "nobody else knows that. He could have dictated it over the phone from anywhere. The main thing, and I tell you this for your own good," he says, "is that you didn't see or hear from him while he was in Baku, nor do you know what he was doing here. OK?" Then he looks at me with those pale-blue eyes of his. Can you imagine? What a bastard! He was just trying to scare me, of course. But I tell you, if they find out that I've been sitting here with you, telling you all this, it's curtains for me. They'll throw me down the sewers, get me killed in a car accident, put poison in my food – anything you like. So I beg you, please . . .'

'But you haven't told me anything yet. Let's get down to brass tacks.'

'I know. And perhaps I won't be able to tell you anything of use. But all the same I want to reach an agreement with you. Everything that you are about to hear from me, you didn't hear, OK? I'll never corroborate this evidence anywhere, understand? Do we have a bargain?'

'All right,' I said, unenthusiastically. 'Agreed.'

'What you really want to do is find out where Belkin is now,' he said. 'Am I right?'

I said nothing in reply, but he obviously wanted verbal confirmation. 'Am I right?' he repeated.

'Yes, you're right,' I said.

'And the only people who could have kidnapped him are this so-called Ziyalov and his sister. Am I right again?'

'Why do you think that?'

'Because Belkin was searching for them all over Baku, and even went to look for them in Moscow. And not because he'd fallen in love with Ziyalov's sister.

313

That's a lot of nonsense. He falls in love with different women all the time.'

At this point he looked across at the girl. 'I'm sorry, Inna,' he said, 'but he's a profligate bastard. There's nothing you can do about it.' Then he turned back to me.

'You see, they stole his border pass! He didn't write that in his diary. In fact he expressly mentions there how all his papers were returned. But he told me that they'd filched the pass which allows him to enter the border zone. And he was afraid that they'd try to use it, they *were* criminals after all! He didn't want to tell the police, however. If he did that, he'd get it in the neck, and he wouldn't be able to travel to Vienna with Brezhnev. So that's why he was rushing about all over Baku, searching for this Ziyalov, you see . . .'

'But his surname isn't Ziyalov,' I said.

'Exactly! That's the whole point! Belkin couldn't remember his surname! He even paid a special visit to the Pioneers' Palace to find his old teacher in the Geographical Society . . .'

'What's the Pioneers' Palace got to do with it?' I asked in surprise. 'He and Ziyalov were at school together.'

"That what he says in the manuscript!' exclaimed Sverdlov. 'In the *manuscript*! But you remember yourself how he said at the very beginning that he had decided to mix fact and fiction. I thought that you would probably be looking for this Ziyalov among Belkin's old school friends. You have been, haven't you? In fact you still are? Am I right?'

'Yes,' I replied.

'There you are!' he exclaimed triumphantly. 'Whereas in fact they weren't at the same school at all, let alone in the same class! But they *were* both members of the Geographical Society at the Pioneers' Palace. It was a very famous society in those days. It used to win all the prizes at competitions bringing young geographers together from all over the country. And the reason was that it was led by a most remarkable man. Or that's what Belkin told me, at any rate. And he paid a special visit to Kyurdamir to find out Ziyalov's real name and his address. The old fellow corresponds with half his ex-pupils to this day . . .'

'And did he find out?' I asked.

'I don't know. Word of honour. Or rather, I think he did, but I'd already left Baku by that time. He went to Kyurdamir the day before he flew back to Moscow, and I had to mess about in Lenkoran that day, taking photographs for an article about cotton-growers. Vadim mentions it in his diary.'

'And what makes you think that he did find out where Ziyalov lives?'

'Well, take a look at this,' said Sverdlov, placing a torn sheet from a notebook down on the table in front of me. I recognized Belkin's bold handwriting. 'Old man!' it said. 'Everything's turning out fantastically. I'll get them. Thanks for everything. Vadim.'

'I found this note at my flat when I got back from Lenkoran,' said Sverdlov.

I looked at my watch.

'Rady, what time are you flying back?'

'Oh, don't come on my flight, please!' he said beseechingly. 'It'll seem obvious enough anyway. I fly out to Moscow and back, and then an investigator turns up straight after me.'

'Listen, Rady Moiseyevich. If you took the decision to pass important information on to us, then you must have realized that I would need to use it. Or else why did you ask to see me?'

'Because I read *this*!' he said, thumping Belkin's manuscript with his fist. 'He calls me Kotovsky in the diary, and at least he writes about me with affection. I'm supposed to have been like a nanny to him, and a doctor. How can I just let these Baku sons of bitches do whatever they like to him? They're dirty crooks, the lot of them! And yet we all let them do what they like with us! If only my grandfather could rise up from his grave.

I'd soon show them what's what!'

He was suddenly interrupted by the telephone. Inna answered and passed the receiver over to me. 'It's for you, Igor Iosifovich!' It was Colonel Serebryannikov.

'Listen, Igor, have you got access to a radio of some kind?'

'What for?' I said uncomprehendingly.

'Can you get "Voice of America"?'

I looked around the flat. There was a radio, of course.

'What's happened, then?' I said to Serebryannikov.

'You listen to "Voice of America". They'll be repeating their news summary in ten minutes. And get Svetlov to listen to it too. He'll also find it interesting. See you later.' With that the colonel rang off.

Svetlov was asleep in the car, but with Inna's and Sverdlov's permision, I brought him upstairs and we all sat down to listen to the Washington announcer's familiar voice.

'This is Vladimir Martin at the microphone. Here is the final summary of the news. According to a Reuter's report, a large number of drug-traffickers were arrested in Moscow today at the hotels Ukraine, Metropole and Peking, at the Zhiguli beer-bar in the Arbat and in various other public places throughout the capital. The agency also reports that one of the traffickers had an accident on the Kaluga Highway, south of Moscow, as a result of which two people were killed. As we know from data provided by UNESCO, the Soviet Union occupies third place in the world narcotics league, with only Turkey and Pakistan producing more. At the same time, huge consignments of opium are exported illegally from the USSR to the West. According to Western correspondents in Moscow, this action on the part of the police proves how widespread drug-addiction is within the country, especially among young people. From Madrid we are told that . . .'

We didn't bother to listen to the latest news-flash from Madrid. We switched off the radio.

'So there you are,' said Svetlov in a puzzled voice. 'We've become famous . . .'

'It's incredible how quickly they find things out!' said Sverdlov. 'That's real workers for you!'

I looked at my watch. It was ten past twelve. Friday had arrived.

'What time does the plane leave for Baku?' I asked Sverdlov once again.

'At 2.40,' he replied.

I'd already filled Svetlov in on the details of my conversation with Sverdlov. 'The best thing for me and you to do,' he said, 'is to leave Moscow right now, before the lightning strikes. And then to fly back tomorrow evening and find Belkin. They're hardly likely to sack us then . . .'

But at that moment the telephone rang once again.

'No, we've left it too late,' said Svetlov.

'Perhaps we should just not answer,' suggested Inna.

'Pointless,' replied Svetlov. 'There's a radio telephone in the car down below, so they'll get us whatever we do.'

I lifted the receiver. 'Hello?'

'Igor?' said the voice of Serebryannikov.

'Yes.'

'You're to appear at the Chief Prosecutor's office at nine o'clock in the morning. He's just rung me himself.'

'Listen, I've got to fly off to Baku in an hour.'

'Well, that's your business. I was just instructed to tell you. You're to appear before Rudenko, and Svetlov is to see Shcholokov – both at nine o'clock. Sleep well, lads!'

I immediately passed the message to Svetlov. 'If there's any trouble,' I said, 'blame it all on me. I am in charge, after all.'

'Sod the lot of them!' he roared. 'Don't any of these bloody ministers ever go to sleep, or do they spend all their time listening to "Voice of America"?'

'We ought to get in touch with your two men in Baku,' I said. 'They ought to give up checking Belkin's old school and start checking the Pioneers' Palace. They'll soon find out who was in charge of this Geographical Society.'

Then I turned to Sverdlov.

'What was his surname, can you remember?'

'No. I had no reason to remember. It was a long, funny name. Jewish, I think.'

'Well, it'll be easy enough to find out at the palace itself,' I added.

'Listen to me,' said Svetlov pensively. 'I don't think we ought to send my men there. Let them carry on sniffing around Belkin's old school. This Vekilov knows very well what they've been up to, but as long as they were on the wrong track, he's left them alone. We've got to go about this quietly, as I see it. Either you or I, Igor, must travel to Baku incognito. Rady Moiseyevich will have to stay in Moscow for the time being. I'm sorry, Comrade Sverdlov, but if you go back to Baku now and Vekilov summons you to his office again, I'm not convinced that you won't crack and tell him all about our little meeting today.' Then he turned back to me. 'Could you get the chief editor of Komsomolka to delay him here in Moscow?'

'I'll do it myself,' said Sverdlov. 'Only I'll have to cancel my booking pretty quickly. Flight registration begins in an hour's time.'

'We can do that over the phone,' I said. Then I took a clean sheet of paper and drafted a telegram to send to Svetlov's lads in Baku.

TELEGRAM

To Comrades Rogozin and Shmuglov
Hotel Azerbaidzhan, Baku

CONTINUE SEARCH FOR BELKIN'S FORMER CLASSMATES
STOP LATEST DESCRIPTION OF SUSPECT AS FOLLOWS STOP

AZERBAIDZHANI AGE 27 MEDIUM HEIGHT BLACK HAIR DARK EYES BOTANY ENTHUSIAST AT SCHOOL STOP REPORT PROGRESS DAILY STOP SHAMRAYEV

Friday, 8 June, 09.22 hours

Secret
To USSR Chief Public Prosecutor
Full State Juridical Counsellor
Comrade R. A. Rudenko

SPECIAL DISPATCH

At 18.42 hours on 7 June 1979, at a point twenty-five miles south of the city centre on the Kaluga Highway, a collision took place between a GAZ–62 cement-carrier and a Zhiguli estate car. As a result of the crash two people died: the driver of the Zhiguli, Citizen Herman Dolgo-Saburov, and an unidentified passenger travelling in the same car.

The incident occurred because the said Zhiguli estate was being pursued by a group of CID operatives under the command of USSR Special Investigator, Comrade I. I. Shamrayev. Because of the unusual nature of the case, I consider it my duty to inform you personally of the circumstances surrounding the incident.

At 18.15 hours at State Automobile Inspection Post No. 7 on the Kaluga Highway, the officer on duty, Captain P. R. Sergeyev, stopped the driver of the Zhiguli estate car registration no. MKTs–22–57, Herman Dolgo-Saburov, for exceeding the speed limit. Because the Moscow CID had circulated all transport police with instructions to seek and detain the said Dolgo-Saburov, Captain Sergeyev decided to take him to Automobile Inspection headquarters. However, the suspect did not do as he was ordered and drove off in his car. Captain Sergeyev therefore gave chase. At the same time Comrade Shamrayev's team, consisting of three vehicles and a CID helicopter, also joined in the pursuit. In his attempt to escape, the suspect drove at maximum speed, crossed into the left-hand lane and collided with a cement-carrier coming in the opposite direction.

As a result of the crash, the bodies of Dolgo-Saburov and his passenger were mutilated beyond recognition, and it has been impossible to identify the woman passenger from her facial features. The boot of the Zhiguli was found to contain a cardboard box filled with banknotes to the sum of approximately 92,000 roubles. This money has been impounded by Comrade Shamrayev and his team.

In my opinion, the actions of my subordinate, Captain P. R. Sergeyev, were in no way the cause of the victims' demise. The car crash was the fault of Investigator I. Shamrayev who, instead of arresting this dangerous criminal at the appropriate time, merely engaged in passive surveillance of his movements resulting in the traffic accident.

Head of State Automobile Inspection
Moscow City Executive Committee
Major-General N. Nozdryakov

7 June 1979

'And that's just for starters,' said the Chief Prosecutor, as he proceeded to move documents across the desk. 'Read these.'

Top Secret
By Special Field Post

To USSR Chief Public Prosecutor
Comrade R. A. Rudenko
Copy to Chief of CPSU Central Committee
Ideological Section
Comrade N. Savinkin (for information)

On 7 June 1979, your subordinate, Special Investigator Comrade I. I. Shamrayev, carried out a series of arrests, as a result of which thirty-seven management staff at a number of hotels and trading enterprises in the centre of Moscow were apprehended.

Comrade Shamrayev's action was not cleared in advance with the Committee of State Security, and as a result three KGB agents were among those arrested. This has had serious repercussions on our undercover work, since for the past three years these agents had been gradually infiltrating an illegal drug-trafficking network. This was expected to facilitate KGB operations for the great influx of foreign tourists into Moscow during the Olympic Games to be held in the summer of 1980.

I request therefore that agents A. I. Gorokhov, P. O. Zhitomirskaya and M. R. Ginzburg should be released as quickly as possible.

At the same time I have to inform you that the unconcealed nature of Comrade Shamrayev's actions, caused by his failure to liaise in advance with the organs of state security, has led to his operation becoming widely known in the capital. It has also caused an unhealthy reaction on the part of the Western news media, particularly undesirable on the eve of Comrade Brezhnev's meeting with President Carter in Vienna.

I ask you to take firm measures to ensure that such dislocations in our work do not recur in future.

KGB First Deputy Chairman
General S. Tsvigun

8 June 1979

Secret, Urgent
By Special Party Messenger

To CPSU Central Committee Member
Comrade R. Rudenko

Dear Roman Andreyevich,

Listened to 'Voice of America' last night. What kind of cock-up is this? Why does America find out about your operations before the First Secretary of the Moscow Party Committee?

You remember what was agreed: no noisy operations in Moscow before the Olympics! And what happens? The city is full of rumours again, just as it was at the time of the Ionesyan murders.

Put a stop to this case right away and calm down the hullabaloo. Let me know the names of the persons responsible so that they can be subjected to disciplinary action by the party.

First Secretary CPSU Moscow Committee
V. Grishin

8 June 1979

As I was reading these documents, I felt sorry I hadn't taken Svetlov's advice and flown to Baku that night. I knew what we were in for: 'Explain your actions', 'How could you allow people to get killed?', 'Why didn't you inform us?', 'Who gave you the right to take the law into your own hands?', 'What am I supposed to say to the Central Committee?', and so on. It wasn't surprising either. After all, two people killed in a road accident, the 'Voice of America' chiming and three KGB agents arrested by accident was hardly bad going! I prepared to weather the storm. I'd probably get a strong reprimand from the party at the very least, and who knew? I might even get taken off the case.

But the Chief Public Prosecutor said nothing. There he was, sitting in Stalin's old chair with his eyes closed, his head tipped slightly to one side with the folds of his chin protruding slightly over the collar of his marshal's uniform. I was waiting for him to open his whitish eyelids and for the fireworks to begin, but then . . . I suddenly realized that he was asleep. That was all. He was breathing evenly with the slightest hint of a snore. His puffy hands were resting on his paunch. So much for the unsleeping eye of the Chief Public Prosecutor, I thought. I didn't know what to do next. Why didn't the telephone ring, or something?

I sat there quietly, waiting for his nibs to wake up. Tsvigun's letter and Grishin's note were burning a hole in my hand. All this General Nozdryakov was doing was simply protecting his own man, of course, but the other two were after my blood. And when you've got the First Deputy Chairman of the KGB and the First Secretary of the Moscow Party Committee gunning for you and the only thing your immediate superior can do is sit fast asleep in Stalin's old chair, what were you to expect next?

Then he opened his eyes and started to speak, as if he hadn't been asleep at all.

'Have you read them all?'

'Yes.'

'Where is Belkin?'

'We haven't got him yet, Roman Andreyevich.'

'When will you have him?'

'We might have got him today. I was supposed to fly off to Baku for half a day or so last night, but . . .'

'I held you up, eh?'

'More or less.'

'Tell me this. Couldn't you get hold of Belkin with less commotion and fewer corpses?'

'Dolgo-Saburov took his own life, you know. Everything's recorded on tape . . .'

'Look, there's no need for all that,' he said with a gentle wave of the hand. 'He doesn't matter. One crook more or less, so what? It's just that you need to work differently. Use more caution. I did warn you. You've made one slip, and there they are, Grishin and Tsvigun, screaming for your blood. A copy to Savinkin indeed! All they want to do is crush our department – any pretext will do. And you've just provided them with one, haven't you?'

'Well . . .' I mumbled.

'Yes you have. Just take my word for it,' he said dogmatically. 'A car chase, mass arrests, KGB agents picked up – you're a regular Superman. Meanwhile, I have to get up at six o'clock in the morning to visit Savinkin at his dacha, to make sure that I get to him before all this lot does,' he said, pointing towards the letters from Tsvigun, Grishin and Nozdryakov. 'What will you all do when I die or retire? Andropov or Shcholokov will make mincemeat of you before six months have passed . . . Well, never mind. You might as well tell me what you've got to report, now that you're here, or else you'll do something else that's stupid . . .'

'Well, basically it amounts to this. Belkin was kidnapped by a group of drug-traffickers who are part of a much larger organization. The top bosses then decided to get the smaller fry for launching out on their own . . .'

'What do you mean by a "much larger organization"?' asked Rudenko, interrupting me angrily.

'Precisely that, Roman Andreyevich. There's a well-organized criminal mafia running this drug show throughout the country. Opium poppies are being cultivated in Central Asia, the Caucasus and the area around Stavropol, partly for the state and partly for the black market. In addition, large quantities of morphine are being stolen from the pharmaceutical warehouses. One of the leaders of the whole show is Viktor Sysoyev, who is also director of the Chief Pharmaceutical Authority. He's away on business in Geneva at present. From him the trail leads upwards towards the Deputy Health Minister, Balayan, and outwards towards the Azerbaidzhani Minister of the Interior and others.'

Rudenko shook his head sadly. 'And all this is recorded in the case file?'

'Yes.'

'It's terrible, this Jewish way you have of making the widest inferences!'

'What's parentage got to do with it, Roman Andreyevich?'

'Now, don't take my words amiss! You may be half-Jewish, but the other half of you is Russian, I know that very well. And you're a good investigator. But you do have a habit of rummaging in the most awkward corners. So what happened to Belkin?'

'He was captured by the same four that Sysoyev threatened to punish for organizing their own drug deals on the side. They were concealing part of the consignment from the rest of the gang and selling it themselves.'

'I see,' said Rudenko with a grin. 'A black market within a black market! That's something new. What else?'

'According to information recovered indirectly from Belkin himself, they have managed to penetrate the border zone and are preparing to flee abroad by helicopter or plane from Charshanga in Uzbekistan.'

The prosecutor frowned. 'Does the KGB know about this?'

'Not yet, Roman Andreyevich. I only found out myself last night . . .'

'For Christ's sake! We've got to tell them right away. Or were you thinking of catching them on the border yourself?' For the first time the prosecutor looked truly furious.

'Well, only one of the criminals has reached the border so far,' I said. 'He's waiting for his three accomplices to join him. Two of them are dead already, and the third . . . The third one I'm looking for myself. That's why I was about to fly to Baku. He knows where Belkin is.'

'I see,' said the prosecutor, striking his fist against the top of his desk. 'We must inform the KGB right away.'

He pressed the button to summon his secretary, and Vera Petelina appeared at the door almost immediately, notebook in hand.

'Write this down, Vera Vasilyevna,' ordered the prosecutor. ' "Secret, urgent, to General Tsvigun, KGB. According to information in the hands of USSR Special Investigator Shamrayev, some criminals are about to attempt an illegal crossing of the Soviet–Afghanistan border by helicopter or plane from the airfield at Charshanga in Uzbekistan. At the same time, I have to inform you that the following are implicated in illegal drug-trafficking: Viktor Sysoyev, head of the Chief Pharmaceutical Authority, and Edward Balayan, USSR Deputy Minister of Health. Signed: Roman Rudenko." '

Then he turned to me and said: 'Can you let those three KGB agents go?'

'Yes,' I replied. About half an hour earlier Pshenichny had told me that none of those arrested claimed to know the doctor, and he had handed them all over to Malenina for further interrogation.

'Add this to the letter, Vera Vasilyevna,' he said. ' "In accordance with your request the three KGB agents will be released today." That's all. Have it sent by special messenger, urgently.'

Petelina left the room and then he said to me: 'That's that! Let them come to us for information now, and not the other way round. When does your plane leave for Baku?'

'I'm going by the regular flight at 12.40,' I replied, looking at my watch. It was already 10.07, and I had yet to fix up my journey, get money from the accounts office and leave instructions for Svetlov and Pshenichny.

'All right,' he said. 'Don't waste any time. And please find this Belkin by Monday, I beg you. Otherwise you and I really are going to get it in the neck from the Central Committee, and I'll have my grand-niece to deal with as well! Understand?'

'Of course, Roman Andreyevich.'

'And now tell me this. Do you have the impression that

yesterday's car crash might not have been an accident?'

'What do you mean?' I said in surprise.

'Well, I'm not certain, but . . . From what I've gathered, you sent instructions that Dolgo-Saburov wasn't to be detained at midday, at 12.10 to be exact. And yet six hours later that transport policeman still didn't know about it. Doesn't that strike you as odd?'

'But who could have wanted it to happen, Roman Andreyevich?' I suddenly felt quite disoriented.

'I've already told you. Shcholokov, for example. And Andropov, too. They want to mess up the operation. Of course, they couldn't have calculated in advance that an accident would happen, but all the same: they do whatever they can to put a spoke in our wheels . . . Nozdryakov doesn't mention that the Automobile Inspection ever received further instructions about Dolgo-Saburov after all. I must ask you once again to be very careful. You're going to need all your Jewish cunning. Does anybody know that you're off to Baku?'

'Only Svetlov and two employees of *Komsomolskaya Pravda.*'

'Keep it like that. Off you go. Ah, just one more thing. I don't think it's worth getting our accounts office to organize your trip to Baku right now. Just to be on the safe side. You can never keep a secret anywhere. Settle up with them when you come back. Meanwhile, I'll sign your travel papers. OK?'

He looked me in the eye, and those eyes of his expressed more than his words. The Chief Public Prosecutor knew that he had to find ways of acting without their knowledge. Here was a man who had survived under Stalin, Malenkov, and Khrushchev, after all. He spent all his time, brain and energy trying to rumble the snares and intrigues of his rivals and enemies.

'But what shall I use for money, Roman Andreyevich?' I asked.

'Why don't you borrow some from somebody? I'd lend you some myself, but I don't have any on me right now.

327

The wife's got it all, in the savings bank, you know . . .'

Of course, why should the Chief Public Prosecutor, a marshal and member of the CPSU Central Committee, carry money about on his person? I doubt if he even knows what it looks like!

Without waiting for the lift, I ran straight up the stairs to my own office. Everybody looked at me as I rushed past, some with curiosity, others in silence, as if they had just seen a corpse, and yet others with a scarcely veiled look of triumph. They had all listened in to the 'Voice of America' the previous night, of course, and they would all have heard about the letters from Tsvigun and Grishin. They obviously thought my days in the department were numbered. For all I knew, they could be right. I hadn't found Belkin yet, after all.

Baklanov appeared out of his office and gave me a questioning glance. 'Still alive then?' he said.

'So far,' I muttered. 'Can you lend me a couple of hundred?'

I quickly opened up my own office and went inside. The telephone was ringing.

'Hello,' I said.

'Mister Shamrayev?' said a cheerful voice with an obviously non-Russian accent. 'This is the *New York Times* correspondent. I'd like to interview you in connection with yesterday's operation. Could we meet in some restaurant perhaps?'

I said nothing in reply. Instead I put down the receiver and went next door to borrow money from Baklanov for my trip to Baku.

17.50 hours, Baku time
The same day, Friday, 8 June
Chingiz Adigezalov, the Director of the Pioneers' Palace in Baku, studied my travel documents and my Prosecutor's Office identity card with great care. I could see that he wasn't so much reading and rereading them as pondering how to deal with me. I'd appeared in Baku like a bolt from the blue on this beautiful June

day. Though it was getting quite late, the sun was still beating down on the buildings outside his office. There was a strong smell of oleanders coming from the public garden next door, and away over the roofs of the houses I could see the calm, translucent green of the Caspian. Adigezalov was about to entertain Komsomol leaders from Azerbaidzhan, Georgia and Armenia. Thus the table in his office was covered with shashlyks, grapes, wine and cognac. The Festival of Friendship between Caucasian Pioneer organizations was being officially opened at that very moment in the palace assembly hall. Then, at the most inconvenient moment, this special investigator turns up from Moscow!

'But couldn't it wait until Monday?'

'No, I'm afraid not,' I replied.

'You see, my chief personnel officer has gone home already . . .'

'Well, you'll just have to ask him or her to come back into work. Either ring up or send a car. I'm here on the express instructions of the Party Central Committee, you know.'

'I can see that from your papers,' he replied. This is what Rudenko had written:

Igor Iosifovich Shamrayev, Special Investigator at the USSR Public Prosecutor's Office, has been sent to the Azerbaidzhani SSR on especially urgent government business, in connection with which all party, government and other administrative organs are to afford him whatever help and assistance he may require.

'All right,' said Adigezalov with a sigh. He'd obviously decided that it would be best to get rid of me as quickly as possible. 'Let's go. I'll open up her room myself. Perhaps I'll be able to find what you're after.'

We walked out of his office and down an old, impressive-looking marble staircase (the Pioneers'

Palace had been built by a pre-revolutionary oil tycoon). On the ground floor we entered what looked like a tiny storeroom. We could hear children's voices coming from the assembly hall, amplified by microphones and punctuated by thunderous applause.

'It's strange,' said Adigezalov. 'Two weeks ago we were visited by a journalist from Moscow who was also asking about the geography teacher. He said that he wanted to pay him a visit in order to write an article about him. And now you turn up from the Public Prosecutor's Office. He must be either a great man or a great criminal!'

We entered the storeroom, which turned out to be a cross between an archive and a personnel office, in fact. The shelves along the wall were filled with piles of children's exercise books, photograph albums, sketch-pads, posters, diagrams, photo-montages and wall broadsheets. There were maps, globes, card indexes and boxes containing letters from all over the world. Each box had the name of the countries of origin written on the side: Cuba, Poland, Brazil, Algeria, Lebanon, France . . .

Adigezalov produced a faded photo-display from one of the boxes. More than a dozen group photographs of former pioneers were mounted on it in a circle, and right in the middle was the picture of a smiling man aged about fifty. Written above it were the following words: 'To our dear Lev Arkadyevich Rozentsveig on his fiftieth birthday – 5 April 1958'.

'Rozentsveig,' said Adigezalov with apparent difficulty. 'No, I'll never be able to pronounce it. What strange surnames some people do have, it's simply amazing! Well, that's your man, and these are all his pupils. The journalist from Moscow is among them somewhere, he showed me himself.'

'And where is this Rozentsveig now?'

'Working at a forest school near Kyurdamir.'

'Where exactly is this school?'

'Look, you can be driven there. You've got a car, of

330

course? Just tell the driver that you want the "Communard" Collective Farm, and he'll take you there straight away. It's an enormous place. Everybody knows it.'

'So I've to go to the forest school on the "Communard" Collective Farm near Kyurdamir,' I said, repeating his directions. 'How long will it take to get there?'

'Well, you'll do it in about three hours by car. What sort of car have you got, a Volga?'

'Listen,' I said. 'Why did this Rozentsveig leave Baku for some collective farm school out in the sticks?'

'Well, it happened before my time,' he said, raising his hands defensively. 'But I can tell you why. Can you really imagine anybody working in the Central Pioneers' Palace with a surname like his?'

I left the building with the sound of fanfares and applause still ringing in my ears. I turned around and saw Adigezalov standing at his window and looking after me in astonishment. There was no car waiting for me at the entrance. He just couldn't understand why a special investigator on urgent government business should be walking off down the road on his own two feet. I could see from his expression that he didn't approve. But there was nothing I could do to oblige either him or myself. By rushing here straight from the airport, I'd already gained knowledge of Rozentsveig's address. Of course, all I needed to do was lift a receiver and dial the Azerbaidzhani Prosecutor's office, the head of the Baku Militia or Central Committee headquarters in the town, and I'd have a Volga placed at my disposal immediately, and a helicopter or motor-launch, if I were to ask. But would they be able to get me to this Rozentsveig?

I went up to a passer-by and said: 'Excuse me, but can you tell me where the bus station is?'

23.00 hours, Baku time
I will leave it for writers like Vadim Belkin and his ilk to

331

describe the 'charms' of the road between Baku and Kyurdamir. I'll say only that the crush for tickets which he described at Baku airport has got nothing on the scene that greeted my eyes at the Baku bus station. The people were the same, however – unshaven for the most part, with huge moustaches and dressed in those enormous Caucasian caps. There they were, storming the mud-bespattered buses as soon as they appeared. It reminded me of the people I'd seen rushing the trains in 1945 when I was small. Now, as then, most of them carried great sacks with them, or ramshackle suitcases, except that now, instead of belongings, their baggage was filled with bread, rice, tea, sugar, butter, buckwheat and other supplies which you can get in big cities these days, but practically nowhere else. It was like any crowded scene at the railway termini in Moscow, except that this Caucasian crowd was even more frenzied and vociferous.

The only way I could get a bus to Kyurdamir was by showing my Prosecutor's Office identity card, otherwise I might not have got there at all. There were no ticket offices. The only thing to do was try your luck in the crush with the crowd of Azerbaidzhanis. After three unsuccessful attempts I realized that I was up against a barely concealed display of national solidarity and that not a single Russian-looking passenger had got on to the last three buses. I found the manager of the bus station and laid my identity papers silently before him. A minute later he obsequiously guided me towards a bus which he placed at my sole disposal, and then I was off. I realized that I had needed to uncover my incognito yet again, but what choice was there?

Meanwhile, the bus station manager naturally rang up his counterpart in Kyurdamir to warn him that a USSR special investigator was on his way. When I finally arrived at 10.30 p.m., waiting for me were Captain Gasanzade, head of the Kyurdamir Militia, and a local party official, Comrade Bagirov. They looked anxious and confused, obviously not knowing what to do with me. I turned down their offer of dinner or a room in a hotel. All I wanted was a car to take me to the 'Communard' Collective Farm. I got one right away. The police officer volunteered to accompany me, but I said no very firmly and went off immediately with nobody but the driver for company – a young Azerbaidzhani with gleaming white teeth. What his boss's parting words to him were, I don't know, as I don't speak the language. But the driver did try to strike up a conversation as we drove through the night. I was determined not to play into the Baku Militia's hands on this occasion however, even though I had more or less already abandoned my anonymity. I said nothing in reply.

When we arrived, the driver handed me over to the chairman of the farm, a fifty-year-old man by the name of Riza-zade. He had obviously just been woken up out of bed by a telephone call from Kyurdamir announcing my visit, and he still looked shell-shocked. Around us lay the silent Azerbaidzhani village, all in darkness now that most of its inhabitants were asleep.

'What's happened?' asked the farm chairman. 'Why are you here?' Obviously the arrival late at night of a special investigator from Moscow was no laughing matter if you were the boss of a huge wine-growing collective buried somewhere deep in the mountains, and a boss who had something to hide.

'I'll tell you everything in the morning,' I said. 'Only right now I'm very tired, and I want to get some sleep. Can you find me somewhere to lie down?'

'Don't offend us, comrade. Of course we can!' replied Riza-zade. Now that he saw a way of obliging his uninvited Moscow guest, he moved quickly into action. 'We've got a whole building set aside for visitors. It's a wonderful place! I'll get you something to eat straight away! Where are your things?'

'I left them in Baku, at the left-luggage office. And I don't want anything to eat. All I want to do is sleep.'

'*Please*, comrade. How can we send you to bed without giving you anything to eat?'

'I'll tell you what. I'll eat a good breakfast in the morning, OK?' I said this with particular emphasis to make him realize that he could show me all his hospitality the next day. He saw what I was getting at, of course, and breathed an inward sigh of relief. He would be able to get off by giving me a bribe, a first-class breakfast or something on those lines. He suddenly became much more cheerful and led me off to the farm guest-house, not forgetting to regale me with a description of the collective's achievements as he did so – how they always exceeded their plan, and what sort of wine and brandy did I like?

The guest-house really was a splendid affair, set in a beautiful garden and fitted throughout with Finnish furniture. My room contained a refrigerator filled with local wine, cognac and vodka, while the table was loaded with fresh fruit and vegetables. I could have sat down to dinner or breakfast on the spot!

But I made a great show of being tired. I collapsed in an armchair and began to take off my shoes.

'That's all, old man, thank you very much,' I said. 'I'll take a shower and then I'll hit the sack. We can talk tomorrow.'

'At what time?' he asked impatiently.

'Oh, I don't know. Let's say nine o'clock, or ten . . .'

'All right. Are you quite sure you don't need anything else? Should I send a woman along to clear up?'

'No, I don't need any woman. I just want to sleep, I'm very tired. Good night.'

He finally went away. Twenty minutes or so later, I switched out all the lights and went outside on to the steps. I was surrounded by darkness. I could see the whole Milky Way up above me, looking extraordinarily immense and close. The village was asleep. The only thing to disturb the silence was the occasional sound of young people's laughter from a little way away. I walked down the steps into the garden and headed in the direction of the laughter.

Half a dozen young people were sitting in the courtyard of another building, drinking tea out of slender, moulded glasses and listening to a 'Voice of America' broadcast in Turkish. When I appeared, the radio was switched off, but a packet of Moscow cigarettes which I'd brought with me was soon being passed around the circle. Then they offered me a glass of tea, which I didn't refuse. They soon started to describe the sights of the collective farm, and within ten minutes or so I had discovered the whereabouts of the forest school. 'Can you see that light over there in the hills? That's their campfire. They'll be singing songs around it until midnight at least.'

After finishing my tea and saying good night, I went back to the guest-house. But instead of going in, I stepped out firmly in the direction of the hills, heading for the light which I could see flickering feebly in the darkness.

It was 11.17 p.m. local time. The light seemed very close. Just a few hundred yards up the hill and you'd be able to touch it ... But it wasn't like that at all, as my thumping heart and my light Moscow shoes bore witness.

Tired, dirty, with scratches on my arms, a thorn in my hand, and one trouser-leg torn against a bush, I finally reached the glowing embers of the campfire at five minutes to midnight exactly. I found my way there in the end by following the direction of the singing.

Lev Arkadyevich was a lively, cheerful, youthful-looking man with a shock of black hair. He looked no older than he had done twenty years earlier on the photograph I had seen. Tall and wiry, with a face burnt by the sun and wind, he was dressed in T-shirt, sports trousers and plimsolls. He was sitting around the fire in this forest glade, surrounded by his pupils, all singing folksongs. When I arrived, everybody stopped. The school itself consisted of a cookhouse and a dozen or so large tents pitched some way from the centre of the collective farm itself. We were right up in the hills, and as you looked around, you seemed to be surrounded by nothing but an ocean of blackness.

About twenty minutes later, when the young people had all gone off to bed, Rozentsveig and I had a chat. As a result, I finally found out the real name of the notorious 'Ziyalov' – it was Boris Khotulyov. He was thirty-two years old and, as we already know, had once been a member of Rozentsveig's Geographical Society at the Baku Pioneers' Palace. He had won many prizes at various national competitions for budding young chemists and had gone on to graduate from the Baku Medical Institute. He'd then done research in psychotherapy at a medical institute in Moscow and was now a consultant at Psychiatric Hospital No. 5 at the settlement of Stolbovaya in the Moscow Region.

Rozentsveig really did seem to know everything about his former pupils, so it had been well worth the trouble of finding him. I felt like a cook who has spent four days baking a cake and who is finally ready to take it out of the oven and open the lid. And because the cake was ready and wouldn't stand another minute's baking, I wanted to get back to Moscow right away and rush along to this Stolbovaya. If the Chief Prosecutor hadn't delayed me that morning, that's exactly what I would have done. I would have been in the Stolbovaya psychiatric hospital at that very moment. It made me very angry to think that I had lost a whole day, but even angrier to realize that I had to carry on losing time even now. There was simply nothing I could do about it. Rozentsveig told me that the last bus from Kyurdamir to Baku had already gone and that there wouldn't be another one till morning. There wasn't any other traffic at night either, not even taxis, because people around there were afraid of being stopped and robbed.

So I spent the rest of the night chatting to him. We were surrounded by sleeping children – forty-five of them from hospitals all over the republic. When Rozentsveig had been made 'redundant' at the Pioneers' Palace, he had had the idea of setting up a boarding-school for children with pulmonary diseases.

He wanted to improve their health through gymnastic exercises in the morning and long walks in the sun during the afternoon. The details of his life have no connection with this story, of course, and I found myself wondering all the time where this Khotulyov was at that moment. Was he still waiting for his sister and Dolgo-Saburov to appear, or had he listened to 'Voice of America' and realized that the two of them had died in the road accident? If he had, he would already be making his escape. But where would he be running to? The Old Man at Charshanga? In that case, he'd find that particular escape route already closed . . .

I asked Rozentsveig how he felt about living there in Azerbaidzhan and whether he harboured any grudge about being made 'redundant'.

'Well, you know, it's the same everywhere,' he said. 'It's the same people, wherever you look – whether you're talking about this collective farm, the district committee in Kyurdamir, Baku or even Moscow. But I've risen above all that now. I live in the mountains, surrounded by fresh air. And look! I've got forty-five children and I teach them all to breathe the fresh air too. I've been surrounded by children all my life, you know, and that helps.'

'But then one of them turns into a Khotulyov.'

'And another into a Belkin. And another turns into you. Khotulyov came to me when he was fifteen years old. His character was already formed by then. And some of my work doesn't turn out right, either, I'm willing to admit it. But you asked me how I felt about this blackness that surrounds me, all this graft and brutality. I feel sorry for them, you know. I look down at them from up here, and I feel sorry for them. I've got fresh air to breathe, while they, well . . .'

Saturday, 9 June, 05.00 hours, Baku time
Just before five o'clock, as dawn was beginning to appear, Rozentsveig showed me the way down to the farm village. Everybody was still asleep. It really was

no distance, and we got there in seven minutes. It had taken me nearly a whole hour to find my way up the hill in the darkness the night before.

But I didn't enter the village. I sent Rozentsveig back the way he had come, and sat on a stone by the side of the road. After twenty minutes or so, my patience was rewarded. Along came a lorry carrying cabbages, heading down the mountain road towards Kyurdamir. I managed to wave him down, and within a quarter of an hour was deposited at the bus station in Kyurdamir. Distances seemed a lot less than they had done the night before.

The bus station was empty, if you could even call it a bus station. It consisted of nothing but a closed wooden hut, a battered concrete shelter and a couple of ramshackle benches. It was only 5.40 a.m., so there were no passengers or buses. I sat down on one of the seats. There was nothing to do but wait for the first bus or taxi which could take me to Baku to catch the next flight to Moscow.

A minute later a police Volga drew up to where I was sitting. The rear door was opened by the Kyurdamir militia captain whom I had met the previous night.

'Are you going to Baku, Comrade Investigator?' he asked obligingly. 'Good morning. Jump in. We'll take you there.'

Apart from him and the driver, there was one other person in the car, sitting at the front. He was a thick-set, broad-shouldered Azerbaidzhani, dressed in civilian clothes. He looked more like an athlete or a wrestler than anything else. I couldn't help but be reminded of Akeyev. He had the same heavy, muscular appearance.

Captain Gasan-zade remained sitting in the back seat. Without getting out, he had opened the car door and was looking at me expectantly with a smile on his face. 'There won't be a bus along today, Comrade Investigator. There's been a landslide in the mountains, and I've had to halt all traffic.'

338

This was an outright lie, of course, and his laughing eyes made no attempt to conceal it. I was alone in a strange Azerbaidzhani village, and there in front of me were the people who ran the place – the local police chief and his henchmen (unless the man in civvies turned out to be one of the bosses himself). There was nobody else around, so I was naturally in their power. If they were to put a bullet in my head there and then, there wouldn't be so much as a dog to bark about it.

I smiled, got up from my bench and got into the Volga, next to Captain Gasan-zade. At that moment the 'wrestler' who had been sitting in the front, got out and came and sat next to me at the back. Now I was well and truly hemmed in by the two of them. Then the car moved off and we began to descend from the heights of Kyurdamir to the lowlands of Baku.

Meanwhile I said nothing but just waited. Of course, they could have bumped me off there and then and tipped my body into some chasm on the way, so that even the most experienced CID sleuths wouldn't find it. The special investigator might have gone anywhere, after all. Who saw him? He didn't even tell anybody that he was making the trip. Yes, he did visit the 'Communard' Collective Farm apparently, then he walked off into the mountains during the night, obviously got lost and, well . . .

But what would be the sense in killing me? After all, Moscow had initiated the investigation. They'd merely send another investigator – Baklanov, for example.

'Listen, old fellow,' said Captain Gasan-zade. 'We're men of the world, so let's talk frankly to each other, man to man. I realize that you're on a case and are just doing what you're told. And you've been making a pretty good job of it, too, I must say! I heard about that Moscow operation of yours on the radio. Whoever did that is a pretty smart worker, I thought! Then last night somebody asks me: who's this Shamrayev fellow that's turned up? From the Moscow Prosecutor's Office, you say? That's the one they were talking about on "Voice of America". Glad to meet you! Amazing how many crooks you managed to pick up in Moscow that day! Now tell me, old lad, have you come to us about the same case?'

I said nothing.

'You see,' he went on, 'it's like this. In Moscow you're in charge. You can arrest whoever you like. It's up to you – and they've got it coming to them for the most part. But we've got our own republic, you know. What do you have to come sniffing around here for? Who are you trying to get?'

I still made no reply. Meanwhile, the car was zigzagging its way down the mountain road. Every minute or two we came to a hair-raising bend with deep chasms yawning beneath us. We hadn't come across any other traffic. The man sitting on the other side of me suddenly coughed into his fist and addressed me in perfect Russian, without any trace of an accent: 'Igor Iosifovich, it's like this. We know that you're investigating Khotulyov, Sysoyev and Balayan. What set the whole ball rolling was that coffin business at Baku airport, and now things have already got as far as Balayan. It's also led you to our republic. But we're not going to let you harm our country, you see. You're in our hands now, you can see that perfectly well yourself. If you don't accept what we propose right away, you'll never leave here alive. But if you do accept, then everything will be all right – for you and us. Now, this is what we've got to offer.'

He leant over the back of the seat and lifted out a small suitcase. It was fairly heavy, and he plumped it down on his lap. Then he undid the locks and opened it up. It contained a large number of neatly arranged piles of banknotes. 'There's 100,000 there,' he said, 'and it's all yours – as long as you agree not to touch anybody in Azerbaidzhan, and to remove all documents relating to our republic from the case file. Do we have a deal?'

I still said nothing. I had no choice, of course. I had to do as they said, but I still kept quiet.

'Stop the car,' he said to the driver.

We stopped by the side of the road – or on the edge of an enormous ravine, to be more exact.

'It's up to you, Igor Iosifovich. Either you take the money, or . . . We haven't got any choice in the matter either, you know. It's our job. We're acting on government instructions, too,' he added with a smile. 'Either you put us in gaol, or we bump you off. But there is another way out.' He stared at me with those tranquil, dark-brown eyes of his.

I took hold of the suitcase, closed the lid and clicked the locks shut. 'OK, let's go,' I said to the driver.

'That's right! Well done!' said Captain Gasan-zade. 'I was certain you'd accept. Praise be to Allah! It would be a crime to kill somebody like you! Let's drop off somewhere for a drink and a bite to eat.'

The 'wrestler' looked at me, too, also waiting for an answer.

'No,' I said, 'I've no time for that on this trip. When is the next flight to Moscow?'

'Nine-twenty a.m., local time.'

'Will you take me to the airport?'

'Of course we will!' replied Captain Gasan-zade. 'What a question!' He really did seem pleased that he hadn't had to kill me.

The same day, after 08.00 hours
They drove me straight to the airport, avoiding Baku itself. On the way there we stopped just once, in Lokbatan, for the 'wrestler' to make a call from a telephone box. He was probably ringing his boss to tell him I'd 'accepted'.

At the airport they helped me buy a ticket for the next flight, wished me a good journey and wondered, with a smile, whether I mightn't lose the suitcase and would I like a bodyguard? I assured them that such suitcases never get lost and that there was certainly no need for anybody to protect me. The 'wrestler' gave me the keys to the case, and in his presence I locked it up and put the key away in a purse. The purse I then placed in the inside pocket of my jacket.

After this they left. There was still twenty minutes to go before checking-in time for the Moscow flight. I didn't much like the fact that they'd gone away without accompanying me as far as the plane. There was something not quite right about that. I entered the waiting room and sat down on one of the seats. Then I pretended to fiddle with the keys in the lock, as if I intended to start opening the case in full view of everyone. I suddenly realized that I was walking into a trap. Two tipsy passengers had followed me into the waiting room. I noticed how they sobered up right away and looked at me in alarm as soon as they thought I was going to open the case. I smiled inwardly, stuffed the key back into my pocket and went up to them. They started pretending to be drunk again, embracing each other and mumbling incoherently, but I went right up to them and said rudely:

'I want you out of this airport within sixty seconds!'

'Why?' said one of them in astonishment.

'The orders have been changed. There's no need for you to protect me. The operation is off.'

'What? You mean that nobody's coming?' said the other one.

'That's exactly what I mean. I said the operation is off, that's all. You can go.'

I was bluffing, of course, but in cases like these attack is often the best means of defence. They gave a shrug and went back to the departure hall in some confusion. That meant that I had a few minutes at my disposal, before they had time to ring their bosses and realize what was going on. I watched them disappear in the direction of the airport militia office and then rushed up to the rows of left-luggage lockers. There was a handful of passengers dozing here and there, but none of them paid any attention to me. All the same, I went down one of the rows as far as I could, found an open locker (No. 54), and then, with my back turned to the room, opened the suitcase and quickly emptied all

342

the money into the cupboard. After that I placed the suitcase on the ground, dialled 675185 on the lock of the cupboard (this was the number of my plane ticket) and shut the door with a bang. I walked out of the waiting room as quickly as I could. Everything seemed peaceful. I spent a few seconds considering what to do next and then crossed the departure hall to the buffet on the other side. I bought a bottle of *kefir* and a slice of cheesecake and stood near the window consuming them and waiting for events to develop.

And develop they did – quite quickly. First of all, policemen came running out of the militia post in all directions, as many as were there, no doubt. Then my two luckless sleuths appeared and, to their total astonishment, found me calmly munching cake and drinking *kefir* in the buffet. One stood there staring at me, while the other rushed back to the militia office to tell them I was still there and hadn't run away.

A few minutes later registration for Flight 247 to Moscow was announced over the tannoy. The militia's eyes were on me all the time now, as I walked over to the check-in desk and stood in the queue. The scene was exemplary. The police made all the passengers queue in a straight line, while the Aeroflot staff were courteous and polite, just like in a film. I realized that the chief actors in this performance were myself, however, and my 'heavy' suitcase. When I reached the front of the queue, the girl stamped my ticket and I placed the case on the scales. At that very moment, cameras clicked and bulbs flashed from all directions. Somebody's heavy arm held my hand against the suitcase. Ahead of me, behind the check-in desk, I noticed a young-looking face with blue eyes and guessed that this must be Vekilov, the Azerbaidzhani Interior Minister's personal assistant, the one who had questioned Belkin and tried to frighten Sverdlov, and quite possibly one of the visitors from Baku who had called at Sysoyev's dacha for the diamonds and gone away with a suitcase full of paper money. Who knows, I might have been carrying that very same suitcase . . .

'Bring the witnesses here!' he ordered, and two airport workers suddenly appeared at his side. They had obviously been warned in advance of what would happen.

'Comrade Shamrayev,' he said. 'We have reason to suspect that you are carrying in that suitcase money which you have accepted as a bribe. Will you open it, please?'

'Please go ahead and open it yourself,' I said calmly, without taking my hand away from the case. I was pressing it down as hard as I could, so that the airport scales wouldn't give the game away.

Vekilov's plan was quite simple. He thought he had me caught red-handed. I would be at his mercy then, and would agree to any conditions. And if I were to prove obstinate, then he had incontrovertible evidence – photographs showing Shamrayev and a suitcase full of money. He would have them sent to Rudenko and the Central Committee immediately, the compromised investigator would be taken off the case and the results of his investigation wouldn't be worth a brass farthing. He thought he had me in a cleft stick.

I produced the key and placed it on the counter in front of Vekilov, letting go of the suitcase as I did so.

'Please, go ahead and open it,' I said.

He didn't even notice how the needle on the scales suddenly slipped back to just over two pounds. He took the key and handed it over to one of his assistants. 'Open it up,' he ordered.

As soon as his assistant removed the suitcase from the scales, Vekilov's face began to register alarm. The case was obviously too light. All the same, the MVD photographers continued to click away, and we were surrounded by a whole host of inquisitive passengers. Vekilov's assistant opened up a perfectly empty suitcase.

I picked up my ticket from the counter and walked

over to the embarkation gate.

The same day, on board the TU–104, after 11.00 hours
After Voronezh we finally made contact with air traffic control at Vnukovo, just outside Moscow. I had made my way to the flight deck and was listening to the captain, Oleg Chubar, talk over the radio.

'Vnukovo, this is fight No. 2546 here. I have a special investigator from the USSR Chief Prosecutor's Office on board. He has an urgent message for CID headquarters on the Petrovka. Can you take it? Over.'

I stood behind the pilot's seat and waited. As soon as we had left the tarmac at Baku, I had shown the stewardess my identity papers and she took me straight to the flight deck. But it turned out that the plane could only contact ground control city by city, and that we wouldn't be able to get through to Moscow until we had passed Voronezh.

Chubar turned to face me and said: 'What number do you want at the Petrovka?

'The duty officer,' I replied. He then relayed this information through to Vnukovo.

'Get up and let the investigator sit down for a bit,' he said to his co-pilot.

'No, there's no need,' I replied, but it was too late. The co-pilot had already vacated his seat and was offering me his headset. I put it on and could immediately hear the voice of the Moscow traffic controller.

'Vnukovo here. We have the Petrovka on the line. Go ahead, please. Over.'

Chubar nodded to me, and I proceeded to dictate the following message: ' "To Lieutenant-Colonel Svetlov. Urgent. Dr Boris Khotulyov, aged thirty-two, place of work – Stolbovaya psychiatric hospital No. 5. Signed Shamrayev." Have you got it? Over.'

'Understood,' came the reply. 'I'll transmit it to the Petrovka now. You can listen in. "To Lieutenant-Colonel Svetlov. Urgent. Dr Boris Khotulyov, aged thirty-two, place of work ..." Hello!' He suddenly stopped talking. He was silent for a few seconds, and then said to me: 'Comrade Shamrayev. I have an urgent message for you from the Petrovka. I'll repeat it sentence by sentence as it is given to me by the duty officer. "Investigation team under the command of Lieutenant-Colonel Svetlov left for the settlement of Stolbovaya at 11.05 a.m. We expect a report on their progress at any moment. Duty Officer, Moscow, Colonel Glazarin." Is that clear? Over.'

I looked at my watch. It was 11.25. That meant that twenty-five minutes ago Svetlov had also got on to the whereabouts of the doctor.

To Investigation Team Leader
Special Investigator
Comrade I. I. Shamrayev

REPORT

Following your instructions to check the personnel at psychiatric hospital and clinics in Moscow and the surrounding district, with a view to discovering the identity of the doctor known as Boris, wanted in connection with the kidnapping of Citizens Belkin and Rybakov, the investigation team visited the following medical establishments over the period 7–8 June 1979:

Psychiatric clinics Nos. 1–21
Psychiatric hospitals Nos. 1–12

The questioning of medical staff and the examination of personnel office records at the above institutions yielded no positive results. However, during my questioning of patients regularly attending clinic No. 21 in the Oktyabrsky district of the city, I found one patient, A. B. Pekarsky, who identified the identikit picture as being of a doctor who had once treated him. The doctor's name was Boris Yuryevich

Khotulyov, who is now in charge of Department 4 at MVD Special Psychiatric Hospital No. 5, near the settlement of Stolbovaya in the Moscow region. This was where, six months ago, the patient, A. B. Pekarsky, underwent a three-month period of treatment at the request of the courts.

Acting USSR Special Investigator
V. Pshenichny

Moscow, 9 June 1979

I didn't get to read this report till some time later, in Moscow, of course. Meanwhile, I said to the air traffic controller at Vnukovo: 'Understood. Thank you very much. Please ask Colonel Glazarin to send a car to pick me up at the airport. Over and out.'

Stolbovaya settlement, after midday

EXTRACTFROM THE REGISTER OF PATIENTS ADMITTED TO DEPARTMENT 4, MVD SPECIAL PSYCHIATRIC HOSPITAL NO. 5

27 May 1979. Patient Ilya Nikolayevich ZAITSEV admitted. Aged 27, no permanent occupation. Reason for treatment: decision of Moscow Health Department Forensic Medical Commission No. 3. Preliminary diagnosis: manic-depressive psychosis. Patient placed in secure cell No. 16 for violent lunatics.

Duty Nurse I. O. Kravtsova

URGENT. BY SPECIAL MESSENGER

To the Doctor in Charge
MVD Special Hospital No. 5
Comrade Zh. F. Galinskaya

We are sending you today Citizen I. N. ZAITSEV, declared uncontrollable by Moscow Health Depart-

347

ment Forensic Medical Commission No. 3. He is to be subjected to compulsory chemo-therapy. The court authorization is appended to this letter.

Secretary to the Cheryomushki District People's Court
N. Khotulyova

27 May 1979

Secret

DECISION OF MOSCOW HEALTH DEPARTMENT FORENSIC MEDICAL COMMISSION NO. 9

On 28 May 1979, the commission, consisting of Dr B. Yu. Khotulyov (Chairman), and psychiatric consultants Dr E. R. Rayenko and Dr S. T. Lunts, examined the patient Ilya Nikolayevich ZAITSEV, admitted for compulsory chemo-therapy on the instructions of the Cheryomushki District People's Court.

The patient is accused of malicious hooliganism under Article 206, Section 2, of the RSFSR Criminal Code. He is accused of publicly burning his identity papers on Kuznetsky Bridge Street while being under the influence of drugs. He is further accused of harassing passers-by by shouting anti-Soviet slogans and through the use of abusive language. He pretends to be a well-known journalist and a member of the CPSU Central Committee Press Corps.

As a result of our examination, we have established that the patient is in a condition of psycho-motor excitation. He displays emotional instability and his mood is explosive. He is unable to adjust to his surroundings and is beyond normal human contact. His psychosis manifests itself in aggressive behaviour and an obsessive belief that he is to travel abroad as part of a delegation from the CPSU Central Committee. He is given to changing his surname periodically. 'Belkin', 'Orlov', 'Volkov', etc., are among the names by which he has referred to himself.

Diagnosis: The patient I. N. Zaitsev is suffering from manic-depressive psychosis and is not responsible for his own actions.

Treatment prescribed: The patient should be subjected to compulsory chemo-therapy for a period of not less than three months. 0.25 gr. Aminazine to be injected intravenously daily.

Commission Chairman B. Khotulyov
Members E. Rayenko
S. Lunts

28 May 1979

And that was all. Two forged documents concocted by a brother and sister were enough to lock away one of the country's best-known journalists (and Brezhnev's favourite, what's more) in an MVD Special Hospital (or rather, prison). It takes just a couple of fictitious documents (the so-called authorization received from the People's Court was never found), and somebody can be clapped behind bars, and not even under his own name. He is placed in a concrete cell with sound-proofed walls and a cohort of hefty medical orderlies to look after him, strait-jacket, wet sheets and a syringe filled with the tranquillizer aminazine always at the ready. And if it hadn't been a question of telling Brezhnev about the disappearance of Belkin on the eve of his trip to Vienna, if Suslov, Churbanov and Shcholokov hadn't got mixed up in it together with a special investigator and the best detectives in the Moscow CID, then say what you like, three months further on this particular 'patient' would have left hospital either with partial amnesia or as a candidate for the local crematorium. I caught myself wondering just how many others like Belkin are to be found in so-called 'special hospitals' in Moscow, Tula, Saratov, Novorossiysk or wherever, and how much aminazine, barbamil, haloperidol, sanapax, frenolon, largactil and other tranquillizers or stimulants are being pumped into completely innocent people . . .

Belkin was asleep, but his rest was far from being that of a normal human being. It was more like a temporary respite in the life of a tortured animal. Who would have imagined that a man who only three weeks before had gone harpooning in the Caspian, climbing and collecting edelweiss in the Pamirs, falling for whichever pretty woman came along next, and finally attempting to uncover a major drugs-ring all by himself – who would have imagined that this young, talented, energetic journalist would now be lying on a bunk in a cell with concrete floor and walls, showing no reaction to the voices of others and only occasionally staring into empty space with clouded eyes, as devoid of understanding as a new-born calf.

'He's been hurling himself about the cell and demanding aminazine all the time,' said Svetlov. 'I thought he'd smash his head in. They had to give him an injection – half a dose. What will happen to him after this I can't even imagine.'

'Where's the head doctor?' I asked.

'She's bellowing away in her office, waiting for you to turn up.'

'And where are Lunts and Rayenko?'

'They're in the consulting room discussing what's to be done next. I told them that I wouldn't let them out of the hospital until Belkin returned to normal. He's turned into an addict, you see, demanding a fresh injection every couple of hours or so.'

'And what's happened to Khotulyov?'

Svetlov spread out his hands helplessly. 'He disappeared yesterday morning. He's most likely gone to join the Old Man in Uzbekistan. I would have flown straight there myself, only I had a talk to Tsvigun at KGB headquarters yesterday. This is between ourselves. He more or less told me that the KGB itself sends drugs out of the country. This is one of its most lucrative sources of foreign currency. Also, if they want to supply one of these "Red Brigades" or whatever with American dollars, it's simpler for them to hand over a case of opium. The "Voice of America" was correct in saying we occupy third place in the world drug league – and that doesn't include the deals they don't know about. Anyway, Tsvigun and Tsinyov deal personally with anybody who breaks this particular state monopoly. Tsvigun takes care of those inside the country, Tsinyov of those outside. He told me that Khotulyov and Gridasov wouldn't be going anywhere. The KGB are already lying in wait for them at Charshanga.'

'And what about Sysoyev?'

'He's flying back from Switzerland the day after tomorrow. Malenina is waiting for him.'

'What are we going to do about Belkin?'

'I don't know. We were waiting for you to arrive.'

'OK. Let's go and join the doctors.'

The consulting room was on the ground floor of the hospital just by the exit. We went down a long white corridor on the first floor, past long rows of freshly painted cells. Everything about this hospital reminded me of a prison, except that here everything was painted white and blue and the brawny, unshaven warders were dressed like medical orderlies in starched, white smocks. By the staircase there was a check-point with a metal door, and there was a similar door on the ground floor by the exit into the courtyard. The courtyard itself was surrounded by a high, barbed-wire fence and watch-towers. On the other side of the fence was the little settlement where the medical staff lived. It was a beautiful place, lots of wooden dachas, spread about in a pine forest with summer-houses and interconnecting paths. Carved fences enclosed flower and vegetable gardens, created and tended by the hospital's quieter inmates.

In actual fact, MVD Special Hospital No. 5 was not

unlike a monastery where the ruling caste of doctors turned their patients into benign and pliant robots.

The six doctors who worked in the hospital's fourth department had control over the more violent patients, and they were all sitting in the consulting room, having been practically arrested by Svetlov. They were under the constant protection of the MVD, which sent any number of dissidents and genuine schizophrenics and other psychotics to them for treatment. There was nobody even to check up on the activity of these medics, let alone to discipline them. Gorged on the fruit and vegetables which their patients cultivated for them, they were in control and sitting pretty. However, they all understood perfectly well that they were now on a kind of knife-edge. Locking somebody up without the knowledge of the MVD was tantamount to turning the place into a private prison. It was an unforgivable crime, since it involved encroaching on the state's monopoly of punishment. Of course, they would do their best to defend themselves by blaming everything on Khotulyov, but I had no intention of discussing with them now exactly how Belkin had got there and how it happened that ostensible experts like themselves had tried to 'cure' a perfectly healthy man by administering monstrous doses of aminazine.

I stared at their frightened faces and said: 'Colonel Svetlov has already told you the circumstances of this case. We have three days in which to get this journalist back to normal. If we succeed, I can't guarantee that you'll be able to carry on your work here unhindered, but I can promise you that if Belkin is in a state to travel to Vienna, this will be taken into account when your future is decided. What do you have to say?'

Nobody uttered a word. A fat woman dressed in a doctor's coat who had a moustache and a face like a trooper, had turned away from me and was looking out of the window. The rest of them – three women of varying age and two men, one an albino, aged about thirty, and the other a wiry old man with an ancient pipe – carried on sitting there, looking down at their feet.

'Look, this isn't a kindergarten and we're not playing games,' I said sharply. 'What I want to know is this. Is it possible for you to cure a drug-addict in two days? Get your brains to work and start remembering what you were taught at medical school. If need be, we'll transfer him to the Sklifosovsky or Serbsky Institutes. Now, how can we bring him around? I'm waiting.'

'I can't understand why you're adopting this tone of voice,' said the moustachioed trooper all of a sudden. 'How dare you address us in this manner? We are carrying out our duty here. That fact that Khotulyov was acting illegally is another matter. I gave warning a long time ago that . . .'

'What's your name?' I asked rudely.

'Eleonora Frantsevna Shpigel. I am secretary of the party organization here.'

'I don't need you. You may go.'

'What?' she shouted indignantly.

'I am waiting for you to go,' I replied.

Fancy there being a party secretary even here! I hadn't expected that! Still, it stands to reason, I suppose. Eighty per cent of doctors are party members, and they need some control.

Eleonora jumped up on her fat legs, moustache bristling, face purple with anger: 'You . . . you . . . you . . .'

I waited. She waddled over to the door.

'You needn't think you're going to get away with this, you spineless idiot!' she shouted. And with that, she slammed the door so hard that it shook some test-tubes and bottles standing in a glass cabinet.

'Now to continue,' I said.

'Listen to me,' said the old man with the pipe. 'What you're asking is impossible. That's to say, people can get unhooked, of course, but not in so short a time. He'll need to be tied down to his bed for a month in case he tries to kill himself. You get cases like this. At the Butyrki prison a dissident called Borisov hanged himself when they stopped injecting him with aminazine. He was twenty-seven, too. Tying him up is the only way to do it. Then all you can do is wait until he pulls through.'

'But addicts do sometimes cure themselves?'

'It's extremely rare and usually only happens at times of severe stress.'

'Like when?'

'I don't know ... During a war, perhaps, or when giving birth. But then he's not a woman.'

'What's your name?'

'I'm Lunts. I was the one who insisted on his being given aminazine. Khotulyov wanted to prescribe sulfozine, and that would have been even worse.'

'Couldn't you have seen to it that he wasn't prescribed anything?' I couldn't help but ask.

He stared at me with an open, frank expression. 'But you see, that's why people are sent to us in the first place. We have to prescribe something. How was I to know that he was brought here illegally?'

'Dr Lunts,' I said, screwing up my eyes. I had suddenly had an idea. 'If we are dealing with a patient who has a particularly strong penchant for the opposite sex, couldn't we make use of that in some way? I know of a case in Baku, for example, where a young addict stopped injecting himself with morphine as soon as he fell in love with a beautiful girl from Riga.'

'Well, it's not easy to find somebody to fall in love with here,' said Lunts wryly. 'Who would you suggest? Madame Shpigel?'

Valentin Pshenichny suddenly looked in at the door.

'Igor Iosifovich, he's off again, shouting for an injection.'

'Tell the nurse to give him some novocaine,' said Lunts. 'It's no more than a placebo, like this empty pipe of mine, but he'll get some involuntary relief from the injection itself, and then the novocaine will act as a painkiller. The lack of drugs will be giving him a terrible aching feeling in the bones.'

Pshenichny disappeared and Lunts carried on talking. 'We could give him ECT I suppose, but we haven't used that since 1953. Many people can't take it . . .'

'All right,' I said. 'We won't give him electrotherapy. Let's try women therapy instead.'

The same day, after 14.30 hours
Svetlov and I were sitting in one of the hospital's summer-houses, like two old procurers, discussing the various possibilities. If Shakh-Rybakov had managed to unhook himself because of Aina Silinya, then we had to find somebody who could do the same thing to Belkin. The first person who came to mind naturally was Inna, the typist from *Komsomolskaya Pravda*. In her favour was the fact that she loved Belkin and would certainly be ready to do anything for him. If this were some sentimental love story or film, then the author would reward her for her self-sacrifice and affection by letting her be the one who enters the hero's cell and brings him salvation. But we were concerned with life in the real world, and we had to be honest about what would actually happen. Belkin had left Inna ages ago. She wouldn't be able to administer any kind of amorous shock to his system, so we had to leave her out of account.

You may think it all sounds terribly cynical, but the next person to be considered was Aina Silinya. I remembered very well the section in Belkin's manuscript where he described her, half-naked on the beach near Baku during the struggle with Mosol. Belkin had Shakh in a full nelson, and while Lina alias Aina was desperately trying to kiss her lover, her breasts inadvertently pressed against Belkin's arms. That made a powerful impact on him, despite the dramatic circumstances of the shooting. In general, he was strongly attracted to minors. I remembered that nymph from Rybachy Island too . . . Svetlov and I spent a long time discussing this possibility. In favour was Belkin's character, inferred from what we already knew of him. But there were many factors which argued against. In the first place, Silinya was still legally a minor, and although she was no longer a little girl, we still had no right to involve her in amorous intrigues. Apart from that, she hadn't really recovered from the death of her bridgegroom-to-be, Yury Rybakov. So, with great regret, we also had to abandon that possibility.

Of course, the best person of all would have been Natasha Khotulyova. It wasn't surprising that he had fallen for her the first time he saw her at Baku airport. If only she hadn't died two days before . . .

'How about Lena Smagina?' said Svetlov.

I made a wry face. Of course, Akeyev's mistress from Kotlas wasn't bad-looking, but Belkin was hardly likely to go for somebody he would consider a commonplace provincial.

'OK,' said Svetlov. 'Now the Moscow CID has got the records of 40,000 prostitutes on file. As a last resort, why don't we choose a seventeen-year-old whore from one of the hard-currency bars and see if she can't do her stuff?'

It was then I had my brilliant idea. It was Svetlov's mention of the currency bars that did it, and the sort of people who frequented the Metropole, the National and other Intourist hotels. I stood up.

'Let's go.' I said. 'I believe I've thought of someone.'

Without waiting for him to catch up, I rushed over towards the office of Dr Zh. F. Galinskaya, who was in charge of the whole hospital. The outraged Zhanna Fyodorovna was closeted with Eleonora Shpigel, but I took no notice of either of them. I picked up the receiver and dialled Chief Prosecutor Rudenko at his private dacha. We were allowed to do this in cases of real emergency.

'Roman Andreyevich?' I said. 'This is Shamrayev. Sorry to disturb you. We've found Belkin alive, but he's in a bad way.'

'What's wrong with him?'

'He was locked up in a mental hospital and has been injected with aminazine. It's not fatal, but it will take some time to break him of the addiction.'

'How much time?' he asked.

'I'll be able to tell you that in a few hours. Meanwhile, I'd like you to tell your grand-niece that he's alive. You told me that she was very keen on him, remember?'

There was a moment's silence at the other end of the line, and then Rudenko coughed in slight embarrassment. 'Do you want to tell her about it yourself?'

'Yes, if you'll let me.'

'Well, why not? Write down her number: 455–12–12. Olga Rudenko. Have you got it? 455–12–12. By the way, there's one more thing. It would be better if as few people as possible discover where you found him and what condition he's in. Do you follow me?'

'More or less,' I said. The prosecutor obviously wanted me to keep Belkin's state of health a secret from the Central Committee for the time being. We'd found him. That was the main thing. I pressed for the dialling-tone and started to dial Olga Rudenko's number straight away.

The same day, 17.30 hours

She arrived in her own car, a white export model Lada. I found it difficult to recognize her, she had changed so much during her time at Moscow University.

None of the tarts I'd seen at the Intourist, Metropole or the Prague Hotels were as enticing as Olga Rudenko. True, I had asked her over the phone to look as enticing as she could, but I hadn't realized that lovesick women could perform such miracles. She was like a beautiful creature from another planet, with velvety eyes and a mass of golden hair gathered into a tight bun. She was wearing some kind of light, diaphanous shift which emphasized her lithe, slender form.

I met her at the hospital gates, got into her car and put her in the picture as best I could.

'Olga, I've got something to tell you. He isn't really

responsible for his actions at present. He's been injected with very large doses of a certain drug, you see. I'm afraid that you may be in for a disappointment. You look absolutely marvellous. I could fall in love with you myself. And I'm sure that if he were in a normal condition, he'd fall for you at first sight, but . . .'

'But what? What do you mean?'

'I'm simply afraid that when you see him, you may change your mind and refuse to . . .'

'Igor Iosifovich,' she said with a smile. 'I'm sorry, but how old are you?'

'Forty-two. So what?'

'Have you had a lot of women?'

'Well . . .'

'I bet that you've never slept with one in a mental hospital, have you? Am I right?'

I have to admit that these young people don't beat about the bush!

'You may be right,' I said, smiling in my turn.

'Well, it's my first time, too, you see. And it's all very interesting. Let's go. I really want to do it!' There was a mischievous expression in her laughing eyes. She obviously regarded it as a challenge. I even felt envious of Belkin at that moment.

'Besides,' she went on, 'making love under the influence of drugs is fantastic!'

She sounded the horn, and a watchman appeared from the check-point. I motioned to him to open up the gates and Olga drove into the hospital.

Ten minutes later

We were standing outside the door of cell No. 18, listening to Belkin screaming and roaring within. One moment he would hammer on the walls with his fist, the next he would hurl the full weight of his body against the door. 'Injection, injection!' he was shouting all the time.

Olga put her eye to the peephole and peered in. Belkin was charging around the cell like a wild animal.

Suddenly she walked away from the door and with one deft movement of the hand let her shift fall to the ground. She was nearly naked. All she had on was a pair of briefs. She wasn't even wearing a bra. The same hand moved to unpin her bun, and the golden hair tumbled on to her sun-tanned shoulders and firm breasts.

'Open up,' she said to the flabbergasted medical orderly.

I pressed a button, and the automatic door moved noisily to one side. The frenzied Belkin immediately charged at us from the depths of the cell, but suddenly stopped as if frozen to the spot. For the first time his eyes appeared to betray some measure of recognition.

He backed as she entered the cell like a lion-tamer about to tame a wild animal.

'Shut the door,' said Olga imperiously, her eyes fixed on Belkin. 'And bring us a mattress of some sort.'

Every twenty minutes or so after that they would ask us for something – food, cognac, clean sheets or cigarettes.

'A definite calming effect,' mused Dr. Lunts. 'Not a complete cure necessarily, but a certain return to normality. I think you may have been right.'

THE END

Epilogue

EXTRACT FROM A TASS REPORT
On 15 June 1979, Comrade L. I. Brezhnev, Secretary-General of the CPSU and Chairman of the Presidium of the Supreme Soviet, left Moscow for Vienna to meet President J. Carter. During their meeting they will be signing the Strategic Arms Limitation Agreement between the USSR and the USA (SALT–2) and will also exchange views on bilateral relations ... Accompanying Comrade Brezhnev at the airport were the following: Politburo members Yu. V. Andropov, V. V. Grishin, A. P. Kirilenko, A. N. Kosygin, A. Ya. Pelshe, M. A. Suslov; Candidate members P. N. Demichov and V. V. Kuznetsov; CPSU Central Committee members B. P. Bugayev and N. A. Shcholokov; Candidate members S. K. Tsvigun and G. K. Tsinyov; Member of the CPSU Central Auditing Commission Yu. M. Churbanov ... Accompanying Comrade Brezhnev on the flight to Vienna were the chief of CPSU Ideological Section L. M. Zamyatin and a group of accredited journalists.

EXTRACT FROM INSTRUCTION NO. 156, ISSUED BY THE
USSR PUBLIC PROSECUTOR ON 15 JUNE 1979
In recognition of the professionalism and drive shown by I. I. Shamrayev and V. N. Pshenichny in carrying out a government task involving the uncovering of a particularly serious criminal action in the shortest possible time, I hereby instruct that the following special preferments be made: Igor Iosifovich SHAMRAYEV

to be given the rank of Senior Juridical Counsellor, and Valentin Nikolayevich PSHENICHNY the rank of Junior Juridical Counsellor.

EXTRACT FROM INSTRUCTION NO. 429, ISSUED BY USSR MINISTER OF INTERNAL AFFAIRS, GENERAL N. SHCHOLOKOV, ON 18 JUNE 1979

In recognition of the professionalism, courage and resourcefulness displayed by Comrade M. A. Svetlov in carrying out a task on behalf of the government, as a member of an inter-departmental investigation team, I hereby authorize that Marat Alekseyevich SVETLOV, head of Moscow CID Second Section, Third Department, be awarded the rank of Colonel of Militia.

EXTRACT FROM INSTRUCTION NO. 336, ISSUED BY THE MOSCOW CITY COUNCIL ON 28 JUNE 1979

As a result of representations made by the USSR Public Prosecutor, the Moscow City Council will make available the following accommodation to Comrade I. I. Shamrayev, Special Investigator and Senior Juridical Counsellor: a one-room apartment measuring 21.8 square metres, address – 6 Red Army Street, Apartment No. 37.

Signed: V. Promyslov
Chairman of Moscow City Council
N. Pegov
Secretary to the Council

EXTRACT FROM THE SECRET CORRESPONDENCE BETWEEN KGB FIRST DEPUTY CHAIRMAN, S. K. TSVIGUN, AND THE USSR PUBLIC PROSECUTOR, R. A. RUDENKO

... I have to inform you that, on 13 June 1979, an attempt was made to steal a military helicopter near

the town of Charshanga in Uzbekistan. In the gun battle which followed, the following wanted citizens were
killed: Boris Yurevich Khotulyov and Semyon Yakovlevich Gridasov. They were found to be in possession of
foreign currency, diamonds and other valuables,
together with five boxes containing narcotics. These
objects to the value of 7.5 million roubles have been
handed over to the USSR Finance Ministry.

EXTRACT FROM PUBLIC PROSECUTOR RUDENKO'S
INSTRUCTION TO SPECIAL INVESTIGATOR SHAMRAYEV,
DATED 17 JUNE 1979

Concerning the illegal imprisonment of
Komsomolskaya Pravda correspondent V. Belkin. In
accordance with Article 211 of the RSFSR Criminal
Code and the regulations concerning surveillance by
the Public Prosecutor's Department, I rule that:

1. All materials relating to the arrest of V. Akeyev and
   thirty-three others on the charge of drug-trafficking
   should be handed over to the MVD Anti-Fraud
   Squad to be incorporated into the investigation of
   the Chief Pharmaceutical Authority being carried
   out by MVD department head, N. P. Malenina.
2. All materials relating to the illegal arrest of Citizen
   V. Belkin at Baku airport, as well as to drug-
   trafficking in Azerbaidzhan, should be passed on
   to the Public Prosecutor of the Azerbaidzhan SSR,
   Comrade A. V. Gasanov.
3. Bearing in mind the instruction received from
   Comrade N. I. Savinkin, the head of the CPSU
   Administrative Organs Department, as well as the
   fact that the Deputy Minister of Health, General
   Balayan, is also the head of a KGB Special Department, responsible for carrying out work of extreme
   importance to the state, all charges against Comrade Balayan concerning abuse of power should
   be dropped.

4. Monies and valuables to the sum of approximately 1.5 million roubles confiscated during the course of the investigation, including the 100,000 roubles recovered from the left-luggage office at Baku airport, are deemed to be the property of the state and have been transferred to the account of the Ministry of Finance.
5. Criminal proceedings relating to the premeditated murder of Yury Rybakov and Olga Dolgo-Saburova should be halted in view of the death of the person accused of both murders, S. Ya. Gridasov.

EXTRACT FROM THE SECRET CORRESPONDENCE OF KGB FIRST DEPUTY CHAIRMAN. S. K. TSVIGUN, AND THE USSR PUBLIC PROSECUTOR, R. A. RUDENKO

As a footnote to our letter of 14 June 1979, I have to inform you that on 10 June in Geneva, V. V. Sysoyev, the head of the USSR Health Ministry's Chief Pharmaceutical Authority, applied to the Swiss government for political asylum. According to information received from our agents, the reason for Sysoyev's defection was a broadcast put out by the 'Voice of America', giving details of the arrest of Sysoyev's own agents on drug-trafficking charges in Moscow. Additional information received in Moscow from Geneva has revealed that, on 14 June, V. Sysoyev died in a car crash in circumstances which remain unexplained.

EXTRACT FROM A LETTER WRITTEN BY R. ROMANOV, CHAIRMAN OF THE COUNCIL OF MINISTERS' CENSORSHIP COMMITTEE, TO L. KORNESHOV, CHIEF EDITOR OF *KOMSOMOLSKAYA PRAVDA*

Regarding the article written by your correspondent, Comrade Belkin, about the misuse of drugs by teenagers in Baku, I have to inform you that this report cannot be published, since *there is no drug-abuse problem in the USSR* : . . .

THE DRAGON
by Alfred Coppel

'Five star fiction . . . highly recommended'
Evening News

'Truly horrific . . . moves with the speed of an Intercontinental Ballistic Missile'
Colin Forbes

A strange Mongol rider drags his Chinese captive across a Central Asian plain . . .

A Russian attaché is shot dead at Dover . . .

The American President plans his visit to Moscow . . .

A Soviet missile base is unaccountably re-aligned on to a new target . . .

A series of apparently unconnected incidents on three continents falls into a pattern that will thrust the world into global nuclear conflict.

Two code-names spell out the answers in the grim puzzle of doomsday: BOYAR, renegade Kremlin warlord and grand master of the scientific theory of holocaust; DRAGON, China's secrecy-shrouded project hidden out in the Turfan Depression, the ultimate death-dealer in the arsenal of Armageddon.

'Slick and fast . . . a rare treat'
Daily Express

0 552 12478 8   £ 2.50

RED SQUARE
by Edward Topol & Fridrikh Neznansky

The ultimate Soviet thriller . . .

Much of this story is factually accurate – the names, the people and the places . . . the death of Brezhnev's brother-in-law was widely reported in the West. 'Death after long illness' said *Pravda* . . . although Andropov told Brezhnev it was suicide. Just *suppose* it was murder . . .

'Fast moving and exciting . . . better than *Gorky Park*'
Good Book Guide

'Meaty entertainment'
Sunday Times

'Gripping and informative fiction that has an unexpected and chilling end'
Yorkshire Post

'Much more fun than *Gorky Park*'
The Spectator

0 552 12307 2   £2.50

SUBMARINE U-137
by Edward Topol

On October 28, 1981, Soviet Submarine U-137 ran aground off the coast of Sweden just ten miles from the Swedish naval base at Karlskrona. The Soviet authorities at the time claimed that this was an accident caused by faulty navigation equipment . . .

But was it?

Colonel Yuryshev has the answer. He offers to trade this secret information in exchange for asylum in the West. The CIA decides to send a Russian emigré named Stavinsky (a look-alike for Yuryshev) to the Soviet Union. He'll stay there while Yuryshev escapes to the U.S. But the plan goes horribly wrong . . .

What are the Soviets really up to?

Will Stavinsky, himself in mortal danger, be able to warn the Western world in time? Before we learn the answer, we are taken on a breathtaking, adventure-laden journey through parts of the Soviet Union which are normally out of bounds.

Submarine U-137 offers an enthralling entertainment of the kind we expect from the author of *Red Square*; but as a speculation based on documented facts, it makes for chilling and uncomfortable reading.

'He writes with an inside knowledge which the Le Carré's and Deightons cannot match'
New Society

0 552 12583 0   £2.50

A SELECTED LIST OF FINE TITLES
AVAILABLE FROM CORGI BOOKS

While every effort is made to keep prices low, it is sometimes necessary to increase prices at short notice. Corgi Books reserve the right to show new retail prices on covers which may differ from those previously advertised in the text or elsewhere.

The prices shown below were correct at the time of going to press.

ORDER FORM

All these books are available at your book shop or newsagent, or can be ordered direct from the publisher. Just tick the titles you want and fill in the form below.

CORGI BOOKS, Cash Sales Department, P.O. Box 11, Falmouth, Cornwall.

Please send cheque or postal order, no currency.

Please allow cost of book(s) plus the following for postage and packing:

U.K. Customers—Allow 55p for the first book, 22p for the second book and 14p for each additional book ordered, to a maximum charge of £1.75.

B.F.P.O. and Eire—Allow 55p for the first book, 22p for the second book plus 14p per copy for the next seven books, thereafter 8p per book.

Overseas Customers—Allow £1.00 for the first book and 25p per copy for each additional book.

NAME (Block Letters) . . . .

ADDRESS . . . .

. . . .